For Amanda, my wife, and Molly, our daughter,
aged six months

In memory of Stephen Milton

Chapters

In Your Dreams

Proposing

'Will you m— me?

Four words! Four! You wouldn't imagine so few words, so few short, simple words, could create such chaos. You might replace them with another four words. For example, 'Please pickle my testicles,' or 'Kindly whisk my brains.' You would expect these words to bring a little hassle, some grief, some madness. But 'Will you m— me?' Only one of the words has more than one syllable, for Chrissakes. The same word I can't even say . . . not yet, anyway.

I guess I'll get used to it. I have to, really. I think it's just a minor, temporary allergy, like hay fever, athlete's foot or scrot-rot. Colin, my dubious hack mate, had scrot-rot once. He'll be there, as an usher, on the big day. I can see him now, scratching his beard while he herds the rest of the lads around with as little success as he manages the pub football team.

Mind you, who won't be there? I wouldn't be surprised to see B Company of the South Wales Borderers (2nd Battalion) and their mascot, Phuq the Goat, at the church on the day. The bride-to-be (BTB) is composing the guest list with months still to go. It's a Proust-sized 'remembrance of friends past who we haven't seen for a decade' composition.

Yup, I am to be wed. I – that is, my fiancée and me – are getting hitched. I have made the lemming-like leap of suicide which is 'the proposal'. I, Johnny Riley, will be taking

11

she, BTB, for my felafel bedded life on 31 May next year.

Sitting here in bed, half awake, I wonder if it was all a sweaty nightmare. In the silence of dawn – no noise of planning, no arguing about whether her twice-removed four-teenth cousin should come, no barking or gunfire – I can't quite believe what I've let myself in for.

A few months ago I made a list of the things I wanted to achieve by the time I was thirty:

Win Oscar for first script.
Run marathon.
Retire to live as a wealthy sloth.

They carried on in the same vein, all a little selfish and a lot fantasy-land, which BTB says is me all over. I started again:

Finally get round to finishing my *Mr Saturday Night* script.
Try to keep place as Blue Boy's left winger by remaining at the fitter end of unhealthy.
Toilet train Muttley (my grungy year-old mongrel), at least a bit anyway.

BTB sighed and said they were now all too achievable and still typically self-centred. I protested and said that I didn't mind Muttley crapping on our kitchen floor, so that one was clearly for her, but she didn't seem to buy it. Anyway, the point is, you'll notice zero reference to getting m—d. Getting hitched wasn't on the first list, and it wasn't on the second. So why slip it in before the big three-o?

Why?

Why? Why? Why? Why? Why?

Repeating this question doesn't actually help.

I don't really know. But I want to find out. I mean, I'm not the first, am I? It's not as if I'm the only plonker to have popped the question without full knowledge of the risks.

Christ, there are 90,000 couples out there right now, in Britain, who have set a date for their own personal dooms-day – that's 'big day' to the optimists. 180,000 people! You realize, unless there are lots of gay weddings, or weddings to inanimate objects – sounds good! Bagsy the Hoover – that 90,000 of those people are blokes. More than eight times the capacity of Craven Cottage! What would it be like?

'Come on ye gro–oms!'

Everything went pear-shaped a month ago. You know the chaos butterfly theory, where fluttering wings in China can cause a hurricane on the other side of the world by toppling a chain of ever-worsening consequences. Well, my chaos, my hurricane, was caused by a mate, a moth and a moment of madness. To be honest, I blame my best mate, Merlin. Back then, in August, I asked Merlin's advice on proposing. Merlin said it was a grand idea. Merlin, the Welsh wanker, was pissed when he said this to me, and pissed when he proposed himself. Merl is a six-foot-five swarthy bloke, who looks and sounds as near as dammit to Darth Vader – without the suit. He has a streak of bright white hair sprouting from his temple, which stands out all the more amidst the scruffy, long black mess. He pretends it went white with fear during a visitation by the ghost of Sid Vicious, twiddles with it constantly, but doesn't seem too bothered when we call him Skunk.

I, on the other hand, am five foot fuck all, with hair that BTB says reminds her of a short-lived Jack Russell her dad bought her when she was a kid. Clearly me and Merl are going to look like spanners at the altar together next year. But, yet again, this is not something I considered in advance. Darth Vader and bloody short-arsed, big-eared Yoda, that's what we'll look like, with Merlin whispering in my ear every five minutes, 'May the force be with you . . . 'cos you're gonna need it!'

We were at one of Merlin's legendary barbecues on a hot

night, smack in the middle of summer. The flat – ground floor and garden of a typical Battersea red-brick semi – looked mildly ransacked. The French windows and kitchen door were wide open, with colourful curtains billowing. Stacks of dirty plates, bin-liners of bottles and cans were strewn throughout, as alcohol had gradually got the better of our efforts to keep the flat vaguely tidy. As usual, the sole survivors of the drunken débâcle were Merl and his wife, Ruth, BTB and me, who were incapable of the ten-minute totter from their flat to our house near Clapham Common. Merl and me slouched on uncomfortable garden furniture, surrounded by post-barbecue waste: half-eaten pork-and-leek sausages, eight trillion fag butts and the ever-present empty bottles. The garden was all pot plants and patio; ease of up-keep and maximum barbecue functionality by design.

I was fishing for proposing tips from Merl. Why the big 'M' was fixed in my thoughts at all is a puzzle. It must have been something biological – colliding neutrons or hazardous chemicals mixing in my head.

I guess that's the whole problem here, I'm confused. I was in a muddle back then and, to be honest, I'm still not out of the woods. You see, on the one hand you've got the 'M' thing – the 'M' word – which scares me more than bank statements. But there it was, lodged in my head like some cartoon arrow shot through one ear and sticking out of the other. So why was it there? Pass. Next question.

On the other hand you've got BTB – formerly known as my girlfriend – who means more to me than my original Ian Dury 'Sex and Drugs and Rock and Roll' 12 inch. We've been seeing each other since college in Scotland and have lived in London together for years now. It's not as tricky as it was back in ye olde days, when the smart women held the best cards till the last hand and made poor sex-starved grooms charge down the aisle for the sake of a virginity-erasing shag. So it's not sex.

Somebody said couples get hitched when they have nothing else left to say. But it can't be that either. We still spark, BTB and me. We still row, we still fight and make up. So she wins, but not all the time. Actually, *all* the time. And when I say *we* say sorry, well, really, I guess *I* say sorry.

Sorry I was drunk.

Sorry Muttley shat on the spare bed.

Sorry I flirted with Maddy.

Sorry I spend my life in a celluloid fantasy.

Sorry I called your mother a contract killer.

Maybe that's why I was thinking of m——. Maybe it was my way of getting back on top. Proposing was the only crack at dominance left for me, other than kinky bondage sessions – which I imagine might chafe.

And then, of course, there's the minor detail that she's beautiful. She's like the sea – frantic, captivating and dangerous in a storm; serene and irresistible on a windless summer's day. I know it's vomit-inducingly soppy, but even that doesn't explain why I suddenly felt the need to get all Neanderthal and possessive, stick little gold tags on our fingers and operate under one name.

Why did I ask her? I don't fucking know. I'm trying to work that one out. Was it the threat of losing her to someone else? Or fear of her eventual boredom with my ineptitude, expanding gut, flatulence and diminishing libido? I don't have a clue. That's what I'm trying to work out. I'd like to just blame Merl, that would be easy. *Fucking twat.*

That bloody barbie was the pivot-point, the watershed. While Ruth and BTB were doing the sofa-white-wine-and-whispering thing, me and Merl chain-smoked in the garden and foolishly cracked open a bottle of Laphroaig. Our conversation wandered aimlessly between irrelevant subjects. We paused to stare at the stars, watch kamikaze moths head-butt the garden spotlight, or refill our tumblers. It was all mainly manly stuff – why Fulham should buy Portsmouth's reserve goalkeeper, which US punk band did a cover of the Banana Splits in '79? Would you have a moral dilemma about silicon implants? Or would you, in fact, be more likely to have an erection? We made our usual trips to the land of make-believe, where I was being wooed by Hollywood and Merl was travelling the world as a famous travel writer, and neatly side-stepped our current job-failures as crap video supremo and never-been-there holiday-brochure writer. We were no better than the moths, flitting between shallow subjects, never pausing too long for fear of burning our wings on the light bulb.

Inside, the girls would be nailing down a subject and sticking to it. It might be any topic, but it would involve them and they would keep at it, focus on it and pin it down. It could be sex with Merlin or me, or whether terracotta kitchen floors have had their day, or why Trish should leave Colin; the merits of a new buttock-toning class at the local gym, or why our bald team captain, Stefano – the Italian Stallion, as the girls call him – would make their perfect bit on the side, or even better, an ideal match for the terminally single Maddy – BTB's buxom blonde best friend. By now their chosen subject would have been dissected under the microscope, like a laboratory rat. It would be easy to pass them off as gossips, but actually they were probably having a *real* conversation, without effort or the agony of forcing things out. Ruth and BTB would probably be putting something right, while me, Merl and the lads might take the piss, but at least the girls could look back on a party or a night in the Blue Boy and say, 'we talked about this subject' or 'sorted that thing out'. Usually, Merl, me and any combination of the lads would simply mutter and wisecrack our way through the night. The most important things remained unsaid, like odd taboos.

I managed to steer one of our fleeting conversational visits on to the subject of proposing. At this point I wasn't entirely sure I would, or even could, ask the big question myself. I hoped Merl would be too pissed to make the link as he happily talked me through his own experience:

'I was knee deep in booze, boyo, wasn't I. I'd 'ave asked fuckin' JPR Williams to marry me that night, you know! It just 'appened to be the case that Ruth was stood next to me. I mean, I've not the faintest idea why it came out. It was only months after we'd graduated, you an' me, Johnny. Mad old time it was, remember? Anyway, back home from Edinburgh, an' I was out with all the old lads, like, an' I went up to the bar in Llandaff – the Malsters, it was. You know, nice pub an' all – an' I was supposed to say, "Forty-five pints of Brain's Skull Attack for the boys," to Billy the barman, and instead I said, "Will you marry me?" to Ruth.'

'So you didn't plan it then, Merl?' I remembered the brain-numbing shock when he'd told me all those years ago. I remembered thinking, You're having a laugh, aren't you? We'd been best mates at college for three years, joined at the hip, never apart for more than a couple of weeks here and there. Then we didn't see each other for a few months after college, and the next thing I knew Merl was hitching himself to his teenage sweetheart.

'Plan it? Plan?' Merlin fell off his seat, landing in a flower bed. 'I've laid more detailed plans for chronic diarrhoea than I did for that proposal!' he said from behind the begonias.

'But you knew. I mean, you'd always said, "That Ruthie; she's my girl." You were always going to ask Ruth to m-m-m . . .'

'Marry me? Course I was. Knew it since the day she shaved me sideburns off at Snippets on the high street. Symbolic, it was. Course, I'd met her on holiday when she had blond hair tied in pigtails and wore one of those silly ra-ra tutu skirts that were all the rage. But I really fell for her a few months before that, when I popped in to get me flick trimmed. I sat in the chair, and her reflection in the mirror stopped me in my tracks. She'd died her hair black and cut it like an Egyptian, but with a peroxide-blond fringe. Remember it made her brown eyes look black. Told me she'd nabbed the idea from a singer on *Top of the Pops* as she cut my hair, but I was too dumbstruck to talk. She must of thought I was a real pillock.'

'So, if you knew all that time, how come you didn't plan it?' I frowned.

'You see, Johnny, that was eventually. I knew I'd ask *eventually*. Not now. I mean, *eventually* I know me hair'll fall out. Eventually, like. But I'm not about to ask you to pull it up by the roots now, am I?'

'But you were glad you asked, though?' I was spending too much time on the topic. This moth was about to melt on the light bulb. Merl looked at me with whisky-red eyes glowing madly in the night.

'Glad? . . . Glad? . . . Well, I suppose I was glad that it was all a blur. You know, glad like glad I was under the anaesthetic when the dentist pulled out one of my wisdom teeth!'

I was rapidly going off the idea of proposing, but it was just too late for a change of heart.

'So you're gonna ask her?'

Like the moth with singed wings, I had remained where I shouldn't have been far too long. Merlin knew for sure why I'd asked the questions, why I'd dwelled on the unspeakable subject.

'You are, aren't you, Johnny? You're going to ask her.' Merlin was on to me now, an angler reeling in a slippery fish. My life flashed before me. Well, actually it didn't. The light bulb firmament was fizzling on the garden spotlight, making it flicker like a very weak strobe. As it did, I fell off my seat to join Merlin in the flower bed. The overall effect with the light and the stars in the sky was, I imagine, a tad like having your life flash before you.

'Yes,' I said, as I landed on my arse next to Merlin. I surprised myself when I said this. Thinking back to that moment of truth, I wonder whether I'd just had the wind knocked out of me and the shocked noise I'd made as I landed just sounded like 'yes', when I meant to say 'ow', or, 'I've hurt me arse'. But Merlin heard 'yes', loud and clear, and that is a very big thing. He became a witness. He became a trustee. He became complicit in the proposal.

If I never propose, Merlin will always be there to haunt me. A physical reminder of one of the few good intentions I've ever had. Now I was committed. I had to do it or . . . well, not do it, but have Merlin take the piss a lot.

That makes it sound trivial, or small, but it's not. It's not just about Merl taking the piss; it's about him knowing what might have happened in my life. About him being party to this great big thing I'd decided. Of course, as my best mate, he knew how much BTB meant to me. He knew how special she was. Merl knew that bluff and bravado was a thin veil, knew that if she left, or if she said 'no', I'd have a personal Armageddon. And if I didn't ask, he would always be there at my shoulder whispering, 'Hey, Johnny, you were onto something there; she was the grooviest chick at the dance, gagging to get it on with you, she was, and you fucked it. You didn't even ask her.'

There was no fooling Merlin; we'd known each other too long. We'd met in freshers' week at college, having happily joined the Sacred Cow Irreverence Unlimited Club in the first few days. As a sort of initiation, we'd agreed to shadow some socialist workers around the university union dressed as gnomes selling copies of the *Beano* while they touted their own newspaper.

'*Socialist Worker*!' shouted the knobbly, bearded militant. 'Fight the class war. Beat Thatcher!'

'*Beano*!' we echoed. 'Bash Street Kids in classroom war!' Gnomes on our knees with round rouge circles on our cheeks. After a near beating, we became inseparable for the next three years.

He can read me like a book, Merlin, and now he knew that

I'd made that big decision to pop the question. The real behemoth of the decision world, and I'd shared it. I had shared it all with Merlin, who went on to say what a grand decision he thought it was, and that I should carry it out as soon as possible.

Looking back to that August night in the flower bed – me, my behemoth, Merlin and the (flattened) begonias – I have a few question marks about the integrity of Merl as chief adviser. He must have been one, or all, of the following when he gave me this advice: too pissed to pay attention, just like the night he could have married JPR; lonely in the sad-bastard married club and attempting to bamboozle me into joining; or perhaps just being honest and stating – in a veiled, best mate sort of way – that if I didn't pin BTB down now I'd be lucky to end up with a wildebeest in a skirt.

I looked through the patio doors at BTB and Ruth, still nattering on the checked sofa. The back of BTB's head bobbed up and down as she blethered, blond curls bouncing. Although pissed, I remember Ruth's face clearly – pine hair pulled back from her sharp features and tied into a French plait. The whites around her dark pupils were bright red, but I couldn't tell whether this was due to tears, or ten too many 'last' glasses of cheap Chardonnay.

For a second I wondered about the state of Merl and Ruth and noticed the way he shuffled over the paving stones, hiding the cracks beneath his feet. My thoughts were random and unanchored, and anything too intense was lost in the peaty fumes of the Laphroaig. I shook my doubt away, deciding Merl's patio, relationship and advice were all equally sound.

So, thanks to Merlin, I decided to ask the question. This may sound like a cop-out. It may sound weak-willed that I couldn't reach this decision unilaterally, like CND, but I couldn't. Nobody, unless they are Robert Maxwell, Margaret Thatcher, Hitler or BTB, makes decisions without recourse to absolutely anyone. Us normal folk humbly seek advice. But where do you go for advice on whether or not to pop the question? There is no place to go for a check. If your car's fucked you go to a mechanic; if your foot's knackered you go to a chiropodist; if your dog's broken you go to a vet (BTB says Muttley won't be at the wedding unless he stops peeing on the floor); but if you want to get hitched to your bird . . . nowhere to go.

I asked Merlin, and look where that got me.

After my life had flashed before me in the begonias, I sought feedback. I sought confirmation that my brain hadn't become a cabbage while I wasn't looking.

'So, Merl . . . er . . . what do you reckon to . . . you know . . . popping the question?'

'Johnny boy, I think that would be a . . . urm . . . super plan . . . Yes, boyo . . . really quite grand.' We toasted my behemoth under the stars, draining our tumblers with another sclerotic liverful of Laphroaig.

In retrospect, what kind of a daft question was that to ask? Try to imagine saying to your best mate, 'I'm going to ask my bird to m— me. What do you think?'

What are his options? What's he really going to say? 'Nah, she's a moose with a personality that's got a wasp up its arse!' Or, 'So, has she stopped shagging her boss then?' Or, 'Who?'

Or, in Merlin's case, 'Yes, boyo, follow the dark side of the Force. Join me, Luke. Leave the Rebel Singlemen Alliance and become a big cheese with me in the Evil Married Empire!'

So I suppose Merlin's simple response – 'grand' – which he followed with a grin, was as good as it gets. We garbled into the early hours, minesweeping his house for signs of booze with complete disregard for the likely severity of our hang-overs. And in this state, in this hazy, surreal summer flower bed, I sealed the deal. I asked Merlin a question that trans-ported him from merely complicit to something integral.

'Merl . . .' I slurred, 'will yooobay thebesss mannnn?'

And in that wonderfully harmonious way that, much like the ancient language of Babel, drunk men always understand each other's slurs, Merl said, 'Jahhnny boy . . . thers nuthin ahhhhhhd raaddrer do.'

In this drunken exchange everything became more than a glimmer in my eye. It was an 'it': an event that had grown from nothing to having a best man. This is how it happens, like mould on bread, starting tiny and growing with monstrous speed into a great big bacterial blob. Before you know, 'it's' grown cars and flowers and lists and guests and china and cards and hymns and ushers and bridesmaids and honeymoons and rings and favours and a budget bigger than a presidential candidate's. It is a monster with a thousand heads and a million legs, and you are a small helpless cell somewhere insignificant inside the matter of that monster – maybe in an arse-cheek, or a toenail. And BTB – or any bride – they become the brain of the beast, with their wicked henchwomen, the bridesmaids and mother-in-law-to-be. Which is rich, really, when you consider that us grooms get it all going in the first place. It's a nemesis we create for no reason I can imagine.

Why?

Lying here, now, in bed with BTB, trying to wrap my mind around the past mad month since I proposed, you might think Merlin's advice wasn't so bad. Both BTB and the house she has styled look calm and serene, like a swan. A cream and white Mediterranean feel in the middle of a south-west London terrace. Above the waterline looks effortless, while below the surface madness ensues, as BTB tidies away the perpetual mess of Muttley and me. It's a pristine screen covering the chaos, a bit like its designer.

Looking at her, under the duvet, you could presume everything was normal. BTB's curled up, snoozing gently like a shark. Balled up, tiny, with blond sleep-tousled hair, delicate limbs, pale sun-kissed skin, freckling as the summer days pass. She looks perfect and sweet and harmless. This is scary. I know, like the house, it's camouflage. Have you seen *Predator*? Where Arnie is hunted by an extraterrestrial whose body armour changes like a chameleon. Looking at BTB now she is equally well disguised. Dozing, you can see no sign of the psycho-fiancée hidden below the surface.

Be warned, potential grooms. We need to form a club and spend money developing hi-tech pre-emptive strike weaponry to defend against BTBs who are hiding behind harmless sweet exteriors. In the future, you too will be able to take your BTB to a branch of Riley's Free Grooms Society™. These will be located on all high streets and look, to the untrained eye, like common-or-garden branches of Jigsaw – which are to BTBs what maggots are to trout. Inside, while trying on clothes that cost more than real estate in Manhattan, special X-rays will be taken and printed out for potential grooms. If an *Alien*-style aura is revealed surrounding their pretty young BTBs, they can quietly be disposed of through trapdoors in the floor, put through a mincer and made into Riley's Tasty Pies and Sausages™. 'She was a monster' we could tell concerned friends and family. At least we could pretend they were monsters if they responded to our proposal in any of the following ways:

'Take a hike.'
'I'd rather m— Russell Grant.'
'Ha, ha, ha, ha, ha, ha (ad infinitum).'
'Excuse me, but who are you again?'
'Barf.'

And then we could spend the next few years saying, 'Yeah, I know she looked lovely . . . Well, yes, I guess she did have a great personality . . . But underneath it all, below the surface, trapped beneath the deceivingly attractive shell, she was a monster. Honest. Fancy a sausage?'

I feel like a lava lamp, in a constant state of flux, molecules all hot, bothered and irritable. One minute staggered by my foolishness, the next by my fortune. I admit BTB's no predator really. She's ... well, she's ... as you'd imagine. She's my bride-to-be. How to describe her? I don't want to use the same old words, in the same old way; they're kind of hollow. Blonde, brunette, pretty, tall, small, gorgeous, thin, fat – they're just descriptors. Words that Merl and I have to apply to holiday brochures and the backs of videotapes. BTB is a 'beautiful, blonde, undiscovered, picturesque, stunning début performance'. It means nothing. It's shallow and insincere, so I have decided to boycott this method.

Instead, I'll use the unfocused technique. I learnt this years ago as a penniless student, up for earning a few quid to piss away pub crawling the Royal Mile with Merl and our perverted landlord, Simon Ratcliffe (or Ratty as he became known, for his rat-up-a-drainpipe behaviour). There were two particular earners that were a good bet and involved little actual work. One was volunteering to be a guinea pig for the university's medical school. This involved signing a piece of paper that removed any responsibility from the university for damage, disability or death. After which they might do anything to you, from giving you a cold and then trying to cure it to testing some new suppository for side effects. The size of the wedge was determined by risk and time. Inducing a heart attack with mink semen over the period of a month might net you a grand.

The second route was faster and easier, but paid a lot less. You put your name on a list held by the Business Studies Department, which they sold to market-research companies. You made sure you answered 'yes' to as many of the questions as possible so that you got invited to the maximum number of focus groups. I was a heavy consumer of wine, cigarettes, business trips abroad, gardening equipment and nappies, according to my profile.

Once selected, researchers would then spend hours talking to us in our focus groups while plying us with wine. Within an hour or so, they were definitely unfocused groups. One of the tactics researchers employed was the if-you-imagined scenario. It went like this:

Research Group for Booze:

'Now, group,' said patronizing, posh, bespectacled research woman. 'Imagine the alcoholic beverage I name and describe it in the form I request, and vice versa. So if I say, "What car would you use to describe Budweiser?" you might say, "Jeep." If I say, "What drink might you use to describe Harvey Nichols?" you might say, "Champagne." I may then ask you to explain why you picked that descriptor. It's important to be spontaneous, OK? Is that all clear?'

The research group mumbled various noises, which didn't include 'yes' or 'no'.

'Guinness,' she says.

'Monster Truck,' I say.

'Why?' she says.

'Why not?' I say.

'Bacardi and Coke,' she says.

'Porsche,' I say

'Why?' she says.

'Wankers' drink,' I say.

'Range Rover,' she says.

'Arse juice,' I say.

I was banned from the focus groups after this incident, which was a bummer, 'cos twenty quid, free red wine and some cheesy snacks were all handy as a student. Anyway, you get the idea. Rather than describing BTB, I'll use the unfocused approach.

Car?

If BTB was a car she'd be a . . . Merc, convertible SLK; sleek, slick, purring and racy. A head-turner, with hand-crafted bodywork you simply can't afford.

Vegetable?

If BTB was a vegetable she'd be a . . . cherry tomato: juicy, rosy, petite, with no pips.

Brand?

If BTB was a brand she'd be . . . Duracell. She's that bastard bunny rabbit clapping cymbals forever.

Dog?

Most of all, most accurately, if BTB was a dog she'd be a . . . Springer Spaniel: mad, energetic, bouncy, lunatic, pleading get-anything-she-wants eyes. She is a human Springer Spaniel. Trapped in a room, she'll whizz round the walls at top speed, like Elvis's motorbike in *Roustabout*'s Wall of Death.

That's the best description you're gonna get – a Duracell-powered, cherry-tomato-eating, Merc-SLK-driving Springer Spaniel impersonating the King's motorbike. And she's going to be my w— . . . Oh my God.

Once I tried this in reverse. According to BTB, I was a Capri with go-faster stripes and no wheels, a retired greyhound salvaged from the pound and some over-boiled cabbage. Odd, but I wouldn't have described myself that way. More of a classic Fifties Porsche, a Weimaraner and asparagus. But there you go, self-perception and reality rarely collide.

I suppose there are crucial questions, like:

'When's the big day?'

'Where's the venue?'

'How many guests will be coming?'

'Will it be a religious ceremony?'

'What hymns will you be singing?'

'Are you going to use the word "obey" for the bride?' Fat chance! BTB is as likely to obey me as Muttley, who shits when I say 'sit', and you don't want to know what the randy little sod does when I say 'roll over'.

'What are you serving as nibbles with the drinks between 2.47 p.m. and 3.34 p.m.?'

AAAAAAARRRRRRRGGGGGGGGHHHHHH.

The details, the details, they make me mad. All I did was ask the damn question. I didn't know there would be a list of seventeen billion things to do, did I?

Actually, there are two sets of critical questions, one for people who givashit (above) and one for those who don't (below).

Q: 'Does it clash with an important fixture?'

A: 'Nope, first thing I did was rule out a few key dates.'

Q: 'Why did you ask her in the first place?'

A: 'Because Merlin said it was a grand idea' – OK, OK, I know this is transparent – 'Because I like her. OK, more than like her, love her.'

Q: 'How can I avoid this happening to me?'

A: 'Stop washing your body now and never look back.'

Q: 'When you asked, were you drunk, drugged, momentarily possessed by a sonnet-vomiting demon, or otherwise mentally impaired?'

A: 'All of the above and generally inept anyway.'

Q: 'Are the bridesmaids shaggable?'

A: 'Well, there's just the one – Maddy – and I can categorically say she is entirely shaggable.'

Q: 'Is BTB pregnant?'

A: 'No, that was not the reason I asked. And, since asking the big question, sex has become a distant memory.'

And most importantly:

Q: 'How in the hell did you manage to ask the question when you can't actually say m—?'

A: 'I didn't.'

Princess Lou and the Reverend Ratty

'Over here, Ratty,' Merlin shouted across the crowded pub, putting his *Evening Standard* down on the scuffed oak bar. A short, soaked, bedraggled pinstripe suit marched over to join Merlin, squeezing past tourists and staff with tottering glass towers.

Merlin chuckled at the sight of his old friend caught in a sudden downpour.

'What the fuck are ye laughin' at, yer bastard!' Ratty was not happy. Merlin continued to laugh, pleased that fate had brought him and Johnny to the door of this strange little man, renting rooms in his flat in Morning Side all those years ago.

'I wiz hopin' fer birds.' Ratty stood in his doorway, wearing a flea-bitten stripy dressing gown.

'Sorry, mate,' said Merlin.

'Youse want some blow?' Ratty asked. They nodded and walked in.

'Fuckin' bastard weather. Bloody forecast said it was gon tae be sunny.' Ratty rattled on in his raw Aberdonian while Merlin sniggered.

'Get me a pint of lager, fer fucksake, ye great gigglin' girlie!' Ratty caught himself in the mirror behind the bar and broke into a smile. His short, normally spiky brown hair was plastered down around his head, making him look like a medieval fashion disaster, and his suit was beginning to steam in the heat of the pub.

'It's nae s'posed to be like this, the weather. It's the summer. It's August for Chrissakes. It's like the monsoon season out there.' Ratty scowled, lines crowding darting eyes, as he peeled off his jacket and shook his hands dry.

'Two lagers, Judy. Thanks,' Merlin shouted to the bottle-blonde barmaid they'd befriended over the years.

Merlin and Ratty had both worked in Holborn for the last three years, and the Princess Louise was an all too easy pit-stop pub on the way home. They both preferred the pub in the old days, when it was independent, the beer was good and the pipes well cleaned, but found the habit hard to break. The customers tended to be casual trade, apart from the odd pub-anorak, *Ye Olde London Pub Guide* clasped in hand. These customers were generally alone, always spent too long perusing the guest ales on the chalkboard and admired the pub in the order described in the guide. They'd begin with the lofty Victorian ceiling, which Ratty said reminded him of the texture of tripe, supported by fluted pillars spread along the original horseshoe bar. Eventually, they'd wander surreptitiously downstairs, to the famed *gigantica Victoriana* urinals.

As ever, Ratty and Merlin looked an odd pair. One short, one tall; one smart, one scruffy. Ratty, in his latest incarnation as a photocopier salesman, was wet but pristine, ironed, creased and polished. Previous Ratty jobs included oil-rigger, fisherman, gigolo (he says), carpenter, chef, postman and weird landlord, of course. He's the type of guy you could guarantee would have the price tags on the soles of his shoes, flashing like a bunny's tush as he tapped along the streets of London.

Merlin, a brochure copywriter for a holiday company, was

29

a 'creative', a broad description for several thousand jobs in London, of which only an estimated 1 per cent are even vaguely creative. As a member of clan creative, Merlin wore the compulsory 'individual' uniform of skate shoes, low-slung trousers and T-shirt. He twiddled his white streak of hair idly.

'Sup on that, Ratty lad.' Merlin passed Ratty his pint.

'Cheers,' they said together.

'How's work?' asked Ratty.

'Shite . . . yours?'

The two men worked through their short list of politeness points as quickly as possible to get them out of the way. Their conversation joined the general din of the pub, which teemed with office evacuees grabbing a swift drink on the way home. Smoke billowed upwards with the noise of the pub talk. The sound was the adult equivalent of children at a swimming pool, more a droning whine than the eardrum-piercing squeal of brats at a pool. The noise and the smoke settled over the crowd like a London dawn smog, nestling under the intricate gold and ochre ceiling.

'Och, you know, work's not so bad . . . er . . . och, pretty shite, I suppose. How's Ruth?' Ratty knew the relationship was struggling and felt obliged to ask.

'Oh grand . . . you know . . . no different really.' Merlin took a dollop of Artex to reality as usual. 'You still shaggin' that bird in admin?'

'No, but I'm tryin'.' Ratty danced about like a sparrow, twitching and jerking.

'And what about that girl you met at Zepher's Bar . . . er . . . ?'

'Elsa. Aye, I'm still seein' her.' Ratty was well known to be monogamously incapable. He could no sooner see one woman for any length of time than walk on water or suck his own dick, both of which he had tried and failed at years ago as a teenager.

'But I'm goin' tae ditch her.'

'Who?'

'Elsa.'

'Why?'

'She's gettin' awfa serious.' Ratty rubbed his stubbly chin as he talked.

'How d'ya mean? Like, movin' in serious, or what?'

'Away tae fuck, ya daft Taff twat. Movin' in!' Merlin might well have accused Ratty of celibacy considering his shocked response. 'Movin' in, Jesus!' Ratty shook his head in disbelief, sipping from his pint in between head-shakes and sighs. 'Movin' in. I'm no soft pillock like you or Johnny, with your lovey-dovey one-woman bollocks. Elsa just wants me to stop shaggin' around.'

Merlin had covered this ground countless times with Ratty, who considered it an indisputable biological fact that men are genetically programmed to shag as many women as possible. In closed male circles this point is often whispered, and men will quickly glance around to check they are free from scrutiny before nodding. Ratty however told this to anyone and everyone. Merlin could picture Ratty wandering the streets of London with a sandwich board and a soapbox, preaching to passers-by like a puritanical Scots reverend.

'Sow yer seed as God intended,' the Reverend Ratty would shout to people passing by. 'Follow yer true path, men, and sow yer seed,' he'd rasp in his too-tight dog collar, handing out pamphlets with a red face and sweaty palms. 'Sow it far and wide, where fallow and fertile.' He'd redden excitedly, fumbling furiously under his smock. 'In the name of God, fuck! Fuck as many women as you can. Fuck all of them if you can, and then, if you want to, fuck pigs and dogs and sheep and fish and watermelons and doors and gravel and spinach.' The Reverend Ratty would collapse in a gibbering fit, semen leaking from his trouser legs.

Merlin winced at this disgusting image and tried to shake it off quickly. 'Stop shagging other women?' Merlin whistled and mopped his brow in fake concern. 'What? The girl in admin?'

'Aye, her as well, but awl women actually.'

'But you're not shaggin' anyone else, are you, Ratty?'

'Well . . . no, but that's nae fer the want o' tryin'.'

Merlin laughed at Ratty's honesty. Ratty reminded him of a jolly kleptomaniac, who knows pinching things is wrong but finds it too enjoyable to stop.

'So "say" you will lad,' Merlin suggested tentatively.

'Don't be daft, Merlin, I cannae!' Ratty fidgeted, playing with a beer mat.

'But just "say" you will.'

'That'd be lying.'

'So?'

'Och, I cannae, Merlin. That would be bad.'

Merlin cracked up again, and Ratty chuckled.

'Well, Johnny boy's about to get seriously serious.'

'He's serious already. They live together. What's more serious than . . . Och don't tell me; he's not!'

'I never told you.' Merlin panicked, remembering Johnny had only told him five days earlier at the drunken barbecue, and called the next day, deeply hungover, to stress the secrecy.

'He's not, is he?'

'Don't say anything, Ratty, or I'm toast.'

'Fuckin' hell. Marriage. The stupid bastard.'

'Honestly, Ratty, this is top fuckin' secret.'

'What's he playing at?'

'She doesn't even know yet.' Merlin broke into a sweat.

'It's against aw the laws o' nature. Another fuck-up like you and Ruth. Jesus.'

'What have I done?' Merlin wanted to push the rewind button so badly he failed to even notice Ratty's derision.

'It's like trying to stop lions fae eatin' antelope on the Serengeti.' Ratty had many rehearsed poetic analogies for why he, and all men, should be allowed to shag constantly without protest or distraction.

'I mean, she's gorgeous, and he can be a right twat, but that's no' the point; it's unnatural,' Ratty ranted.

'Oh God, I'm supposed to be the best bloody man,' Merlin muttered to himself while Ratty wittered on oblivious. 'Best man, not worst confidant!' Merlin held his head in his hands.

Ratty suddenly stopped and turned to Merlin.

'What d'ya say there, Merl?' Ratty was intense.

'I'm the best man.'

'No, not that bit, the bit about her knowing.'

'Well, she doesn't; she doesn't know yet. He's in Barcelona, and she's flying out there tonight.'

'He's no' asked her yet?'

'No, he's asking some time this weekend.'

'So it might no' happen after all.'

'What? Oh, you mean she might say no?'

'Errr . . . somethin' like that . . . I'm burstin' fer a pee. I'm off to the palace, get us another lager, would ya, Merl.' Ratty scuttled off in the direction of London's poshest pub urinals. Merlin turned to the bar and tried to catch Judy's attention. As he did, Ratty glanced back, saw that Merl wasn't looking and made a dart for the exit through heavy double doors.

'Same again, Judy.' Judy frowned and looked confused.

'Is someone else joining you, Merlin?' Judy had been serving Merlin and Ratty and a few other regulars for years now.

'Eh?'

'Ratty's left, I just saw him leave.' Judy pointed to the exit, and Merlin's gaze followed her finger as he scratched his temple nervously.

'No, he's popped to the loo . . .' With a start, he spotted Ratty through the leaded windows at the front of the pub. He was frantically punching numbers into his mobile. Merlin thought for a second, pieced it together and made a dash for the door, barging through, shoulder first.

'. . . It's fuckin' unnatural only shaggin' one woman, listen to yer pal, don't do it . . .'

He lurched for Ratty's mobile, wrestling it from his hands.

'Hello, hello. Anybody there? Fuck, fuck. Ratty!' Merlin shouted into the receiver. 'Tell me you didn't call who I think you called!' Merlin's face was pale.

'Who d'ya think it was?' Ratty looked guilty, failing to meet Merlin's eye. A wee schoolboy caught shoplifting, a packet of Refreshers tucked inside nylon Ys. The pair stood still in the rain as commuters rushed to tubes and buses.

'You rang Johnny, didn't you?'

'Maybe.'

'What did you say?'

Preparing

It was in Barcelona, a week after my barbecued babbling with Merlin, that I failed to say 'Will you m— me?' to BTB. We'd been to Barcelona together previously, BTB and me. We fell in love with each other at the same time as we fell for the city.

We'd met as students at a gig, when Merl, me and Ratty tripped the M8 across to the Glasgow Union in my rusty old Maestro. From then on, the M8, me and the gold Maestro became intimately familiar with each other, as I nipped over to see BTB in her trendy West End flat.

For a year or so we enjoyed playing the non-committed-this-will-never-last-but-let's-have-fun game. In fact, for a large part of that period she refused to allow me to describe her as my girlfriend. It was during this easy-going party time that the one-night stand with her schoolfriend, Maddy, occurred. Nobody ever mentions this any more. It's a sort of self-imposed censorship.

In the final year we became as serious as students ever are. After graduating we moved to London – via Scunthorpe for me and Manchester for BTB – to live in a succession of separate shitty rooms and flats.

Barcelona the first time, three years ago, was a seminal trip for the two of us. It was here, amid the Gaudi and Gothic spires, in the palm-edged squares, strolling down the

Ramblas, full-to-brimming with parakeets and lilies, news-stands and caricature artists, here in Barcelona's passionate madness, that we decided to live together and face the wrath of our parents.

Their responses were predictable:

BTB's Dad, Gerry Donnelly, smiled at his daughter while he whispered in my ear, 'If you hurt a hair on my daughter's head I will kneecap you and your whole damn football team.'

My father, Henry, said, 'Mmmm, save on bills, I suppose. Have you seen the *Sunday Times*, old boy?'

My mum looked wistfully at us and said, 'Ah, young lovers, just like *Breakfast at Tiffany's*.' Mum was daydreaming again. I guess I've inherited her fantasy-land genes.

BTB's deceptively gentle-looking, white-haired mother's response was the most frightening. No threats, no disagreements, just a single, simple tear rolling down her cheek, and the unspoken thought I could hear thundering through the ether into my subconscious: *He's not good enough for you!*

BTB's mother was only beaten in the sinister stakes by my cookie Grandma Victoria, who is now ninety-seven. She stared at BTB, gnarled white face, blue eyes as bright and piercing as antique forks, pretending to look frail and weak in a rocking chair.

'You are sinners, children of the devil, and she' – crooked finger unfurled to point at a blushing BTB – 'she's just after the money. Fetch my stick, boy.' Granny Victor (pet name) had been watching *Gone With the Wind* again. Once she was my wise old nan, who had a saying for every eventuality up her sleeve, along with the crumpled linen handkerchiefs that shared the same space. Since senility had set in, she'd forgotten that the only inheritance to be had in the Riley family was debt, and the reality was that BTB was my own financial equivalent of a Zimmer frame.

So, Barcelona seemed perfect; it seemed a suitable place for a proposal. The place where I hoped I would rediscover that earlier, reckless courage and overcome my fear. Of course, the fact that I had been asked to talk to some guff industry gathering – the International Video Collation Expo – meant that my flight and hotel were already paid for. The truth is that my boss, the head of Extraordinary Film & Company, had been asked to speak, but had passed the offer on to me when it clashed with some freeloading trip to Brazil. Nonetheless, all I had to do was get BTB air-freighted over on some cheap haulage plane for twenty quid and I had a bargain romantic break that any travel agent would be chuffed with.

So I flew over first class on Poshasfuk Airways on Thursday to speak at the expo, and BTB was flying in on Cheapaschips Airways on Friday night. I remember the flight vividly, like a video I can replay at will. I don't know whether it was the flying or the fear and nervousness I was experiencing at first and second hand that kept it clear in my mind. Maybe it was because I met someone on the plane who was literally larger than life, who seemed intent on invading my thoughts from that moment onwards.

Here I was, flying to Barcelona in first class (first time) to speak at an international video conference (another début) with someone else picking up the tab (result). I took in my surroundings, trying to work out what was worth the extra grand to elevate you to first class. The stewardesses were the same, a bit more polite and less rushed, but the same. The seats, patterned a little less grotesquely, felt an inch or two roomier in every direction. Not much, I know, but I was revelling in the limited luxury. What jarred was the thought that I'd got away with both the aisle and the window seat to my selfish, expansive self. You know how it feels to want that room, to keep that personal space surrounding you free from threat. But with seconds to spare, while the stewards and stewardesses were battening down the hatches and I was settling in to the kind of comfort I'd never had before, chaos arrived. Half running, dripping with sweat, pissed and clueless, Mr Big could not help but take centre stage for the passengers. My heart fell when a steward pointed him in the direction of the vacant window seat next to me.

Watching him squeeze into the space reminded me of my recent waist expansion. I used to be thin, although I'm hardly fat now. Let me rephrase that: I used to be effortlessly thin, in the face of attack from gallons of beer and acres of fried, fatty food. I used to laugh in the face of fatness. Mates, like Colin the football managing bearded hack, would say, 'One day, Johnny. One day it'll hit you and your waist will expand overnight, like a balloon filling with water.' And he was right, the bastard. Course, Colin was just after company. Since marrying Trish, Colin had gained a beard, ten pounds and misplaced both his and his wife's libidos like lost sets of keys.

I met Colin Carter in my first job, when we were both younger and slimmer. After graduating, I landed a prime position on the *Scunthorpe Gazette* as cub reporter. Colin, star reporter, as he had me believe, took me under his dubious wing. He sub-let me a room in his toilet-like house for way above the going rate. It wasn't long before I realized I was a hopeless dyslexic with more of a future in celluloid than print. Colin was fired for a quip about the local MP, and personal friend of our editor, Jonathon Smythe-Bailey the turkey farmer. Colin flattered the personal friend of the editor in a piece campaigning against a local tax windfall for foul breeders. Colin described Smythe-Bailey as a community man at the very centre of Scunthorpe '. . . after the "S" and before the "H", to be precise.' He was marched out of the building by security.

My brief journalistic career lasted less than a month. I back-pedalled stupendously and persuaded BTB to ditch her mundane corporate Marks & Sparks milk-round job in

Manchester, and leg it down to the Big Smoke with me. She moved in with her lunatic Uncle Alfie in East Dulwich. Colin landed a job on the *Sun*, who considered the Scunthorpe–Smythe incident a master stroke, and never looked back. I moved in with Colin and entered the wonderful world of video collation.

'Shorry, shorry.' Loud 'tutting' and 'tssking' came from the seat in front. My own seat buffeted up and down while Mr Big shifted nervously, checking for the nearest exits. He felt for his lifejacket.

'Mine's there. I think yoursh is, too,' he said with inebriated concentration and a hint of Geordie. I nodded, trying to avoid a conversation.

'Can't shtand flying,' he said.

'You don't say.' I smiled.

'Medical condition, you know. Fear of flying, like.'

'Fear of falling rather than flying, surely?' I said, regretting it as I watched his face whiten further, deciding I should try to avoid making things worse for Mr Big. A stomach of his scale could probably hold a sizeable quantity of vomit.

'I'm sure it'll be fine,' I muttered. The hostess wandered past.

'Missh, missh. Hey, lady.' She kept on walking.

'Oi!' Mr Big shouted. I pointed to the steward button. He pushed it, several times. It pinged like an annoying doorbell. She returned.

'How 'bout a drink for me and me pal here.' I cringed at the association.

'Of course, sir, once in flight.'

'Flight, oh aye. Don't want to cause problems, don't want to mess up anything, don't want a crash.' He was sweating again.

'First flight, is it, sir?'

'No, just a little trapped wind.' His shiny face and wide eyes glared at the hostess.

'You'll be fine, just relax.'

'Should be's, like, I've drunk enough to relax a ferkin' elephant,' he said and belched.

You'd need to, I thought. She wandered off.

'Sick bags. SICK BAGS,' he shouted after her. She calmly strolled back, no sign of anger showing.

'Right there in the pocket.'

Mr Big pulled the bag out and examined it. 'Won't fit much in there, like,' he said to me. 'Can I have yours, pal?' I nodded and passed it over.

'Would sir like another drink?' An hour into the flight the stewardess still wore a forced smile. It was as starchy as her oversprayed big hair and ugly uniform, patterned without thought for the potential fits caused to flying epileptics or pissed passengers, like myself.

'Bloody Mary.' I think it was the fifth.

'That's five, you sad man!' she snapped.

'What! I don't think that's any of your bus—'

'I said, would you like lemon?' she repeated, caustically.

'Yes, please.'

'Arse?' she said. I looked at her again, shocked. She held up the ice bucket and tongs with a smile.

'Ice . . . oh.' I nodded and accepted the plastic tumbler, small tomato-juice tin and miniature vodka bottle.

'And for your friend?'

'He's not my friend.' We both looked at the vast crumple-suited catastrophe sitting next to me. Well, I say sitting, but he was really too huge to sit in any single aeroplane seat. He was as big as they come. As a result, he didn't seem to fit. He didn't seem to fit into anything – his beige linen suit, which bulged and strained at the seams in all sorts of unlikely places; his snakeskin loafers, the leather of which was losing a battle to contain what I imagined were feet the size of foot-balls. Flabby limbs – elbows, knees, and arms – all escaped from his space and helplessly invaded my own.

'You seem very close.'

She was really enjoying this, the bitch. We both looked at Mr Big. His head was resting on my shoulder, like a huge grotesque baby. His puffy, pale orange-peel face had a life all of its own. As he snored, sour alcohol breath puffed his cheeks in and out and rattled his jowls, like a demented whinnying horse. His tongue lolled around, a pink slick slug, perilously close to my ear.

'I've never met him before in my life.'

'Oh, I just assumed, over the course of the last six drinks you've had together . . .'

'Five.'

'Five drinks.'

'In fact, this is the fifth now, so actually we only shared four.'

'Uh-hmm.' The hostess paused and tapped her feet impatiently.

'Four,' I emphasized.

'Four, sir. Well, I'd assumed you were friends.'

'No. Never.' The fat man snorted loudly in his sleep, while we looked on with expressions of mild disgust.

'Shall I wake him?' she asked.

'No, no please. Let's leave him be.' Better a slumbering, drunk, fat, space-invading man than an awake one.

So I was left to face my own demons on the remaining hour of the flight. As he shifted in his seat again, I stared down at my notepad, headed, BARCELONA CONFERENCE. Three or four lines were scribbled beneath the heading, all of which had been scored out. I was getting nowhere. In less than twenty-four hours I'd face a room full of delegates from the video collation world, and I didn't have a Scooby Doo what I was going to say.

I don't know how I ended up in my job. Once, life revolved around parties, chatting up the opposite sex, football and fun. I dreamed of being an actor or a director; a 'something'

41

or 'somebody'. The next thing I knew, I'd learnt to say things like 'profitability', 'efficiency', 'resource', 'networking' and 'proactive'.

I'm the marketing manager for the Extraordinary Film & Company (EF&Co) who make videos for the 'grey market' – marketing jargon/bollocks for 'elderly' – using old TV footage from around the world. My first film was called *Wartime Women* – a completely crap and very ordinary collection of unrelated clips of women at war. Anything from Vera Lynn to a bomb factory in Japan to Minnie Mouse cartoons, all packaged together and sold using blatant jingoistic nonsense about Britain and the good old days, even though 80 per cent of the clips were foreign, as usual, as they're the cheapest.

We're the market leaders in this niche area. Our latest release is very exciting and is provisionally entitled *Amusing Clips of Cats with Balls of String*. Of course, this is just the working title. I expect we'll come up with something left field like *Cute Cats 'n' String Special* closer to worldwide launch.

It may surprise you to learn that I had no intention of doing this when I was a kid.

Johnson Riley, aged ten:
  'What do you want to be when you grow up, Johnny?' asks Mum through a cloud of lavender water. Mum always wore this and, as a result, motherhood and the smell of lavender are intertwined for me.

  I am silent; a nasty ten-year-old with a classic Seventies helmet haircut in a dirty tracksuit, picking his nose.

  'An astronaut maybe?' Mum tries. 'Or a footballer? . . . How about a butcher? . . . Or baker? . . . Or a drug-pushing Gangsta-Rapper?'

  'I want to be' – I spoke through a stubborn sneer – 'a marketing manager.'

  'You do, Johnny?' This shocked Mum. 'Not a stuntman or a contract killer?' she offered.

'No, a marketing manager.'

'Not a porn star or pirate?' she kept trying.

'No, a marketing manager. Ideally in the video collation sector, perhaps targeting the "grey market".'

'And what do they do, then, Johnny?'

'Nothing ... of consequence. But Granny Victor says that's fine, that's what most men do.'

'Oh,' says Mum, clearly a bit despondent that her son isn't going to do anything worthy of a Women's Institute lecture (Cornwall branch). Her eyes rapidly glaze over as she drifts into her own faraway dream world.

Mum often did this, drifting off planet into her own fuzzy orbit. She would do it at all sorts of times in all sorts of inappropriate places. Away she would be, dancing with Fred Astaire, crooning with Gene Kelly, singing and swinging in her celluloid world. Mum dreamed of the people she would have liked me to have been, not EF&Co's marketing manager, with launch plans for *Gardens on Film* or budgets and revenue forecasts for *Kids on Camera*, but a tap-dancer with a good voice, or a film star – a Valentino hero with puffy silk trousers and thigh-length riding boots. Even a director or producer's assistant; a gopher or film critic. A bloody projectionist's assistant would have been better than a marketing manager. For a few years I fooled Mum, who thought I'd become one of her fantasies. She would gush at her coffee mornings, 'Yes, Johnson's in the film industry, my dears. I'm sure he'll be directing in no time.'

Of course, Mum knew that her and my Hollywood ambitions were one and the same, deep down. But gradually, to save face, I'd buried them and allowed them to be worn away by EF&Co, like tread on a tyre. Less and less grip for the infamous *Mr Saturday Night*, and more and more rubber burnt fruitlessly in pubs at lunchtime and after work. My whingeing joined the sound of the other workers, complaining at the injustice of a world that failed to spot the brilliant flame of their talent, wasting away on a barstool and capitulating to a 'career' in the video collation – VC – industry.

And now, here I was, at the zenith of my career, about to speak to the globe's VC experts (failed Hollywood hopefuls) in less than a day.

Mr Big spluttered and twitched in his sleep, a fat finger sending my Bloody Mary spilling colourfully across my pad, swamping the few notes I'd made in tomato juice and vodka. I swore loudly, turning the notebook over to see another set of notes: REASONS WHY I SHOULD ASK HER TO M— ME. This was the serious list. This was the real demon, the real cause of my nervousness. Beneath the heading was a series of scribbled pros and cons, in no particular order, revealing my lingering doubt. Eventually, frustrated that I couldn't rationalize an argument for the big 'M', I'd scored them out and had to talk myself out of the hole I was in. OK, forget logic, assume you want to ask her and focus on the plan.

I reckoned on asking the question straight away, on Friday night. This way I'd avoid weekend-long nerves and have a slim chance of enjoying Barcelona. I'd tried to do some homework on the art of proposing. I mean, how do you propose? Who tells you what to do? I flicked through a dictionary of quotations which I'd pinched from the office, thinking it might do the job by providing a few examples of prime proposals from the great and good.

After all, if you were to look back on your life and think of your top sentences, the proposal must be pretty damn significant. If you are a normal person, then 'Will you m— me?' must vie for the number-one slot. OK, if you're the prime minister or a dictator or someone famous, then maybe there are more important sentences, but surely, even for famous folk, the personal rather than the public bit of life is the part that counts.

'I came, I saw, I conquered.' – Will you m— me?

'I have a dream . . .' – Will you m— me?

'Float like a butterfly, sting like a bee.' – Will you m— me?

But could I find anything of use? Could I bollocks. Before I left the office on Thursday morning, all I found was some good advice from Kafka and one brilliant Darwinian theory to help me prepare for Barcelona.

Kafka appreciated the impending doom of wedlock, was twice engaged to the same woman, Felice, and twice broke it off. I think we can take a tip from this. Engagement can be escaped from. It is not Devil's Island or, if it is, you too can be Papillon. Kafka said, '*Alone, I could perhaps some day really give up my job. Married, it will never be possible.*'

I can relate to this; I wouldn't mind waving bye-bye to marketing videos at EF&Co. The trouble is, I've got more chance of doing this with the help of BTB than without her. As a serious high-earning career chick, who pays far more than her fair share of the rent and bills in our house, I was half hoping to get her accidentally up the duff and offer to look after the resulting sprog. I would then do such a crap job of looking after said sprog that BTB would eventually hire a nanny for fear of sprog becoming Mowgli the wolf-child. Mowgli would have zero manners and develop the single skill of cheering gleefully at the TV while slobbering down its front, just like its father. By the time a nanny was coping with the child, I would have joined the ranks of the long-term unemployed and have to stay at home, watching the nanny, the child and *The Richard and Judy Show*. I would end up the Darwinian antithesis, de-volving happily, filling out my ecological niche on a comfy sofa.

Which leads me to the Darwinian theory. Now this isn't, as you might expect, a theory of natural selection applied to the big 'M', although it's fun to imagine how that might work. I guess that a natural-selection theory might argue that blokes like Merlin, who pop the question early, are more secure in their chance of siring children – as is their biological requirement – than those who don't pop the question, like Ratty. While Ratty would argue conversely that his seed, due to the lack of any marital tie, has probably sown more little acorns than any married man could ever hope. Colin would just be confused about him and Trish. She was a press officer in a merchant bank and admitted that she'd deluded herself into ambitions of a 2D Barbour lifestyle with some stockbroker called Eric. Colin reckons it was his superhuman sexual prowess that lured Trish away from Eric. In the early days he'd describe her as 'a cross between Nicole Kidman and a Tasmanian Devil' between the sheets. 'I've had a redhead on my red head' he used to tell a crowd down the Blue Boy with a grin. But since tying the knot, in his own words, his little swimming fish have been 'leaping to their death on the giant tissue mountain sperm graveyard'.

No, the Darwinian theory I'd picked up on wasn't actually about natural selection, which is lucky seeing as comparing the lads seems completely inconclusive. No, old Charlie Darwin might have got all intellectual about genus, class and finches, but he was far more down-to-earth about getting hitched. The Darwinian theory of m— was a list. Charlie D. wrote a list. Or, in fact, two lists regarding proposing to his bird, Emma. In his inimitable, logical, batty-as-a-beagle way, he decided that whichever of the two lists was longer would resolve his dilemma and decide whether or not he should propose. I suppose he was a sort of Victorian botanist dice-man. On the plane to Spain, with a tranquillized bull elephant for company, in my desperate, soul-searching, pre-proposal state, this seemed the soundest advice around.

Darwin's (paraphrased) lists went:

1. Why I shouldn't m— Emma	2. Why I should m— Emma
Freedom to go where one likes	Sprogs (if it so please God)
Gentlemen's club conversations	The charms of music and female chit-chat
Don't have to visit out-laws	Good for health
No cost of sprogs	Companion for life
No quarrelling	Object to be loved and played with
Terrible loss of time	Better than having a dog anyway!

Darwin wrote this in July 1838, when he was my age, twenty-nine. And this was the state of his list, the Darwinian criteria for m—. Now, I may be just an amateur biologist but, if you ask me, list one, 'Why I shouldn't', is looking more of a winner than list two. There's more substance in the first list, far more stony, heartfelt sentiment. I mean, by the second point of list two – 'charms of music and female chit-chat' – Darwin's already scraping the barrel. As for the dog oversight, I mean, how could a wife compete with Muttley? Even if you accept some of the spurious entries on list two, it's still neck and neck.

Therefore you'll be surprised to learn that Charlie asked Emma to be his BTB. How? How could this happen when the lists were equal, not to mention the fact that list two was mainly garbage? He added one final sentence to list two, which went, *'My God, it is intolerable to think of spending one's whole working life like a neuter bee, working, working and nothing after all. No, no won't do. Imagine living all one's days in a smoky, dirty London house.'*

This final point was so long that it blew the 'Don't marry' list away. Darwin then wrote conclusively across the bottom of the two lists, 'Marry, Marry, Marry – QED.'

He bloody cheated, didn't he! He might as well have written 'because, because, because' over and over in the 'Marry' list like a big snivelling cheat. Liar, liar, pants on fire, I say to Darwin's list, if playground terminology must be used.

But I was desperate for any help. After nearly two hours, five Bloody Marys, three gin and tonics and acres of fantasizing about joining the mile-high club with all three of the air stewardesses, I read over my scrawled 'Why I should/shouldn't ask BTB' lists.

1. Why I shouldn't m— BTB	2. Why I should m— BTB
Sprogs (whether God is pleased or not, I am not ready for nappy attack just yet!)	She knows how to magic the bills away, I would be sent to gaol if left to me
Freedom to fart without fear of reprisals	I think all my friends prefer her to me
Her three brothers and father (armed and dangerous)	Her three brothers and father (armed and dangerous)
Footy	Muttley loves her
A chance to play the field again	Can't remember how to play the field, can't find the field, don't think they'd let me in field anyway
Can't say m—	Her smile

Like Darwin, I decided to leave the casting vote to a final scrawl across the bottom, 'Because, because, because . . . because she's wonderful . . . because she's . . . because to not have her share my life would be total bollocks.'

Conclusive proof, QED (suck on that, Darwin.)

'Do it.' Mr Big belched the words out as he woke up. I covered my pad like a protective child swot at a test.

'Excuse me?'

'Excused, pal.' Mr Big's face, like Playdoh, had creased comically on my shoulder, where he'd left a pool of drool.

'It's none of your business,' I said defensively.

'I can help you.'

'How?'

'Wisdom.'

'How? You're . . . you're just a fat drunk northern bloke.' The man roared with deafening laughter like a great grizzly bear. The decibel level made me realize that I'd just taken the piss out of someone who could probably snap my spine in half with an accidental sneeze, or eat me mistakenly, thinking I was a light salad. I was glad he was laughing and tried to make amends.

'Bad experience?' I asked. He stopped laughing suddenly, and brought his wild-eyed face to within an inch of my own.

'Never, never, ever miss your moment.'

'What?'

'Never let something you want slip through your fingers like so much sand. Never let self-centred thoughts cloak you, like a Klingon vessel, so you can't smell the coffee.' I tried to keep up with what sounded, and smelled, like weird, pissed rambling.

'Capture your firefly, keep it tight in your hand, never let it go. You can chase it for ever, and ever, and ever, looking for that thing that you didn't think you wanted when it wanted you and then, by the time you realize you do, it's *hasta la vista*, baby.'

'So you're saying ask her.'

'I'M SAYING, FUCKING RIGHT *ASK*, YOU LITTLE TWAT!' Other passengers looked nervously at the shouting bear next to me. 'Don't think life is about this shit.' He picked up my conference material. 'This is piss; this is nothing.'

He ate the conference programme. 'This doesn't even taste any bastard good.' I stayed stock-still, as if I was caught in a loo with a lion.

'I swapped my soul for little slice of ladder-rung action; I let them cut out my heart for a pile of magic powder, planted the seeds and grew a beanstalk.' A big, fat blob of a tear plopped from his heavily bagged eyes like brimming china cups.

'Now I can't find her. I look; look everywhere. I spend money on people looking. Can't fuckin' fly, can't find her fast enough. Always gone from where I get to next, like a rumour, like the last good show in town.'

For the rest of the flight Mr Big sobbed. I held him. I tried to wrap my arm around his shoulders and, at full stretch, I could just see my fingers waggling on the far side of the sad planet beside me. Just before descent, the caustic trolley dolly came to offer help.

'Is he OK, your friend? Does he need anything?' She wasn't so bad.

'My friend's fine,' I said. 'Just fine.'

At the end of the flight, Mr Big apologized, and gave me his card, bouncing away into the Barcelona night, for all I knew to chase his firefly again, the one he lost some time earlier in his life.

Presenting

Barcelona continued to crash and burn. By the time I'd checked in to the hotel, nerves had well and truly got the better of my alcohol-to-blood ratio. Nerves always affect me before addressing an audience; the trouble is those nerves, the speaking ones, were being dwarfed by giant big-fucker proposal nerves.

Post check-in, I continued the alcohol binge started on the plane with more *cerveza* than was sensible. Conference hotels are the same the world over, and the combination of my worsening inebriation and the banal interior ensured that it failed to register with my senses in any meaningful way. The over-riding feeling was placid and predictable. My bedroom was an oblong assembly-line job, with standard striped wallpaper, glass-topped desk, ugly lampshade and beige bathroom. A tiny balcony looked promising, but it was hard to tell in the dark. Heading for the bar, I stumbled through the wash of pale fitted carpets, brass fixtures, soft lighting, uninspiring paintings, listless wood and drab fake marble. Eventually I located the hotel bar, after asking my reflection for a drink in a large mirror in the foyer. The barman kindly humoured me, putting up with my sad stereotypical term of endearment for him. 'Manuel,' I shouted pathetically.

'*Sí, señor*,' he said drolly.

'Teach me the Spanish for . . .' I'd always wanted to learn

a language, and randomly fed Manuel words and phrases to translate into Spanish.

'Sí, señor,' he would reply. This carried on for way too long. I returned to my hotel room arseholed, with a few hours to sober up and prepare my speech.

On the day of the conference, I was an odd concoction of hungover, sleepy, smelly and scared of the weekend coming. Not a good mix. That morning, crowded by the tan-coloured bathroom tiles, I was shocked by my reflection. I could have been in an advert for a hangover cure. I attempted to disguise myself with the pristine new suit and shirt BTB had chosen for me – dramatically improving the chances of it looking OK. On the hanger the brown cotton designer suit and brilliant white shirt shone. I put them on carefully, daintily trying to avoid creasing them. I looked in the mirror again to wonder at the transformation. I had converted the stylish suit and shirt into limp, bedraggled clothing. It was as if my hungover, parboiled face had spread its constituency through the threads of cotton and wool.

I snuck into the darkened auditorium where the expo was being staged after the first speaker had already begun, and was directed to a reserved front-row seat. Sinking into my chair, I gripped my pounding head and mentally gripped my bowels, which were having a hard time with the hat-trick gut hassle of beer, tapas and the prospect of proposing. I sat smack in front of a sign saying, 'Have You Turned Your Mobile Off?' I checked. It was still off from the night before when, on Poshasfuck Airways, they'd announced something like, 'Use of mobile phones will cause the plane to plummet into a mountain,' scaring Mr Big into a sudden bout of suffocating flatulence. I made a mental note to ring the office and pick up my messages at the end of the conference. The day rolled on and the speakers came and went. It was all humdrum monotony until . . .

*

'And now, please give a big Barcelona welcome to ...'
Conferences aren't normally this glamorous, I thought,
dazzled by the light show that had started. '... the wonderful ...' As I stood up, overhead spotlights zoomed about like
a scene from the blitz in which my head was a zeppelin. '...
the world-famous ...' Steady on, this is supposed to be a
boring work presentation with slides and charts, it can't be
me they're talking about. '... JOHNSON RILEY!'
Ohfuckohfuck. I looked at the audience, expecting maybe a
hundred bored executives to stare back, indifferent as usual.
Ninety thousand men were lit up in waves by the sweeping
spotlights. They cheered hysterically as I walked slowly
towards the stage, suddenly feeling as though I knew the
moves, that this moment was somehow choreographed.

As I stood on the steps to the stage, each one lit up as the
spotlight focused on me. A drum roll started and I kicked left
and right. I reached to my left to catch a top hat, perching it
jauntily on my head. In my right hand, a silver cane
appeared, which doubled up as a microphone. Finally, at the
top of the stairs, I turned to face the 90,000 grooms in
the audience. In one movement, I pulled off my suit and shirt,
cleverly fixed with Velcro. Underneath I'm wearing an all-in-
one white Lycra jumpsuit, with JR embroidered in diamanté
on each arse-cheek and the crotch. I notice that I've grown a
heavy black moustache, horse's teeth and a larger lunch box
than I'm used to. I'm Freddie Mercury. It couldn't be worse.
The crowd scream as I begin with the song they are all
expecting:

'Baaaarrrrceeeeloooooonnnnaaaaaaaaaaaa.'

'Such a beautiful horizon'

'Baaaarrrrceeeeloooooonnnnaaaaaaaaaaaa.'

'Such a shame I am proposing . . .'

'Hmmmppp.' I woke with a start, slobber on my suit, my head in the lap of the Japanese lady sitting on my left. Being Japanese, she had been too polite to wake me from my slumber. I managed to time my awakening perfectly with a request from the Spanish chairman for questions from the floor regarding the last presentation from the German speaker. My loud 'Hmmmppp' had been mistaken for an offer of a question.

'Yes, a question from Mr Riley of England's EF&Co,' said the chairman.

'Ah yes . . .' *Ah shit*, I begin. 'A fascinating presentation from our German colleague . . .' *Which I slept through*, I bullshit. *Ohgodwhatamigoingtoask?* 'I would love to know what the opinion of . . . er . . .' Name? Name? Name? 'The speaker is . . . er . . . regarding his home market of . . . er . . .' *A suicide pill, a sawn-off shotgun in the mouth, a mercy killing from a kind-hearted assassin in the audience would all be welcome at this particular point in time.* 'Er . . . the Bertlesmann TV copyright battle?'

I had read about this somewhere recently and it sounded pretty good. Saved, thank God, from international embarrassment. The speaker looked at the chairman in confusion, who in turn said, 'Mr Riley, Mr Spiegel has spent the last hour doing just that in his presentation entitled "A Victory for VC, Bertlesmann TV Beat the Regulators".' *Shit, I had read about this recently – in the fucking programme!*

Everything was falling apart. So far I had listened to eight speakers from around the world without taking in a single word. I had sat nervously, knowing that I fully intended to meet my girlfriend at the airport later that night, spend a romantic weekend with her in Barcelona and ask her a question which would ultimately recreate, re-form and reanimate her as the monster, Psycho Fiancée! After the next speaker, it would be my turn, so I had roughly twenty minutes to get my head together.

Normally at a conference I crap my pants copiously before having to make a presentation, and then make a stuttering, incompetent pillock of myself in any debates or workshops. In my defence, this is not uncommon.

Do you know what the vast majority of Brits are most scared of?

Not spiders, not snakes, not vertigo, not flying, not even claustrophobia, but public speaking. Amazing, isn't it? I mean, you'd think it would be the big 'M', having children, mothers-in-law or Granny Victor. But no, it's public speaking. I can understand this actually. In fact, my company have sent me on courses to stop me spewing profusely before presentations. And yet, here I am again, nervous, no sleep last night, palms sweating, can't hold my food down. But all for the wrong/right/wrong reasons. I have thoughts for only one thing, one sentence, four words, five syllables – and one specific word I still haven't been able to successfully say yet: mmm . . . nope, still not possible. I was scared spineless, but not about the presentation, about something far more frightening and indelible. I looked at the conference programme for inspiration.

Johnson Riley, marketing manager from Extraordinary Film & Company, will present on his company's UK experiences. Johnson has seven years' experience in his industry. His successes include the Guff Video Initiative in 1998 and the Crap TV Plan of 1999. Johnson is about to make the biggest mistake of his life and propose to his girlfriend like a fool. In America his name means 'penis'.

I thought back to the advice of the wiry, long-limbed American sales evangelist who ran the course I'd recently been sent on: 'Nerves are nothing to fear.' A hundred or so scared presenters cowered in the room like shivering puppies at the vets.

'Nerves are good, nerves are Neanderthal! It's all about the science of fight or flight,' he explained, as if he was some guru, some world-altering scientist, instead of a tin-pot, two-bit preacher. I remember looking around to see if any of the other delegates were falling for his shit, and realized they weren't even listening, they were praying. Praying that he wouldn't ask them to speak or make a presentation, so it didn't matter a toss what he said, which is precisely why he was talking shit.

I have to admit that he did give me a good tip on controlling anxiety. He explained that nervousness can be controlled by left-brain activity. The right side of your brain is the creative bit, while the left side is your rationality, memory and logic – I think God skimped a bit on this side of my brain. The trick to overcome your nerves is to get the left side into gear. If you can do this, if you can wake it up, then whatever you're nervous about – presentations, proposals, wedding speeches – becomes automatic. You flip into auto-pilot and the creative side of your brain takes a nap. To get the left side going, he advised reciting something you have learned: repeating telephone numbers you know, doing a crossword puzzle, or reciting multiplication tables in your head. This bit of advice from the wiry Yank has since become an entrenched habit. When I'm nervous I say them over and over in my mind, just like we used to at school, in that sing-songy, perfectly harmonious parrot-fashion way, while Mr Smith, the maths teacher, conducted with delusions of André Previn.

Now it was my turn to speak and I wished that I'd worn a nappy as I approached the lectern.

Ohfuckohfuckohshitohshit, nervous as hell.

Three fours are twelve.

Trying desperately to control myself.

Two twelves are twenty-five.
I'monlytwentyninewhatthehellamidoing.
Two nines are four.
I'mtooyoungtogetmmmmmmm . . .
One one is single.
Seconds before they called me to the podium my nerve wires were still crossed.

'So we are pleased to welcome' – the chairman sounded neither pleased nor welcoming – 'Mr Johnson Riley of Britain.' The speaker seemed to spit the word 'Britain' out like a bad oyster.

I stood up and large sections of the already dwindling audience left. I looked at the script that I'd thought was good at 3 a.m. *'¡Buenas noches!'* I said, although it came out as 'bonus knockers'. The chairman shook his head, and I realized I was about to talk nonsense for the next forty minutes.

At the end the applause was similar to the deafening clapping at a village-green cricket match when a batsman actually manages to hit the ball. Barcelona was not going well. Barcelona had sunk without trace. Barcelona was a sun-dried, cracked white turd.

Returning to my seat, humiliated, I was struck by a sudden flash of clarity. I decided not to tempt fate a second time in Barcelona. One Spanish disaster was plenty for this year, proposing could wait. After all, it was only Merlin who knew, my mate, my best buddy, my trusty confidant. Merl would support me. After all, it was just a delayed fixture, a postponement, not a full-blown cancellation.

Of course, there was the problem of BTB; of catching my firefly, like Mr Big said. He would definitely disapprove, but hey, what did he know, he was just a fat drunk. I fished his card out of my wallet where I'd stuffed it, unread, along with taxi receipts and meeting debris.

Lord Norbert Camberly
Gold Sparrow Films Worldwide Inc.

Film Producer & CEO

A fat, drunk, nobody, world-renowned, Hollywood-hunted producer of the best of British film. Lord Camberly, who did all his business out of the back of a limousine driving around London. Norbert Camberly – famous for refusing to be lured (physically) to Hollywood, famous as the big Geordie boy made good, and famous for his fear of flying. I'd dissed the kind of contact most people trying to break into film would swap a bollock for. Lord Norbert Camberly. What a load of pants.

Flapping Camel Coat

'Four, four, two. Four, four, two!' shouted Colin from the touchline. The rain was relentless on another grey Sunday morning in Battersea.

The pitch was one of six that crowded a poorly kept stretch of wasteland, hidden in the suburbs east of the power station and just to the south of the Thames.

From a distance they looked like proper footballers in a proper match. Eleven men, good and true, battling it out on the chalk-scoured mud. Their plain blue, long-sleeved, round-necked shirts made them look like a bunch of Fifties throwbacks as they huffed and puffed around the pitch.

'Four, four, two!' Colin shouted relentlessly.

'Go fuck yersell!' Ratty shouted back, as he charged down the left wing, low-riding on stumpy legs and snorting like a warthog. Failing to pass his marker, he hastily cross-bred a swallow-dive with a bellyflop in a feeble attempt to gain a foul.

'Foul!' shouted Ratty, gripping his shin as his marker, now in delirious possession, trampled up the wing unchallenged.

Up close, you realized they weren't real footballers, but real people, real men, better suited to barstools than football matches. Aged anything between twenty-five and thirty-seven, they were young enough to stagger around the pitch for ninety minutes – just – and old enough to have given up hope of Wembley, or even Craven Cottage.

'Up and after him, Ratty! Come on!' Colin used to play with the lads, but since his marriage and subsequent loss of stamina, speed and hair, he strutted along the touchline with the self-importance of a cock.

'Come on, four, four, two, like I said! Tell him, Stef!' Colin shouted to Stefano, the sole skilful footballer on the team.

'No!' Stef shouted back to Colin.

'GOALLLL!' shouted the red-and-black-striped opposition – the Hope and Anchor – as the ref blew his whistle in confirmation.

Ratty's marker had strolled past the defence and slotted the ball insultingly through the legs of the keeper, Merlin.

'Jesus, Merl!' Stef stuck his hands on his hips and hung his head low, and for all the world looked like Ronaldo, disappointed at the failings of his team-mates. Stef was built like a real footballer, was fitter than the rest of the team put together and had once tried out for Brentford. He also, dubiously, claimed he was of Italian descent (Stefano) even though his surname was Smith. Of course, he claimed it was on his mum's side, but she'd run off back to Italy with the local fishmonger when he was eight, so there was no way of checking.

The rest of the team was more like a schoolyard rabble having a kick-about. The whistle blew for half-time and Colin strolled determinedly to the centre circle, where the Blue Boys had gathered around Stef. As both a solid footballer and a PE teacher, Stef kept in shape and was a natural captain for the team. He looked the part, sounded the part and played the part well.

Colin's new goatee partially hid his triple chin. He'd nurtured the beard, taken up cigars and bought a second-hand flea-bitten camel coat to look the part of team manager. Unlike Stef, it somehow seemed pretend. Colin was a little boy playing at dressing up, convinced that he's a superhero in his outfit of red wellies and pyjamas.

'Fuck me, here comes Cloughy,' muttered Merlin.

Stefano was in full flow when Colin arrived. 'Lads, we've gotta hang back and cover their ten; he's a bastard on the break. And Skunk, for fuck's sake, *this* is a football.' He held up the ball. 'We want to stop it – the ball – going in the back of our net!'

'No, no, no. What you need is a four, four, two formation,' interrupted Colin. With unified and practised discipline, the entire team ignored him.

'Oh, come on, Stef, that was keyhole-surgery shooting,' protested Merlin.

'It went through your bleedin' legs, which were spread-eagled like *Penthouse*'s September centrefold,' continued Stef.

'Aye, she wiz all right, her, right enough,' Ratty piped up from the back, alternately wheezing and puffing on his third half-time cigarette. 'No' as good as May, though.' He looked thoughtful, and the team momentarily joined in, mentally conjuring the September and May *Penthouse* centrefolds.

'And it was your bloody fault Hope and Anchor broke, Ratty, which led to the last goal. *Passing* is what we do when we are about to lose the ball. That's called *passing*, Ratty.'

'Ha fuckin' ha, Ronaldo!' Ratty scowled.

Stef glanced at the ref and saw that he was preparing to start the second half. 'Right, now a word from our manager. Over to you, Col.'

'Right, boys, it's all in the formation—' With precision timing, the ref blew for the start of the second half. The boys trotted off at once, leaving Colin crouching alone in the centre circle, scratching his stubbly beard, his camel coat flapping in the wind.

Ratty and Stef kicked off. 'Have you heard about Johnny?' Ratty asked, receiving Stef's tap and feeding the ball back to the defence.

'No, what?' Stef watched the ball dawdle back to Merlin

and started walking forward, ready for a deep kick into the opposition half.

'Have they split up?' Stef shouted, moving further away from Ratty, ready to break.

'You wish, you'd love to have a pop at her, eh?' Ratty's crude instincts were often accurate.

'Oi, steady, Rat, me and Maddy are supposed to be an item nowadays.'

Merlin thudded the ball forward and Stef jumped for it. Out-leaping his marker, he nodded the ball through to Ratty.

'Yeh right.' Ratty pushed up the left wing and Stef kept with him.

'You know they're in Barcelona for a romantic weekend?' Ratty said as he fed through to Stef who had found space on the left.

Stef was tackled and the ball went out for a throw-in in the last third. He shook his head and blamed Ratty. 'Stop yabbering, you blouse. Get on with the game.'

A defender came up for a long ball, and Ratty and Stef goal-hunted twelve yards out.

'Anyway, so what about Barcelona?' Stef couldn't scrub the conversation from his mind, even though it was distracting him from the game. The ball sailed through the air *en route* to a perfect top-left-hand-corner volleying opportunity for Stef, who had already lined up his shot.

'Johnny's proposing,' shouted Ratty. Stef sliced the shot three miles wide of the left post.

'Fuck! Fuck, fuck, bastard.'

Nobody knew what Stef was cursing.

Within ten minutes almost every player on the field knew that Johnny was proposing in Barcelona and were chatting about the pros and cons of marriage.

'Foul!' The ref blew against Ratty.

'You know, scientists reckon, nowadays, that it's bio-logically impossible for a man to remain with just one partner.' The ref chatted idly to Ratty and the player he'd just fouled, who joined in as Ratty helped him to his feet, 'Yeah, that's right, it's to do with longer life expectancies and eating natural yoghurt.'

Ratty sighed and slapped his forehead. 'It's to do with shaggin' as many birds as ye can, ya daft bastard.'

'So when's he asking?' Stef asked, on another doomed foray into the opposition's half with the unhelpful assistance of Ratty.

'Probably has already, daft fucker. He flies back Monday night, so you never know, he might be saving the best for last.' Ratty wheezed as he spoke.

Only Merlin, the lonely keeper, was unaware of the topic of conversation that kept the players engrossed for the majority of the second half.

In the last five minutes, the opposition scored their fifth goal to the Blue Boys' bugger all. 'The decider that put them out of reach,' as Colin later described it. While Merlin lay in a heap on the ground, the Hope and Anchor number ten, who'd scored a hat-trick, ambled past him to collect the ball from the back of the net.

'So I hear you're gonna be Johnny's best man.'

'Hmm? Oh yeah, that's right. I . . .' In the gaps between the mud, Merlin's skin blanched to match his white streak. 'What the fuck! How in the hell . . . ?'

'Let's hope you make a better best man than goalkeeper,' he sniggered, and strolled off as the final whistle went.

Colin met Merlin as he stomped towards the concrete oblong changing rooms, fuming. 'How about Dublin?' Colin said. Merlin ignored him and seethed, massaging his temples. He imagined castrating Ratty, or worse, nailing his knob to his femur and taking him to a lap-dancing club.

'Little bleedin' jock bastard!' muttered Merlin.

'Or Amsterdam?' continued Colin. 'Or maybe we could use that girl, Tina?'

'What the bloody hell are you on about, Colin lad?'

'You know, Tina, that Kiwi you always go on about. Works in your post room by day, gets her kit off at night. Although, thinking about it, I know some hookers who'll do specials for stags and—'

'FUCKING HELLLLLL!' Merlin shouted and clapped his palms over his ears. What had he done?

Supposing

Would I propose?
  It didn't seem likely.
  Could I propose?
  'Mmmmm . . . nope!'
  I sat alone in the hotel bar post-conference, sulking. Even though the majority of delegates were asleep, or had left when I'd been presenting, their avoidance of me suggested that news of my lacklustre presentation had spread like a nasty rash. Forget it, I thought. Fuck 'em. Self-important film failures; who needs their plaudits? Not me, all I need to do is dust down *Mr Saturday Night*, pop it in the post to Lord Camberly and it's arrivedérci VC. I fantasized about success, about cheers from the crowd at Cannes, about slaps on the back from Norbert, about BTB smiling and laughing, delighted, as I popped the question.
  POP! The bubble burst. It was no good. I was a failure. Mr Big would probably bin my script and BTB would respond to my question with 'What? You, Johnny? Is this some sort of sick joke?' I was glad I'd decided to ditch the proposal.
  Delegates were scattered among the hazily familiar brass and wood of the hotel bar. They huddled for comfort in small groups of threes and fours, discussing monotonous VC stuff, fixing phone calls and visits, exchanging handshakes and business cards, adding to the standard conference

practice of copious bodily fluid exchange.

I spotted the Japanese lady I'd slobbered over earlier among a small group of women at the bar. She smiled. I smiled back hesitantly, presuming she was simply laughing at a joke at my expense. *Look at the English tool, wasn't his talk cack*, I imagined her saying to her colleagues.

Earlier, in my nervous, hungover stupor, I had somehow failed to notice that the polite Japanese lady was, in fact, stunning, in a shy and understated way. Her charcoal hair hung in a short, sharp cut, which framed her delicate waxen face. As she laughed, large black eyes danced like jet-flecked jewels. Japanese women – kinky oriental sex slaves, I mentally stereotyped from my sad-lads' library of fantasy porn.

Gambling further humiliation, I strolled casually to the bar and ordered a beer. Remaining there, awkwardly, I stood slightly too close to the group, next to the Japanese lady. Searching for some status, I pulled out my mobile phone. It was off. I turned it on. It bleeped. The digital display flashed 'One Message'. I presumed it was from BTB, checking in, telling me she was in the departure lounge at Heathrow and would be in Barcelona pretty soon. I gulped, realizing the imminence of her arrival brought my supposed proposal ever closer. I thought it through again, thought about the consequences of the question lodged in my head like a piece of shrapnel. Soon I'd meet her at the airport and alter her irretrievably into my betrothed – sounds like death-rowed.

Fuck it! I couldn't do it! I wouldn't do it. I turned the phone off again. I could pick up the message another time. I could ask her to mmm . . . thingy me another time. It's all just too permanent.

I swallowed hard and sat on a stool at the bar, glancing across at the group of women to my right. Did I really think there would never be another woman after BTB? Because that's what it all boils down to, you know. Either that, or you accept lies and infidelity; and while I confess to being a typical bloke, I'm no serial shagger like Ratty.

We'd lived together for three years now, and making that decision had been hard enough. So far I'd managed to delay the inevitable house buying and joint mortgage with various excuses, ranging from 'the property market is collapsing like a house of cards' to 'no chance of getting a mortgage, I'm a credit fugitive'. But living together is one thing, the big 'M' is quite another. Living together could be seen as chic, bohemian, relatively painless, separable. It even sounds temporary. While m— sounds middle-aged, permanent, the final countdown. A bit like retired, or put out to pasture.

I slumped on my stool, head resting on my hand, necking my beer. Just the thought of proposing brought a million questions flying through my brain, like bats in a cave, each one screeching through my mind.

What about sex? It's good now, living together, but will it all take on a functional sprog-orientated connotation post m—? What about the potential for GBH from her family when they find out? Apart from the incongruous, gentle younger brother, Seamus, the rest of them look violent – silent mother and ranting dad, Jack and Paddy, the brothers grim. Somehow, I get the feeling they see me as temporary, a bit like the hyperactive Jack Russell her dad threw in the canal when she was a little girl.

Will that be the final whistle for the lads? Sad husbands – me, Merl and Colin – outweighing single beaver-hounds – Ratty and Stef.

What about money and the dreaded joint bank account? She'd finally find out for sure just how much I piss away on booze, fags, CDs, videos and leisure flotsam. And would she mind if we only spent seventy pence – my savings – on the big day?

Does it have to be a religious ceremony? My only God is the King.

And on that subject, how about Elvis impersonating priests and tattoo-swapping in Vegas?

Would I scriptwrite – skint and hopeful – or spout shit in bill-paying video collation? Way too rhetorical.

Am I supposed to stop fantasizing about Maddy? I still remember that night at college too clearly. Maybe hypnosis would work. And is that ditto for the kinky oriental sex slave on my right?

Do I have to be a grown-up? I think that's less likely than world peace.

Did Dad have the same questions in his head before he asked Mum?

I could go on for ever.

Millions of bastard bats in the cave, some big fat life-changing questions; some tiny, incey-wincey detail ones. But they're all there, all screeching. Forget them. The real choice is the to-be-or-not-to-BTB question:

Do I, Johnson Riley, take her, BTB, to be my lawful wadded wolf, because I will never love another more?

Or, Do I, Johnson Riley, take her, BTB, to be my leerful welded waif, but accept that there is every chance I will shag a few other women on the way to an average fourteen-year-long stretch before divorce and the messy by-products of children and mortgages?

That's it. That is the choice. You either lie, but say 'I do' anyway, or you love her and say 'I do' genuinely. Liar or lover, you choose. The Japanese lady was smiling at me. I spilt my beer on my shirt, surprised to have been caught staring. I panicked and looked away, hiding in my messed-up thoughts.

You see, this is the whole trouble with life; it's what Mr Big was trying to grasp in his slurred stream of consciousness on the plane. Being happy, accepting your lot willingly with a smile, is all about whether you imagine the grass is always greener. Everything can be reduced to the nature of your grass and whether you're happy with it. If you're not, but you pretend you are, all you're doing is covering a yellow patch on the turf, pretending Muttley hasn't dumped a steamer in the middle of the lawn or ignoring the moss below the surface. You're deceiving yourself – it'll go away, it won't screw up our lawn, everything's OK really.

But accepting your lot happily often means living in the real world and not a parallel universe where women fall at your feet and beers guts are in vogue.

BTB says there are two kinds of women, women who like chocolate and complete bitches. I think there are two types of men, men who want to be James Bond, and men who want to be James Bond but either pretend they don't or have been anaesthetized to zombie their way through life in a coma.

Every man wants beautiful women who can also fight. We want fast cars, guns, commitment-free shags and pens that you can blow things up with.

I returned the smile of the Japanese lady.

Nope. No-way José. Uh-uh. Forget it. I abstain from voting, I postpone making the choice. I'll decide about my grass later. No proposals for me today, I'm playing 007. Another day, some other time, I'll sit and think about whether BTB's greener than the greenest grass I can imagine. OK, she's green, she's lush, she's a verdant velvet bowling green. But won't it ever be greener?

The trouble is, I haven't seen all the grass in the world. I've seen the grass in the gardens of our street, and in streets all over Clapham, Battersea and right across London. I saw grass up at Edinburgh and back home in Cornwall, where I grew up, and my grass is greenest by a mile. But I haven't seen all the grass there is. Japanese grass, for example, remains hidden away in some secret walled garden.

Eventually, in a few years, or perhaps five, a decade maybe – at the end of my days I'll be able to make an educated and intelligent judgement about the comparative greenness of grass. And nothing will have been lost but a bit of time, eh? No offence caused, no-one would know – just my pal, Merl. After all, BTB never expected a Barcelona proposal, so why worry? Ratty would back me up, if he knew, which of course he doesn't. And Stef, too. Mind you, I reckon he fancies BTB, so maybe he'd be biased. I'll just take my time and think things through. See if I can find a few answers to the bat-questions, check out a few more lawns to ease my mind.

Of course, you might think I've backed down because of bruised confidence after a pants presentation, or fear of rejection from BTB, or of the consequences of the big 'M'. But you'd be wrong. In my mind it's all about certainty. Honest. And I guess, when she's not here, laughing and loving and fizzling, it's easy to fool myself, to temporarily forget, to be a love amnesiac. But it isn't that, either, really it isn't. My phone beeps again, I still haven't retrieved my message. I put the phone away, like the proposal. *I'll worry about that later*, I think.

I watch the women in the bar from the corner of my eye as I pocket my mobile, happy that it has performed its status-rescuing function. The ladies on my right, and indeed the majority of the bar, would be thinking, Look at that guy, he's an important businessman, I bet he works for a cool company like EF&Co, who make cool videos like *Bird-love – The Mating Dances of Birds Around the Planet*.

I wish I was James Bond.

I pull out my wallet. Searching for pesetas, I find the crumpled piece of paper I'd torn from my pad on Poshasfuck Airways. I read over my Darwinian Criteria for m— list.

About to throw the list away, I notice faint writing on the other side of the paper.
The barman appears.
'Sir?'
'Ah, Manuel, a Martini please. Shaken, not stirred.' I

return to the note. The words are written in flammable ink. I reach into my dinner-suit jacket pocket for my standard-issue solid-silver combined cigarette case and lighter. After lighting a cigarette, I heat the paper with the flame and the words begin to form:

007, you have ten seconds to digest your mission before this ink dissolves. SPECTRE are suspected of an international plot to distribute videos containing subliminal messages that cause the viewers to behave in a way that contravenes the security of the British Empire. They are currently targeting Her Majesty's Secret Service agents. We have already lost three field operatives, 004, 005 and 006. All good agents who previously womanized gratuitously in between heavy bouts of violence, driving fast cars and spending taxpayers' cash in casinos. All three agents, after only one lethal viewing of the SPECTRE videos, have married and settled down. 004 has a baby on the way and 005 marries Moneypenny next weekend (see you at the service). 007, the fate of the Service and safety of the nation and the planet is in your hands.

M

P.S. 004 wants you to be a godfather, and 005 has asked if you could be an usher.

The words fade on the paper as quickly as they had formed. 'Manuel, some Tabasco sauce.' I screw the paper up, douse the ball in sauce and pop it in my mouth.

'Excuse me, I'm a bit peckish,' I quip to the polite Japanese lady watching me as I down my Martini and swallow.

'Allow me to introduce myself, my name is Bond, Johnson Bond. May I buy you a drink?' Manuel returns. 'Champagne for madame and I'll have a—'

'Martini. Shaken, not stirred?' guesses Manuel.

'No, a pint of Guinness.'

'But, Mr Bond?'

'I'm bored with bloody Martini, it's a poof's drink.' The waiter nods and disappears.

'And for whom do I have the pleasure of buying champagne?'

'My name is Slo Lee Cumming,' spoke the Japanese lady.

'Hmm, Opium. What an appropriate fragrance,' I say as Manuel arrives with the champagne.

'Tattinger 'forty-three!' I exclaim as the bottle arrives in a silver ice bucket. I lean over the bar.

'Yes, Mr Bond?' Manuel sighs, bored of my demands.

I whisper, 'Haven't you got some cheap stuff, Pomagne or Lambrusco; she'll never know the difference.'

'Certainly, Mr Bond . . . Anus,' he mutters as he walks away.

'What was that?'

'I was thinking of retiring to a more private place, Mr Bond. Why not join me in my suite?' Slo Lee talks slowly as she strokes my inner thigh. She hands me the key to her suite and slinks out of the bar elegantly.

I wink at Manuel.

'I'm in there, definitely in there.' I grin.

'Yes, Mr Bond, of course . . . Arse,' I'm sure I heard him add quietly.

'I say, what was that?'

I came to my senses suddenly at the hotel bar. After five beers and one sickly Martini, I had still failed to engage the Japanese lady in conversation. To be honest, I didn't really want to. Not in the real world, anyway. As ever, I was far happier in my threat-free fantasy land.

Looking at my watch, I realized I was in danger of missing BTB's flight, so I drained my glass, thanking Manuel with a slur.

Somewhere, mixed into the background noise of the hotel bar, I could hear music – 'We Have All The Time In The World' by Louis Armstrong. I remembered that even the average male alter ego, James Bond, had once popped the question. It was a sobering thought. If Bond, every man's id, can do the m— thing, then anyone can. Tragically, Mrs Bond was shot by Blofeld on their honeymoon in the saddest ending to any film ever devised, and in the background 'We Have All The Time In The World' played.

I didn't; I was late.

Lost-cause Armpits and Rhino Skin

'I'm telling you, lads, that fifth goal was the decider.' Colin paced edgily in the corridor outside the white-tiled shower cubicles, muttering while reading a paper. Every few minutes he would shout something into the steam, directed at Stef, Merl or Ratty, who were the last of the team still showering.

Colin was now without camel coat, but comically kitted out in his own, too-clean, Blue Boys' strip – Chelsea, late Sixties – which rose up over his gut, showing off a hairy roll of fat.

'Fuck off, Colin.' Merlin's words were lost in the din of the shower.

'What did you say there, Merl?' shouted Colin, peering into the gloom, before carrying on with his managerial dissection of the game, in between glances at the *News of the World*.

Merlin sat silently on the tiles, angry that the whole world seemed to know about Johnny.

'We've got to work on formation and . . . and goal-keeping.' The corridor outside the showers was the only place where Colin's diatribes would go unchallenged and uninterrupted, mainly because no-one could hear him over the noise of the streaming water. Most of the team had left the showers already and hurried down the corridor into the changing rooms, where they were quickly tugging on socks, shirts and shoes over wet, half-clean bodies in the rush to get their first Sunday pint. Merlin, Ratty and Stef dawdled under the showers, sulking and chatting.

'I'll sort some training on Wednesday, shall I?'

'Shut up, Colin!' shouted Stef in the direction of the corridor before turning back to Ratty. 'I wish Col'd give this manager thing a break. He thinks he's Arsene fuckin' Wenger; it's becoming an obsession.' He talked quietly to Ratty, genuinely concerned about Colin. Stef sort of acted as Colin's minder; he'd known him since their East London schooldays, and had been his best man only six months before. 'I think it's to do with Trish,' Stef said even more quietly.

'What, being a bollocks manager?' Ratty missed the point.

'No, I think it's all over for him and Trish.'

'See, this marriage thing's nae fuckin' use to anybody. Johnny shouldn't be—'

'Ratty, shut the fuck up. You're like a bleedin' tape-recorder on a loop,' Merlin grunted from the floor.

'Who rattled your cage?' said Ratty.

'A daft Aberdonian who follows his cock around and has a larger mouth than Béatrice Dalle. Jesus!' Merlin slumped back down.

'Fitness and focus, that's what it's all about,' Colin shouted.

'I've seen him do this before,' Stef said. 'He gets all obsessive when he's depressed. Remember when he split up with the one before Trish? . . . Er?' While he searched for the name, Stef shampooed his bald head, the habit of his own mild amputee syndrome.

'Helen,' Merlin grumbled sulkily.

'Helen, I shagged her when— Ow!' a Merlin-hurled shampoo bottle accurately bounced off Ratty's head.

'Yeah, Helen. Well, Col went out and bought this huge home-cinema system – Home Entertainment 2000 it was called – and then bought the entire *Star Trek* video collection. Every single episode.'

'Aye, and we christened the TV Helen Mark II.' Ratty nodded and grinned.

'And then there was the time his grandad died and he got all weird about jigsaws. Completely addicted; two or three a day. He'd drive miles to some jigsaw shop in Thurrock Lakeside to get his fix.'

They both chuckled at the memory. Stef and Ratty turned their showers off and the noise dimmed significantly.

'What do you reckon about an away kit?' Colin was relentless.

Ratty and Stef grabbed their towels, looked at Merlin sulking inconsolably in the corner and walked towards the changing rooms, past Colin. Stef made a last-ditch effort to cheer Merl up.

'Come on, mate, look on the bright side: at least Johnny won't need to tell everyone the news when he gets back from Barcelona.'

Merlin looked up and stared at Stef, shaking his head. As they passed Colin in the corridor he said, 'So what do you think, Stef? Training on Wednesday night?' They ignored him.

'The Skunk's taking this all a bit seriously, isn't he?' said Stef.

'Och, he'll get over it. He let in six goals two weeks ago.'

Stef stopped and checked to make sure Ratty was joking.

'Och, well, never mind. It's aw Johnny's fault.'

'You mean, for telling Merl before he'd proposed?'

'Nah, for proposing at all, daft bastard. Anyway, I've a cracking idea to help Merlin, and to take the sting out of him tellin' aw the lads.'

'He only told *you* Ratty, not *all* the lads. That's what *you* did.' Stef used his teacher tone and waggled a finger at Ratty.

'Aye, whatever, but it's a good idea, listen—' Ratty's face carried a mischievous grin as the pair opened the changing-room doors and their words became drowned by the noisy

76

banter of the two teams. They were swamped in the usual chaos of twenty-five men chucking wet, muddy clothes around, cracking jokes and spraying deodorant on lost-cause armpits.

'You know what, mate?' Colin could now speak at normal pitch to Merlin, who was still sitting on his arse with water battering his back. 'I'm not sure the lads take me seriously as a manager.'

Merlin's face finally cracked and he snorted at his friend, bemused by his unintentional wit. Merlin stood and turned the shower off.

'How's Trish, mate?' The question seemed to throw Colin off balance slightly. He hopped from one foot to the other, nervously, and folded up his paper.

'Oh, you know. OK, I guess.' Merlin knew this meant worse than you can imagine, but stuck to the unwritten male rule of keeping your emotions tucked away.

'How about Ruth?' Colin returned the shot.

'Ruth's . . .' Merlin wondered for a second whether to break the rules, suddenly change the game, rewrite the book and tell the truth. 'Ruth's fine.' Merlin's messed-up life would remain, like Colin's, his own private concern, his secret fuck-up. He remembered that, as a child, secrets were exciting, precious things, like jewels clutched in a tight-clenched fist, buried deep in a pocket. But it wasn't true, it didn't last. Adult secrets are nasty pus-filled boils in the crack of your arse, which grow and fester and stink and swell unseen.

Merlin knew that his and Colin's marriages were not exactly models that you would proudly recommend to your mates with a smile and say, 'Go on, it worked for me.'

'Think Ruth could fit in a trim tomorrow?' All the lads benefited from Ruth's free haircuts.

'Yeah, sure. Listen, Colin, do you think it's good for Johnny? You know, marriage and all that?'

Colin puzzled over Merlin's question. 'Well, to be honest,

yeah. I mean, look at me? Trish would never say yes to me now, but I caught her early, before I gave up football for management, and—'

'But are you guys really happy, Col, lad? I mean, I don't mean to pick on you, like, but, you know, take Ruth and me. Well, I don't know if we'll last. She . . . we fight . . . we . . . I don't know, it's hard to explain, but I don't think we'll go the distance.'

'You will. You'll be fine, you'll see. Like me and Trish, you know, solid.' Colin balled his fist into the shape of a stone. It was an open secret that Trish was on the verge of walking out, and was already averaging two or three nights a week stopping over with girlfriends.

'I think we'll have kids soon, you know, seal the deal, good and proper with a family. I'll be a dad, and Trish could give up working in the City and . . .' Colin's mumble tailed off into nothing. Merlin knew this was unmentionable, another dirty secret, another sham.

Merlin decided to let their own marriages lie, undisturbed, and brought the spotlight back to Johnny. 'Apart from that, the other question is will she say yes to Johnny?'

'I tell you, mate, he'd be one lucky fucker. She's gorgeous, she's fun, she earns a wedge . . . and . . . and she gives good head.' Colin relaxed now as the pressure was let off the raw nerve of his relationship.

'Col? Jesus!'

'Johnny told me. Said she got a record-breaking nine point nine from the British judge, which was him, and the rest of the judges could piss off, 'cos they weren't getting a go!'

'Work OK?' Merl asked, and Colin's face lit up, suddenly remembering his news.

'Oh yeah, good. I think I've got a crack at a column. Well, just holiday cover for a mate really, who pulled a few strings with the editor.'

'A column? Who for?'

'The *Mail on Sunday*?'

'Fantastic, Colin, lad. Bloody brilliant.' Colin had been trying to break into columns as an escape route from the gutter press for years.

'Yeah, I'm chuffed. You know, good money, but only for a month, so I need to make one fuck of an impression in that time.'

'So what's the column about?' Merlin probed and Colin started shuffling awkwardly again.

'Well . . . I'm not sure, the editor wants to get younger male readers and thinks a sort of blokey emotional thing might work. But he wants a hook. You know, a theme. The guy before me was slowly going round the bend and used to write about his trips to the therapist. Now he's well and truly flipped, and I think he's in a loony bin.'

'So what are you gonna do?' Merlin towelled himself while they talked.

'Well, I'm going to have to use a pseudonym, but I was thinking of maybe a column based on the footy lads.'

'Eh? What d'you mean?' Merlin asked anxiously.

'Actually, come to think of it, Johnny would be a good character and—' Colin thought aloud.

'Johnny?'

'Yeah, the editor was saying how women have invaded the columns. A plague of cellulite and PMT, he said. He reckons that all the real-life subjects are from a woman's perspective. Blokes are left with sport, cars and engineering. But a man's take on matrimony, Johnny's perspective on the whole marriage thing, now that would be brilliant.' Colin bobbed excitedly on his toes.

'You can't fuckin' do that, you bastard. Jesus!' Merlin suddenly remembered why he'd been sulking in the shower. 'Christ, for all I know the poor sod hasn't even proposed yet, or she might have told him to get stuffed. And he only told me, confi-bloody-dentially, eight days ago. Now, not only does the entire football team know, plus the other team and the ref, plus all the wives who'll be told it when the boys get home pissed at the end of the night, but now he's also starring in a bleedin' column in the *Mail on Sunday* every week, telling a few million strangers about it, too. Fuck, fuck, fuck!'

'He won't mind. You're over-reacting.' Colin's skin was thicker than a rhino's. Merlin shoved past him and marched off to the changing rooms. Approaching the door, he could hear a muffled song coming from the other side. He opened the door to be greeted by the pitiful sight and sound of men attempting to sing.

'Johnny's gettin' married in the morning . . .'

Twenty-five grown men in various states of undress had formed a semicircle facing away from Merlin and the door, and were singing at the tops of their tuneless baritones.

'Ding dong his life's about to end . . .'

Merlin laughed. It was funny, after all, and Johnny wouldn't really mind the team knowing. He walked towards them, half joining in.

'Johnson's proposing . . .'

Merlin peered over the tops of heads to see Ratty conducting the rabble like a regular maestro.

'And we're supposing . . .'

Who else would it be but Ratty, but what was that he was holding in his hand facing the singing footballers?

'If she says yes his life's about to end!'

A mobile phone, a mobile fucking phone . . .

Postponing

I joined the rows of expectant faces at the airport, staring at the automatic doors under the arrivals board. I scanned the crowd to see who these people were and with whom, for a short time, I shared a common cause. All of us waiting for planes that held people we'd come to meet and greet. Strangers, business associates, family or friends; lovers, mothers, husbands or wives; brides-to-be?

The airport had the veneer of luxury attached to Barcelona for the general Olympic overhaul in 1992, like cheap varnish or a strip of pine on chipboard. The shine on the marble floor was scuffed and littered with a thousand Spanish filterless fag ends.

The air was hot and heavy with smoke and the pregnant tension of people nearly here. My nerves jangled after the day's events: international embarrassment at the Video Collation Expo and a near marital miss. My career was fucked, but I'd escaped the clutches of the big 'M'. I felt like Steve McQueen would have felt if he'd actually made that jump across the wire to freedom on his Triumph. I lit a cigarette to celebrate, needing that soul-massaging feeling of a lungful of smoke, unlocking its nicotine fix. I smiled; I wanted to laugh out loud. I wanted to sing, or better yet, whistle the theme tune to *The Great Escape*. So I did. In my head it sounded Dolby.

No proposal, thank God. I could just enjoy the bank

holiday weekend in Barcelona, a city of half-formed dreams, half-hearted promises and half-empty bottles.

I watched the sliding arrivals doors. They were made of smoked glass, and I tried, in the few quieter moments when there were no departing passengers, to spot my reflection when the doors closed. It wasn't hard; there I was, the grinning, crumpled buffoon. My face was pale with the 'ill' tinge that comes with London living. Among the teak complexions of the Catalonians, I stood out like a town-hall clock face at midnight. My new BTB-chosen suit now looked as weary and overused as my unshaven, puffy face.

And suddenly, on the other side of the sliding doors, I saw BTB for a few seconds before they closed, in a long security clearance queue. There she was again as they opened. After a day's work, after a four-hour journey and a two-hour flight, she looked neatly pressed and fresh. She looked unsullied, a photo from a magazine that you looked at cynically thinking, *Must have been staged*, because people never really look that good. The doors shut and there I was again, a dull reflection, grubby and shambolic. They opened. Now BTB was walking towards me on the far side of the doors with the swagger of a film star, all slow-mo and shades. Her white-toothed, wide grin was framed by feathered sunshine curls, which curved around her dimpled cheeks and oval chin. In that moment, in a reflection, her very presence reminded me why I couldn't just forget everything and walk away from the proposal. The doors shut again and there I was, unkempt, broiled.

What the fuck are you doing, Johnson? Look at you. You look like a scrotum. Ask her, ask her for fuck's sake, I thought. *Before she notices. Ask her to marry you, before she realizes you're broken and can't be fixed.*

We met, we hugged. I held her for a moment longer than I would normally. She lifted her shades and her sparkling emerald eyes looked into my poached watery pools in puzzlement.

'Hello, gorgeous. Have you been on the beer?' She smiled and stroked my cheek.

'*Cerveza*,' I announced proudly, like a schoolboy. Happy, for once, to have drunkenness to hide behind. Incapable of finding words for my thoughts, which swirled between vague notions of beauty, commitment, duality and the greenness of my grass.

'*Sí, señorita, cerveza* and, er . . . *tapas*,' I said, searching among my extensive catalogue of Spanish phrases and words.

Out of the corner of my eye I was sure I saw a huge great blob of a man shuffling towards departures, tearful and desperate, another wild firefly chase.

'Mr Big. Norbert,' I said aloud and scanned the crowd.

'Who's Mr Big Norbert?' BTB asked. But he was gone, a whale that shows a fin and hides its bulk, as if it was never there at all.

'Who is it, Johnny? Sounds like a gangster. Mr Big Norbert.'

'Oh, just this guy I know. A guy who's looking for something he lost.'

'What, in Barcelona?'

'I guess that's where he thought he'd find it.'

'You are pissed.'

'It's a good city to find things.'

I smiled and she took my hand as we sauntered off towards the taxi rank, a couple once more, complementary, easy with each other.

'You remember the last time we were here?' I asked, wondering how BTB had travelled so lightly.

'Ye-es.' A cautious, two-syllable answer.

'You remember what we did?'

'Maybe.' She knew, she bloody knew. She couldn't have forgotten such a momentous decision as let's live together and face the wrath of the evil families. But she was playing it carefully, all wily and slow.

'Hang on, where are your bags?' I asked.

'Oh, a nice man offered to push the trolley. Now where is he?' She scanned the crowd, pointing in the direction of a mountain of luggage on wheels, seemingly pushing itself.

A sweaty little man popped his head up nervously from behind the mound. His face fell when he noticed me clinging possessively to his damsel in distress.

'Four bags? Four bags for one weekend? For a petite . . . scrub petite . . . for a tiny blonde chick!'

She giggled. She knew it was ridiculous.

'Couldn't decide, Johnny. Don't be mad,' she mock-pleaded, like I had a choice.

Instinctively, I let BTB do the talking at the airport, picking up the taxi to the hotel. Language is as natural to BTB as belching is to me. She's fluent in Spanish, French, German, Italian, Arabic and fifth-century Visigoth. I am fluent only in alco-babble, as are Merl and most of the lads.

I tried to butt in on BTB's fluent chats with the weather-beaten driver, about which I rapidly became paranoid:

'You speak Spanish beautifully, madam, but your man-friend seems to be an English imbecile who expects the world to understand his bleating. Tell me, he is an associate? A distant friend?'

'My boyfriend.' She giggles flirtatiously.

'My God, it cannot be that a woman who I mistook for an angel, with eyes plucked from the night skies and the voice of the music of love, can be with . . . with . . . with such a thing as this, which I could not even imagine shitting from my hairy Spanish arse.'

'What are you talking about?' I asked.

'Oh just er . . . directions, things to see, you know,' she lied.

'So what shall we do?' I wasn't letting the Casanova cabby steal my lady with his slavering silvery tongue.

'Whatever,' BTB said distractedly and looked like

she was about to start another chat with the driver.

'Um, you haven't asked me how my talk went,' I pre-empted.

'Well?' she said. I realized I didn't really want to tell her about that.

'Well what?'

'Well, how did it go?'

'Er . . . I've decided to change my career,' I said.

'Why? Didn't it go well, sweetheart?' BTB looked genuinely concerned. I didn't want to get into this. She seemed to sail through the obstacles and pitfalls in her career as if nothing was even slightly strenuous. She was happy with her work and they seemed happy with her. Whereas I wanted to be Spielberg or Coppola, or a scriptwriter, or something famous and successful. Yet, here I was, a middling-sized fish in a tiny backwater, only just attached to the film industry. BTB was about to become a managing partner in her ad agency and *wanted* to be a managing partner in that agency. She had it sussed, the smug bint. Her ultimate desire and the likelihood of her achieving it were almost exactly the same. Mine were so far apart it was like saying, I want to be a mountaineer, and ending up a chandelier.

'Video collation's not for me,' I said.

'So what is?' BTB had heard this before and didn't really believe I would change anything.

'I'm gonna finish that script.'

'Uh-hmm.' I hate that noise, 'Uh-hmm'. It's so brief and simple, yet, said with a sarcastic tone, it can be soul-destroying. That noise means, Yeah, right, like in your dreams.

'I bloody am,' I said, overdefensively.

'Whoa there, I didn't say you wouldn't.'

'You said the "uh-hmm" thing.'

'Johnny, I know what you're capable of, but you've said that a thousand times before. Where's your motivation? Where's your enthusiasm?'

I pulled out my wallet and thrust the impressive Lord Norbert Camberly's card in front of her.

'I've got a perfect contact. I met this guy; he's . . . he'd be interested.'

'Wow, Lord Camberly. Was he at the conference?' *Wouldn't be seen dead there*, I thought.

'No.'

'So how d'you meet him?'

'On the plane.'

'Oh.' *That's cheating*, she was thinking. He had to be there, he was stuck on the plane, constrained. She was more right than she knew.

'Well, at least it's a contact.'

'Yeah, sure, Johnny. You finish the script, you send it off, then you change your career. I'm sure it'll be brilliant.' This was BTB's way of saying, Go on then, I dare you. 'It's just . . . it's just that you rarely have the courage of your convictions. You so rarely do the good things in life that I know you can do. And it's a shame. One day, one day it'll all be too late and you'll look back on a life that's a long list of might-have-beens and could-have-beens all racked up, Johnny.'

And she was right, of course, in a horribly incisive way. Years ago, when we met in college, when everything seemed to last a long time – sex was all night, and after sex was talking, and in the morning was more sex, and energy was on tap – back then I'd shown her my stuff: poems, plays, scripts. I'd shared my dreams and she'd been so impressed. She'd stroke my hair while I lay on her lap and read things to herself. Every once in a while she'd smile, or a tear would well in her eyes, and she'd kiss me proudly.

But now it feels old and faded and grey. Even the words are lost. The taxi driver butted into my thoughts, noticing I'd stopped hogging BTB. I translated:

'Beautiful lady, forget El Loser, he has as much chance of

writing a good script as I have of making my lovely taxi fly up into the sky. But I can make you fly. I can make you fly with me through the skies in the back of my taxi, once we get rid of the boy-fool . . .'

Bastard. I knew some Spanish. Manuel, the barman, had taught me plenty. While BTB and the driver chatted, I mentally recounted the phrases I knew:

1: *Dos cervezas, por favor.*
2: *Donde está las zapaterías?*
3: *Mis cojones son tan grandes como melones, y tuyos son pequeños como los chícharos.*
4: *Quieres chuparme los dedos del pie?*

Watch out Collins, you're buggered. Riley's slim-edition phrase books are set to take over the world. I vowed to use each phrase in turn over the course of the weekend.

On Friday night I said, '*Dos cervezas, por favor.*' Which means, 'Two beers, please.' That's '*Dos cervezas, por favor.*' Repeat, '*Dos cervezas, por favor.*'

By the end of the night I'd used it so frequently that it slopped off my tongue with the familiarity of 'a pint of Guinness please, Frankie' at the Blue Boy on a Sunday afternoon, post-football, pre-pissed coma. I wondered whether the boys would miss me back in Battersea on Sunday.

After dropping BTB's bags – one wardrobe on wheels, one hold-all and two shoe trunks – at the hotel, we tried to out-party the locals. This involved downing *cerveza* and gin and tonics alternately, dancing to any and all music in a parody of flamenco – which made BTB look good and me look like a dancing bear – and eating a hearty meal – tapas at 2 a.m., which consisted of three cold prawns, some balls of something and a pint of garlic sauce. Something clicked as we tuned in to each other and grinned the night away like a couple of kids. We could have lived and laughed and licked every second off each other twice over.

After tapas we moved on to a series of glass-fronted clubs and bars along the Olympic Port, staggering between them, indiscriminately happy. Lambada'ing in gay bars and twisting in trendy dance haunts.

'Johnny!' BTB had to shout, her lips to my ear, as we danced, our bodies glued together with sweat. 'I love you. This is fantastic.' A night of talking over loud music had left her with a bourbon-coated, bluesy voice. Her breath on my face, the dancing and her words made me shiver with exhilaration, like a sudden shot of coke bursting in my brain.

'I . . . I . . .' Come on, Johnny, you can do it. I'd conquered the I-love-you fear years ago, but maybe I'd conquered it in a false way. Maybe I'd said the words but detached them from the meaning they conveyed – the meaning BTB imparted when she whispered them as we danced.

'I love you,' I said, and meant it, maybe for the first time. She stopped dancing suddenly but stayed in my arms.

'Come on, we're going.' She kissed me heavily on the lips, the salt of her sweat, gin, vodka, tequila, garlic and lemon all mixing into a taste of purest, 100 per cent proof Barcelona. She dragged me off the dance floor and into the night.

It was a magical time – the night reluctant to end, the morning straining to begin. The stars blurred across our dilated pupils. Pickpockets eyed us hungrily, eager hyenas stalking soft, slow prey. Elaborate news-stands shone like paper palaces in the night. The flower and bird stalls on the Ramblas and the meat, fish and vegetable stands in the covered market were busily building colourful masterpieces as we drowsily meandered home. The dawn arrived to cast an unnecessary light on what remained of the night before, of which we were a tired, tawdry part.

Sex was attempted in the smoky half-light, in a drunken

fumbling way that I'd bet, like myself, BTB has no detailed memory of, simply a vague, warm awareness that it was wild and hazardous. Fragments of thoughts and feelings floated like seeds in the wind. While we rode on the wave of adrenalin that only comes with a chaotic night such as this, I thought of the passion we were rediscovering, the mad, ceaseless sex and desire of the early days. I remember wondering if she would be, could be, would have me as her sole lover for ever. Whether my love, our love, was the kind that could last a lifetime, and whether I would be happy with this woman until the end of time. As we collapsed on the covers of the creased Spanish linen in a slick, bruised, satiated heap; as our synapses clashed and clattered like bubbles bursting deep within, with the soles of my feet prickling, as if little crystals were forming beneath the skin, I remember thinking, *God, yes. Yes.*

I woke a few hours later overwhelmingly happy. The night before had been perfect. It had been everything I loved about BTB, about our relationship – wild, drunken, debauched, extravagant, carefree – single people together for a moment, comets kissing and passing in the cosmos. I was still drunk. I had a childlike smirk and a teenage erection – life couldn't be better. I sank into a dream in which I was a barman who was absolutely happy perfecting Martinis, sours and slings.

In what seemed like a matter of moments I awoke, close to death. My head galloped, my stomach slewed, my eyes shrivelled. I had the devil's own cock of a hangover, all fierce, fiery anguish. I would have wept with the pain if I hadn't converted all the water in my body into pure alcohol.

I cast a single gluey eye over BTB during a pain trough. Eyes as deep and clear as wishing pools looked back.

'Sightseeing and shopping!' She giggled and shot out of bed like a toddler on Christmas morning.

'Come on, Johnny,' she shouted.

'Shhhhhh,' I whispered.

Perspiring

It was the most nauseous of days, though I took strength from the fact that it could have been worse. At least now there was a hole in the day where previously a proposal was pencilled in.

In the morning we (supposedly) sightsaw. I sight-squinted, hiding my bruised eyes behind shot-glass sun shields. I baulked in the Sagrada Familia among Gaudi's dizzy spires and spiral staircases. I retched in the Gothic Quarter, crowded by the claustrophobic ancient creaking streets and cracked flag-stones. I chundered in Café de l'Opera on the Ramblas, while BTB bolted a tortilla breakfast and a hairy Spanish coffee that stuck to my tongue when I tried to break the clench of my rancid hangover with a fistful of caffeine.

At lunchtime we sought out a hotly tipped tapas bar at the harbour end of the Gothic Quarter. My beer, chorizo and cold squid left me revived but bemused by the odd antidote. 'Hair of the dog,' BTB explained.

'Do you remember all of last night?' I asked BTB cautiously, wondering if she too had felt the energy, search-ing for a mutual epiphany.

'Ye-es.' Again, the caution.

'All of it?'

'I remember it was dangerous. I remember that I said it didn't matter that you didn't have anything, if that's what you mean.' She smiled, even though she knew we'd been foolish.

'You said it was OK to . . .' I looked around and whispered . . . *come.*'

'Johnny, last night I'd have said it was OK for you to tie me up, cover me in fudge and whip me with nettles,' BTB said loudly.

'Shhh.'

'They're Spanish.' She laughed. We looked around. No-one was paying any attention. 'My God.' She laughed. 'Your anchovies escaped! Let's hope they swam downstream.'

'Hey, my boys would know what to do. Christ, they've been training long enough.'

'You'd think they'd have wised up by now,' she babbled, 'and worked out that it's either a rubber bounce-back, or worse, the great white void of the outside world.' Our conversation was mischievous, and underlined how close we were. For BTB and me, sex had always been frequent and free, like rainstorms. With the proposal parked, I was happy that it should remain an unfettered leisure activity.

'But I was good last night?'

'Maybe.' She was coy.

'Stamina of an ox, issue of a bull?' I said.

'More like hamster.'

'What? Issue or stamina?'

'Both.'

'Right,' I decided to embarrass her. 'Doggy-style does it for you, huh?' I tried, loudly, enjoying the game.

'Oh yeah. You know, it's the depth, and the control. You need all the help you can get from me in that department.' My intention to embarrass her failed miserably.

At this point, a dignified-looking, white-haired, well-tanned man leant over from the table beside us. 'I'm pleased to hear *señorita* and *señor* are enjoying the Barcelona nightlife,' he said in perfect English, as we looked at each other, wondering if he meant what we thought. 'And I'm glad you have the stamina of an ox and the issue of a bull, young

91

man. May your fulfilled sex life continue for many years to come. I bid you good day.' He stood and left, while we sat still, scarlet-faced and red-handed. BTB giggled nervously, crinkling her nose.

After lunch, constitution restored, I was ready to open my eyes and actually *see* some sights when BTB informed me that tourism was over for the day and shopping would commence. I protested.

'But—'

'Johnny.'

She won. I let her. After all, it was her weekend. She wasn't to know, but I felt guilty for not proposing. So, to ease my conscience, I offered BTB the present of her choice in Barcelona. It wasn't difficult to guess what this would be, knowing that she had a particular leather-and-straps style fetish. Hence phrase *numero dos* from Manuel.

We strolled back up the Ramblas, unconsciously retracing our drunken return from clubbing the night before. We headed north to the main shopping districts of Barcelona near our hotel. The market was quieter now. We sauntered past the half-empty stalls and littered pavements arm in arm. BTB nestled in my armpit, and I wondered at the way she fitted so well; her head to my shoulder, her hand in my hand, like a book-jacket or cigarettes in their packet.

I chose the moment to try the phrase I had learnt specifically to delight her. Strolling up to a friendly-looking policeman with his thick moustache and machine-gun, I said gruffly, *'Donde está las zapaterías?'* Spanish should, in my linguistically sparse opinion, always be spoken with a pleuritic tone. The policeman muttered back to me gruffly, gesticulating and pointing as if I could understand. It was great. I nodded, pretending to follow his directions with my best sage expression, knowing BTB would understand full well what he was saying. I was conscious, as we stood on the Ramblas with the policeman giving directions, of the sun beating down and the market packing away their cages and shutters, that BTB was staring at me as though I was something precious – but only to her. A gem, but one that was really a crystal, flawed and rough-edged. A stone a jeweller would examine and discard, but which, to BTB, was all the more special for its roughness. 'Johnny,' she said adoringly as we walked away, 'you learnt to say where are the shoe shops? just for me.'

And I had.

Phrase two is, '*Donde está las zapaterías?*' Repeat after me, '*Donde está las zapaterías?*' Which means, 'Where are the shoe shops?'

Knowing this phrase is 100 per cent essential if your BTB is a *serious* collector. I knew that BTB would look on starry-eyed, devoted to the man who knew her innermost feelings and desires – shoes. BTB loves shoes, loves clothes and loves to shop – but only for clothes and shoes. And why not. She looks good in most things, so I suppose she *would* find it enjoyable. I think I enjoyed it once. Now it's kind of functional – Oops, just upped another inch on the trouser front, better buy a new pair, sort of thing.

Of course, BTB always argues that she honestly needs a new pair of shoes. Even though she could wear a different pair every day for the next decade, and still have two cupboards full left over.

More annoyingly 50 per cent of BTB's collection – the largest private collection in Europe – looks, to the untrained eye, exactly the friggin' same. Countless Saturday evenings have been spent like this:

'*Do you like my new shoes, Johnny?*' BTB will grin, high *on fulfilling her daily shoe-buying fix.*

'Yes . . . yes . . . I, er . . . yes . . . but . . . yes.'

'*What, don't you like them?*' BTB wafts around our house *like a catwalk model, pausing and twirling in front of various mirrors, while Muttley scampers around her feet.*

'They were a bargain, Johnny, only eight hundred and fifty-seven pounds.'

'How much?'

'Reduced from two thousand five hundred, which is a thousand per cent discount.'

'Oh, well that's fine then, cheap at half the price. But aren't they a replica of about fifty other pairs of loafers you own?'

'Loafers? What loafers?' BTB answers distractedly, still flouncing in front of mirrors.

'You know, in the Loafer Closet.'

'Oh yeah, the Loafer Closet. Get off, Muttley. No, you're thinking of the coffee-coloured Gucci suede ones; these are sandstone,' she protests calmly.

'No, no, not them.'

'Oh, you mean the cream nubuck ones. No, these shoes are completely different, Johnny!'

'Yes, silly me, I forgot to put them under a microscope and do DNA tests to ensure they're not exact replicas!'

Shopping normally bores me faster than Jimmy Hill. In Barcelona, I tried. I tried really, really hard, but after we'd acquired only a few shopping bags I was struggling. Hot, hassled and laden down with pastel plastic bags whose handles cut into your hands, we had somehow moved quickly on from shoe to clothes shopping. By this time I'd even begun to tire of the sole pleasure a man has when shopping with his girlfriend: innocent voyeurism. Sitting in plush velvet armchairs, facing flimsy changing-room curtains while semi-clad women dash back and forth, curtains flapping, you become invisible. No attention whatsoever is paid to the poor male dragged along to shop with his other half. He pretends to be engrossed in brochures and magazines while energetically hoping for an eyeful of unprotected brassiere.

Unfortunately for me, BTB spotted my wandering eyes. Reappearing from the changing room for the seventy-fourth time with the words, 'Does this make my bum look big?' BTB noticed I was paying her no attention at all, but was captivated by a bum far larger and less attractive than her own – another symptom of the grass-is-greener syndrome. I was looking simply because the bum I was beholding was a Spanish, brown, forbidden bum, with a bit too much wobble. BTB's bum is pert, white, wobble-free, but, most importantly, available for my personal private viewing on an almost limitless basis. This is one of the great downfalls of man.

I hoped to make amends in the evening over a candlelit meal at Cochinillos. After all, originally, this was to be the proposal venue, supposedly imbued with 'an irrepressible romance' (according to the guidebook). It wasn't to be. Our mutual aggravation gathered speed like a tidal wave. *Thank God I cried off*, I thought as we rowed bitterly. We cultured the most poisonous of arguments in the restaurant's 'serene rustic ambience'. It started almost jokingly, with a dig about my bum-watching indiscretions earlier in the day, but was added to carefully, like ingredients in a big boiling paella, steaming and bubbling violently.

'Johnny, I saw you. You were staring as if you'd only just realized you had eyes in your head!' She loved to argue; it was an addiction.

'I wasn't,' I said, sitting helplessly, like a lobster in pot.

'You were, too, you lying tosser,' BTB said politely.

My chicken arrived. It was horse. 'OK, so I was looking at her arse,' I said, trying a new, untried tactic, 'but only in wonder at its worthlessness in comparison to yours.'

BTB laughed for so long that I understood why this tactic had never been recommended by my mates.

BTB's lobster arrived. It was lobster. 'So what do you think about porn?' she asked, hunting out an argument like a leopard looking for the weak or wounded.

'Prawn is tastiest with ginger and oyster sauce,' I said, blanching.

'Porn!'

'What?'

'Porn!'

'A chess piece which is limited but critical.'

'Porn!'

'Porn?' I said, as if the word was alien and unknown. As if I had never come across this particular order of letters, this strange jumble of syntax.

'Yes, Johnny, porn, like the stuff Colin lends you.'

'Colin?' I said, continuing my flawed strategy of pretending I'd never heard particular words before.

'Yes, *Colin*, your gutter-press mate,' BTB said. 'Trish says Colin lends you pornography.'

'Pornography?' I said, lacking conviction now, realizing the game was up and that bluff about buff and muff won't work.

'Do you, Johnny? Do you borrow pornography from Colin?' BTB swigged her wine, really getting into the row. Her hair was swept back and her face glowed with the pleasure of the kill.

Yes, I toss myself off to it when you're not around. Care to m— me, by the way? I thought.

'Do you?' she repeated, knocking back another glass.

'No,' I lied in a weak and wounded way.

'Liar.' She chewed on my leg. I considered this and decided I wasn't lying as I hadn't 'borrowed' porn mags from Colin, but had accepted them as kind gifts which I had no intention of returning . . .

'I bet you keep them somewhere sad and predictable, like under the mattress.'

. . . until now.

'My, my, Johnny. You're blushing. Did I hit the spot? Like the little teenagers in your dirty magazines?'

I ate my horse, felt nauseous and gulped at the wine. I tried to think how I could possibly remove the magazines from under the mattress without BTB noticing.

Time passed. I masticated while BTB slandered me about

masturbation. By the time coffee came it was hopeless. She had reduced me to little more than an uncontrollable gristly little willy.

During the kill, I became captivated by BTB's beauty. I wondered whether antelope considered the elegance of the leopards that ate them. BTB shone in a row. A sun on a clear winter's day, stunning, cold and dazzling. Her words clipped, leaving her mouth like bullets from a Beretta, lips spitting them out with an angry pout, hands pale and pointed, with absolute control, like a ballerina, shoulders leaping, eyebrows dancing. It was a masterpiece. And at the centre of it all were her eyes, those hypnotic eyes, mesmerizing their prey, the softness of the verdigris pared back, absorbed into the cold copper below. I was immersed. I was a male praying mantis, praying for, and joyful at, the very thought of being eaten.

'But I love you,' I said pathetically. 'I only have eyes for you.' Christ, desperate lines for desperate times.

'Liar! I've seen the way you look at women. And I've seen the way you look at Maddy!' Now we were getting seriously serious. The Maddy line of attack was only used on special occasions, a bazooka in the BTB armoury. The trouble is, she is gorgeous, I do fancy her pants off and there was the infamous incident we don't mention when she visited BTB for a party at college.

'You fancy her,' she accused.

'I do not,' I said with a hefty dose of indignation. Back when I was going to propose, rather than postpone, I'd tried to work out what would happen and what kind of wedding BTB would want. I wasn't sure what sort of service or reception she'd like, but the one thing I would have bet money on was that she would ask Maddy to be her bridesmaid, and vice versa, if the time ever came. She might even ask Maddy to do a turn at the reception. Maddy's a pianist, waiting tables by day and playing hotel bars and restaurants by night, crooning sultrily and drawing the eyes of men like a dancing flame. The Maddy one-nighter had followed all three of us around for years. Of course, BTB couldn't really complain. She and I were in no way an item back then, more a half-planned succession of tangled duvets. But they were best friends, her and Maddy, and below the surface the knotted roots of tension grew.

'I don't fancy Maddy,' I lied, trying to sound dismissive with a hollow chuckle and a 'tsk' added on the end of the sentence for good measure.

'I've seen the way you look at her. Your eyes light up. You turn on that smarmy smile, and I bet the chipolata you keep knotted in your Y-fronts stirs when Maddy's around.' BTB's alcohol-fuelled cheeks flushed rosé to match the wine.

'Don't be daft, darling.'

'And her *tits*.' She whispered the word 'tits' as if it was blasphemous. 'You're always staring at her . . . *tits*.' I sat thinking. In truth, as I could well remember, Maddy did have quite the most distracting breasts. Captivating, like televisions, or what I imagine real fires were like before technology. Chairs could be arranged around Maddy's breasts so that people would always be pointing in the right direction. Crowds could gather in the evenings and watch Maddy's breasts perform in the limelight, shamelessly grabbing the attention of their audience. Even Maddy herself, it seemed, would often be interrupted by them, a sentence cut short, a song interrupted by a distracting jiggle.

BTB read my sordid mind. 'Bastard,' she said, throwing the remainder of her Rioja over me and leaping for the door. I hurriedly left a bundle of cash on the table and ran after her into the oily night.

I caught up with BTB, but she refused to acknowledge me. Spotting the same policeman I had conversed with previously, I decided to make use of phrase *numero tres*, in a foolish attempt to win BTB over again with my mastery of the local lingo.

Manuel described this third phrase as a friendly colloquialism and heartily suggested that I should try it out on locals in rural Spain. On olive wrinkle-faced farmers in crumbling brown bars, or black-cloaked, white-haired, little Spanish old ladies, rocking gently on ancient wooden chairs in narrow medieval back streets. Manuel went on to inform me that the phrase could be used as a greeting, a farewell, a joke, or simply a term of endearment.

'*Mis cojones son tan grandes como melones, y tuyos son pequeños como los chícharos,*' I said to the policeman.

The policeman punched me very hard. As consciousness vanished, I cursed Manuel and imagined him laughing at the bar, mixing perfect Martinis. Fading away I thought, *She'll have to look after me now.* And she did. BTB sat with me in the back of the ambulance while I was carted off to an emergency room. Apparently I threw up a lot, but no-one could decide whether this was due to booze or concussion.

BTB later translated. The phrase means, 'My balls are the size of melons, and yours are the size of garden peas.'

Manuel had explained that the sentence is best said with *mucho* gesticulation – big hands for *melones*, tiny finger and thumb pressed together for *chícharos*. He said people would love me for knowing such a funny local phrase.

'You stupid, stupid, stupid arse, Johnny.' I woke in what looked like a tacky Brazilian soap opera. Lying on a hospital bed in casualty while white-jacketed medical matadors charged bull-trolleys back and forth. I was staring up at BTB, who provided some solace for the experimental, nouveau-industrial music playing in my left temple. I raised my arm to my head and noticed I was in a white robe.

'Blood and vomit,' BTB explained, shaking her head. I knew she'd been here before, countless times. I'd made ineptitude and blunder an art form. She remembered the time I'd been arrested for drunkenly digging up a sapling from a roundabout, having forgotten to buy her a birthday present.

She remembered missing our flight to Greece the previous year when I confidently drove to the wrong airport. Then there was the time she came and collected me and Colin from the Derby, butt-naked after we'd lost one bet too many.

'God, I'm so, so sorry. I am a bit of shit on a shoe, just like the taxi-driver said . . .'

'Shhh. It's OK, baby,' she stroked.

'And I fucked up everything else, just like Mr Big said I shouldn't. And that was the moment, that was the moment it was all meant to fit together, and I punched the pornographer, arsed Maddy and policed Colin and—'

'Shhh, baby. It's OK, you're delirious. I forgive you, for now.'

I touched my eye and tried to brush off the flamenco dancers who'd obviously mistaken my head for a well-sprung floor.

'Careful, Johnny.'

'Owwww!' Christ, even through what felt like a whole roll of bandages elastoplasted over my eye, it was agony.

'And I'm sorry about the porn.'

'But you had chicken, Johnny.' She laughed quietly.

I slipped off to sleep again, dreaming I was a fatally wounded First World War hero, being ministered to by a beautiful nurse, who had foolishly fallen in love with me.

Before falling asleep, I heard her tenderly whisper, 'For God's sake, Johnny, it's just a bloody black eye. And to be honest, you deserved it. I'm on the policeman's side; I'd have punched you if you'd said that to me.'

I groaned theatrically.

'Ohhh, there, there, poor thing,' she whispered, kissing me lightly on the temple.

I awoke the next day, Sunday, with my flamboyant purple, gold and green black eye. The following day, bank holiday Monday, we would be travelling back early in the morning.

The casualty experience seemed to have restored our balance, albeit temporarily. The Saturday-night argument was forgotten, like so many previous drunken night-time rows we'd had before. BTB gently nursed me through the morning while I lapped up her sympathy. I sprawled on a sun-lounger on the tiny white balcony of our hotel room while BTB dabbed at my battered face with a cool flannel that smelled of peppermint. A thin blue line of sea was just visible in the distance, but the smell of the coast was drowned by the city. BTB had removed my merely decorative bandage in the morning. 'Just a little bruising, Johnny. Nothing to worry about.'

I checked it out in the mirror. It was an ugly purple mess. I looked tough, with a serious don't-fuck-with-me-I've-already-been-there face.

Eventually, BTB coaxed me into a stroll with the promise of zero shopping and minimal sightseeing. By early afternoon, we ended up on a bench in Gaudi Park, watching the Spanish walking their armies of straggly dogs, which they encouraged to shit everywhere. It was blissful, my head lolling in BTB's lap, the sun mixing with her fingers as they stroked my face.

'Have you got the mobile, Johnny? I promised I'd ring Mum today.'

A dorsal fin sliced the surface of my thoughts as she mentioned her mother. 'Sure.' I flipped the phone open and it beeped again. Two messages this time. I handed it over and stood up.

'You've got messages,' she said.

'Yeah, I'll get them later. One's from you anyway, isn't it?'

'Hmm?' BTB spoke distractedly while she concentrated on dialling. 'No, I didn't call you.'

This was vaguely puzzling but nothing serious, probably just work calling which would have to wait until Tuesday in the office.

'One's probably the lads. They'll have just finished footy. They're playing the Hope and Anchor this week. Or maybe it's one of your friends trying to track you down.' We'd learnt to share my mobile phone outside working hours for all things social. My office seemed to appreciate that evenings, weekends and holidays were sacred, while BTB's did not.

'Hi, Mum,' BTB, as normal, shouted into the receiver as if it were a tin can on a string.

'I'm just off to find a loo,' I said. BTB, who was already rattling words into the receiver at frightening speed, nodded and waved me away regally.

Standing at the urinal, I thought about the weekend and decided it had sort of been a success. I'd need to do some explaining to EF&Co and the lads about my black eye. Merl would need to be silenced about the aborted proposal, but it had been good, all in all. Strolling back to the bench, I watched BTB press the 'End Call' button and put the phone down.

While I'd been away, something had changed. I tried to lie back down on the bench and snuggle up for some sympathy, only to find that BTB seemed to have run out of the stuff.

'Are you going to pick up your messages, Johnny? They might be important.' BTB's voice was clipped and cold again, as if she'd slipped back eighteen hours to the night before.

'What's up?' I asked.

'Nothing. Pick up your messages,' she insisted.

'Have you heard them?' I asked. She shot me a knowing look and grunted huffily, turning her head away as she spoke.

I shrugged. 'They can wait. Let's head back and grab a coffee.'

BTB reluctantly agreed, and we strolled back through the Gothic Quarter in a confusing silence. BTB seemed to be weighing things up. By the time we arrived at Café de l'Opera in the Ramblas, she had changed her posture and was smiling cynically at me. We slotted into the crowded Spanish bar close to the window and ordered coffees. A pianist crooned and tinkled in the corner, wearing a black shirt and blue-lensed glasses, with a voice like velvet-coated gravel.

'All of me, why not take all of me?'

He sang in a way that seemed wise and indifferent, almost as if he was doing it for himself. 'He's good,' I said. 'I'd love to be able to do that.'

'Hmmmp,' grunted BTB. 'You wouldn't have the patience.'

'I would.'

'Or the persistence.'

'Would too.' I was conscious that I sounded like a child.

'And you certainly wouldn't have the skill.'

'I . . .' I shut up, and mentally challenged BTB's view, making a silent promise to myself. *I'll show her. From now on I'll do whatever I set my sights on – film scripts, piano playing, nothing will stop me.*

'Go on, pick up your messages, Johnny.' The phone sat dumbly on the table.

I shrugged at her insistence, and pressed the hash button to pick them up, smiling at BTB as she sipped her coffee and narrowed her eyes.

'You have two messages,' came the autovoice. 'Message one.'

'Johnny. Johnny, it's Ratty . . .'

'It's Ratty,' I said jovially to BTB.

'. . . I hope it is nae too late. Merl says you're away to ask the big question . . .'

My smile turned to stone.

'What's he say?' BTB asked. I tried to think things through, confused.

'. . . Do *not* fuckin' do it, Johnny. Marriage is a right load of nonsense . . .'

Ratty's message rang loudly in my ear. 'He says . . . er . . .

103

have you heard these messages, sweetheart?'

BTB shrugged ambiguously and turned her head away.

'. . . It's fuckin' unnatural only shaggin' one woman. Listen to yer pal, don't do it . . .'

I was paler than bleached paper. My nausea returned in a sudden, heavy wave. My battered eye throbbed. Ratty was cut short by a frantic Merlin.

'Hello, hello . . . anybody there . . . fuck, fuck . . . Ratty.'

BTB glanced at my scared eyes. Sweat blistered on my lower lip. *Stupid bastard. Stupid fucking Welsh twat*, I thought, trying badly to look calm. BTB's head turned away again and her shoulders gently rocked. Was she laughing? Crying? Had she heard? Did she know? I couldn't tell, I couldn't concentrate, I couldn't believe what was happening. I realized quickly that it was up to me to guess. I mean, she wasn't going to admit that she'd heard about the proposal from a sordid little Scot who thought the whole idea was nonsense.

'Message two:'

What was I going to do? I listened to the sound of a changing room full of men clatter and grunt before . . .

'Ready? Right, one, two, three . . .'

'Johnny's gettin' married in the morning . . .'

The boys sang loudly. My bowels began to loosen.

'Ding-dong his life's about to end . . .'

'Who's the other message from?' BTB's question pierced through the singing footballers like a mace.

She must have picked the messages up back on the bench in the park, Christ! Christ on a bloody bike!

'Johnson's proposing . . .'

104

Fuck, fuck, fuck . . . Every fucking body knows, fuck, fuck . . .

'And we're supposing . . .'

'Oh, uh . . . the lads,' I managed to stumble.

'If she says yes his life's about to end!'

Laughter, then 'Click'.
'Press hash to delete all messages.'
I pressed the button as though it were the stop switch for an atom bomb with only nanoseconds left on the clock.
'They . . . won; they won.' I lost. 'Loo,' I mumbled, making a sharp exit.
I tried to wash away the dilemma with cold water, but it was stuck, irremovable. I looked at my reflection in the mirror above the sink. My eye was a technicolour mound mounted on my temple, and the rest of my face seemed to have distorted oddly to account for the lump, like a latex mask. I grabbed at the rubbery flesh and tried to push it into shape, pull it back to what it once was, all those years ago, when I first met BTB. Fresh-faced, young, horizon-free.
Fuck! She's just waiting. Waiting for me to say, 'Will you mmm . . .' and I still can't bloody say it, and she'll know I've bottled out. Hang on, maybe she didn't hear Ratty and the boys. Maybe she didn't pick up the messages. I tried to convince myself that this made everything OK. *So get a grip, Johnny boy.* I pointed aggressively at myself in the mirror. *It's gonna be just fine. I just gotta kill Merl, the fucker, then silence Ratty and Colin and Stef and . . . the rest of the team. And I guess they'll be in the Blue Boy now, so that's Frankie the Abacus and . . . I guess the wives will know and . . . Fuck, fuck, fuck, it's over. The game's up, it's all too late. I'm toast. There's no way out. Practise, I need to practise.*

'Will you mmm . . . Fuck!'

'Will you mmm . . . Arrgghhh. Get a grip, Johnny.' I kept trying in the mirror.

'Mmmm . . . me?'

'Mmmm . . . me?' I wondered if I might get away with a mumble.

'Mmmm . . . me?' Maybe if I did it through a mouthful of tapas.

What was I going to do? I had to ask her, but I couldn't ask her. 'OK,' I admitted defeat to myself, 'time for plan B. Time for the contingency proposal.' This was my only hope. Delaying tactics – sticking my head in the sand, suddenly fainting or feigning amnesia – all flashed through my mind, but none of them would work. I had no choice, I had to act.

'You OK, Johnny?' BTB asked with a sinister smile as I sat down. *She's bloody enjoying this. Enjoying me squirming around in this slimy mess.*

'*Garçon?*' I waved at the waiter. If I had to do this it would be with style. My palms began to sweat. This was it. I was about to press the big red button marked 'Do Not Push', and from here on there'd be no turning back.

'*Camarero,*' BTB corrected, and the waiter magically appeared.

'*Champagne, por fabor, camaroono,*' I said firmly but entirely incorrectly. BTB shook her head smiling.

'*Cava, por favor, camarero.*' She and the waiter chatted for a few minutes in perfect Spanish. She explained that Catalan was just a little too tricky for her, and anyway, everyone spoke Spanish. I didn't care, I was too distracted by the giant butterflies that had returned to my stomach. I tried to keep my cool, resorting instinctively to habit.

Two fours are eight. Seven fives are seventy.

Ohmigodohmigodohmigod!

The cava arrived and we supped. BTB looked at me with

wide eyes and a mischievous grin.

'*Slangivar,*' I said.

'*Salud,*' she said.

We raised and clinked glasses; sweat trickled down my neck.

Six twelves are fifty-four.

'What are we celebrating, Johnny?' She carried on the impish, innocent act.

Hearwegothisisit . . . Geronimoooooo!

One times one is . . . two?

'*Quieres chuparme los dedos del pie?*' Thank you, Manuel. Thank you, thank you for saving me from saying the 'M' word. He had taught me a Spanish proposal to solve my allergy.

BTB was snorting hysterically.

'What? What's the joke?' *Had it all been a wind-up?*

'What here? Now?' BTB asked, giggling.

'Uh . . . I dunno!' *Did she mean answer me or actually do it?*

'Come on, just say yes or no,' I pleaded, wanting an end to it all.

'You just asked me if I would . . .' BTB explained.

'Yes?' I said.

'. . . . like to . . .' she continued.

'Yes?' I said.

'. . . suck your toes!' She laughed long and loud.

Fuck, fuck, fuck.

'Bastard, Manuel,' I said aloud.

'Who?'

'Forget it. Listen, I'm trying to ask you to mmm . . .'

She smiled.

'Mmmm . . .' I kept trying.

'Mmmm . . .' I was determined, gripping the edge of the table.

'Say it, Johnny. Why can't you say it?'

'Mmmm . . . Mmmm . . . Oh, I dunno, it's just not in my

. . . my . . . er . . . my . . . er . . . thingy. You know . . . er . . .
What's that word that means knowing lots of words?'

And in that moment, in that fraction of time, that second
of ineptitude, I had won her. She collapsed, spluttering with
laughter, managing eventually to pause for breath and say,
'Vocabulary. And yes, I would love to mmmm . . . marry you,
Johnny.'

'*Cameroono, mascara, mas, mascara!*' I excitedly mis-
pronounced to the waiter, trying desperately to order more
champagne.

The night dissolved into a long train of golden champagne
bubbles, fizzling into our mouths, onto our tongues, into our
minds and enveloping everything that surrounded us. That
night, I was both the happiest and most terrified man in all
the world.

Engaged

I spent the following week in a strange, proposal-induced coma. To warn those who haven't experienced the feeling, it is similar in effect to falling out of an aeroplane over the Atlantic at 30,000 feet with no parachute in pitch-darkness, plummeting into the middle of a freezing ocean, swimming for thousands of miles before finding a lonely, icy-cold rock to perch upon and await the 'big day'.

You're in a state of shock. Not the sort of shock that a nice cup of tea or a couple of pints with the lads will sort out, either. A deep, numb-brained confusion. You feel like a circuit in your noddle has shorted and the same question repeats itself over and over like a scratched CD.

'So why did I do that then?'

'So why did I do that then?'

'So why did I do that then?'

In the days that follow, you blunder about in a blurry haze, but at certain points suffer severe moments of awareness, like the cramps; moments of clarity, where you suddenly realize the horrific scale and implication of the four words you have spouted. These moments of clarity can be triggered by things people say, things you see or do. When they come it feels as though someone has removed a metal tray from your stomach, the normal purpose of which is to hold up your internal organs. With the tray missing, you feel them rush towards the floor, filling up your legs and dangling uncomfortably out of your arse. One wrong word and you've got soggy liver in your big toe and a prickly pancreas in your scrotum.

Anything can cause these moments and they become more frequent as the shock wears off and your brain slowly defrosts, like Tesco's reduced, special-offer minced beef. Some moments have obvious triggers. Ratty is good at setting the organs plummeting with a question like, '*Och well, Johnny, I suppose you've had a good life, and you picked a fair darlin' and all, but fit're gonna dee when her rump balloons and her titties droop like empty sacks?*'

Or Colin being honest and overfrank: '*Trish says that she shags me nowadays more for sympathy or nostalgia than satisfaction. Says I'm like an old heavyweight after too many comebacks: flabby, unfit and lasting less time in the ring with every fight.*'

Or my mum on the phone: '*Johnny, I think the Royal Doulton with the golden pears and silver rim is the nicest for your list. I think it's called . . . er . . . the Expensive-Gaudy-Fruity-China-Arse line.*'

Sprog-talk has always sent me diving to the loo. OK, I know you aren't actually given a baby by the vicar on the day, but everyone implies, and even seems to know, one will come along sooner or later. I have vowed to keep my eye out for the little crawling buggers; they're not taking me by surprise and smothering me in soiled nappies and peach-purée vomit.

Then there's the more obscure things, like a documentary about natural disasters: '*The fatal power of the avalanche is deadly for the lone skier. The slightest noise can set in motion a chain of events from which there is no escape. Ultimately, the skier will be engulfed in the huge hurtling weight of the avalanche as it gathers speed. Triggered by those four seemingly harmless words, "Will you mmmm . . . me?"*'

After Barcelona, I threw a sicky on Tuesday, and carried on refusing to confront EF&Co for the remainder of the post-proposal week. I feigned some unimaginative ailment, like stomach flu, incapable of facing the office with the result of my début in the international video collation world.

Result: one black eye, four useless Spanish sentences that will get you locked up, beaten up or hitched up, one fiancée.

I couldn't face the lads, either, and put off any beers and get-togethers until the following weekend, hoping that my swollen eye and addled brain would both regain their former hue by then. Don't get me wrong, I hadn't changed my mind. I mean, I'd finally asked her and I wasn't about to U-turn yet again. But it's . . . well, it's hard to explain; it had all happened so fast.

Do you remember sherbet-filled rice-paper flying saucers? Well, Barcelona was like one of those, full to the brim with pure powdered pleasure, exploding on your tongue and filling your mind with laughter. Thinking of it brought more of a sensation to mind than a memory. Like when you jump in a dream and just keep on going, high into the sky. Higher and higher . . . and then you stop. That's the feeling; that weird, boiled adrenalin moment of in-betweenness.

But now the high was gone. Now was 'meanwhile, back in the real world, Johnson cried'. The first person BTB rang was Maddy: '. . . and then he asked me' – she sounded like she'd explode with excitement – 'you know, the question . . . the big question.' I could hear Maddy screaming down the line from forty feet away. 'Yes, of course you're the bridesmaid . . . Well, I don't know about white.' They launched into an hour-long wedding witter. 'About two hundred, I guess.' I hoped she was estimating the age of Granny Victor. 'No I am not pregnant Maddy.' She giggled. 'Well, it was sooo romantic . . . in a gorgeous little café just off the Ramblas . . . No, I had no idea; it was completely out of the blue.' For some reason I couldn't quite place I spiralled further into depression.

111

I wasn't really mentally prepared for this situation, for being engaged. I thought I'd put the whole malarkey on hold, thought I'd pressed the pause button, like freeze-framing a rogue nipple on some dodgy video as a teenager. I'd tried to extend my childhood, tried to put off another stagger to adulthood, like a wobbly loose tooth that I was too scared to pull. But everything went blurry and mad, and here I was, back in Clapham, a *husband* for Chrissakes – or as good as anyway. *Husband!* My God. A word used to describe people other than myself.

Johnson Riley, film scriptwriter, superhero and *husband*, I practised. It sounded knob.

Over the week, gradually trashing the clean look of the house, I slumped further into post-proposal trauma. All I had for company was antique pine everything, daytime TV and Muttley, who was doing a particularly poor job of cheering me up. In fact Muttley was sulking and skulking more than I was. Perhaps he hadn't forgiven me for putting him in kennels over the weekend.

We developed a slovenly routine together, Muttley and me. BTB would wake at an illegally early hour, with a smug grin and cat-with-cream bearing. She would bounce around the house like an India rubber ball, singing Tigger's bouncity-bounce song, while me and Muttley shot identical withering looks at the too-cheerful blonde whirlwind. 'What's up, sulky chops?' she would say.

'Mmm . . . uh I . . .' I tried to excuse my sullenness without casting doubt on the proposal.

'Let's open a nice tin of Chum – rabbit flavour, that'll cheer you up.' She was speaking to the dog, hopefully. Half asleep, I'd hear her natter. 'Johnny would probably forget to feed you, wouldn't he, my little cuddle-bucket. But we'll forgive him; he's had a traumatic time lately and seems to have got himself trapped in the bedclothes this week.'

I would drift back into a dream and wake, suddenly, at the in-between up-and-down point.

As soon as BTB had left for work, Muttley would pad down the hall and peek into the bedroom, a hopeful look on his beardy grey face.

'Hello, boy.' He'd take this as a 'yes' and charge into the bedroom – out of bounds when BTB's around – wag his tail for a polite minute or so, before flopping down and curling up on the rug beside the bed.

Muttley was all of a year old now, but still the odd inexplicable puddle or stain would appear around the house. On these occasions, Muttley would pace around the house pretending to look for the pissing culprit: *'It wasn't me, must have been someone in here . . . or maybe in the kitchen . . . I know, Johnny, I reckon it's that mad bouncy blonde woman.'* I'd imagined Muttley talking to me from the day he arrived.

BTB bought Muttley for me as a birthday present last year. I think he ranks up there with the PlayStation in the chart of presents BTB has bought me but wishes she hadn't. PlayStation arrived several Christmases ago to shrieks of glee from me, Stef and Colin, with whom I shared a flat at the time.

Three weeks later, I emerged from a stinking room, strewn with beer cans and pizza boxes. I was pale, unshaven, eyes sunken and red, muscles wasted apart from two enormous overdeveloped thumbs.

'Ugh,' I grunted, standing dishevelled on BTB's doorstep. She looked scared, as if she might phone the police to rescue her from the dangerous escaped convict at the door.

'Just off to buy a new game. Thought you might want to come for a quick beer with me. Can't be long, though, Stef and Col are waiti—'

'SLAM!'

BTB has never been the patient sort. A couple of weeks later, I came home from work to find a tell-tale dust-hole

113

where the console used to live. After checking under the beer cans and up-turning and emptying the pizza boxes, I realized that it was gone and that I was panicking like a crack addict. Stolen. Damn. Who to call? The police? Mulder and Scully? – Aliens vaporize PlayStations – BTB? Of course, BTB.

'What d'ya mean you lent it to your cousin? I don't care if he's got seven kids and has just been sacked, I want it baaaaaack!'

I never saw it again.

So far, I've managed to keep hold of Muttley. But I've noticed him beginning to cower when BTB gently whispers 'Battersea Dogs' Home' in his ear.

Me and Muttley have been partners in crime since the Saturday morning he arrived. BTB had taken me somewhere chaotic the night before to celebrate my birthday. I had a slurred memory of mozzarella and ham *panini* in Soho, at Bar Italia, consumed as a pre-emptive anti-hangover strike. I'd ignored noise and movement at some horribly early time and remained immobile under the duvet, like a boulder.

An hour or so later a lidded cardboard box was placed on top of me. BTB stood at the end of the bed, wearing one of her indulgent grins. Two things were strange about the box. Firstly, it moved, irregularly and noisily, and I started to mentally tot up potential presents – tortoise, giant sewer rat, the world's largest Mexican jumping bean. Secondly, for a world-class present wrapper such as BTB, this box was a shoddy job, with only a single blue bow tied around the outside. BTB would be a multiple gold-medal winner if any of the following were Olympic sports:

Present wrapping.
Gossiping.
Networking (last count 85,002,374).
Smiling.

But wrapping is her true talent. Unlike me, or Merl, or most people I know, BTB actually derives copious amounts of pleasure from the act of wrapping. She will happily wrap all day and night, never tiring, but laughing, a kitten with a ball of wool.

In the run up to Christmas it all becomes slightly excessive. I have to subtly warn hosts at dinner parties about her proclivity to wrap.

'Just move that ornament out of arm's reach, would you,' I whisper urgently to our host.

'Yes. Why?' Worried thoughts of thievery, or perhaps severe clumsiness.

'She may wrap it up.' Surprised look from host.

'She often wraps up indiscriminate objects at this time of year,' I explain. 'As long as your kids don't have any hamsters. That really was embarrassing.'

So this lurching, sparsely wrapped present on my lap was unusual.

'Open it, open it, open it!' BTB clapped with excitement. I didn't need to. The lid flew off and a ball of grey fluff with too-big paws and outsized eyes leapt out of the box, landing in a heap on my chest.

The disorientated puppy whimpered with fear, wagged its tail tentatively and spun around and around before settling and looking up at me, head cocked to one side.

'It's brilliant. It's the best present I've ever had.' The puppy slobbered on me, licking my arms and face. 'What kind of dog is it?' I asked, looking at its gangly limbs, uneven, fluffy fur, patched in grey and off-white, and a long muzzle that was oddly white-bearded, even as a puppy.

'Bit of everything I think. The dogs' home picked him up last week. What'll we call him?'

'It's a boy?'

'Think I'd let another woman under this roof?'

'What about Joe Strummer?' I tried.

'Elvis?' BTB was always slightly more mainstream musically than me.

'Hmm.' I looked at the puppy. 'He's got the sneer, but I'm not sure the pelvic movement is up to the King.'

'Brad?'

'OK, OK, no famous names, I'm not ending up with a dog called Brad bloody Pitt.'

'How about Wolfie; he looks like a wolf,' BTB tried.

'A very small, soft, cute wolf. I know, I know – Muttley.' Muttley seemed to prick up his ears and snigger like his namesake before peeing all over my lap.

Presents can be used as a reward, a message of love or commitment, or, as I found out, a weapon. A present finally hauled me out of the post-proposal trauma, although not one as fun as a PlayStation or a puppy. The other resuscitator was Muttley, holding up a mirror, reflecting the morose, self-centred fuckwit I'd become.

Most mornings on the lazy post-proposal week, BTB would flap about the house like a trapped bird, turning the Chris Balls breakfast show up full blast. BTB would mutter ceaselessly to Muttley, who followed her around, and in my half-asleep state I was never sure whether she'd really said the phrases I remembered, or if I'd imagined them. 'You know, I think I'd rather marry you, Muttley. You're more mature, you smell less, you're awake.' They seemed to become angrier and louder as the days rolled through the week. 'If he thinks I'll wander up the aisle for some pathetic child who can't come to terms with adulthood . . .'

Typically, me and Muttley roused ourselves at eleven or so. We'd take a slow stroll around Battersea Park, before picking up a video and some grazing food for an inert afternoon. I wallowed. We wallowed. Muttley picked up on my mood and skulked around the house, the two of us doing even the most pleasurable things with a melancholy indifference.

I'd flick on *The Godfather* trilogy again, and crack open a can of beer with a sad sigh, or put my feet up in the garden in the sunshine, with a bowl of olives, a good book and a face like a slapped arse.

Likewise, Muttley would chew a bone as if it was cardboard and sniff other dogs' backsides as if he just didn't care. It was this reflected sullenness, this odd dog mimicry, that made me realize just how pathetic I was being. The reality is that me and Muttley are winners in Loserville. We are emperors of the underdog world. Muttley had escaped the dog's own version of death row and ended up with caring, considerate owners, who, currently at least, did not respond to his partial bladder control with a sack in the canal.

Similarly, I had bagged a winner. As a failed almost-been, with a foie-gras liver and a dead-end job, I had somehow managed to persuade a delectable Delilah to meet me at the altar.

We were lucky consorts, me and Muttley. We were Butch Cassidy and the Sundance Kid, the way I'd always imagined them as a child. In innocent youth I refused to even consider the possibility that the two heroes were all shot to hell by Mexican soldiers in the final scene. Instead I saw them shooting their way to freedom, singing, 'Raindrops keep falling on your head'. Successful failures, Muttley and me.

Sort yourself out, Johnny, I told myself. I mean, I should be happy. In some parallel universe an alter-BTB had said she'd rather marry a lemon than an alter-Johnny. It's not so bad; she loves me, she still fancies me, we've a roof over our heads and beer in the fridge. By Friday, my personal pep talk had sunk in and I was smiling again.

But Friday was also the day BTB finally snapped. My first, and her last, bouncy day. She returned from work in a fury and threw a small oblong present into my lap. I waited for it to explode, but it didn't.

I read the tag: 'Thought you might appreciate some organizational assistance now you have a wedding to plan.

117

Use it or die, Johnny.' Inside was an electronic organizer. I would have needed thicker skin than Colin to fail to get the hint.

'You have the sensitivity of a buffalo.' Her lips trembled as she spoke. Even by my standards I'd behaved like a gold-plated tosser. BTB had tried to Tigger her way through the week, announcing our engagement to friends and her colleagues at work, deciding to hold off telling the parents until a face-to-face meeting could be engineered. Gradually, being bubbly and lively and lovable while I was morose became too wearing.

I had sulked. Veiled, very thinly, under the pretence of a black eye, I had sulked like a child and moped around with Muttley like a couple of gravediggers, scooping out mud for our own burials. I had grieved for the loss of my freedom without a second thought for BTB. Dismantling her happiness like an adult stealing Santa from the imagination of a child.

I repeated the words 'sorry, I was a twat' three thousand times that evening. About halfway through she began to actually believe me. Although it wasn't much in the way of an apology, I persuaded BTB to let me buy her a meal at the local Italian, Bucci's, the following night.

I love Bucci's. It's not the food, which is magnificent. It's not the décor or ambience, which are equally flawless. It's the service. In Bucci's, I am the Godfather. I am Don Rileone – shown to the best table and treated with awesome respect and deference. Better yet, Bucci's have a traditional Italian view of courting.

Stef recounted a splendid evening of maltreatment at the hands of Bucci's recently. A month ago, the three of us – me, BTB and Stef – had planned a trip to the white tiles of Bucci's to catch up on a skiing holiday that Stef was organizing for an extended group of friends. Funnily enough, they managed to pick one of the few nights I couldn't make. In fact, they always seem to pick nights I can't make.

Bucci's were brilliantly indignant at what they thought was definitely illegal. Stef might as well have been Judas at the supper after the last one, when the head of the table was vacant. The owner, Carlo, obviously recognized BTB from our countless visits together, but thought her presence as Stefano's companion treacherous. Carlo was having none of it. I could just imagine him ruffling his short grey hair and twiddling his thin moustache. I laughed as Stef told me he was treated with total disdain. He was ignored and hidden in a dusty corner under an arch and behind an overgrown rubber plant. His arm became weary as he had to hold it aloft so long for service. On five occasions he was brought the wrong order, and at least two of these incorrect dishes contained offal of some description. He said he was sure the waiters were laughing at his shiny noggin, and reckoned they were insinuating it was due to a lack of masculinity. Red wine was spilt on Stef's classy clothes and soup arrived with a clatter, slopping across the marble table-top and dripping onto his trousers.

Eventually, they left embarrassed. Stef said he'd half expected a black Mercedes to pull up and gun him down on the way home, walking hastily down Lavender Hill.

It was Saturday night with BTB and, once again, I was Don Rilcone, shaking hands with the humble, welcoming Carlo, who showed us to the best table, flicking the wrought-iron chairs and marble table-tops with a white cloth, impatiently beckoning waiters to help with coats, pull chairs and offer drinks.

We were already back on the ever-present subject of weddings by the time a Peroni for me and a G&T for BTB had arrived. I belched.

Every second of the day, every half-hour through the night, every phone call, everything, it seemed, revolved around the wedding. In only a matter of days it had become our very gravity. Wedding talk gave me wind. Inwardly my stomach bubbled as we talked about dresses (£EEK), cars (vintage Aston?), guests (several hundred), ushers (buffoons to a man), speeches (damn lies) and on and on. Worse than that, tasks kept landing on my plate like hunks of fresh-baked olive bread. In one conversation she added DJ, band, photographer and video.

'I know, love, I reckon your Uncle Alfie could do all four jobs for a bellyful of mild.' I ducked as bread whistled past my ear, landing in the tiramisu on the dessert trolley.

'Johnny, Uncle Alfie'll be horizontal before dinner and start stripping at the disco, just like he did at Julie's christening.'

'See, Chris Balls, David Bailey and the Chippendales all wrapped up in one lovely bundle.'

Lately, we were preoccupied by the ongoing ignorance of our parents and the fact that BTB had help from all of her girlfriends but not her own mother. Maddy had already enlisted the support of Ruth to do hair and source dress-makers and Trish to sort make-up. Maddy said wickedly, 'If Trish can hide her king-size hooter, she has to be a sheer genius with the old warpaint.' Apparently, though, there's no substitute for a mother's support.

'We can't tell them over the phone.' BTB was going in circles.

'OK, OK, so let's go and see your mum and dad in St Helens this weekend and tell them face to face.' Call me a kipper, but this seemed the most sensible plan.

'What about your parents, Johnny?'

'We'll tell them over the phone, or go and see them,' I said.

'But they haven't even met each other.'

'So.' I considered this a positive. Why risk the possibility of conflict?

'Johnny, my mum and dad are traditional. For a start, Dad will have expected you to ask his permission, and you didn't.'

'He'd have said no,' I interrupted.

'He wouldn't,' BTB said half-heartedly.

'Would.' I was emphatic. I had thought of this prior to Barcelona. A couple of times, when my nerves got too jiggered, I'd even considered it a possible escape route.

'Well . . .' BTB knew this was true.

'He'd have said, "Over my dead body, yer shitebag. An' if yer want her, we can fight." Or something.'

BTB protested while I imagined trying to ask her father's permission:

I pictured him in the darkness of his office, taking appointments and accepting gifts from the local community. I was next in line.

'Next.' BTB's father seems to have stuffed olives into his cheeks and set his mouth in a down-turned grimace. One day, I promise myself, I will be Don, I will hold the respect of the family in my palm like a key.

'Don Donnelli, it is I, Johnny Rileone.' The Don nods, holds his sneer and tilts his head back, pushing his chin out and peering down his nose at me ominously.

'Sit down, Johnny.' He wheezes his words painfully through a barrel chest and Grappa'd vocal chords.

'Don Donnelli, it is with respect that I come to you today and graciously ask for the hand of your daughter.' The Don holds his expression, outstretches his arms and slowly stands. I cautiously walk towards him and he brings my head to his chest gently.

'Johnny, Johnny, Johnny.' The old Don sounds tearful and emotional. 'I knew your father in the old country. The Rileone family and the Donnelli family, we go back, we have respect.' He places his hands on either side of my face, clasping it close to his own. 'You, Johnny, are like a son to me, and a brother, and a leetle puppy dog.' He kisses me on the forehead. 'And it is because of the love and respect I have for you . . . that I have to kill you . . . myself.'

121

'And my parents haven't met Janet and Henry yet.' BTB was still on the same subject when I gratefully returned to the real world.

'Ugh.' Not this one again. Whenever BTB discussed our two sets of parents – collective noun 'an interference of parents' – I had visions of trench warfare with bayonets and mud.

'They'll meet on the . . . well, they'll definitely meet . . . you know, at the . . .'

'For God's sake, Johnny, how much practice do you need to get over this wedding dyslexia? We are getting *married*. Repeat after me, Johnny – *married*.'

'Mmmm . . .' I said with a constipated grunt. She laughed, even though I frustrated her.

'Who was the lead guitarist of the Smiths?'

'Johnny Marr.'

'Just the surname.'

'Marr.'

'Say the word "weed" without the "w".'

'Eeed,' I said.

'Good boy. Now put them together.'

'EeedMarr,' I mumbled stubbornly.

'Johnny,' she cautioned, 'stop being a child.' Behind her smiling eyes I could see the defiant Donnelly glint, reminding me that much more nonsense would result in violence.

'Marr . . . eeed,' I said.

'Now try it out in a sentence.' I spotted Carlo passing by.

'Carlo.'

'Yes, Johnny.' Carlo bowed gracefully. He had me sussed as a sucker for service.

'We are getting marr . . . eeed, marr-eed.'

'Marr-eed.' Carlo rolled his 'r's which made all the difference to the coherence of the word.

'Marr-eed. Married. *Splendido. Questo matrimonio!*' he

shouted to his sons. '*Presto, Luca, vai a prendere lo champagne per celebrare.*' Carlo clicked his fingers excitedly at his sons. I didn't expect this result from saying 'marr–eed'. Carlo and his family nearly brought the restaurant to a standstill for half an hour while he patted me on the back, kissed BTB on each cheek approximately ten times and fed us complimentary champagne. I watched BTB blossom in the attention; she watched me retract in the same light.

I enjoyed the break in planning but, yet again, we were doing something as a direct consequence of the big 'M'. It was as though an all-powerful God was mapping our every move towards the day. When we surfaced for air, I tried, unsuccessfully, to steer us towards a subject other than weddings.

'So, it's the Blue Boy after this. All the gang are there and—'

'What about telling the parents together at Christmas?'

'Hmm?' This sounded like a bad concoction. Christmas *and* a vast interference of parents. At least it was a few months away.

'I thought we'd do our own thing like . . .' Look after a spooky hotel in the mountains, go mad, chase each other with axes – where I'd get to say 'Here's Johnny' a lot.

'Yes, that's perfect, Christmas. They'll all meet and then we can tell them the news. Perfect.' *Perfect!* I thought. Since when did perfect translate into suffering a trauma worse than waking up to discover that you've accidentally put your bollocks in the Moulinex?

'OK,' I said quickly, with little thought for the consequences.

'Good, that's all agreed then.'

'Mmm.'

'Now what about the—' I knew this would be more bloody planning and had to intervene.

'Did I mention we're meeting the gang in the Blue Boy at

half ten?' I had to keep trying to turn the talk from all-invasive wedding speak to something less likely to give me indigestion.

'Four times, Johnny. What's the matter with you, for God's sake? It's as if you're not interested in this damn wedding. Christ, Johnny!' BTB's eyes flickered and I had memories of Barcelona. What was it with BTB, rows and restaurants?

'But I . . .' *But I started it in the first place*, I wanted to say, but showed rare restraint. I'd popped the question. That's all I'm supposed to do. Job done. Now it's over to you, your mum and my mum and your friends and whoever the hell else comes out of the woodwork – is there a wedding fairy? – when there's a wedding to organize.

'But I am interested,' I lied.

'You started this in the first bloody place,' she snapped.

'Err, yeah, but . . .'

'So no bloody walking away, Johnny. You've started this and you'll finish it.'

Fuck, I thought, pushing my whitebait around the plate so quickly it looked like they were swimming.

Sonar, Sharks and Microwaves

You could guess they were together, but it wasn't obvious. In the blue gloom of the pub the friends had segregated themselves in that ancient way – men at the bar, women at the table. The Blue Boy was an average pub, modelled in the style-free Seventies with fitted carpet, green velvet seat covers and dark overvarnished wood.

Colin and Merlin muttered, with half an eye on a third-division match on the TV. Ratty was jittery as he shoved coin after coin into the fruit machine next to them, swearing regularly. The three wore the usual mixture of jeans, shirts and sweatshirts. Merlin, a bit bolder in colour, a bit less obvious by brand; Colin, slightly scruffier, a tracksuit instead of jeans and a badly hidden belly overhang beneath a checked shirt; Ratty, always with a thought for shag potential, the smartest of the three and the only clean-shaven one.

Beneath the surface, this pattern would continue. The two over-settled, horizon-free men would probably not have put on clean pants for the evening; they certainly wouldn't have considered the aesthetics of those pants over their crustiness, as Ratty would.

'Och, you friggin' shitebag bastard.' Ratty kicked the fruit machine.

'Oi, Ratty,' Frankie the Abacus shouted half-heartedly from behind the bar.

'Set sixty-three years after the original, but still with the prime directive and . . .' Colin's hushed tone suggested a self-awareness that he was being an anorak.

'And still set on the Enterprise?'

'Well now, hang on there, Merlin. You see, there've been five Enterprises. The original was number one seven zero one, which was destroyed in . . .' Colin patted his belly when he spoke on a subject he knew.

'Fuck's sake, why did I no' hold the melons, fuckin' eejit.' Ratty swore to himself, before turning to join Merlin and Colin at the bar. 'Yer not still talkin' about *Star Trek*. Jesus! Who's fer a drink?'

They nodded, holding up their glasses.

'I'll check if the girls want a top-up. Hey, d'ya think they'se two lassies a' the back are wi' the guys playing pool?' Only Ratty still had a fully operational sixth-sense pulling sonar.

'Who?'

'Where?'

Ratty held up his hands, palms forward, realizing his mistake.

'Just forget it. Go back to yer Trekkie bollocks. When's Johnny arriving?'

'Hour or so,' Merlin mumbled.

Ratty shook his head and walked towards Ruth and Trish, huddled together at a table nursing drinks, immersed in whispers.

'Drinks, ladies?' Ratty always spoke to Trish's nose. 'Never seen a more sexual nose in aw ma life,' he would say enviously to Colin.

'I'm fine for now thanks, Ratty.' Trish shook her defiant red sprawl of hair.

'Me, too,' said Ruth. The pair paused for the minimum possible time to answer the question. If Ratty had been alert, he would have noticed the similarity between the two sets of girls – Ruth and Trish and the two schoolgirls – straddling the age range. Both close, both touching and tactile, both aware of every minute gesture, continually and unconsciously reading each other's body language.

'Do youse ken if they'se lassies are wi' the lads playing pool?' Ratty cut in rudely.

'Hmm?' The pair looked up, surprised, as though released from some hypnotic trance by a click of the fingers.

'The two lassies—' Ratty pointed, but by now it was too obvious and the schoolgirls were giggling self-consciously.

'They don't look old enough to be in here, let alone . . .' Trish peered across the pub snootily.

Ratty had already turned and was walking back to the bar. 'Jesus! Friggin' couples, like OAPs. Not old enough. Old enough tae drink, tae fuck, tae tak it up the arse,' he said to himself. 'Same again for the lads, no girlie drinks. Cheers, Frankie.'

Frankie nodded to Ratty as he polished his glasses methodically.

'What the hell are those two yappin' about so intensely anyway?' Merl pointed with his pint as he spoke.

'Oh, Christ knows. Soap operas, I think.'

'Soaps! Huh, women,' joined in Colin. 'Anyway, then, in Voyager, they're stuck ninety years from home and . . .' Ratty wandered off in the direction of the pool table, passing Ruth and Trish on the way.

'And then he said *I* was out of shape! Can you believe it, Ruth? He sits on that bloody sofa like a potato every day, waiting for the porn channels to come on at night, and moans if I go to bed early with a book.'

'Just leave him, Trish. Come and stay with me full time.'

'What about Merl?'

'He can have Colin.' They laughed together. 'Made for each other, they are.' Trish giggled. 'The pair of them could watch videos, play computers games and, when they get the urge, get a hooker or, even better, a rubber doll,' she elaborated.

An ear-piercing screech of laughter made them look over, to see Ratty sat with the two girls.

'Honestly, he could be their dad,' Ruth frowned. 'How does he do it?'

'He's like a shark. That's it, a shark. You know, Col, relentless like. Always up for the kill, that's Ratty.'

'If you ask me, Merl, he's more like Muttley.'

'D'you know a shark will kill, even when they've just eaten, just for the hell of it. Programmed in. Can't help themselves.' They looked over, riveted by Ratty's cocky approach. 'Just like Ratty,' Merl said.

'Or the Borg. They're relentless, and they're ugly, too,' Colin mused. 'Although I have seen Muttley hump the floor.'

'The thing is, Col, Ratty's technique's more sophisticated than Muttley's. You see, unlike Muttley, but like a shark, Ratty has finely tuned his skills, like, and heightened his senses, and therefore his chances of success.'

'Now hang on there, Merl, he still gets rejections – loads of 'em.'

'True, but he rarely fails to home in on a shag.'

'But that's just desperate, if all he's doing is trying it on with any old moose.'

'No, there's method in his madness, lad. Listen, Ratty has combined a variety of techniques. Firstly' – Merl extends his first finger, counting – 'he uses the old-fashioned numbers routine. Just like door-to-door double-glazing reps, he racks up the numbers. More hits, more chances. Completely relentless, he is.'

Colin is captivated.

'Secondly, Ratty is acutely aware of levels. In any hunting ground – a bar, a supermarket, a car park – Ratty instantly discounts the upper end of the shag spectrum.'

'Right,' nodded Colin.

'He knows, like a maestro, that the top ten to fifteen per cent of the women at the hunt will be too used to offers. He calls it the savannah syndrome.'

'Like the Renault?'

'Like lions. Lions, right, might be attracted to the most beautiful, most elegant antelope. But those buggers are the fastest, too, see. So, instead, they'll go after the one with three legs if they can, for least effort.'

'Got you. So has Ratty shagged a three-legged antelope?'

'And finally, in harmony with the first and second techniques, he applies the third and final failsafe.' Merlin pauses, conscious of Colin's raised anticipation.

'Which is?'

'Which is the swiftest possible route to the kill.'

'Eh?'

'*Time*, right. Time is of the essence.' He paused to underline the gravity of the statement. 'Time is what ticks away before the next kill. Same as the next door if you're selling double-glazing, see. So he closes in as quickly as possible and asks for a shag as soon as he can.'

Ratty returned to the bar. 'Fuck,' he said, dripping with the Hooch that covered his face and shirt.

'Good technique, is it, Merl mate?' Colin laughed.

'No luck there, Ratty lad?' Merlin looked slightly surprised.

'I wuz a bit ambitious, I s'pose. Asked for a menajatwa.'

'A what?'

'Menajatwa. You know, Froggy-style, three in a bed nonsense. Trouble is, these days, unless it's a wee bit different, I cannae get it up.' Ratty returned nonchalantly to the fruit machine, entirely unaffected by the fact that he'd just asked two teenage girls, who might be anything from fifteen to nineteen, for sex, together, at once.

'I know it'll be hard on him, but it's for the best,' Trish explained.

'Does he know, Trish? I mean, is he expecting this?'

'You know Colin, he hardly notices anything. He's got the emotional awareness of a dinosaur. I think he only recently worked out I was spending more time at Mum's than with him. If I divorce him, it'll take a good year before it sinks in.'

Ruth placed a comforting hand on Trish's knee, aware of the sadness below the surface. 'I don't know, Ruth, nobody tells you it's like this. Nobody says how it's really going to be. It's all fairy-tale romances, strong men, beautiful children, golden retrievers and Agas. No-one mentions Sky Sports, beer guts, flatulence and McDonald's. No-one tells you that the man you marry quickly deteriorates into an ape, forgetting the power of speech and thinking a bloody bunch of flowers will buy him out of any problem.'

'Oh, Ruth.' Tears flow freely. 'I need a tissue.' Trish sniffs. 'Just popping to the loo.'

'She all right, Col?' Merlin watches Trish dash for the ladies'.

'Allergy.'

'Allergy? What, to you?'

'Ha bloody ha.'

'Seriously, mate, she doesn't look good. She still spending time at her mum's?'

'Less these days, you know. It'll be fine.'

The similarity between Colin and Merlin's marriages was their equally thin foundation. Both couples had met and married in the blink of an eye. Merlin proposed to his teenage sweetheart in the long bender of a post-graduation summer, while Colin had met Trish only seven months before they'd tied themselves together – the same length of time it takes to make an episode of *The Simpsons*, as Colin proudly commented.

'This column'll help. More regular income, something to focus on.'

'Not still on this wedding countdown lark, are you?'

'Merl, I tried to back down, mate, honest. But the editor, Hargreaves, he's completely hooked on the fucking wedding thing. I sold the bastard idea too well.'

'Well I'm having nothing to do with it. I haven't seen Johnny since he got back, and I don't think he'll ever let me off for fucking up his proposal so badly. Now Stef's gone and dropped him from the squad and you're writing a bloody diary of his life.' Merlin rubbed his temples.

'Saw Hargreaves yesterday. I thought I could at least get him to change the name of the column, but before I could say anything he'd pulled out the artwork. I mean, it's good stuff. Over the next month he's got four cartoons of a confused groom, no expense spared. It's a big break for me. If it works, he'll either keep it regular or build a space into their new culture and review section.'

'Colin Carter and culture, that's a strange combination.'

'Piss off, Skunk. Anyway, what about you? Still got the call of the wild?'

'Hmm?'

'You know, travel, writing and all that?'

'Yeah, yeah.' Merlin gazed out of the window at rain clouding the amber streetlight outside the pub.

'One day. One day, maybe.' His gaze lowered and focused inside the Blue Boy, coming to rest on his wife. 'Maybe not,' he muttered.

Maddy and Stef arrived, laughing and flushed. On the other side of the pub, Ruth and Trish raised their eyebrows and nodded to each other, like old women.

'Shaggin' again,' Ratty said, in a matter-of-fact way.

'What, those two?' Merl's expression revealed more than a passing interest.

'Oh aye, no strings, it just keeps Stef's balls out o' the barrow, like.'

Enraged

By the time we left Bucci's our potential row had been defused by my special absolute-silence technique – a dodgy method at the best of times, which sometimes backfires and enrages BTB into a Vesuvius-like state. We left Bucci's on talking terms, but tepid. In fact, not even tepid, cold. I only hoped that the solace of friends, the warmth of a Guinness and the homeliness of the smelly, swirly pub carpet would smother our mutual aggravation. I needed to escape the wedding cocoon that had grown around us in the last few days like a musty shroud. I needed to see friends, talk trivia, drink Guinness, forget.

The Blue Boy is our local. It's important in life to have a local. A place you can call your own. A Guinness-soaked comfort blanket. A haven of lively barstool banter. A barman, like Frankie the Abacus, who has your regular tipple waiting for you before you even slot yourself into the barstool cushion moulded perfectly to the shape of your buttcheeks. A simple, heart-warming, smoke-filled, putridsmelling hideaway.

The Blue Boy is a fifty-yard stagger from our front door, and no more than half a mile from Bucci's on Lavender Hill. Three years ago, when BTB and me were about to move in together – or, in Granny Victor's words, 'become disciples of Satan, living in sin like dogs' – this was a critical factor on my list of things a place must possess. BTB had her list:

Central heating.
Garden (for barbecues which I was apparently supposed to
master, just like swotty Merlin Masterchef).
Too many bedrooms (to entertain huge quantities of
family and friends every weekend).
Gas stove (all the better to cook with, my dear).
Wooden floors – because, because . . .
Minimum upkeep, no potential fixing or DIY necessary (I
inherited Dad's DIY skills, which are metaphorically
similar to the flying skills of cod).
Within a taxi ride of Jigsaw, Karen Millen (Kings Road)
and other women's' money-spending emporiums
(obviously).

And I had mine:

Local pub.
Other local pub, just in case.

On that particular Saturday night I felt somehow dis-
associated from our friends in the Blue Boy. I felt like a
spectator, a ghost.

There was a slight celebratory air. People cheered, vaguely,
when we arrived, and we quickly donned our happy masks.
Maddy squealed and ran the length of the crowded pub to
hug BTB. They giggled together like schoolgirls for a few
seconds, and BTB confirmed a night out at the local Greek
restaurant in the week. They pretended this would simply be
a cosy private retreat where they could celebrate and plan,
but I just happened to know they both fancied Michaeles, the
head waiter – 'Like a rude Ryan Giggs that you want to
butter all over,' Maddy explained vividly.

A token champagne cork popped before the lads returned

hurriedly to their pints. Merlin and Ratty made great, long-winded and elaborate apologies for telling everyone I was proposing, and pleaded for a public pardon. A few polite questions were asked:

'When?' Trish.

'May thirty-first.' BTB.

'Isn't that World Cup qualifiers?' Merl.

'No, I checked.' Me.

'Tsk.' BTB.

'Where?'

'In Clapham.' (News to me.)

'How?' Ruth.

'Church, Catholic. We fancy something big.' BTB (organ-dropping news to me).

I tried desperately to prevent my facial expression from giving away my sudden sense of fear and confusion. Eyebrows, lips and cheeks twitched and jumped nervously, attempting to rearrange my face into a frightened sneer. I stared at the whirling green carpet and concentrated on remaining calm. Thankfully, the questions stopped, and that was the end of it. That was the extent to which the wedding encroached on the evening. *Oh joy*, I thought, waiting for the rush of freedom to kick in. Waiting. Expecting to be over-whelmed by our friends' underwhelmedness. But it wasn't that simple. No matter how hard I tried, I couldn't shrug off my dislocation, my in-betweenness.

Watching the gang, I began to feel that I could see beneath the collective skin, see straining vessels, see malfunctions, lumps and pustules forming below the surface. Perhaps it was the proposal-induced coma I'd been in for the past week, but I felt as though we were at the beginning of some strange group dysfunction. In retrospect, it was all there, all evident that night in the Blue Boy. If you looked hard, if you looked deep into pores and pits and crannies, everything that followed for the group was there to see.

BTB joined Trish, Ruth and Ratty, sinking into seats around a table in the corner. Alternately, the group planned weddings and argued about whether people should wed – girls – or whether marriage is as natural as cloning super-warriors – Ratty. Ratty rabbited, firing his bigoted views through a pointed finger, trying to goad the girls into a flushed, red-faced fight, at which point he would smile and destroy their attack by commenting on how beautiful he finds feisty women. Ruth had known Ratty long enough not to rise to the bait, and coolly dismissed his views as she would a child's. Spurning him with practised off-handedness while she tied her hair into a French plait, sometimes even laughing at Ratty's desperate attempts to heat the blood. Trish was less experienced in matters Ratty. She raged, red curls springing vigorously in time with her expletives, eyes alight, a twitching nose entrancing Ratty as they rowed.

Colin and Merl went back to playing pool with inspired crapness. Maddy returned to Stef and flirted outrageously, under the pretence of attempting to win money from the trivia machine – known as Unconquerable.

I watched BTB slot back in, as if Barcelona had been some weird time pause and, back in reality, nothing had changed, while I felt like Superman in Bizarro World, where everything is slightly out of kilter. I couldn't believe that the same thing that had made me barf and sweat and lurch was as inconsequential as this. To our friends, it was simply a five-minute 'cheers', a glass of champagne and something for Ratty to have a row about.

This was what I needed. I needed anonymity. I needed to talk about anything but m—.

I downed my warm champagne, stifled a retch, looked at the company options and chose the pool table and trivia machine choice at the back of the pub. Maddy, Stef, Colin and Merl all looked as though they would be as likely to talk weddings as Swahili.

I paused at the bar for a more drinkable drink, and smiled while I considered the benefits of having a local, being a local, playing for the pub team and knowing the landlord.

'Aye, aye, Frankie, the usual, mate.' I nodded. He strolled over slowly, ignored me and served an old wrinkled bloke standing next to me at the bar.

'There you go, Harry.' Then he turned to me.

'Sorry, young man . . . a pint of the usual? That'll be . . . er . . . ?'

'Guinness.' I sighed.

'Guinness. Right you are. Erm . . . er . . . ?' He searched for my name.

'Johnny,' I grumbled. Three years, three fucking years, every weekend and at least two nights a week, and fucking Frankie still didn't know who I was.

'Winner stays on?' I gatecrashed the pool table as Colin accidentally snookered himself behind one of Merlin's balls.

'Fuck!'

'Ha ha, Col boy, still thinking ahead as ever.' Merl cleaned up his remaining balls and slotted the black in the top corner with a flippant, carefree stroke, gloating while Colin frowned.

'I had you, I should have won. I'd bloody beaten you fair and—'

'Next,' Merlin called, with fake boredom, throwing his cue casually onto the baize.

'I owe you a beating for that loose tongue.' I piled in the coins and pushed the metal slot, patiently waiting for the pool balls to trundle.

Colin ordered drinks at the bar.

'Hi, Col, same again for you and Merlin?' said Frankie.

'Yeah. Oh, plus a Guinness.'

'Right you are, Col,' said Frankie. *Bollocks*, I thought.

While Colin jingled the change in his tracksuit pocket and

clinked and fussed at the bar, Merlin lowered his voice like a conspirator: 'I'm sorry, Johnny boy,' Merlin mumbled, 'I feel like a right wazzock, telling Ratty, you know.' Merlin flushed beneath his weekend bristle and kept his eyes down deep in the baize.

'I just wasn't . . . I didn't . . . I don't,' he stuttered.

'Forget it, Merl,' I said, trying to provide an easy exit. 'Just remember you owe me one, big time. No fucking around on the stag do and I get the right of veto when you do your speech.'

'Deal.'

We played, we chalked, we potted. Colin drifted over to the trivia machine left of the pool table, next to the bar. He slotted his body awkwardly in between Stef and Maddy, a fat thumb between two lips.

'Why don't you go sit with Trish, Sofa boy?' goaded Stef.

'Er, I don't actually think she wants me to. Not exactly flavour of the month.'

Maddy saw that behind Colin's opaque eyes a glimmer of melancholy stirred. As anchor woman in the battle with Unconquerable, she smiled at Colin and focused her attention on making him feel welcome.

'OK, Colin, we're bound to beat this bloody machine now you're here.'

'You told lover boy about your column yet, Col?' Stef was conveniently tactless.

'Shh.' Colin frantically gestured a cutting motion across his throat.

'So you haven't told him yet?' Stef grinned wickedly as Colin shook his head.

'Just give us a warning, would you, mate. Don't want any blood on this shirt, you know.'

'Shh, boys, here comes the question: "What proportion of murders are committed by someone known to the victim?" '

'Whatever it is, it's about to go up when you tell Johnny.'

Stef chuckled and Colin sighed, adding, 'That's if Trish doesn't get in there first.'

'It wasn't just plain stupidity, you know, Johnny.' At the table, Merlin spoke in a hushed whisper, without context.

'Eh?'

'Telling Ratty. I wasn't just being a twat; it was more complicated than that.' I laughed loudly and Merlin frowned.

'Merl, don't play the post-rationalizing game with me.' Merlin looked hurt.

'No, shh, listen.' He burrowed into his pocket for a Silk Cut. 'I had to ask someone, Johnny. I mean, I know Ratty's not exactly even, or balanced, but he . . . well, I . . .'

'What, Merl? What's up, mate?' I had been chalking my cue-tip for minutes, and Merlin had been lining up the same shot for an equally long period of time. We were on hold, freeze-framed. Something fundamental was attempting to free itself from Merl's emotionally static brain. A fly wearily, but eventually, tearing itself free from a sticky amber almost-grave.

He breathed deeply and looked up. 'Are you sure?' he said, dark eyes fixing my gaze, pulling away the tray holding up my innards.

I paled. I staggered. My best mate, my best man. The grand wizard who'd magicked us together in the first place with amateur alchemy.

'Are you sure about this marriage malarkey, Johnny boy?' he whispered.

'I . . .' I gagged. 'I . . .' I couldn't answer. I threw Guinness down my throat trying to clear blocked passages. 'Merl . . . I,' I stuttered weakly, no conception of where my sentence or thoughts were going. Conversely, Merlin seemed to have become calm and certain.

'Because I'm not, Johnny.' He looked over to the far corner of the Blue Boy, watching his wife, animated and happy in his absence. 'I'm not,' he repeated. 'Everything fades,' he said profoundly. 'I should be up a fuckin' mountain in Nepal, or swimming with luminous eels in Papua New Guinea. But here I am, earning enough to keep the mortgage ticking over, commuting every day to write tacky brochure reviews of places I've never been. Everything fades, dreams included. Life's like a fuckin' boil wash.'

' "What percentage of marriages today end in divorce?" '

Maddy reeled the question off awkwardly as Colin sighed. 'All. Except the ones that end up buried under the patio, I expect.'

I listened silently to Merl's rare monologue, wondering how things had become so stale between him and Ruth without me knowing. I remembered him telling me how they had met – on an 18–30 holiday when he was seventeen and had lied about his age on the form. It was his and his mate Barry's first holiday abroad. They'd saved for months, working nights in a Birds Eye frozen-pea plant. Ruth's pigtails had jutted out from the head-rest in front of Merl on the coach from the airport, and he'd recognized them straight away as belonging to the girl he'd fancied for years down at Snippets on the high street. He was chained to Ruth from the moment they arrived in Costa Crappa. While Barry shagged everything that moved for a fortnight, Merl was smitten by teatime, and had a promise of a shag back in Cardiff a fortnight later – just as long as he behaved himself in Spain.

'You buy a new shirt, like, an' it becomes your favourite shirt.' He whacked the ball and the target thumped off a cushion and flew cleanly into the corner pocket. 'You love it, you wear it. You know, you wear it as often as possible.' Another ball cut delicately into a middle pocket. He could see all the angles like a geometric map. 'It fades, but you love it all the more for the comfort. It knows your body, your moods and moves. It's forgiving.' His last ball dribbled slowly into the top corner, leaving only the black. 'Then one day, Johnny boy, one day it falls apart at the seams.' He tapped a corner with his cue-tip. I stood in silence, holding an unsipped pint in one hand and a cigarette turned to ash in the other. The black rattled in the pocket, but stayed up stubbornly.

'Bollocks!'

I looked at his face. It had altered since the last time I'd looked properly. The pale skin had greyed and given recently. He seemed somehow smaller than I remembered him. A missed black hurt slightly more than it should.

'Bollocks,' he said again, wearily.

'Merl, what's up?' I asked quietly as I lined up a shot. He shook his head, turned away, cutting me off, joining the trivia team.

'Loser!' Colin shouted, missing the atmosphere as he would a bus.

Merlin shuffled over to Unconquerable.

'Thank God, a real man,' Maddy cooed loudly, slipping her arm through Merlin's. Shining in the clutch of men, alive in the innuendo of male company, Maddy seemed to instantly fill Merlin's grey face with colour.

Colin, equally, was out of character. He, too, lowered his voice to create the illusion of a private, quiet chat. 'So, Johnny, I need to check something with you, buddy.' In Colin's rhino-skin world this was extreme sensitivity. 'You know how I've always wanted a column?'

I nodded. I'd known this for years, and had truly hoped it would come off for him some time. Like Colin himself, we all knew he needed some sort of purpose to keep him on the rails, or more aptly, off the sofa. Something to recreate the energy that had enticed Trish away from Eric, her banker fiancé, all those years ago. Back then, after Scunthorpe, Colin was unstoppable at work and play, scooping and clubbing, door-stepping and dancing. Back then, he'd wooed Trish with poems of love and infatuation, but time had crumpled his passion like wet paper.

Over the years, there'd been talk of film scripts and screen-plays, novels, fiction, faction and documentaries; each fad passing as fields through a train window. Colin was a hack. Any imagination he'd ever had had been filed away, subbed to death. A column would be perfect, but it was so hard to break into the cliquey circles that controlled them.

'Well, I've been offered one. Well, sort of.' Colin, normally the shameless braggart, spoke with uncharacteristic humbleness.

'Wow, that's bloody brilliant, mate.' Colin gestured to me to lower my voice as I loudly congratulated him, shaking his hand.

'Shh, shh.' Shushing me at the pool table seemed a strangely popular sport tonight. We carried on playing.

'Who for?' I never imagined getting such good news from King big-head Colin would be so tough.

'The *Mail on Sunday*. It's just holiday cover but, you know, if it goes well, if it works . . .'

'Great. That's great, really. So what did you want to check?'

'Well, it's nothing really, but you know how columns have an angle?' He wandered over to the newspaper rack by the bar and pulled down a couple of papers to illustrate his point. 'This guy, he's an alcoholic, on step six. The column's called "There's a Bear in the Room". It's an AA code – good title, eh? Makes good reading, too, but it can be a bit depressing when he fucks up. Last week he stole his son's piggy bank for a bottle of vodka.' I nodded, wondering where we were headed. 'And this woman. I hate this woman. Her husband has left her and she just whinges about it bitterly, week after bloody week.'

'So?'

'So you gotta have an angle, Johnny, and a good title.'

'So what's yours?'

'Well, here's the thing. I mentioned a title and subject – off

141

the top of my head, you know – but the bloody editor loves the fuckin' thing and I can't change his mind. Course, it doesn't need to be the truth, so I ... well, I'm using a pseudonym.'

'A pseudonym.' I laughed. 'You pretentious git. I know, I know, why don't you call yourself Cardinal Colin Cock-Spuckle, the confessions of a serial wanking priest?'

'No, you don't understand . . .'

'Or Colin Cack's Crack Column, world-famous explorer Colin Cack leads globe's first expedition up his own back passage?'

'It's called "The Life of Riley".' Colin was deadpan.

' "The Life of Riley"?' I laughed nervously. 'That's a good one.'

Colin wasn't laughing. He shrugged and shuffled.

'The Life of fucking Riley!'

'Yeah.'

'What's it about?' I clenched my cue like a javelin. Colin began to back away.

'It's a blow-by-blow account of getting hitched from a bloke's-eye view.' Colin rushed out the words – obviously taken straight from the strap line in the column – and dashed for the door. The trivia team looked on calmly, their unfazed faces showing that they had expected this to happen. My cue clattered into the door frame and splintered.

'Oi!' shouted Frankie. It took some heavyweight flirting and fluttering from Maddy, and fifteen quid from Merl, to calm Frankie down. Colin failed to reappear for the remainder of the evening, like a coward.

Eventually Trish followed him home, apologizing behind him. 'I'm sure it won't be too bad,' she said, with zero conviction, cheeks blazing. 'Probably no likeness to you at all, Johnny. Silly bastard. At this rate he'll have to write a column about a bloke's-eye view of divorce.'

Trish left as people laughed without confidence.

Stef and Maddy tried to sneak off without saying good-byes, so I decided to ruin their tryst and draw attention to their departure.

'Bye-bye, Stefano,' I shouted. He pulled a pissed-off face. 'See you at football tomorrow,' I called. Stef rubbed his bald head and glanced at Ratty, who was still sitting with Ruth and BTB, and then at Merl. Both men studiously ignored him.

'Erm, actually, Johnny, you're not playing.'

'What?' This was rapidly becoming the worst night out in living memory.

'We've got a full squad this season. Had to file the names last weekend when you weren't around.'

'Thanks, Stef.'

'Sorry, mate, thought you had other things planned this season. Maybe someone will drop out.'

He left with Maddy dangling drunkenly on his arm. At the door, she suddenly pulled back and shouted, 'See you at my place next Tuesday, Johnny.'

Bitch, I thought. This was Maddy's warped way of causing chaos. With one sentence she'd made Stef jealous, Ratty and Ruth curious, and BTB suspicious. After the Spanish-bottom incident, I was already on borrowed time, but the ancient history of Maddy and my drunk one-nighter stung BTB even now.

But Maddy was drunk and I wasn't about to blow cover in the Blue Boy and open myself up to ridicule from the lads for having piano lessons. Nor was I about to fuck up the surprise for BTB.

BTB looked hurt. She and Ruth whispered for a while, clocked Ratty, Merl and me on a non-stop mission to oblivion, and decided to leave us to it and go. We elected Ratty, as most coherent member of the group, to persuade Frankie to have a lock-in. Amazingly, he succeeded. We reckoned Ratty either paid Frankie, or offered him some sort of deviant S&M-orientated sexual favour. '*Go on, Frankie, I'll tickle your testes with nettles if you do.*'

'Right, a toast to the nearly-weds.' Merlin raised a glass in the stale aftermath of a Saturday night.

'I'm no' fuckin' toastin' that,' Ratty grumbled. 'Just another wake for a single man.'

'Ratty, for fuck's sake, lad, not everyone needs to be like you.' Merlin's defence was weak.

'Dis'nae work. Marriage dis'nae work. Eh, Frankie, what's the odds?'

Frankie stood, methodically drying glasses. He raised thick grey eyebrows at the question, pushed black plastic rectangular specs up his nose and brushed back long, thinning, grey hair. We sipped our whiskies as Frankie stroked his chin.

'Hello, Frankie? Anybody in there?'

'He's thinking, Merl.' It was well known to the locals that Frankie was a bit of a sage. 'Frankie the human abacus', they called him. He used a technique whereby he would attempt to calculate answers to posed questions by adding and subtracting the confessions of the locals at the Blue Boy.

Frankie muttered, 'An' Phil's wife pissed off with that Dutch bloke. Arty's still going strong with his wife, but he tries it on with Jean. Does it count if they're faithful, even though they try not to be?' he asked.

'Yes,' I answered quickly, anything to up my chances.

'No. Does it fuck. 'At's like any guy could wander around with his troosers round his ankles but end up classed "happily married" 'cos he's too laupin' to get a shag.'

'Sixty per cent,' announced Frankie proudly.

'Success rate. Well, that's OK.'

'Failure. Sixty per cent likelihood to fail.'

'Oh,' I said.

'Can we talk about something else?' Merlin spoke wearily.

'You'll be shagging Maddy night 'afore the wedding.

144

You're probably shaggin' her now, doin' tag with Ronaldo like those wrestlin' teams in spangly leotards.' Ratty's comments were body blows to the ribcage.

Frankie looked up, wondering who the accusations were aimed at. I shook my head, amazed at the rancidity of Ratty's mind.

'No? So what's this "See you at my place, Johnny" all about?' Ratty mimicked Maddy's candy-coated voice.

'Nothing.'

'Aye, fer sure.'

'Yeah, what was that about?' Even the ever-supportive Merl turned on me.

'Nothing.' They all looked suspicious. Frankie suddenly stopped drying the glasses, like a Mexican stand-off.

'Nothing. She's helping me with something . . . honest.'

'Sperm-count reduction?'

'Fucking hell, Ratty, why's everything have to boil down to sex with you?'

'Eh?' Ratty looked bemused. The question simply did not compute for him.

I tried to deflect the attention. 'Come on, Frankie, back me up here. We can be faithful, can't we? Men can be faithful. What are the odds?'

'Faithful?' he pondered and returned to rubbing his glasses.

'My mum and dad are still together.' I built my argument unconvincingly.

I could see no hope of winning the row and tried to change the subject instead.

'Listen, guess who I met on the way to Barcelona?'

'Ronaldo?' said Merlin.

'That poncey flamingo dancer who looks like a girl?' said Ratty.

'Lord Norbert Camberly.' I spoke his name solemnly, with the gravity and weight required.

'Who?' said Merlin.

'Fat Geordie. Films. Size of a planet.' Ratty's description was simple but sufficient.

'Sat next to me . . . Scared of flying, you know?'

'Hmm, I would be if I was that size, probably should have gone in the hold for ballast.'

'Would he no' explode in the hold?' We all imagined the vast Norbert Camberly exploding in a plane.

'Anyway, he asked me to send him my script,' I exaggerated.

'Which one's this, now?' asked Merlin.

'*Mr Saturday Night.*' *The only one.*

'The pub landlord in Shrewsbury?' I'd given a copy to Merlin.

'That's the one.'

'You read it?' Ratty directed the question to Merlin.

'Yup.'

'Good?'

'Er, needs work, but it's OK.'

'You mean it's shite?'

'No, no. It's . . . it's good.' Merlin turned to me and a little flame of energy suddenly lit. 'That's great, though, Johnny boy. Good for you, a contact. Make sure you send it. Don't waste a chance like that; gotta take the chances in life when they come.' Merlin wittered as the alcohol finally beat his blood in a battle with sobriety.

'Eh-hmm.' Frankie coughed loudly. He had stopped drying glasses again and was resting both hands on the counter, attempting to look authoritative. 'Football, then cigarettes, then beers, then wives . . . just ahead of religion.'

'What?' I said.

'You asked if men could be faithful, so I worked out a few things as well as wives, you know, to give you a bit of context.'

'Football was bottom?' It was a hopeless clutch at straws, but I had to try.

'Top! Men are most faithful to their team, rarely change

their cigarette brands, do change their beers slightly more often, but less often than their wives.'

'Men are more faithful to the beer they drink than their wives?' confirmed Merlin.

'That's right, but they do rank more highly than God.'

'What, wives?'

'Yes. And now, gentlemen, on that note, I'll politely request that you leave the premises, as Jean's upstairs waiting for me in her silks.'

'Silks?' repeated Ratty, a hint of spittle vibrating in the corner of his mouth. Frankie's wife, Jean, was built like a pug.

'So how long have you been with Jean?' I still searched for hope.

'Twenty-six years.'

'Faithful?' I asked and winced, expecting the worst.

'Loyal as a dog.' *A chance*, I thought, *a slim chance*. A Jean-and-Frankie-type chance.

'What, like sexy underwear, silks?' Ratty was somewhere else in the sordid recesses of his mind.

'Yes, well, for me anyway. It's the Fulham away strip. Really gets me going, you know. Better than that Viagra stuff.'

We left, dragging Ratty behind us, drooling uncontrollably and threatening to gatecrash Frankie and Jean's vigorous lovemaking with another menajatwa offer.

Fifty yards isn't far, but it's amazing how many times you can change your mind in that distance. In between the Blue Boy and my front door I ricocheted between a whole series of opposites, as well as a couple of walls. I bounced uncontrollably between naively optimistic to wildly cynical, from loyal as a pug to fickle as Ratty, blissfully betrothed to brutally condemned. It didn't really matter, by the time I'd fumbled haplessly with the keys, dropped them, fallen through the front door, fallen up the stairs and into bed, I'd forgotten all previous thoughts and contradictions and was left with only the inevitable:

'Ahhhreaalllllyluvvvvyouu.'

'Ssh, Johnny, you moron.'

Muttley's Satiated Smile

'Kill, kill!' shouted Johnny in the cold November sunshine.

'Get him off me. Get him off!' Johnny chased Muttley, who chased Colin across the muddy pitch as the ref tried to intervene.

'Manager pitch infringement . . . and dog and er . . .' The ref blew his whistle vaguely and fumbled with his notebook. It was the Blue Boys' third game without Johnny, with no noticeable decline in standards.

The mud-streaked players stopped to watch a spectacle infinitely more entertaining than their own feeble footy efforts. They steamed and shivered, huddling together, passing bottles of water and tossing comments across the field.

Colin half ran and half hopped across the field, keeping a good distance from Johnny, who was wearing a skiing jacket over blue-checked pyjama trousers. Muttley was attached to Colin's leg like a limpet.

'Kill. Kill him, Muttley!' Johnny brandished a rolled-up *Mail on Sunday* containing the first 'Life of Riley' column.

The Blue Boy players began to take sides and lay bets. 'Run for it, Cloughy,' shouted Stef.

'Get him, Muttley,' cheered Merlin. 'Fiver on the dog. Any takers?' Muttley had grasped the wrong end of the stick and was desperately humping Colin's leg.

"At'll be the best shag Colin's had in a wee while.' Ratty

sniggered, already puffing on a cigarette, slumping down in the centre circle.

'Think we should call him off?' asked Stef, impatient to restart.

'You fucking cock-sucker, Colin. What's this shit?' Johnny waved the newspaper, gaining on him.

'Call off who, Stef? Johnny or Muttley?' Merlin had wandered up from the goal line to join Stef and the rest of the lads enjoying the show. It was the perfect vantage point, and they swivelled in unison as Johnny, Colin and Muttley charged around the touchline. 'Ah, the cat's here.' Stef threw the ball at Merlin, who kept his arms crossed and his hands pressed deep into his armpits against the cold.

'Fuck off, Ronaldo. The ground's too hard to dive.' The ball bounced off Merlin's chest and rolled back to Stefano.

'An' you're too soft, Skunk, ya big jessy.' Smoke merged with the cold air to cover Ratty in gold-tinted billows.

'Not exactly been his best day ever, has it?' Stef tossed the ball in his hands as he talked.

The voices of the trio carried easily across the pitch. 'What? It's nothing, Johnny, just a column. Call Muttley off, Johnny. God, you wouldn't know it was you. Call him off.' Colin waggled his leg furiously, now behind the Thames-end goal at the far end of the field.

'Whose worst day? Johnny boy's?' Merlin tugged his gloves off with his armpits as he spoke and rubbed his hands together for warmth.

'No, Col's. Trish moved out this morning.' Stefano said this without emotion, sniffed loudly and spat into the mud. It was almost inevitable, the final step of a journey that Trish had begun long ago.

'Oh.' Merl, likewise, had little sadness or surprise left in him.

From behind the goal in the distance, they heard, 'He's gonna mess up my bloody coat.'

'Piss on your frigging coat, Colin. Explain this worthless piece of shit.'

'You're taking it well considering, Merl mate.' Stef stopped spinning the ball, turning to face Merlin.

'Considering what?'

'Trish. You know, moving in with you and Ruth.'

'You're fuckin' 'avin me on, Ronaldo.'

'Oops,' Stef said quietly.

The team fell silent and Merlin kicked the ground like a schoolboy. 'Pass us a fag, Ratty.' Ratty stuck his hand inside his shorts unpleasantly, digging the packet out.

The threesome were now getting closer again, coming up to the opposite touchline, still shouting, 'It's not really you, Johnny. Don't be ridiculous. You wouldn't know. Nobody would know. There are only a few similarities.'

'It's called "The Life of fucking Riley", Colin, you bastard!'

'THWACK!'

Finally, Johnny had managed to get within arm's reach of Colin and swung the paper in a powerful forehand volley. Colin cowered and Muttley humped his heart out.

'Look at the wee bugger go.' A hint of admiration crept into Ratty's voice.

'Wouldn't bloody know! He's called Riley, he lives in Clapham, he works for a video company, he's the same bloody height as me, for Chrissakes.'

'THWACK!'

'He supports the same team as me, drinks in the same pubs, eats at the same restaurants.'

'THWACK!'

'He's getting hitched on the same frigging day as me, in the same place, he likes the same music, drives the same car, even wears the same pants that came free with four-packs of Boddingtons.'

'But—'

'And, according to you, the only woman who would

have me would be blind, deaf and very, very, very dumb.'

'THWACK!' They were nearing a full circuit now.

'Johnny, it's not you – obviously.'

'And, supposedly, we haven't had sex since I proposed.'

'But that's tr—'

'THWACK!'

Back where they'd started, Muttley stopped humping abruptly. The surprise made the two men look down.

'I think he's come,' said Johnny.

Colin stared miserably at the sticky mess on his precious camel coat, while Muttley swaggered away with a satiated smile.

The ref restarted the game with a flourish. 'Show's over, folks. Move along there. There's nothing to see here.'

Ring Rage

I stepped into a burning ring o' fire,
I went down, down, down and the flames went higher,
The ring of fi–re,
The ring of fire . . .

Muttley was singing in the back of the Audi. Taking the piss,
as usual. Well, actually he wasn't, it was the radio, the
motion of the car and him chewing on a chewy shoe. He just
looked like he was singing the song, which harshly summed
up my situation. I winced and clenched my wallet and
buttocks together as best I could.

BTB turned the music down as we slipped through south
London like a raindrop on a window pane. Not for me, you
understand, but because it was interfering with the hands-
free phone chat she was having with Trish. 'Oh, I know, Trish
. . . Oh, you poor darling . . . Well, his mother would say
that, wouldn't she . . . Yes, well actually, no . . .' BTB looked
me up and down. '. . . No, he's not quite that bad . . . He's
here. We're on the way to buy the rings . . . Yup, the full
works . . .'

As we followed the flow of the Thames, I tried to cut out
BTB's chat, mainly because I was filling in Trish's side of the
conversation, and didn't like what I heard. To silence her, and
take my mind off the little band of gold at the end of the

road, I fantasized my way through south London's landmarks.

As the upturned table of Battersea Power Station reluctantly sank behind a bland glass tower, we passed through the concrete mess of Vauxhall before MI5's Gothic gateau HQ hove into view. Banks of hidden security cameras would be recording our approach. Inside, I suspected, would be one of the many alter-egos of my mother-in-law-to-be.

'Ahhh, Agent Johnson seems to have resurfaced after Operation Ringpiece. Have him gutted; he's not good enough for my . . .'

First Big Ben, in its *ITN* splendour, and then the rest of the Houses of Parliament, slid into a patriotic picture-postcard view. The intricate stonework and tiny mock-Gothic windows toyed with your perspective and made the buildings seem even more ludicrously grandiose than they really were; a bit like the puffer-fish MPs inside.

'Order, order, order,' shouted Madam Speaker, BTB's mother.

'Does the prime minister deny Agent Johnson accepted a diamond-encrusted gold ring as a bribe?' Gerry Donnelly made a disarmingly good MP.

'Er . . .' said my dad, the baffled PM. Jeers, shouting and booing rose from the floor like rattled cattle after gunfire.

Just before Waterloo's weird, prawn-shell-topped Euro-hub, an ambulance screeched past us and sharp-turned into the glass and concrete of St Thomas's Hospital.

'Scalpel, Nurse Donnelly.' BTB's mum holds up a machete for the blood-spattered Welsh surgeon. Unnervingly, it suits her.

'Nurse, this is a delicate operation, see.' Merl was an unconvincing doctor. 'Johnny boy's gone an' lost control of his sphincter and we gotta replace it with this.' He held the twenty-four-carat-gold, diamond-encrusted anal ring before dropping it on the floor. 'Oh, shitebags.'

I shook away my daymares as we parked on a meter next to Gabriel's Wharf. 'Why here again, petal?' I asked BTB.

'Well, Abby at the office bought hers here' – *EEEEEK, Abby the sloane with the husband who brokes nations for a living* – 'and it's gorgeous, and apart from that, I thought you might want to buy me dinner to celebrate afterwards.' She nodded in the direction of a blue-awninged bar, plastered pleasingly with the word 'Hoegaarden'.

'Hmm, sounds good.' I licked my lips at the thought of a cold beer. 'How about before we shop?'

'The table's not booked for an hour, Johnny.' I puzzled, peering at the empty bar, which didn't look like the kind of place you needed to book. With a fright, I saw the Oxo Tower rising up behind the happy Hoegaarden bar, a vast steel boil lance. Bloody Abby, bloody little Mrs rich tits and her Chesterfield of a husband.

Gabriel's Wharf was a quarter-mile square of eclecticness in the drab grey wash of south London. Wherever you cast your eye in this part of London, things were just not quite right somehow. Soulless building sites, equally empty Eighties-designed new developments, or brand-new, vacuous, ultra-chic glass and wire. But nothing human, or lived-in, apart from Gabriel's Wharf.

Children played on hand-carved rocking animals in the middle of the square – a duck, a hippo and an alligator. An odd mix of bemused tourists, skate-boarding kids, wealthy shoppers and a knot of three or four homeless people sharing a can of Tennent's Super were scattered across the colourful square. Like rich velvet tassels that bring a rug to life, the shops fringed the edges.

I was pleasantly surprised. Nowhere could I see the Abby-style glitzorama I was expecting. Thinking about it, my Abby view was out-dated, formed in the big-haired, gold-dripping Eighties. I had to admit that nowadays, while still annoyingly

155

sloaney, and still with a tightly stuffed sofa for a husband, she had definitely become 'more Prada than Gucci, darling', as she would say. In fact, asking BTB to describe Abby's ring gave me hope. She had used words like 'simple' and 'minimalist', as opposed to 'opulent' or 'mountainous'. I calmed myself down, remembering BTB's description of Trish's engagement ring as 'an ice rink in a gold mine'.

BTB led us to an innocent-looking shop, with a curvy yellow hand-painted sign above the door, giving it a craft-fair feel. A few warning signs were present which should have tipped me off: the window display was beautiful and suspiciously price-tag free, there was a buzzer on the door and only room for two in the shop.

Forty minutes later I'd still seen no prices. BTB and the happy-clappy, hippyish assistant had developed a shortlist of ten or so engagement rings, ranging from 'scary' to 'simple', which they'd lined up on the counter. By now we had learned everything there was to know about diamonds and gold and carats and clarity and cut and mounting. My credit card cowered in my pocket. Worse still, behind the engagement rings, a series of potential wedding rings were lined up to match BTB's chosen ring. And even worse than that . . . was just about to come.

'And will sir be wanting a matching wedding ring?' The assistant grinned inanely, like some lobotomized religious-cult devotee. BTB was already smiling in that assured of-course-you-want-one-don't-you-my-darling-lovey-wovey-Johnny-pants way.

'Er . . .' I remembered agreeing to this, accidentally, some time ago. 'I . . . er . . .' I could try 'allergy' or 'manual labourer'. You know, 'Might slice my finger off if the ring gets caught in the corn-chaffer down on the farm,' but these were both bare-faced lies.

'Yes, of course,' I said. It was just a ring, after all. The happy-clappy hippy passed me one to try on.

Holy fuck! I thought, trying not to scream. *There goes the metal tray.*

'I've changed my mind . . . I don't think it . . . er, suits me.' I was pale and slick, wide-eyed and staring at the married man in the mirror with a ring on.

'Johnny, what's wrong with you? You said you wanted one.'

I made a high-pitched nervous whimpering noise and panicked, trying to pull the ring off my finger.

Nobody tips you off about this. Nobody tells you to watch out for the moment you put a ring on, when suddenly you realize that what you thought was a harmless, quaint tradition has clear and brutal motives. It must be similar to the moment when kids connect a bacon sandwich with the cute cuddly porkers they see in cartoons and Disney films.

'It suits you,' said BTB, looking suspiciously like a gaoler.

'I feel like a pigeon.'

'A what?'

'A pigeon,' I said.

'That's nice. Why?'

'Tagged, you know. Like when they tag birds and clip their wings. Well, I feel . . .' I noticed BTB's dagger eyes and the happy-hippy's awkwardness, and bit my tongue.

'I've never been so embarrassed, Johnny.' We sat in the clinical sheen of the Oxo Tower restaurant, my now flaccid credit card feeling hopelessly inadequate and incapable of rising to the challenge of the bound-to-be-vast food bill. Abby's ring might have been simple but, apparently, simple doesn't come cheap. BTB had finally settled on a plain rose-gold band with a single sunken diamond. I was presented with the bill, offered a part exchange for one of my organs – kidneys, heart, liver – and thanked God that she had steered clear of the chunky platinum ring with diamond cluster option.

'Sorry, it just came out.' Pigeon was the least of it. Pigeon

157

was the nice image that sprang to mind. The other image, with the bounty-hunting lesbians on Harleys, would really have upset her: *Tripped by flailing bolas and slotted into a waiting body bag. 'Bagged and tagged, ladies,' they hollered. 'Bagged and tagged.'* I vowed to keep the leather-clad lesbians locked away in my imagination.

I looked down at my lap and slipped the napkin that covered my hand away. There it was, aaaarghhh! BTB and the hippy-git girl had conspired against me in the shop and fought off my complaints about the ring not suiting me, not fitting me and just not *being* me (barrel scraping). I had been forced into a 'sizing' ring, which I was to wear, like an electronic tag, for a week or so to see how it felt (like I couldn't fly).

'Let's see, Johnny.' I picked my left arm up with my right arm and flopped it on the table.

'It looks lovely, darling.' I looked down at the alien hand.

'Would sir and madam like more time?'

'Er . . .' *Do you have main courses for less than twenty pounds a pop?* I wondered.

'*We 'ave some specials. As a starter, a ring of squid in chilli oil with a salad of rocket and shavings of red pine from Canada, and, as a main course, we 'ave the warm breast of wood pigeon, bought live and frightened to death this morning, served on a bed of risotto rice in a piquant sauce which is pensive.*'

I sighed. We ordered.

'It's all connected, you know, Johnny. You can't keep on sticking your head in the ground.'

'What? What's all connected?' *Already in the bad-books, credit card still smarting.*

'Not wanting to wear a ring, not being able to say "marry". You're just not being honest, Johnny.'

'I am.'

'Why can't you say "married"?'

158

'Marr-eed,' I said.

'Why don't you want to wear a ring? Because it's a sign? Because it means you're taken, Johnny? Is that it?'

'I . . . er . . .'

'Not so easy to pick up slappers, Johnny?'

'No . . . I . . . how could you think . . .'

'Well, where the hell were you last Thursday? Tell me that. 'Cos you weren't with Merl or Colin or Ratty.' I wondered whether to gamble on Stef, or whether it was a trick.

'Nowhere.' Duff answer. Her fingers drummed the table, waiting for a better one.

'You know, just out after work.' *Strictly speaking, not quite a lie.*

'Oh.'

'What do you mean, "Oh"?'

'I mean, oh how bloody convenient, Johnny. I mean, how come it's always work? Or something vague and non-specific, Johnny. How come?'

I could see her mind racing, see connections, sums and equations reeling. She decided not to finish, not to make the final assumption. No X + Y = fuck you, Johnny, for BTB. Perhaps the evidence wasn't there, perhaps she doubted her logic and her suspicions were unfounded, perhaps it didn't matter and I'd already lost the game. All this because of my reaction to a measly little band of gold.

Messing with my squid, I considered my position. I was being pathetic, baulking at a badge. A badge that I should wear with honour, just like I did as a teenage Madness fan, when that little black-and-white badge took pride of place on my Harrington jacket. Like the sad little red star on my second-hand leather at university, which epitomized my stubborn idealism. Yet here I was, incapable of such a small, simple gesture as 'I am married', 'I am in love'. I felt these things but, as usual, couldn't say them. Not out loud. Not here in the restaurant.

How can you explain such irrational things? I mean, I wasn't questioning me and BTB through fear of the ring, it was just a shock. Nobody warned me. Nobody said the ring was more than just a ring. But it is. You might as well tattoo 'Me and BTB For Ever' on your forehead. And, yes, I loved her, yes, I wanted it to be for ever, but . . . your mind races away with you.

Here I was, in the Oxo Tower, wearing a silver sizing ring. So self-centred and self-conscious that I thought everyone was looking, that everyone could tell.

'Hello, married sir, here's your pigeon. Would husband sir like to see the dessert menu, or will hen-pecking wife be ordering everything?' said the waiter.

'Heeelllllooo, sir, your drinks.' Stunning, flirtatious waitress. 'Oh, I see you're tagged and bagged. Too bad, I was going to offer you no-strings sex behind the coat-stand over there.'

Of course, the reality is that nobody cares. Nobody givesa-fuck. Nobody, apart from you, that is. And you should be proud. Proud like a Madness badge, like a red star. Proud like a Fulham scarf, proud like a wedding ring.

. . . And it burns, burns, burns and the flames went higher,
The ring of fi-re
The ring of fire . . .

Deranged

BTB and I arrived on Christmas Eve, sliding down the M3 to Cornwall, another rain-slicked metal slug stuck in Christmas traffic, escaping droning London. Cars crammed with over-Christmased parents and TV-ad hyperstressed kids, worrying that Father Christmas will fail to meet their hopes and greed.

BTB's engagement ring throbbed in my pocket like uranium, hidden from the gaze of our unaware families.

Even the ever-cheery Santa's little helper BTB was dreading this Christmas. We had created a gruesomely stressful experience, an accidental assault course. Not only was it the first meeting of the families, not only was it Christmas, with all of its traditional tripwires and beartraps, but, as the fairy topping to this doomed Christmas tree of fun, we had decided to announce our engagement.

It had to be the worst plan since the Welsh Guards decided to defend Rorke's Drift against 17 million attacking Zulu warriors with fourteen soldiers – most of whom had one leg or TB or were mad as minks in a cage.

Everything had started well enough. For at least a few minutes we were all quite civil. BTB was greeted like the long-lost daughter she was to become. Granny Victor was sedated and non-violent. Dad was charming, giving BTB the same guided tour she'd had several times before of the converted farmhouse that had been the Riley family home for twenty years. Mum was the perfect hostess, fussing over BTB with mugs of steaming coffee, running baths, telling her stories about the history of the village and the friendly ghosts and spirits she sees around the house. 'Happy spirits, my dear. Friends from another age, returned for a visit to their happy home.'

BTB laughed graciously, slipping me a does-she-need-medicine look, while Mum busily rummaged through great piles of old black-and-white photos, via which she told the family history in a puzzling muddle of sequence, event, name and place.

'And that's Great Aunt Edith. Now she was really fat. I think she was the one who fell into a ditch and died because she couldn't get out.'

BTB looked startled, and a little nauseous, as they sat on a rug in front of a log fire. BTB idly stroked Muttley, whom I'd been allowed to bring on the strict promise that he would behave more like a dog than an incontinent flea-bitten rug. Muttley, in turn, was watched with distrust from the mantel by Wedgwood, Granny Victor's ancient, malicious, bony blue cat.

'And this is Uncle Douglas – the one wearing the boater – he has a metal plate in his forehead,' Mum said, as though the plate was a complete inventory of Uncle Douglas's contribution to life. 'He's with Granny Victor.' Granny Victor huffed disapprovingly from her chair. 'That's Johnny, holding her hand. She doted on Johnny, like a second mother—'

'Johnny-bloody-bladder-pants!' Granny Victor hollered.

I smiled, remembering the stories she used to tell me, the long sea-walks and beach expeditions she'd lead me on as a curious child. Before. When she was lucid and wise. Before. When she was young, with a lead-free mind.

I played chess with Dad; mostly in silence. It was the perfect environment for Dad. Freed from conversation by the game, he could mutter the odd polite nicety without tripping over anything complex or emotional.

'How's the old film thing going then, Johnson?' Dad, like me, was poor on the detail. His strengths lay in the shambolic clutter of academia – an eccentric wit, an encyclopedic knowledge and an endearing charm.

'Fine, fine.' It was pointless elaborating and burdening Dad with specifics that would struggle to find shelf space in his overcrowded mind. I heard BTB 'tsk' in the background, aware that everything was far from fine at EF&Co. Mr Big filled my thoughts like a too-long limo, but now was not the time to unburden my bruised dreams on the family.

'Yours?' I returned, realizing chess was also the perfect environment for me.

'Oh excellent, excellent. Have you seen the new journal?' Dad had retired a year ago from a research position in a biotechnics company. Now he edited an international academic journal, entitled *Basidiomycete Genealogy and Genotypicity*. Dad was cited on the inside cover – Dr Henry R. Riley – R for Roysten – Ph.D, M.Sc., M.I. Biochem. Contributing Editor. Dad had devoted his entire life to the study of genetics in mushrooms and related fungi. His lifetime achievement was widely known and well-rewarded. Dr Henry Roysten Riley had isolated the gene which determines the buttoniness of button mushrooms. You will have noticed in recent years that button mushrooms in supermarkets have become more and more buttony. Well, you have Dr Riley to thank for the buttoniness of the mushrooms you chop into pastas or toss into salads. I nodded at the journal and muttered encouraging words.

'Fix that central-heating problem you had?' he asked after moving his knight into a queen-rook pin that really pissed me off. I'd inherited Dad's ineptitude with all things domestic and practical, although we both made a pretence of understanding such things. Dad lives life through a spectroscope, where unseen minutiae matter, but larger things, seen through normal eyes, like bills, DIY and wives, are unmanageably large.

'Yes it was the pump; it was dirty,' I said uncertainly. BTB was too involved in Mum's monochrome to question my knowledge of our heating system. In reality, BTB had fixed the heating herself, with a spanner, a book and phone instructions from Paddy, one of her brothers.

'And is Merlin well?' Dad had warmed to Merlin when he'd discovered they had a shared passion for mushrooms. 'I sent the lad a bag of the latest *Lentinus edodes*. Damn tasty lot, too. Did he like them?'

'Yes,' I lied. Merlin's fake mushroom hobby sprang solely from a passion for the magic sort, and he'd quickly realized the value of cultivating the subject. As a student, he'd managed to bamboozle Dad into sending him a cling-film bag full of severe mythical hallucinogenic mushrooms called Mexican Bastards. Merlin missed an entire term.

'Good, good. Nice lad that Merlin.' Muttley distracted us from our chess as he loudly snuffled and snorted, licking his balls.

'My advice would be to have him neutered,' said Dad offhandedly.

Muttley whimpered and moved on to licking his arse. Elsewhere, I pictured Merlin crossing his legs.

It looked like a normal, happy family scene. I warmed to the idea of telling the families and celebrating our engagement. I began to imagine an idyllic Christmas. Good food, good wine, good humour. I pictured the two families after our announcement, merging and mixing together easily, like ingredients in a Christmas cake. Mothers making mince pies in the kitchen, helping BTB plan wedding-type things. Dads drinking brandy and smoking cigars together, standing in front of the fire; talking politics, the importance of family and regular bowel movements. Me sitting with a smiling

Granny Victor recounting stories of her and Grandpa Jonah (who died of gout the year before I was born).

In the late afternoon, I walked BTB around Cawsand several times with Muttley in tow, pissing promiscuously on the crumbling sandstone cottages that tumbled towards the sea.

It was dreary and drizzling. Grey seas and skies, grey eyes and minds. Our white-Christmas hopes looked muted and improbable. Muttley, as ever, caught the mood and padded around nervously on the beach off the leash, keeping his distance from BTB and me. Normally, a visit to Cawsand and a trip down the beach was the doggy version of a dose of speed for Muttley. He would loopily lope, chasing sandflies, fighting seaweed monsters and biting the heads off the white horses that charged towards him. A game of ducks and drakes was usually ecstasy for Muttley, hopelessly chasing pebbles bouncing between the waves. Today, on Christmas Eve, Muttley knew the mood was bleak and kept beyond a safety zone he'd drawn around BTB and me, choosing instead the company of a dead seagull or some sheep shit to roll around in.

'It'll be fine, Johnny.' BTB's eyes had absorbed the dreich Atlantic melancholy. She gripped my hand tightly. Through sheepskin mitts, borrowed from Mum, I could feel the reassurance of her small hands. 'Don't worry, it'll all be fine.' She reached up and kissed me gently on the cheek. A teacher reassuring a pupil on their first school day, a mother and child freshly back from being almost lost. A ruddy, ruffled Granny Victor wrapping me in her pink lamb's wool cardi, while I dripped, exhausted, on the beach, having nearly drowned after swimming out too far.

How was it that someone as small and fragile as BTB had become the guardian, the adult? When would I take that responsibility? When would I lift the weight of our little world from BTB's shoulders? Now? Once happily m—d? As a result of a sprog or similar shock treatment?

Or was this just another Johnson Riley flaw? Was I destined to remain a shorts-wearing, mud-spattered child? School-cap squint, replica Spitfire in hand, charging around the house and garden, beach and park, re-enacting the Battle of Britain. 'ACK-ACK-ACK-ACK-ACK' of the machine-guns, fists clenched, thumbs pumping imaginary triggers. Arms outstretched for the 'NNNNEEEEEOOOWWW' of dive-bombing planes. 'KA-BOOM!' as a piece of Spitfire driftwood smashed into the Nazi sandcastle.

Would this be for ever me?

BTB looked back at me, smiling. Almost, I hoped, accepting me for what I was, a small boy playing on a beach. I struggled to raise myself higher.

I watched BTB lean into the buffeting, salty wind and wrapped myself around her, hoping I felt strong and protective. I had a sense of timelessness standing on the same beach that I'd stood upon so often as a child. The view felt familiar and eternal. I thought back to the countless walks and wanders I'd had on the beach as a careering child or sullen teenager. Stolen cigarettes and miniature whisky bottles whipped from Dad's dresser after his travels abroad, moping and sloping after slights in the schoolyard from pals and first loves.

The very smells and rushing noise of the place, the sense of salt stretching your skin, all reminded me of mulling. Mulling over what would become of me, where I would end up. So how right it felt, in this place, to know I would wonder no more.

For here, I realized, nestled in my arms against the cold, was my future. From now on, for ever, there would be no more mulling, no pondering and wondering. She would be all. Childhood fantasies tumbled towards insignificance.

'Beaches remind me of childhood,' I said, staring out to sea. I held a vivid image of Granny Victor, crouching on the shoreline, her greying hair, still holding a hint of strawberry, flicking across her face in the wind. She would painstakingly select coloured pebbles for me to give to Mum or Dad on their return from work or travels or holidays.

'Me, too.'

'What?' Mind elsewhere.

'Beaches remind me of childhood, too, Johnny.'

'Really?' I'd forgotten that BTB had an existence before me. I couldn't picture her as a child. I couldn't picture BTB before me.

'Johnny, you're not the only one you know. I feel just as uncertain and scared as you.'

'You do?'

'Johnny, you've moped around all day. I know what's in your head. You think that you're the victim, that you're the only one who's suddenly been asked to grow up and become an adult.'

'I do?' I said unhelpfully.

'What about me?' she asked.

'What?'

'I didn't ask you to ask me to marry you.'

'I . . .' *Couldn't get my head around this.*

'That was one of the few things in life you've managed to come up with on your own.'

'You could have said no,' I jabbed back.

'Really?'

'Yes, really.'

BTB nodded sarcastically at my comment and stared out to sea. We were silent for a few seconds, only the rush of the waves surrounded us. I licked the salt from my lips.

'Would you *really* have said no?' I whimpered.

BTB laughed and shook her head. You could tell she was trying to shake her thoughts away.

'Don't be silly, Johnny, just remember that there's two of us in shock, and the two of us have got to present a unified front over the next twenty-four hours, or we'll be hung, drawn and quartered. So snap out of it.' She smiled and gave my hand an encouraging clinch. 'Alternatively, we could still change our minds, you know.' As she spoke, I wondered whether 'we' didn't mean 'us' but 'her'.

'Do you really want to go through with this, Johnny?' Was she asking whether I had changed my mind?

'Are you still sure?' Had I changed my mind?

'Yes.'

'You would be truthful wouldn't you?'

Why did she keep chiselling and chipping away? I couldn't help but hold the questions back to her in a mirror. Didn't she believe me? Am I telling the truth? Is she?

'Yes,' I said again, failing to do justice to my somersaulting mind. BTB looked puzzled, glowering hard at me, as if she were an X-ray machine. Trying to work me out, trying to find the facts, unsatisfied with her suspicious, superficial view.

'I don't know, Johnny. Are you really?' With those words she drifted out of my arms and into the wind, smoke wisping between my fingertips.

In the evening, BTB wrapped everybody's presents beautifully, and anything else that wasn't mobile – Muttley just escaped – and Mum prepared a honey-roast-ham dinner and popped next door to borrow some mustard.

I took the chance to carry out one of the great Riley Christmas traditions, and trotted off to disturb Dad, hiding under mildewed newspapers and corner-curled mushroom journals, in his study. This was my annual mission impossible: 'Operation Christmas Fairy'.

In the Seventies, when my age was still a single figure, before settling in Cawsand, the family had moved frequently to keep pace with Dad's sparkling fungal career. But whatever the house, Dad's studies were always other-worldly, on the outer reaches, in the basement bowels, dusty attics or isolated outhouses. Always on the fringes of the family, they would take on the semblance of a separate place, a different, agaric world on the edge of our own. In his study, Dad was not in, he was out of contact, *incommunicado*. I suppose, with a brat like me scampering over him like a gerbil, this was absolutely necessary. But I often wondered if it wasn't also a hideaway, a den that sheltered him from the cold world of conflict and expressed feeling, in the warmth of mushrooms and academia.

Tramping up the stairs this Christmas brought back memories of breaching his study borders as a child, like Vietnam-vet flashbacks – doors slamming, shouting and cursing, and running away with the taste of my heartbeat throbbing in my mouth. Even now, as a grown man with a nearly-wife, I could feel my hackles rise as I approached the final flight of stairs. I tramped loudly, trying to provide Dad with advance warning of my approach.

As a child, it was a forbidden paradise, which I was always tempted to taste. Sometimes my courage would drain away and I'd run and hide. On other occasions, I'd overcome my fears, tunnel in and spend happy hours in a playground of crumpled paper, curios, documents, leather-bound books, maps made meaningless by time and a bewildering array of strange objects.

Once, I remembered, I'd miscalculated badly. Creeping past the kitchen, where Granny Victor chopped rhubarb to the sound of Abba singing 'Waterloo' on the radio, I was so certain that the study was empty, so sure that Dad was out somewhere, that I didn't even bother with the safety-net token 'knock-knock'. My very motion, my every move, betrayed my motives. Clearly trespassing, I snuck, crept and tiptoed.

'WHAT ARE YOU DOING, JOHNSON!' Dad's younger voice boomed as he shouted, rising from his desk, towering above me, silhouetted against the window. I jumped out of my skin.

'ANSWER ME BOY!' I was witless and shaking. Unable to speak, I opened the door and charged down the corridor. I knew what would follow next.

'GET BACK HERE, JOHNSON! I'LL HAVE YOUR GUTS FOR GARTERS!' he shouted from the threshold of his other-world. Dad had the best repertoire of Victorian cusses I've ever heard.

'Stone the crows, I'll pickle that child,' he muttered, as he charged around the house after me.

'Knock-knock'. I finally conquered the childhood memories seeping into my mind and resumed my mission.

'Hello?' Dad's voice was rich, calm and warm. His youthful temper worn down by the wind.

'It's Johnny.'

'Come in, Johnson.' The scene was familiar. Dad in tweed and tie – always dressing for his desk. Time had softened him, like a malt. The texture of the tweed over the years seemed to have entered his skin and calmed his soul. Looking at him now, this seemed to be his time, his zenith. If we all have a pivot at which our lives and minds are most balanced, where before and after could not be better, then this was Dad's time. He sat peacefully at his desk, grand and dignified, grey-haired and bold eyebrowed. He was mellow, no longer angry; pensive, no longer rushing.

'Hi.'

'Hello.' We both knew why I was here. This had been my burden since I was ten.

'So, have you bought Mum a present, then?' Dad was hopelessly forgetful and stereotypically scatty when it came to present-buying. The rule was that, for anniversaries, birthdays and Christmases, a day or so before D-Day, I would have to remind Dad – possibly pestering him three or four times a day – and, more often than not, I'd have to buy the present for him. This time, I'd even brought a couple of spares with me, just in case.

Over time, this had become so accepted that I felt unavoidably linked to Dad's present performance. Mum, while never entirely forgiving of Henry's absolute ineptitude, knew that when she'd said 'yes' to his proposal, she was committing herself to life with 'a man with an eye for a mushroom under a microscope', and she seemed to accept this. But over the years it had wearied her. Over time she had begun to talk of missed opportunities and hoped-for other lives. Her fantasies teetered on the brink of reality.

'Yes, of course. What do you take me for?' Dad huffed. This, too, was familiar territory. Dad's snooty how-could-you-think-such-a-thing response had been perfected over the years, even though, in the main, he usually hadn't bought anything.

'You have?'

'Yes, of course. Bought it ages ago.'

'Really?'

'Yes, Johnson, really.' This was more stubborn than usual.

'Really?' I kept trying.

'Yes, that's it over there.' He pointed to an impressive-looking box in the corner, balancing on a pile of books and half-buried under copies of *National Geographic*. I smiled when I noticed Dad hadn't outgrown another of his enduring habits: he had wrapped the box in last year's paper. I don't think this habit was born out of any sense of economy, or tight-fistedness, it was simply his way of compensating for the fact that he knew, a year later, he would forget to buy wrapping paper again, and having a hoard of last year's slightly crumpled, slightly faded stock was better than nothing.

I examined the box. For Dad, it was a large and suspiciously well-planned present. Perhaps his mellowed tweediness had not only soothed his nature but reconnected a few loose cranial wires, too?

'What is it?'

'It's perfume.'

'Perfume?' I said anxiously. 'What kind?' I envisaged a vat of rancid out-of-date Yardley, palmed off by a nasty, stained door-to-door salesman, like Clark, the ever-tanned neighbour.

'Her favourite,' he said proudly.

'Favourite?' Mum's favourite and Dad's favourite would not necessarily collide.

'You know, Crabtree and Evelyn's Lavender.' I was impressed.

'Oh,' I said. Although this was a great achievement for Dad, I felt a slight sense of loss. It was like coming home to Muttley and saying, 'Walkies,' expecting him to leap about and pee on the floor, and instead hearing, 'I've been, I can look after myself, thanks, mate. Walk yourself.' Dad had raised himself a rung up a ladder I'd always thought out of his reach. It was sad, but it was also relevant to my situation. It suggested that, perhaps, even I could grow up. Perhaps, one day, I could pay a bill or organize a direct debit for BTB and me.

But mainly I was sad. Like stockings on the bedpost, this was a tradition I had thought would always be there. I wondered what strange traditions, habits and eccentricities would grow out of BTB and me and . . . our family.

'Mum seems a bit stressed-out, Dad.'

Dad shuffled his papers and twiddled a pen.

'Christmas, Johnson. Busy and all that. Lots to do. Sure she's fine.' He picked up a black-and-white framed photo of his father, who'd died two years ago. Grandpa was dressed in his RAF uniform, looking dashing and film-starry.

'Shame Dad's not here.' Was he changing the subject, or was this all connected? Dad felt loss severely, but internalized everything. He let the pain build up over time, out of sight.

'We all miss Grandpa, Dad.' I wanted to give him a hug, find out more about him and Mum, about grief and Grandpa, but extracting it was harder than sniffing out a

172

truffle. I wanted desperately to ask him about the leap that me and BTB were about to make, the Butch and Sundance cliff-jump at Christmas dinner. But the stiff upper lip was in the way, as it always seemed to be in my family. The stiff upper lip that was represented by Grandpa and his uniform. The stiff upper lip that had caused the emotional paralysis of generations of men, and was still going strong today. War had meant that Dad's dad, and to an extent Dad himself, could never fully grieve loss; for loss was so great, so total, during war, that if every man had stopped and paused and broken down, then everything would have stopped. For him and Grandpa, emotional paralysis was almost necessary. It was, I thought, as we headed back to dinner, a tradition I could do without, while the honey-roast ham, seasoned with heated debates and rambling stories, was a tradition I held altogether more fondly. I found myself thinking what a proud and glowing grandpa he might make.

'Johnny, Johnny, what's wrong? Wake up, Johnny.' BTB prodded me violently with spear-like nails in the breaking Christmas morning dawn. I retreated under the sheets and into the dark warmth of the duvet.

In my dream it was also dawn. The sun had begun its slow crawl across the big skies covering the Natal valley, further scorching the dry brown earth of Riley's Drift – the last outpost and wedding venue for the South Wales Borderers, B Company, 2nd Battalion.

In the distance, we could hear the drone of yet more warrior guests, beating their spears on their cow-hide shields, like a distant steam train, as they prepared for yet another attack. The ushers tried to look calm and dignified in their red uniforms.

'Can't believe you've got us in this bleedin' get-up,' complained Colin. 'What's wrong with bloody morning suits?'

'Do roll-call Sergeant Major Merlin,' I said, dusting down my tunic and fixing my helmet. Merlin stuck his chest out, sergeant-like, as best he could. He wore a flamboyant moustache, like a stoat lounging on his lower lip.

'Yes sir, Lieutenant Riley, sir. Fall in, men, officer on parade,' he shouted. The two surviving soldiers lined up. 'Jones, Private, seven one three,' shouted Sergeant Major Merlin.

'Sir,' said Private Colin, hopping awkwardly on his one remaining leg, using a rifle as a crutch. 'How come we're friggin' privates and Johnny gets to be Michael bloomin' Caine?' he whispered to Ratty on his left.

'Jones, Private, seven one four.'

'Aye, but I'm no' a fuckin' Welshman, you understand,' said Private Ratty.

'Shut it, Jones, and polish your dirty helmet, you slovenly soldier.'

'Actually, Sergeant, I was hoping tae get one of the bridesmaids to do that.' Ratty grinned pervertedly.

Merlin ignored him. 'All present and correct, Lieutenant Riley, sir.'

I picked my way through the debris of the reception and sat on some dead Zulus in what remained of the blackened skeleton of the chapel. Lieutenant Stefano Chard of the Royal Engineers joined me, battle-grilled. He was bleeding heavily from the stump of his left arm, amputated at the elbow.

'So, you saw your first action, Riley.' Stefano's Stanley Baker sideburns and mop-top were obviously false.

'Yes,' I said, wondering why Stef always had to be in charge of everything.

'How do you feel, now you're married?' he asked.

'Sick! Is that normal? Is that how everyone feels?' I stared into the distance with hard-boiled eyes, unfocused, innocence lost.

'I don't know, I'm single.' Stef still had the energy to sound arrogant.

'I didn't know.'

'I told you, Riley, I came here to build a bridge, not get hitched, like you, you daft twat.'

Suddenly the horizon wobbled, and a wave of warrior guests unfurled across the vista, like cards dealt from a pack. 'My God, look, there's thousands of the bastards.' My voice wavered.

'Sing, boys. Sing like mad Welsh choristers,' shouted Sergeant Merlin, leading the song. 'Come an' have a go if you think you're hard enough!' he sang.

Richard Burton's rich voiceover rolled across the parched valley with the credits. 'In the entire history of the Victoria Cross, only 1,344 medals have been awarded for bravery and valour above and beyond the call of duty . . . and only five at a wedding service . . .'

On Christmas morning, the house slipped into an ominous wait, like a cloaking sea mist. After breakfast, everyone sat around, twiddling and tinkering, making banal small talk.

Five minutes before the Donnellys arrived, Wedgwood rose from his velvet cushion and slunk across the room, soundlessly slipping through the ajar door. A second later the backdoor cat flap snapped.

Wedgwood was an early-warning system for incidents, his feline senses honed not to the crude human or canine sensory planes of noise or smell, but to atmospheres and happenings. A barometer of events.

Five minutes later, Muttley stirred. His ears pricked up and he began to bark in a feeble coughing way, which made him sound like a dog with laryngitis. The crunch of car tyres on gravel gave the arrival away to the rest of us. BTB rushed to the door, and I followed behind. In our wake, chaos ensued.

'I'll put the kettle on,' said Mum.

'I'll light the fire,' said Dad.

'Kippers please,' shouted Granny Victor loudly, disorientated as she woke from her morning nap.

'Come and meet them first.' I tried to calm the family down.

'Of course, of course,' they muttered, as if they had temporarily forgotten the rules.

'Poached,' shouted Granny Victor from the lounge, while BTB, me, Mum and Dad lined up on the front doorstep, doing our best impression of a happy family. It felt like an awful, stage-managed PR façade for some politician who'd been caught with his dick in a donkey and needed the support of his family as an emotional Arab strap.

The big Donnelly car seemed to crunch across the gravel for ever. Even though I'd seen the car countless times before, it never failed to frighten me, and I looked sideways to see Mum and Dad rearing as it invaded the driveway, dwarfing Dad's rusting Volvo. It was the kind of car that a modern-day Grim Reaper might drive. I suppose, these days, he'd swap his sickle for a sawn-off shotgun (which he'd probably find in the boot where the spare tyre should be).

It was a liquid-black Range Rover with shot-glass windows. Gerry Donnelly's pride and joy.

'Anybody know a drug baron?' Dad muttered under his breath, nervous wit surfacing.

Muttley slipped between our legs and sped round to the far side of the car, out of sight, where I just knew he would be either shitting, pissing on the Reaper-mobile, or, worst of all, humping Gerry Donnelly's leg in welcome. As the driver's door opened and shut, the dog howled and tumbled head over tail into a rhododendron bush. Gerry Donnelly didn't know he had an audience.

'Damn ferkin' dog,' he muttered, emerging from the place where Muttley had been.

'Why in the name of God would you want to live in a Godfersak—'

'Hello, Dad.' BTB rescued his sentence.

'JESUS!' He jumped. 'Daughter.' Mr Donnelly was dressed in a dark suit and tie. Small and wiry, he had a charisma contrary to his physique. In a second, his demeanour changed and a sparkling white-toothed smile shot across his weathered face like lightning. He opened his arms and she ran from mine.

Gerry looked like an ex-flyweight boxer, with muscles in unnerving places – forearms, jaw, eyes. He ran a large family, which in turn ran a large number of businesses that required muscles in unnerving places. The family and the business were one and same, with only BTB, as daughter, escaping. Jack, Paddy and Seamus, the three brothers, along with countless uncles, ran various Merseyside businesses, including, Donnelly's Builders and Decorators, Donnelly's Scrap and Donnelly's Landscape Gardening. The last, a recent arrival to the empire, had been set up by Seamus – the uniquely gentle, slightly effete, youngest Donnelly brother.

Gerry, as father of the clan, would be presumed to be the master of all things family. This was nearly, but not quite, true. After hugging his daughter, Mr Donnelly walked to the passenger door and opened it, like a private guard, holding his arm out for Mrs Donnelly to take when she chose to step down. A tiny, white-haired woman, dressed in black, blinked out innocently from the dark car. Mrs Donnelly stepped down gingerly from the Range Rover.

She had an odd conundrum of characteristics, which travelled up and down the spiralling helices of the women in the Donnelly clan. Mrs Donnelly was serene, yet one look would bring her burly sons to their knees. She was quietly loud, gently brutal, tiny but colossal. A judder ran down my spine as I recognized the future BTB in her mother. In the curls of her hair and jade flecks of her eyes, I could see the same stubbornness, the same look of total calm control that was at once real, but also disguised emotion,

177

like false eyes on an angel fish.

From an early point in my relationship with her daughter, I began to associate the *Jaws* theme tune with Mrs Donnelly. She always looked at me as though I was the insignificant bait, not the hook. I didn't fancy revealing myself as the threat, the shark-hunter. I wasn't ready, the hull was too leaky and the sea too rough. But the boat was chartered – we were announcing our engagement in a matter of hours over turkey and sprouts.

Welcomes were stilted and uncertain, like a baby's first steps. Everyone weighed each other up cautiously. Within seconds, odd connections began to form and a fuzzy image of people enjoying themselves appeared.

In the lounge, Granny Victor was having a saner moment and Mum and Dad had flipped into host and hostess auto-pilot. The connections were odd because they were unexpected. Gerry's mischievous blue eyes and silver tongue were bringing out the teenage, tittering girl in Mum – something I'd never seen before. His rough, tough, lovable-rogue character was almost the exact opposite to her husband, which must have been the appeal.

'My, what a grand place you have, Janet, and how could such a scruff of a boy have a beautiful mother like yerself?' Gerry sparkled while his wife 'tutted' and 'tsked' as she settled herself in an armchair, next to Granny Victor's ancient, creaking rocking chair. The cat, having weighed the guests up from a distance, returned to his mistress silently.

'Well, Mr Donnelly,' Mum answered.

'Gerald, please.'

'Gerald! Gerry not good enough now?' muttered Mrs Donnelly to herself, shaking her head.

'Well, Gerald, he obviously takes after his father,' Mum smiled.

'Thank you, dear,' Henry cut in. 'Drinks anyone? Tea, coffee . . .'

178

'Whisky will be fine there, Henry.' Triggering another frown from Mrs Donnelly, who was as dedicated to temperance as her husband was to drinking.

'Whisky . . . er . . . yes, of course, whisky. What a good idea for Christmas.' Dad failed to disguise his surprise at this request. He looked at his watch with confusion, wondering if we had somehow slipped past the lunchtime law that he lived by, even on Christmas Day.

'Hmph, drought in this part of the world, then?' Gerry drank the thimbleful of Singleton in one. Gerry could drink whisky by the pint, do a good impersonation of sobriety after a bottle, but, once past the bottle mark, became a serious hellraiser. Henry felt obliged to do the same, like a couple of cowboys in the Wild West.

'Bleuch! Mother of Jesus, what's this awful pish yer feedin' me here, Henry?'

Dad fretted. 'Well . . . well, it's a rather good single malt, to be honest.' Dad also didn't know that Gerry liked a basic blend. Bells, Grouse, J&B, Johnny Walker. Nothing acquired, nothing complex. Something you could drink hard, fast and often.

'None of yer fancy fine bouquets and after-note, high-falutin shite, young Jonathon,' he'd once said to me after I bought him a bottle of Laphroaig for his birthday.

Wedgwood, a famously unfriendly cat, behaved in an unprecedented way, jumping on to Mary Donnelly's lap and purring like a kitten. Granny Victor, of course, took this as the right royal recommendation that it was, and decided that she and Mary were of the same mould. They wittered quietly to each other, and I strained my ears, attempting to eavesdrop. I caught only odd words and phrases: 'rations', 'worked our fingers to the bone', 'good Christians', 'don't know how lucky they are', 'wrapped in cotton wool'. They seemed to be comparing moral positions and childhood hardships in the same way as teenage boys compare motorbikes or female conquests. More worryingly I'm sure I heard 'never make a man of that boy', 'lazy as sin' and 'not good enough for my daughter'. I panicked, the *Jaws* theme racing through my mind. Then I realized that I couldn't attach the voices to the phrases and concluded, with relief, that they were as likely to come from Granny Victor about Henry, as from Mary Donnelly about me. I laughed at the consistency of the world.

Three tumblerfuls later, Dad was slurring while Gerry had just warmed up his tonsils. The pre-dinner present-giving was already in full flow.

'It's a . . . pair of socks . . . with Mickey Mouse, no, no Minnie Mouse, on them. Well, that's just great. Thank you, Grandma.' I wandered over to Granny Victor in the time-honoured tradition and pecked her on the cheek. Already, my jaw ached from the effort of maintaining a false thanks-that's-just-what-I-wanted grimace.

I suppose nothing defines the nature of individual families better than festivals and ceremony. Christmases, birthdays, anniversaries, births, deaths and . . . weddings. This succession of ceremonies, lined up across the generations, row upon row in a wonderful procession of life. Happy, sad, celebratory, tragic. These are the defining moments, not the minutiae, or the detail of the daily grind. Try to remember an insignificant or uneventful day with your family, and compare that to the clarity of your sister's wedding, your grandfather's funeral, the birth of your daughter. These are the moments that make a family, that make a life.

Families are fermented over years, over decades. Like Madeira barrels for whisky, the flavour is gradually imparted. BTB's and my mistake was simply haste. Naively, we'd tried to mix two previously separate family ceremonies together, violently shaking together Donnelly oil and Riley water.

I added the pair of socks to my pile of book tokens and ties from various aunts and uncles, a shirt and tie combo, or mismatch, from Mum – pink shirt, blue tie with waves and gaudy goldfish swimming across it – and a massive encyclopedia of mushrooms from Dad, which I was sure I'd seen on his bookshelf only a day, or two, ago.

Up until this Christmas, I'd had a clear winner in the stakes of worst present ever. It was from Granny Victor, a few years earlier, after my first term as a student in Edinburgh. 'You'll need one of these,' it said on the tag. It was a mug. *Thank God*, I thought, *now I'll be able to avoid trying to drink tea by putting a tea bag in my mouth and pouring boiling water straight from the kettle down my throat.* It was a special mug. It had a picture of a large green boat – a tug-boat, I think – on the front and, when you filled the mug with hot water, the hull of the tug-boat went blue. Fan-fuckin'-tastic. Actually, I became rather attached to the mug over the years. It stayed with me through halls of residence to Ratty's flat in the final year, where Merlin eventually smashed it to smithereens using it as a golf tee for a half-eaten Big Mac at a graduation party.

BTB's parents outdid the mug, storming straight into the charts to take the number-one slot with a box of place mats. They were gold-rimmed and coloured an ugly burgundy, which surrounded poorly painted 'Famous British Battles'. They were outstandingly crap. My parents quickly followed their lead with a furry sheepskin hat for BTB. It looked as though this particular sheep had died fairly recently from sheep mange. I guessed BTB would place the shrivelled thing on her head as frequently as she danced around the house wearing only a boa constrictor. She could hardly bring herself to place the hat on her head now to show how pleased she was with her gift.

Surveying the scene, I imagined the post-present catastrophe as a picture place mat 'Famous British Battle' – patterned-paper debris strewn across the room, boxes and cellophane littered like artillery shells and bullet cases, casualties everywhere, wounded by this gift and revived by the other.

I tried to work out who'd done well. Dad couldn't be more chuffed with his brand-new coffee percolator from Mum, about which he was childishly joyful. Months later, looking at the Christmas photos, we noticed that the glass jug of the coffee percolator appeared with Dad in every shot, proudly carried like the World Cup or an OBE. As we were to discover, Dad was far more aware of the aesthetic qualities of that jug than its practical application.

BTB seemed to have survived well. The cuddly crocodile I'd bought her was somehow insignificant next to an expensive shiny new leather coat from her parents. As BTB opened my present, I suddenly wished we were on our own, secure in a family-free, log-fire and flickering-Christmas-tree cocoon. But BTB flashed a smile at me, while her parents raised eyebrows and Granny Victor lost it for a second, shouting, 'Cock-cock-cockodile,' loudly. Granny Victor was easily pleased; so long as she received an industrial-sized crate of foul jellied fruits, her Christmas was complete.

Muttley seemed content with a catnip mouse, while Wedgwood was bemused by a chewy shoe – 'Mixed-up, bit embarrassing to swap them now,' said Dad. Mum loved the *Illustrated History of Lavender* I'd bought her, and had a feast of chocolates to gorge on, but seemed a little bit quiet . . . Hang on. I realized, paling, that Mum hadn't received her main present from Dad. Frantically, I scanned the base of the tree, but could see no sign of a small present, let alone the vast, party-perfume box that I knew Dad had bought. But I needn't have worried, Dad had saved the best till last, and was now entering from the hall. He'd kept the big present hidden for suspense, and carried the box with ceremony, like a birthday cake, or a diplomatic gift for some fearsome tribal chief.

Dad peeked around the corner of the enormous box, cardboard showing under last year's tatty wrapping paper. BTB's

eyes lit up and she clapped like a child. She had a great fond-
ness for the eccentric, bumbling Henry, and was now rooting
for the underdog, knowing Dad's normal form was failure on
the present-buying front.

'Happy Christmas, Janet.' Dad smiled. For some reason,
Mum's eyes had lit down.

'Hmm . . .' she said vaguely, hesitating with the big box on
her lap.

'Open it then, Janet, I've a throat like a nun's . . .'

'Gerry!' Mary Donnelly gagged her husband.

'Yes, go on, Janet,' said Henry, a faraway look in his eye
now, as if trying to place something.

Slowly, painfully, she unwrapped her gift, the colour peel-
ing from her face like the cheap wrapping paper from the
box. Mum's cheeks washed white, before gradually regaining
colour, then turning pink and finally settling on an angry
scarlet. Opening the box, she turned with a crooked grin to
look at her husband.

'It's perfume, Henry. How nice.' Curt, clipped, sarcastic.

'Yes, dear.'

'A whole box of perfume.'

'Yes, all different, dear. Isn't it good.'

'And where did you buy this lovely selection from, Henry
darling?'

'From . . . well . . . I can't remember now.'

'It's from the catalogue shop, isn't it, Henry?' Dad's eyebrows
raised as his mind grappled with the concept of a shop that
sold catalogues. 'This is the *missing* perfume box.' Mum's voice
had raised an octave. I started sweating. Wedgwood left
the room, dragging his chewy shoe, and Muttley hid under the
tree.

'Anyone for sherry? Coffee perhaps?' Henry tried a feeble
distraction tactic. The men rallied instinctively behind one of
their own, wounded.

'Whisky,' said Gerry, a little too quickly.

'Hmm, sherry, yes please, Dad,' I joined in over-enthusiastically. Granny Victor eyed me suspiciously, remembering that I'd called her precious sherry 'rancid gravy' the year before.

'I bought this for the Red Cross ladies six months ago.' Mum was standing now, the missing box exhumed on the floor. She rifled through the contents, blustering, 'Ann's Tweed, Jenny's Opium, Sandra's Poison, Ruth's Elizabeth Arden, my Lavender Water – it's all here. It was easier, and we got a good discount if all the ladies bought together through the catalogue.'

Henry edged coffeeward, clasping his percolator to his chest.

'They kept asking me where their perfume was. Oh, Henry, really.' He'd already left when she asked nobody in particular, 'How can I ever show my face at another tombola?'

I was flabbergasted, staggered by the combination of daring and ineptitude involved. The selection perfume box had obviously been delivered by some anonymous innocent. Coincidentally, Dad had collected it on the doorstep, and opened it to magically discover the perfect Christmas present for his wife. He had taken the box, wrapped it in jolly dancing snowmen paper and presented it to Janet for Christmas. Stunning. Taking something from someone, wrapping it and giving it back to them ceremoniously as a Christmas present.

His only defence was the fact that, because he joined so many book clubs, music clubs, wine clubs and gift clubs – all of which he'd failed to keep track of – he was quite used to having various items that he hadn't ordered delivered to the house. He'd never read the small print, so was blissfully ignorant of the line saying, 'If you fail to order something from our list of dross, which deteriorates monthly, we will send you the crappest of the crap and bill you for it later.'

The room was quiet. Shaking my head, I couldn't think

of anything to say. BTB looked at me, turned to Henry and back again, silently calculating genetic possibilities.

Sitting down to the ceremony of Christmas dinner, I wondered why on earth we had ever thought this was a good idea. A month ago, when BTB had suggested it as we snuggled up, I'd had my doubts, but in the end agreed it could be a good plan.

OK, so we accepted that we should really have told the parents straight away, when we touched down from my Barcelona bruising. But we didn't. The families had never met and, at some point, like the Second World War, we knew this conflict would become inevitable, so we decided to do the meeting and announcement in one go. Somehow, we had lulled ourselves into thoughts of a cheery, sleigh-belly, tinga-bloody-lingy Capraesque Christmas. In Clapham, we'd imagined a Yuletide happy-families fairy tale. Christmas would be a joyous, magical event; it would snow on Christmas Eve, everyone would be delighted with our engagement and Granny Victor wouldn't say 'buggeration' over and over, like a demented parrot.

'Stuffing!' shouted Granny Victor like a foghorn.

'Crackers?' pleaded Mum, tensely, to the table, which ignored her.

'Is the tide out then?' said Gerry Donnelly, impatiently waving an empty wineglass.

It had the feel of a children's party. A desperate, every-man-for-himself battle for the requisite plateful of Christmas fare. I glanced at BTB, who had 'nightmare' written all over her face. Was it too late, I wondered, to change our minds? Tell the parents over the phone separately? Or maybe just call the whole thing off?

Glancing from face to face around the table brought to mind a feast of cannibals. I felt like a missionary preaching from a pot-shaped pulpit roasting over the fire, preaching

185

irrelevantly to the unconvertible who drool and salivate while my meat tenderizes. Dad demolished Mum's precious prize turkey that she'd won at the local Red Cross raffle.

'Carve away from the bone, Henry dear.' She spoke through gritted teeth, her cheeks scarlet from a combination of the kitchen stove, the morning's sherry tippling, and her as yet untamed anger at Henry's present-buying catastrophe.

'Yes, Janet dear, I am.' Henry was as ruffled as his crumpled tweed Christmas jacket and tartan tie. He diced the turkey, viciously hacking hunks off the mauled carcass.

'Coffee smells good, Dad.' I tried to set him up with a staged compliment for Mum. In the background, beneath the hullabaloo, the 'pleuch, pleuch, pleuch' of the coffee percolator was audible.

'Yes, lovely. What a wonderful idea for a present, Janet dear. Really excellent.'

Pleuch . . . pleuch . . . pleuch.

'Is that all right for you, my dear?' Henry sarcastically thrust a tiny sliver of shredded white meat towards Granny Victor.

'Arse-face!' said Granny Victor, like a violent Tourette's-syndrome victim.

'Mother!' Mum paled. Mrs Donnelly nodded seriously, but it was hard to tell whether she was agreeing with Granny Victor or Janet Riley.

Gerry Donnelly laughed heartily and said, 'To be sure, now pass those taters over here, would you, young Jonathon lad.'

I passed them silently.

'Johnson, Dad.' BTB sighed.

'Crackers?' cried Mum for the tenth time, waggling the battered red-foiled cardboard.

'Uh-hmm,' I confirmed. Only BTB noticed, raising a scolding eyebrow.

'Mum, where are these crackers from?' My own cracker seemed to be held together with Sellotape and kite string.

'I made them from a kit,' she said proudly. I pulled my cracker with BTB. It phutted like a dog's fart, and a small brown wrinkled object that looked like faeces landed on my parsnips. I prodded it with my fork, and noticed Mr and Mrs Donnelly doing the same with their own brown things.

Granny Victor had quickly stuffed hers into her mouth and was stretching Nosferatu fingers in the direction of BTB's plate when Mum spotted her chewing.

'Don't eat them, Mum.' Granny Victor chomped furiously. Every wrinkle seemed to dive into her mouth like a black hole, pulsating and quivering as her cheeks sucked in and out and her false teeth jabbered.

'What are they?' I asked anxiously.

'Chocolate-covered dates stuffed with marzipan. Spit it out.' Mum had hold of Granny Victor's mouth and was trying to stop her swallowing it.

'Spit it out, Mum.' Granny Victor swallowed and smiled imperiously.

'Oh well, she ate cat food last week, so I'm sure she'll be OK. Nobody else eat them; they're last year's crackers,' Mum said casually, failing to acknowledge that she could have poisoned the two families.

For a second I regretted this wasn't the case. Mass food poisoning couldn't be any worse than telling these two, hopelessly incompatible families that they were to become united.

'Ow!' I grunted as BTB kicked me for the third time under the table. I reached for yet another top-up of Shiraz to dull the pain and give me the courage to make the announcement.

'What the hell's up with you, boy?' BTB's dad needed little confirmation that I was a wimp, and must have presumed I'd bitten my tongue or chipped a fingernail.

Pleuch . . . pleuch . . . pleuch.

The percolator drip-drip-dropped in the corner, perched on a red leather-topped table near the fire. Wedgwood watched the contraption cautiously from his cushion on the mantel, while Muttley snoozed, his head resting on the cuddly catnip mouse.

'Nothing.' I tried to avoid eye contact with BTB, who was staring at me like a lunatic. Every time I caught her eye, her face contorted horribly. The first time she did this I thought she'd accidentally eaten one of last year's stuffed dates and was about to collapse. Gradually, I realized it was a subtle form of code. Early translations of her facial gymnastics and under-table kicks had proved incorrect. But I persisted like the Bletchley Park code-breakers, trying to defeat the Nazis and crack the infamous U-boat code, Shark.

'Are you trying to tell me you're sitting on a pineapple?' I said, unhelpfully. BTB crossed her eyes and sucked in her cheeks.

'You look like a whippet,' I whispered.

Pleuch . . . pleuch . . . pleuch.

'Tell them,' BTB growled.

'Oh, I was just about to. Why didn't you say that?' I lied.

Mum and Dad were having a similar struggle at the far end of the table. In an odd parallel, which I presumed was to do with the mauled turkey carcass, my parents seemed deep into their own red-faced, whispering row.

Granny Victor looked the way I imagined the turkey we were tucking into had looked only weeks before, her cheeks stuffed with food as she gobbled away happily to herself, the loose skin on her neck quivering as she hard-swallowed partially-false-teeth-chewed Christmas fare. Opposite me, within a right-hook's reach, Gerry eyeballed me menacingly.

Pleuch . . . pleuch . . . pleuch.

Dad, not used to Mr Donnelly's pace, had been mumbling and swaying for the length of the meal, and had managed to cover his tie in gravy and drop his handkerchief in his wine.

'Ferkin' amateur,' I'm sure I heard Gerry mumble in between stories about Irish ancestors, ghosts, giants and family curses. BTB's father held court like a rampant Richard Harris: 'And Cousin Connolly was struck dumb by a lightning bolt during a horse race that he'd won, but he never spoke again. The village reckoned it was a deal with the devil himself. And then there was Great Uncle Casie Donnelly. Now he was the Wild West hero that John Wayne based that *Shootist* fella on.' Gerry was in a mischievous mood that I had seen several times before. He was an artist, captivating an audience with tall tales before boring of the task. To entertain himself, he would begin to test the mettle of the group, lobbing in contentious and controversial comments like mortars.

Pleuch . . . pleuch . . . pleuch.

Mr Donnelly scanned the table like an old Gatling gun. 'So, when're ye gonna get a real job to look after my daughter?' I was the obvious fodder.

'I can look after myself, thanks.' BTB instinctively defended her self-sufficiency, but in doing so made me sound small and irrelevant to her happiness.

'Bet you never got your hands dirty in yer life, did ye, young Johna—'

'Johnson,' I semi-shouted, angrily. BTB glanced sideways and could see my jaw clenched with pent-up tension. 'I did.' This was a reflex, and the table waited in silence while we all wondered what I was going to say. 'I used to pick potatoes on the local farms for pocket money.' I unearthed the muddy recollection like a ruddy King Edward. 'Up at the crack of dawn, fingers raw by lunchtime, caked in mud, nails cragged with grit . . .' Mum's giggling stopped me from continuing to elaborate my story into some epic of childhood hardship and poverty in the Granny Victor vein.

'For a half a day.' Mum sniggered. I went scarlet, realizing the potato memory I'd picked was badly blighted.

'At a time?' asked BTB, thinking she was helping me out.

'No, dear. Ever.' Even the stone-faced Mrs Donnelly found Mum's answer amusing.

Pleuch . . . pleuch . . . pleuch.

'He was brought home in a tractor by that nice farmer over at Yorbay, Fred Morris. Fred said Johnny was the slowest picker he'd ever seen, apart from a young girl before the war from Polperro, who was a bit loopy, ate the raw potatoes and threw herself under a tractor.'

'Lazy. Told you. Sent home for shirking, was he, Janet?' Gerry wheezed with laughter as he spoke.

'Well, that's not all, Gerald. Fred said he was . . . now, I think his words were "a flaming Trotskyist". He said Johnny had tried, single-handedly, to form a potato-picking union and organize a strike at the first tea break.'

'A milksop and a militant. My God, I'm surprised you missed the priesthood and politics as vocations, lad.' He chuckled. 'You need a proper job, sonny. Come and work with the Donnellys, hard-working bulls to a man, except that young Seamus, who should've been a girl.'

'Dad,' chided BTB.

'It's true! Seamus with his bloody arty landscape balhooey. Never thought a son of mine, a Donnelly, would grow up a—'

'Gerald Donnelly, will you be wanting me to recount a few stories about yerself as a young lad?' Mary Donnelly was quick to defend her own.

'Anyway, the offer's there. Work with the Donnelly boys and we'll make a man of you yet.'

'No thanks.' I spoke through gritted teeth.

'NO?!' Gerry boomed, while I looked sheepish. BTB stepped in to protect me, only inflaming Gerry's irritated thoughts that I was not, as his wife kept telling him, worthy of their daughter.

'He has a career in film, Dad.' Once again, BTB played the grown-up, the guardian.

'Career! What sort of ponce has a *career*? He should come and get a proper job in the family. Stuff his bloody *career* up his arse. Sorry, Janet,' he added quickly. My parents were too polite to contradict the overbearing Gerald.

'Young people today, they're just work-shy, layabout idlers.' Granny Victor joined in on her favourite subject, Why young people today are crap.

'Damn right,' nodded Gerry. 'Layabouts the lot, young people today. No different to the Johnny Foreigners we got in the Fifties. Running every shop on every bloody corner, and you lazy young people doing bugger all about it, with your poncey, noncey advertising and films, and . . . and . . . and landscape bloody gardening,' he ranted.

'Dad!' scolded BTB.

'Gerald Donnelly, will you not be warned, another word against our Seamus and we'll hear more about your own upbringing, and see just how hard you worked in your pop band, with yer long hair and yer tight pants and yer—'

'OK. OK there, Mary, just hold your horses. Not another word, I promise.'

But Granny Victor was too far gone. 'Young people and darkies, all the same, lazy as the day they were born. Wouldn't know one end of a spade from the other.' In full flight now, Granny Victor twitched energetically.

'I'm with you, Victoria.' Gerry geed her on, winking furiously.

'And the bloody gypsies, too, and the good-for-nothing, layabout Irish.'

Gerry had nodded too often to stop in time, and found the momentum carried him through to agreeing that his own countrymen were also good-for-nothing layabouts.

Granny Victor's bright eyes danced. 'Cock sprocket!' she said, victoriously.

Pleuch . . . pleuch . . . pleuch.

The table was silenced, and BTB began to prod me once again.

'Look, we've got something to say,' I said quietly. Nobody

191

paid any attention. Grandma gobbled, Mary seemed to be ticking off her husband and Mum and Dad's row spilt across the table bedlam.

'How could you, Henry?' Mum's face was beetroot. All they seemed to do these days was row. I'd never questioned whether their marriage would survive, but suddenly, with inappropriate timing, I realized it might not.

Mum gulped at her wine.

'Christopher Columbus!' Dad swore Dickensianly.

'Go on, Johnny,' BTB whispered again.

Pleuch . . . pleuch . . . pleuch.

'I say, Gerald, what do you think of the mushroom tapenade?' Henry tried to wriggle away from his wife's anger.

'Oh, for crying out loud, Henry,' Mum moaned, banging her glass on the table and spilling her wine.

'The wha'd'yama'flip, Henry?' Gerry shouted back.

'Tapenade.'

Pleuch . . . pleuch . . . pleuch.

'You mean this black paste?' He pointed to a pot of goo.

'Yes, you see, it's made from a rare wild mushroom only found—'

'Henry!' Mum was shouting at her husband.

'To be sure, Henry, I've been a bit diverted by the Christmas dinner to try yer mushroom jam.'

A shrill pinging noise slowly drew everyone's attention to BTB, who was repeatedly tapping her crystal wineglass with her fork. 'We've an announcement, haven't we, Johnny.' BTB spoke through gritted teeth as she jabbed my thigh with her fork. I stood involuntarily and gained a clear view of the room. Over the heads of Mum and Dad, at the opposite end of the room, I noticed something odd about Dad's precious coffee percolator.

'Oh, how lovely, dears.' Two glasses of wine and Mum was drunk. Her nose rosy, her body slipping slowly under the table. Mum had a legendary limited tolerance for alcohol.

'Oh goody gumdrops, pass the tawny port time,' wittered Granny Victor through a mouthful of broccoli.

Pleuch . . . pleuch . . . pleuch.

'Right,' I said loudly, gaining the table's attention. With everyone expectant, I stammered, 'I . . . er . . . we are . . . I'm happy . . . yes . . . er . . . happy to announce that we are . . .' All eyes were on me. 'We are getting . . .' I reverted to mental trickery – (Johnny) 'Marr . . .' (W) 'eeed.'

Pleuch . . . pleuch . . . pleuch.

Mr Donnelly was the first to rant: 'Jesus, Mother of Mary and Joseph, what in the . . .' He carried on incomprehensibly for a minute or two. The only words which surfaced were things like 'ponce', 'ferkin', 'kneecap', 'no permission', 'over my dead body' and suchlike.

Mary Donnelly was tellingly silent. Granny Victor, on the other hand, coughed and spluttered, trying to get the word 'married' out of her full gullet, but muddled and mangled the word into 'rammied', 'whammied' and 'rampheed', gurgling as she tried to swallow her food.

Muttley barked before moving away from the now brown-stained leather table and the rapidly spreading dark puddle on the rug in front of the fire.

Pleuch . . . pleuch . . . pleuch.

'Shouldn't there be a jug underneath the percolator to catch the coffee?' I asked.

'Jug . . . jug . . . Ah, yes, wondered what that was for.' Dad jumped to his feet, looking for the jug.

'Oh, Henry.' Mum sighed.

Granny Victor continued to cough and began to sound like Wedgwood hacking up a fur-ball.

I checked Mary Donnelly's reaction. Her eyes were tightly closed and her lips pursed, as if she were balancing a slice of lemon on her tongue. I imagined she was thinking *Please let me wake up now. Please let my daughter marry a normal lad, like that one Julie the hairdresser told me about*

. . . Trevor, I think his name was. Works for Group 4.

'Um, shall I fetch some water?' BTB was concentrating on Granny Victor, who was still spluttering.

'By bloody Christ,' said Gerry, shaking his head.

'Someone get some water, she's in shock,' BTB said urgently, patting Granny Victor's back as an unholy whistling sound rose from her clogged throat.

'Mother!' shouted Mum.

'She's choking,' said Gerry, darting around the table. Granny Victor's eyes were popping out of her head and the veins on her temples raised and pulsed like overflowing candle wax. Gerry Donnelly slapped her hard, full on the back, and a half-chewed broccoli floret shot across the table and bounced off Mary Donnelly's head. Granny Victor inhaled heavily, croaked, 'Brockfuckle arse!' and collapsed on the table.

Nice Baubles

'Right, my lovely boys, let's pull crackers, stuff ourselves silly, snog under the mistletoe, get dreadfully drunk in front of the Queen's speech and play truth or dare with mince pies and port for tea.' Maddy was a Christmas princess, trussed up in red velvet and diamanté.

Maddy's alternative Christmas dinners for the 'loners' had become almost as much of a tradition as the family gatherings across the country that the trio of Ratty, Stef and Maddy either avoided, or didn't have available to them as an option.

'Nice baubles, Maddy.' Ratty smiled into Maddy's velvet-cushioned cleavage, before nodding towards the blinking fake silver Christmas tree balancing unsteadily in the corner.

'Well, thank you, my little Scottish dumpling.' She turned to Stef. 'Come on, Mr Jolly, let's get you Alka-Seltzered before Christmas turns into one long vom-session.' Stef groaned, while Maddy dashed off to rake around in her cluttered kitchen drawers and overflowing medicine cabinet.

Frank Sinatra crooned cool Christmas tunes in the background.

This was the third year that Maddy had played Santa, and converted her cramped Parson's Green second-floor flat into a veritable grotto of kitsch Christmas crap. Beneath the superficial tinge of spray-on snow and limp straggling tinsel draped around door frames and mirrors, Maddy's distinctive taste shone through.

Her flat was a cluttered, mystical boudoir. Plush velvets mixed with tasselled ethnic drapes, woven with glittering beads and sequins. Patterned cushions and throws covered the two deep sofas and single chaise longue; so much so that any original fabrics were lost in the swathes of colour. Rustic reds, oranges and browns combined with the textures of raw silk and satin to create a visual heat.

Every available space – mantelpiece, table top and dresser – was covered with ornaments and photo frames, mementoes and trinkets. Walls, too, were crammed with posters and paintings, mirrors and yet more patterned drapes. In the bay window, overlooking the green and Maddy's favourite pulling joint, the White Horse, Maddy kept her pride and joy: the grand piano. Here, she captivated private audiences, or practised songs, before letting them loose on suitable clubs, cafés and restaurants in the West End and south London.

It was a woman's place, a pampering place. But strangely, one that men felt at home in far more than other women. It was all too permanently feminine for Maddy's girlfriends. All too hedonistic. She had inherited the flat from her mad grandmother, who Maddy reckoned was some kind of a British Mata Hari. Maddy had preferred to add layers to the existing embroidered, patchwork decor, rather than start from scratch. The end result was, at once, Parisian, Russian, Indian and oriental. But mainly, it was Maddy: exotic, flamboyant, erotic, erratic and contradictory.

Once again, this Christmas, the guest list wrote itself. Maddy, Stef and Ratty were the founder members of the tradition, started when they discovered a shared lack of family with whom to celebrate Christmas. Maddy's parents were acrimoniously divorced, and she was expected, but refused, to choose between them every year. Stef had grown up to despise his father, after his mother flew back to Italy with the fishmonger when Stef was a kid. 'He'd bring home the pub dregs with him every night and expect me to respect whichever local slapper was in his bed.' Ratty rarely discussed his past, but, over the years, they had gleaned the fact that Ratty's mum had died in childbirth. His childhood was spent with a bitter drunk for a father, who'd blamed Ratty for his loss. 'Used tae beat me raw with a strap, 'fore his lungs caved in,' he said.

Today, Stef was struggling in vain with a hangover from hell. He had barfed in the bathroom twice already, and had to pass the honour of carving the goose to Ratty. He coped admirably, using cruise-liner carvery-chef skills. Typically, he couldn't help but mutter non-stop innuendo about 'being good with birds', 'liking a good goose' and anything at all to do with 'stuffing'.

'So how come Col's no' here, Maddy?' Ratty dropped a clanger.

'He's with Trish isn't . . . oops.' She raised her hand to her mouth, realizing her mistake immediately. 'What about his mum and dad?' she asked desperately.

'Always go to Tenerife for Christmas. Fuck, I should have warned you, Mads. Sorry.' Stef guiltily tripped back from his hangover.

Maddy pounced on someone other than herself to blame. 'For God's sake, Stef, you're supposed to be his best pal. Ring him.'

'What, now?' Stef looked confused.

'Yes, now, it'll be no use getting him over for bloody Boxing Day, will it? The poor lad's probably sat in his pit on his lonesome, having Pot Noodle for lunch and feeling as Christmassy as a pina-bloody-colada.' Maddy pointed at the old-fashioned telephone next to the chaise longue.

'But he eats like a horse!'

'Stefano.' Maddy pointed.

'And he farts like a horse, too.'

197

'Ring him.' Maddy kept pointing until Stef rose and walked to the phone. Ratty chuckled and continued carving.

'What're you laughing at?'

'Och, just thinkin' there aren't many people you take orders fae, Ronaldo.'

'Shut it!' Stefano spat, while Maddy raised her hand to her lips and zipped them shut in a silent gesture to Ratty to stop him stirring.

'Yeah ... Hello, mate, it's me ...' Stef spoke with a monotone disinterest. 'Oh, yeah ... Happy Christmas to you, an' all that.'

'Jesus, you boys on the phone; it's painful.' Maddy tugged her low neckline upward, conscious that Ratty was attempting to get an eyeful from his carving vantage point.

'Mind you don't hurt yourself, Ratty dear,' she said drily.

'What's that noise? ... Scalextric? ... Excellent.' Stef perked up instantly. 'Who bought you that? ... We? Who's we? What? ... Is he there as well?' Ratty stopped carving, and he and Maddy listened intently. 'Well bring him over, too ... And the Scalextric ... Yeah, Maddy's. For a bit of goose ... No, not that kind ...' Maddy wrinkled her eyebrows into a mild frown. Stef put the phone down and returned to his seat. 'Pass the roast potatoes, Mads.'

'Well?' she said, as she passed the dish.

'Er, please?' Stef tried, like a little boy, unsure what response would get him what he wanted.

'OhforGod'ssake, what's happened?' Maddy lost patience.

'Oh, well, Merlin's at Colin's place, and they've bought themselves Scalextric.'

'Why?' asked Maddy, looking concerned.

'To race with, it's the rally motor-cross version.'

Maddy sighed and adopted a *Janet and John* tone. 'I *mean*, why is Merlin at Colin's?'

'I ... erm ... I didn't ask.'

'How can you not ask?' Maddy shook her head in disbelief.

''At'll be another marriage doun the pan.' Ratty sat down and began to eat.

'Ever thought about a career in talk shows, Ratty darling? You know, an Aberdonian version of *Oprah* or *Parkinson*, or perhaps some sort of caring counselling job?' Maddy was as hooked on insulting Ratty as he was on insulting her.

'I think there's room for a more honest line in marriage counselling.' Stef was warming slowly. 'None of your "Why don't you talk it through, Mr and Mrs Smith? Share your problems, take a massage course." No, no, Dr Ratty could just steam in with "Fuck it, don't waste your time, go your separate ways. A partner's not for life it's for . . .' Stef paused, trawling his alcohol-clogged memory.

'Christmas?' Maddy asked with a giggle.

'Screwin',' Ratty stated with worrying sombreness.

'Anyway, you're wrong, boys, the pair of you.' Maddy led a familiar charge. 'Did you know that emperor penguins mate once in their lifetimes and reproduce every year? And, after the females drop the sproglet penguins, the girls piss off somewhere hot for their hols, while the boys keep the eggs warm under their beer guts.'

'Twat-heeds,' spluttered Ratty through his goose. 'Any creature that's fucked up its ecological niche so badly it's below zero most of the year is bound tae be a half-wit.'

'Ratty, it simply demonstrates that nature's way can be loyal and lifelong.'

'Thirty per cent of the seagulls in New York are gay,' said Stef randomly.

'Aye,' Ratty agreed too quickly, before doing a double-take, presuming his friend would be backing him up. 'Gay seagulls, Stef? Fit planet're you on?'

'It's true. I read it in the paper.'

'Stefano, dear, Colin writes in the paper. Need I say more.' Maddy's tone remained teacherly.

'Gay seagulls, Jesus! Anyways, Maddy, what I wuz tryin' to

say, 'fore His Randomness butted in, wuz that there are far more examples of promiscuous loons shaggin' in the natural world than penguin-type, lifetime-partner shite.'

'You mean, like chimpanzees, Ratty dear?'

'Aye, 'at documentary last week on BBC2, showed king monkeys huv a whole harem of lassie monkeys to choose from.' Ratty chewed on a celery stalk, looking mildly primate-like.

'And dogs?'

'Aye, dogs an' aw. Muttley gave Colin and his beanbag a right good seein' to, within hours of each other, the other week.' Ratty smiled as he said this, as though Muttley were a younger brother, or a protégé.

'And rats?'

'Rats are good breeders and . . .' Ratty's words dwindled as he realized he was being led, like a donkey.

'How convenient for you to be able to work to the lowest common denominator, my sweet.' Maddy popped a sprout in her mouth and made it look like a triumphal full stop.

The three friends had barely dented the enormous goose and mountain of vegetables when Merlin and Colin arrived, and Maddy rushed to buzz them in and meet them on the landing.

'No, three–one, mate, you didn't have to answer the phone,' Merlin argued.

'It could've been Trish,' Colin protested.

'Could've been the friggin' Pope. You lost, three-one, fair and square, mate.'

Maddy had taught herself not to let the thoughtlessness of her male friends needle her. The fact that the phone call meant they could come to *her* house and join in *her* Christmas meal had obviously been blocked out by their sensitivity bypass.

'I'm sorry, my dears, didn't Stef pass on the invitations? I'm so sorry. Happy Christmas.' She stretched on tiptoes to kiss Colin on both cheeks, before moving on to Merlin.

'And you? What are you doing here, Mr Wiz?'

Before Merlin could open his mouth, Colin bowled in with a response as they entered the flat. Ratty and Stef turned as he said, 'Ruth's left him. She's had enough and is going travelling. Completely made her mind up, no going back. Irreversible, it is. Much more serious than Trish and me.' Colin dumped his coat on the sofa and sat down where Maddy had been sitting, immediately picking at her food. It would be wrong to say he didn't intend to hurt Merlin; intention presumes forethought, and therefore some tact and a little sensitivity. Colin had neither and was just being Colin – talking without thinking, talking like he farted.

Merlin was left standing, gloomy and silent, in the middle of the flat. Maddy rescued him. 'Come on, love, let's take your coat into the kitchen and you can tell me all about it over a glass of wine while the lads catch up.' With all the care of a mother, she ushered the listless Merlin into the cluttered kitchen ahead of her.

Amid the spice racks, pots and jars, Maddy cut to the chase. 'Where is she?' She sat on the Formica top, while Merlin perched on a barstool, both sipping huge balloons of red wine.

'Her parents made it clear to me I'm not welcome. I can't go to mine. Can't face them. She means everything to them.' Merlin paused and swallowed. Maddy knew enough about Merlin to know that tears would be sacrilege.

'It'll work out, won't it?' Maddy stroked his thick black curls gently. Merlin shook his head, feeling silence was less likely to betray his feelings.

'This has happened before, hasn't it?' Maddy mined for hope. Merlin shook his head more vigorously. 'It's over . . . fucked,' he managed to squeeze out.

'Come on now, Merlin, you two can work it out. Is she seeing someone else?'

More shaking. 'Not now, anyway. Can't say she hasn't.

Can't say anything. Says she might travel, take a year or two and cut and blow-dry her way across the States. Like it's that easy for her to do. We were going to do that together, once. She says there's nothing left between us, just a mortgage, and I'm welcome to it. A pair of husks, she said we were, last night.'

'Do you want her back?' He shrugged at her question and glugged his Barolo.

'You poor thing. Come here.' Maddy drew him into her embrace. She thought she felt a delicate droplet land on the skin of her shoulder and kissed him gently on his crown.

'I want you . . .' he mumbled, his voice muffled in her velvet so that Maddy couldn't be sure of what he'd said.

'What? What did you say?' She was greeted with a long pause. She could hear the men laughing and grunting in the room beyond. How many times had she done this? she thought, rocking gently in time to the tree-tops outside. How many male friends had found their voice with her, behind closed doors, away from prying eyes, predators and partners alike? Was this her life? For ever a sister, an agony aunt, a mistress?

Merl finally broke his silence. 'You know, you and Stef. You've got it made, everything before you, all to play for.'

'Me and Stef?' Maddy couldn't help but laugh. 'Me and Stef is convenient, that's all. Company, easy, like a take-away meal. Suits Stef, suits me. But you need solid foundations to build on, like loyalty and trust, and neither one of us can claim either.'

'What do you want, Maddy?'

'Nothing much – zero-cholesterol chocolate, Brad Pitt on tap, to stop being the bloody bridesmaid all the time.' Maddy reached for the wine bottle and refilled their glasses.

'You're the bridesmaid in May, aren't you?'

'Yup, third time unlucky. Just like third light off the match is unlucky.'

'Yeah, my grandpa used to say it was 'cos of the trenches in the First World War: snipers got their sightings and, bang!'

'Well, it's the reverse at weddings, you know, three sights and the snipers just think, Wonder what's wrong with that old bint. Christ, there she is again, old moose.'

'Moose? Come off it, Maddy, everyone fancies you.' Maddy blushed, although Merlin couldn't see her. 'So you just wanna get hitched, do you, Maddy? 'Cos after Ruthy and me, I'm not so sure.'

'All I want's a bit of stability, Merlin, I want someone safe and certain. Johnny's a catch, lucky cow. That's the sort of thing I'd like, you know.'

Merlin frowned. 'Funny, I'd 've said he was the lucky one.'

'She thinks there's something between me and Johnny, you know. Like he's got some unfinished business from ten years back, when I jumped on him at that party.'

'Well, maybe he does.' Merl dug into a long-term mystery.

'Merlin, you don't understand, I don't want to be some bloody bike everyone wishes they'd tried. Johnny's getting married to my best friend . . . my best friend, who's always had bloody everything go her way. More brains, more blokes, great jobs . . . and now Johnny. And I could have had Johnny, trouble is, I don't bloomin' well want Johnny. I want . . . I want . . . I want what other people have got.' Maddy bit her lip in frustration, unable to articulate her thoughts.

'See, telt youse, 'nither marriage bolloxed.' Ratty was in righteous mood. 'Is it no' time to start writin' 'bout divorce, Col?'

Colin shook his head. 'Editor's happy the way it is. D'you read it this week?'

'Aye. D'ye no' think it's a wee bit harsh to write that Johnny thinks his father-in-law-to-be maims people for cash?'

Colin laughed nervously. 'I just made it up. Pure fiction.'

'But Johnny really does think that.' Stef joined the debate.

Colin changed the subject. 'So, Ruth gone, who'd of thought it, eh?'

'Probably be in the friggin' column next week,' Ratty jibed.

'Ruth'll be back, eh, Col, just like Trish 'n' all?' Stef had never progressed beyond more than a few months of seriousness. He had no sense of depth or longevity in relationships, and ended up treating his own and everyone else's with a bemused flippancy.

'Don't know about Ruth, but Trish'll be back, definitely. I've got a cunning plan, you know.'

'Nae fuckin' chance, Col. Trish's gone. You've got more hope of losing that lard bucket strapped round yer stomach.' Ratty scooped dollops of cranberry sauce on to his plate.

'You'll see, she'll run back to the new me – Colin Carter Mark Two, turbo-charged, super-fit and double romantic.' Colin paused while his two mates coughed, snorted and spluttered for a minute or so, trying to picture Colin's romantic gestures. 'What? I can be romantic. You'll see, bastards. Maddy'll help. She's romantic, isn't she, Stef?'

'How would I know? I wish you lot would drop the Maddy and me thing. We're just casual, you know.' Stef's face didn't give away whether he was unhappy, joyous or indifferent about the easiness of their situation.

'You get on well, don't you?' Deep down, past the pisstaking, Colin and Stef were old friends. The two had looked out for each other from playground punch-ups, through lost virginity, underage club-blagging, minor STD traumas, college and beyond, into the too-early, grim reality of adulthood.

'And she's a babe, mate,' Colin continued, trying to make his mate see sense.

'Yup.'

'I bet she's like a cat in the sack?' Ratty's one-track mind joined in.

'Uh-huh.'

'And she's fun, she's a laugh.' Colin felt he was on a roll.

'Mmm.'

'And she's . . . er . . .' Sadly, probing remained an undeveloped skill for Colin.

'Got miraculous . . .' Ratty's hands cupped imaginary breasts.

'Listen, I admit she's special, all right. But I'm not in it for the long term.' Stef's slim response wasn't going to satisfy Colin.

'Why not? Jesus, man, how many babes who are special, good in the sack and have fantasy tits are there out there?' Colin asked rhetorically.

'In London? I reckon about . . . sixteen thousand,' Ratty calculated.

'Bollocks! Is that according to your standards, Ratty?'

'Nope, 'ats the women I dinnae touch wi' a barge pole. You know, the antelopes, the women wi' way too much competition fer 'em.'

'Sixteen thousand?' Stef grappled with the figure.

'Oh, about fifteen thousand nine hundred of them are taken. You know, married or co-opting.'

'Co-habiting,' corrected Stef.

'Whatever.'

'So that leaves . . . not many.'

'I reckon, on yer average night, yuv got as much chance of finding a woman like Mads, who'll even consider meeting up with you again on a date, as shitting a solid-gold turd.' Ratty waved a golden roast potato, pinned to his fork, as he spoke.

'See, even Rat-man agrees, mate. Bag her, before she fucks off.' Colin was surprised to have Ratty's support.

'Whoa! I agree Mads is special, but I dinnae think Stef should settle down. Christ, Col, 'ats not what I wiz sayin'. He should enjoy the high life while it's goin', make hay when the sun shines, like, but after she's buggered off with some big rugby broker bloke, he should lower his sights and shag in the Vauxhall Conference fer a wee while.'

Colin shook his head in defeat, and Stef breathed heavily, preparing himself. 'Look, Maddy's special. Maddy's a one-off, an original. But she's like a little bit of Kryptonite in your pocket, or a jaguar in your bedroom. You can't keep it. It's something that everyone else wants, or something that needs its freedom too much.'

'Bollocks, Ronaldo, she'd settle down with you if you wanted to.'

'No, no, you don't know what I mean. It's the stress. We've talked about it, me an' Mads. We've discussed being serious, but . . . but everyone looks at her, and Maddy, well, she looks back. She'd flirt with a friggin' corpse. I haven't got the energy or the patience to watch my back, to look round corners. I don't know if I even trust her.'

'Cannae trust 'em fer a second.' Ratty nodded.

'And she's worse than ever at the moment. Never in, or never answering the bloody phone. Says I need the mystery of never knowing where she's going or who she's with.' Stef clutched his bald head as his hangover hit second wind.

'Oh, and I suppose we're all trusty honest Injuns, are we?' Colin asked Ratty, sarcastically.

'Oh, fuck no. No way. We're worse, like. But at least we know we're lying. Or at least we do if it's us . . . well, I mean, if I'm lying, I know I'm lying.' Ratty talked himself into a cul-de-sac and gave up.

'I won, I won, I won again. Enough Scalextric,' Maddy slurred slightly. Merlin, Colin and Ratty sat in a captivated semicircle around Maddy, on the far side of the track set up on the floor. Stef tirelessly zapped at the TV screen, lounging moodily on the chaise longue. Maddy and him had jarred and prickled all afternoon.

Time had ticked by to the tune of a Queen's speech, a vat of red wine, two bottles of port and one James Bond film.

They'd been playing winner stays on for the past hour or so. Maddy had won every single race which, at face value, seeing as it was her first attempt, may sound a little surprising. Yet more surprising, unless explained, was the polite, sportsman-like behaviour of the three lads. The normal course of events would be a no-holds-barred, anything-goes race, followed by a battle to wrench the controls off one another before the next race. But today, everything had entered the twilight zone.

'Well done, Maddy. Winner stays on then. In fact, why don't you have another try, Ratty?' said Merlin, who had been a spectator.

'No, no, I lost, can't stay on. Your go, Colin.' Ratty threw the control at his friend.

'Are you sure about winner stays on, boys? I've won the last seven races, doesn't someone else want a go?' Maddy looked flushed and puzzled.

'No, no, Maddy, winner stays on,' they said in unison.

The cause for this behaviour was simple, and to be found not in the smell of burning metal and the drone of the cars, but wrapped tightly, in red velvet, and bouncing with wild excitement through every race.

The boys were blissfully captivated by Maddy, as they sat cross-legged like a row of silent Buddhas or drugged lab monkeys wearing distant smiles. Their collusion was unspoken and instinctive. From Maddy's first race, the jiggling, giggling, strap-slipping action had dictated the racing strategy of team Menetton. Winning male drivers were nudged off the track by a stray foot from a spectator. When Maddy's car span off the track on an uncontrolled corner, the competing car simply stopped dead, while Maddy leant, bent and bustled, retrieving her red Mini Cooper.

'Come on, Maddy, just one more race.' Colin whinged pathetically.

'Nope, time for coffees.' Maddy stood and staggered into the kitchen, leaving the men looking glum.

'Grand. Grand that was,' Merlin muttered, almost to himself. Colin and Ratty were dazed into dumbdom.

'You're pathetic, you really are.' Stef stood frowning at the transparent voyeurism of his friends, as if it was yet another reason why he should keep Maddy in the casual-sex bracket.

Once, the unfettered ogling of the lads had been something Stef had happily joined in with, but now he and Maddy had something going, albeit vague and relaxed, it had begun to irritate and annoy him. Today, especially, it seemed to compound his short-fused frustration.

'It's all right fer you, you're flying first class, Ronaldo.'

Stefano had to laugh at Ratty's honesty. Stef's problem was the history. How could he change his tune now and chastise his mates for leching after Maddy, when he'd been doing the same thing for years? And anyway, what did he and Maddy really have going?

'Maybe, mate, but I reckon I'll be back in economy with you lot in no time. Look at this place.' He drew his arm in a wide arc across the room, pointing to the mantelpiece and shelves. 'I've seen less cards in friggin' WH Smith. So far I've only found two from bloody women.' Colin stood to join Stef, and randomly plucked cards from the shelves: 'Mike, Phil, Mr Bump – Mr Bump? – Dave, Marky . . . Who the hell are all these guys?'

Merlin joined in the game: 'Sam, Billy. 'To my lambikins, from Roger.'

'Roger's her dad.' Stef seemed happy to be able to trace a source.

'Vince – something foreign – from Alphonse, Johnny, Rick.'

'*Johnny*. Johnny?' Stef interrupted, reminded of yet more Maddy history that made him uneasy. Merlin returned to pick up the tasteful, hand-made happy snowman card that occupied a prime position on the piano. He cleared his throat. 'Happy Christmas, Maddy, I'd be lost without you. All my love, Johnny.'

The kitchen door opened and Merlin hurriedly returned the card to its slot, knocking a whole row down, dominostyle, in the process. Stef's frown etched ever deeper.

'Coffee and mince pies?' Maddy carried a tray piled high with china.

'Lots of cards, Maddy.' Merlin tried to explain himself.

'Of course, popular gal me, Merl. Got to keep the contacts up, being a woman of no fixed abode and all,' she sang out, shooting a glance at Stef.

The men sank contentedly into deep velvet cushions and sofas with their strong coffee and mince pies. 'The mince pies are a Delia spesh,' Maddy explained, handing the plate around.

'Sing us a tune, Maddy.' Ratty, for all his caveman sensibility, loved listening to Maddy on the piano. He said it reminded him of watching the northern lights on the foothills of the Grampians as a teenager, sitting in his Datsun Cherry with a bottle of whisky, a tartan rug, an old blues tape whipped from his dad, who worked out on the rigs, and his hand tugging at the knicker elastic of some timid schoolgirl.

Merlin poured whiskies while Maddy settled herself in front of the piano. 'OK, this is a new one I'm learning, so it's a bit of a trial run for this special hand-picked audience.' Maddy sparkled like a glitter ball behind the piano.

Merlin, film buff and muso, recognized the song in the first few notes of the intro and tried to place it. 'Sting, "My One and Only Love" from – let me think – *Leaving Las Vegas*,' he whispered to Stef, who was standing next to him. Stef looked at him with a pained expression. It was a slow, breathy, easy-listening love song.

The very thought of you makes my heart sing,
Like an April breeze,
On the wings of spring,
And you appear in all your splendour,
My one and only love . . .

A simple song of complete and utter devotion. Maddy's deep, smooth voice swirled around the room and entered the minds of the men who held their breath, bewitched. Her fingers tumbled down the ivory steps, dancing, while her eyes glowed.

In the moment after she finished playing, before Ratty cheered and the lads clapped loudly, the silence was tangible. Pressed into that fraction of a second was so much raw emotion, so much unsaid thought.

'So what d'ya think, boyz?' She spoke with a mock-American showbiz voice.

'Fuckin' brilliant, Mads. Bloomin' marvellous.' Merlin was the first to wade in with thick buttery compliments.

'Aye, fairly brought a tear to my eye, darlin',' Ratty agreed. Maddy turned to Colin, who just mumbled, dumbstruck. Wallowing in the admiration, Maddy turned to Stefano for more praise.

'It's Johnny's song, isn't it?' The mention of his name was like an off-key note.

'No. Sting's, petal.' She raised her guard with the speed of a flyweight.

'Johnny plays it all the time. It's from the *Leaving Las Vegas* soundtrack.'

'Well, he's not the only person to have seen the film and heard Sting, is he? More whisky?' Maddy stood, knocking her stool over, and snatching the bottle from the table.

'No,' Stef mused. 'Who was in the film again?'

'Er . . . Merlin, top-up?'

'Who starred in the film, Mads?' Stefano dug while Maddy flustered.

'Yes, please,' Merlin cut in, holding out his tumbler for a top-up, and saying, 'Nicholas Cage, wasn't it, mate?' Merlin's rescue didn't go unnoticed by Stef.

'Yes, I bloody know you've seen it, mate.' Stef scowled. 'Fuck it. I'm off.' He picked up his coat, strode towards Maddy, snatched Johnny's card from the piano and threw it at her, before storming out of the flat, slamming the door.

She shrugged. 'Hates snowmen,' she said, as she picked up her stool and sat back down. 'Right, and then there were four. So . . . any requests?'

Endangered

I was finding the piano lessons increasingly difficult. Maddy had taken to dressing up – or down – and seemed to be clad more skimpily every time I trotted over to Parson's Green. She would snuggle up close in some flimsy flowery number on the piano stool, flip off her mules and wriggle cherry-painted toenails, pressing the pedal and slowly brushing my leg. Maybe I was imagining the squeeze of my hand when she placed it on the keys, the tilt of her head when I made a mistake, the coyness of her eyes flickering across mine before darting away, like a thief's fingers. But it seemed that here was a woman, a very attractive woman, doing a full-on fertility dance in my face. She couldn't have been more explicit if she'd stood on the table and belly danced.

Now, I'm no saint, but I'm no sinner, either. I did what any man with good intentions would do in such a position: I mentally pictured fish guts, trying to stop my old man from making a marquee out of my trousers. It wasn't easy. Call me pathetic, call me sad and primeval, but I'm just being honest when I say that often man and 'old man' are at odds. The very moments that you would prefer him to sleep harmlessly, curled up on your thigh, he says, 'Oi! No, I'm here. I'm here, look at me. I'm going to stand up, right now. I'm standing, look. LOOK AT ME!'

Every lesson was a sweaty, tense battle of wits between

Maddy, me and my member. Just think about this for a second: I'm alone, in the erotic boudoir of a seriously sexy woman, who is rubbing herself against me while we sing love songs to one another. She is blowing in my ear, brushing her wrist against the proposed site of my marquee, and I'm thinking, halibut, maggots, gills, phooaaarrr, blood, scales, cod.

Now women may find it distressing that men are subservient to their knobs. But sadly, it's a fact, and it should simply be accepted. The short, bald bastard that dictates to us from our trousers will henceforth be called Mussolini, sharing, as they do, a diminutive stature, a polished noggin, and an Italian temperament. We can consider the facts for a second if you wish:

I love BTB.

I am here to learn BTB's favourite song.

Maddy is BTB's best buddy and probably just mucking about.

But she smells sooo good I can almost taste . . . no, no, don't go there.

On this occasion, in early February, I was fighting a losing battle and eventually cracked. 'Right, Mads.' I stood, sweating, and stumbled across the room, willing Il Duce to go to sleep. Maddy was smiling victoriously, glancing crotchward as I tried to hide behind the table.

'We're going out . . . for some air . . . and coffee.' I was agitated and panicked.

'We've got coffee here, Johnny. My, my, you seem all steamed up. Why don't you take a shower?' Maddy was loving this, loving her elemental dominance.

'No, no, come on, Mads, I'm hungry, too. Come on, let's go eat.'

I wasn't really hungry, and we weren't on a date, and, as I've explained, I was trying to play the good guy and remove myself from a situation in which Mussolini seemed more in control than me. It turned out that Maddy was meeting Stef in Battersea later, so it made sense for her to drive and we dropped into Bistro 7, on Lavender Hill, for an entirely chivalrous lunch.

Maddy was better behaved in public, at least for a while.

'So, after that, I told Colin why I was spending time with you, and—'

'Tsk,' Maddy tutted and sighed flamboyantly. She looked to her left, out of the floor-to-ceiling plate-glass windows, at the Arts Centre opposite on Lavender Hill. The cherry blossom had come early, and the pink shock seemed out of place – old ladies in cream-cake hats.

'What? I can tell Colin, can't I? I mean, I know he's got a big mouth, but . . .'

'It was so much more fun when it was all clandestine and everyone was suspicious,' Maddy rued.

'Suspicious about what?'

'You and me, darling. You should see Stef; he's like a wounded bull. I hope Colin doesn't tell him. Although I think he's more interested in winning back Trish at the moment. He has a cunning plan, you know.' Maddy sipped chilled white wine while I studied the menu.

'What's his plan?' I asked, shutting the menu decisively. Maddy tapped her elegant nose.

'Top secret, my love.' She smiled mischievously. 'Sworn to secrecy.'

'But I'm just worried about the calibre of his plan, that's all,' I explained.

'He's hell bent on it, whatever you or I say, Johnny.' Maddy smoked in an affected, theatrical way.

'Come on, Maddy, what's the plan?'

'Look,' Maddy sighed, 'it's got something to do with the Chris Balls breakfast show next Monday. That's all I'm saying; ask him the rest. He's your mate, isn't he?'

'Oh come on, Maddy.'

'In return for special favours, maybe I'll tell you.' Maddy's flirting was interrupted by the arrival of the camp waiter. While I picked up the menu to remind myself what I'd decided on, he handed us a Valentine's Day promotional flyer.

'Just printed, love birds, make sure you book quickly.'

I blushed and Maddy grinned, reaching over to hold my hand. 'Oh we must, mustn't we darling,' she hammed.

'But . . .' I began, but trailed off. The waiter looked unimpressed by our show, and tapped his foot on the wooden floor, impatiently. 'Shall I come back when you're less busy?' he asked, while Maddy pulled a face, mimicking his stroppiness.

'No, no, I'll have sausage and mash, please, and another Guinness.' I wasn't hungry, but it was too habitual a choice to avoid.

'For mmmaadame.' The waiter must have trained on a week-long course, learning how to say 'madam' and make it sound just like 'trollop'.

'Just wine. I'll save myself for dessert.' Maddy handed the waiter back the menu.

'Dessert. Right.' The camp waiter looked Maddy up and down, visually questioning her figure's need for any pudding, before turning on his heels and voguing across the restaurant.

'Rude bastard,' I said.

'But at least *he* thinks we're together,' Maddy smiled, picking up the Valentine's Day menu. 'Oysters, salmon, strawberries. Sounds good; how about it, Johnny, my sweet?'

'Maddy, listen, I . . .' Maddy threw down the menu in a huff, mind-reading what I was about to say.

'Oh, for God's sake, Johnny, I'm just having fun. Stop being such a bloody bore.'

Was I being a paranoid fool, while Maddy was just being herself?

The trouble is, I quite enjoyed the idea of Maddy really being interested in me rather than messing about. My devoted husband-to-be Jekyll side was affronted by the glimmer of seduction, while my Ratty-type, Hyde side was dancing.

'Johnny, I'm just playing.' It was like hearing a magician's secrets. 'You're going to be my best friend's husband and I'm the chief bridesmaid. If that isn't enough, I'm also seeing, admittedly on a hugely casual and pretty crap basis, your mate Stef. So stop being so bloody stressed out about everything, darling.'

Maddy made me feel so utterly immature that, when she started flirting again, to question her motives, to suspect that she was even slightly serious, was to reveal myself as a spotty pre-pubescent pup.

In between courses, Maddy returned to the special Valentine's Day menu. 'So I take it you're dissing me on Valentine's Day, Johnny?' She was being sarcastic again, demonstrating how large a buffoon I was being. She meant, Of course you're busy, Johnny, don't you think I know that. Durrrr.

'Hmm.' I shrugged. 'So, are you off somewhere romantic with Ronaldo?'

'Hmph,' Maddy snorted dismissively. 'Stef is as romantic as Bernard Manning. I'll probably have another lonely night in.' She pulled her injured puppy face. 'What about you two?'

'Don't know. Every year we go to one of the local restaurants. It's all a bit predictable. What's the ideal Valentine's night, Maddy? What would you want?' I realized my mistake in personalizing the question, but it was too late.

'What would I want . . . from Johnny Riley, for Valentine's Day?' Maddy moved into overdrive, her chestnut eyes flicking up to her left as she placed her first finger on her bottom lip, thinking. 'Hmm.' She raised herself on to her elbows and leant forward on to the table. Her pale arms pushed her chest together like a vice, giving her a cleavage like

Boadicea's breastplate. *Calm down, Mussolini. Calm.*

'First, I would like,' she whispered gently, forcing me to move closer, 'a candlelit meal prepared by your own fair hands.' She placed her hand on mine and, after the jibes, I felt it would seem childish to withdraw my own.

'And there's nothing quite like one of Agent Provocateur's racy lacys to get the pulse going,' she purred.

'Agent Provocateur? Lacys?' I repeated innocently.

'Top-class, seriously sexy lingerie, my sweet,' she whispered. 'Silk, lace, crotchless, nipple-clamps, diamond-studded dog collars – you name it.'

'So,' I coughed, nervously, 'that would be an ideal night?' I tried to return the question to the hypothetical, while thinking about the innards of a pilchard.

'Hmm.' She sighed, closing her eyes and leaning her head back, as if fantasizing. I was losing my battle of wits to the bald dictator.

Get a bloody grip, Riley. This whole Maddy trip was increasingly frustrating. Why was it that Maddy could make me this hot and bothered? Was it just red blood cells, or was there more to it? How could I marry BTB when another woman, her best friend, could have this effect on me at the click of her fingers?

'Excuse me.' The camp waiter enjoyed disturbing us. Clearly pleased with his timing, he said, 'So, shall I put you two down for the fourteenth?'

'No, no.' I looked at her hand holding mine and wriggled it free, while she giggled and he frowned. 'We're not together,' I flustered.

'Yes . . . and I'm as straight as the Grand Canal.'

Maddy broke into a giggle. 'Desserts?' he enquired, with regal indifference.

'Strudel,' Maddy mumbled between chuckles, trying to wrestle my hand back into her own and playfully tickling me under my arms.

'Erm.' I picked up the menu, quickly checking the options. 'Cheesecake,' I said, squirming. He looked at us derisively, wholly unimpressed, before twirling and mincing away like a matador.

In desperation, I started tickling Maddy back, and she giggled uncontrollably. I realized how harmless it all was. We were old friends, for Chrissakes; I could tickle her and she could flirt with me all she wanted. We were just friends.

For some reason I can't explain, I looked to my left through the plate glass. It's always hard to tell whether you are unconsciously aware of someone else watching you, but my eyes connected with another set in a stationary Golf Cabriolet on the opposite side of the road, under the cherry blossom. They were coldly, immovably, fixed on my own.

It was impossible to know how long Ruth had been watching us. Had she been there as long as we had? Had she watched the entire act, with every second of innuendo?

Realizing how ludicrously infatuated we looked, I jumped back with a start, trying to drop Maddy's hand like a murder weapon, probably just adding to my guilt in Ruth's dark eyes.

It was unusual for me to be up at the same time as BTB. Generally, she had long since bounced out of the door by the time I stumbled downstairs, looking like one of the walking dead.

But today was Colin's big day. This was the day we'd all been instructed to tune in to Chris Balls' breakfast show at 7.30 a.m. I fiddled with the radio while BTB made coffee and flicked through the post.

'Bill, bill, bill, bill,' she muttered.

'Make sure you have Balls for breakfast.'

The annoying jingle blasted across the kitchen, woke

Muttley with a start and seemed to rock BTB, like a willow in a gust of wind. Muttley padded over to welcome his favourite two-legged being.

'Get off, Muttley. Johnny, will you feed the bloody dog?'

I looked at BTB, swaying by the kettle, standing barefoot on the grey lino floor, wrapped in an old powder-blue towelling gown. She faced the French windows at the end of the galley kitchen, frosted lightly with ice, and seemed oblivious to the cold. BTB was rubbing her face and flicking, repeatedly, through the clutch of unfriendly envelopes, looking as though she didn't want to plunge into any individual bill.

Me and Muttley were both thinking the same thing at the same time: Where had Tigger gone? Where was the bouncing blonde whirlwind that we had grown accustomed to, like a couple of storm chasers? I looked at BTB, her gaze fixed on the chalk-board, shaped like a shopping basket, hanging on the kitchen wall to the left of the French windows. The board had a long, long list of wedding-related tasks on it, covering its entire length: 'Cars, photographer, cake, dress, bridesmaids' dresses, honeymoon, hotel, invites, flowers, Father Derek, booze, band, DJ, video, ushers, seating plan.' I watched BTB's eyes scan the board, as she swore, unintelligibly, under her breath.

I realized that I couldn't remember our last conversation. We had become a pair of automatons, working mechanically through our daily processes. We ate together, sat on the sofa and watched some toss video together and we slept in the same bed, but all of this was like so much padding on a sore. The things that we wanted to talk about, needed to talk about, were invisible, like infections running through our blood, unseen. We ended up discussing the details of our wedding plans over and over, like some kind of mantra. The 'M' subject gave us an excuse to nimbly sidestep our real problems, pretending everything was fine.

*

'Goood morning. It's seven thirty-eight and you're listening to Balls for breakfast, and the Fun Lovin' Posse. Hey, Polly, let's twiddle your tuning knobs. Ooopps, only joking, listeners, too early for that, eh. Don't touch that dial, we've got a special feature starting today called Desperados, jilted people so desperate to win back the affections of their loved ones that they'll do absolutely anything to get them back. But first, Robbie Williams . . .'

'That must be our boy – a desperado sounds apt.' I looked for a smile on BTB's grey face. She sipped her coffee and sat down on a barstool, finally opening the bills. How had this crept up on me? When did BTB stop singing the bouncity-bounce song in the morning? Where did the down-turned crow's feet and black eye sockets come from?

'Love, are you OK?' She turned away, looking out into the plain paved backyard, eclipsing me.

'OK, first up on Desperados it's – drum-roll – Colin Carter from Clapham. Hello, Colin.'

'Yeah, hi, Chris mate, how are you?' I smiled and pointed at the radio, turning the volume up.

'So, you are totally desperate, is that right, Colin?'

'Completely desperate, yes, Chris.' Colin sounded muffled and distant.

'And what's the lovely lady called, Chris?'

'Trish.'

'OK, Trish, I hope you're listening out there in radio land, 'cos you have the chance of a lifetime. Colin, here, wants you so badly that every morning for a week, starting tomorrow, you can ring us at Fun FM and tell us what you want Colin to do to pledge his love to you. Isn't that right, Colin?'

'That's right, Chris . . . er . . .' Colin sounded unnatural and scripted. Someone had obviously given him his lines.

'Go on . . . you've got a poem, haven't you, Colin?' Chris Balls prompted.

'Yeah . . . what now?'

'Yes, do the poem now, Colin.'

'OK . . . right . . . Dear Trish, to prove my love to you, There's not a thing I wouldn't do, Just name your task and I will show, How low a desperate man can go.'

'Well, that's a really beautiful thing, Colin. Right, time for an ad break, but don't go away, 'cos in five minutes, Colin, who I can guarantee has around about the worst voice in the history of radio broadcasting, will be singing Trish's favourite love song. I hope you're listening, Trish, 'cos Colin will do anything for you. The man has no dignity.'

'I can't believe he's doing this. What's he doing? Jesus!'

'At least he's trying.' BTB's eyes were narrow and red.

'What does that mean exactly?' Muttley left the room.

'Look at us, Johnny, this is pathetic. This is the longest conversation we've had in weeks, and it's a row.'

'What? What have I done?' I wondered if Ruth had already become a supergrass.

'It's not *what* you've done as much as not done, Johnny.' She pushed me away as I went in for the this-will-solve-everything hug. *Bollocks, my one and only plan, foiled.*

'Well, what have I not done?' I fumbled.

'Look, look around you. Wake up, these are bills.' BTB held up the fistful of paper, accusingly.

'Uh-huh,' I said, nervously.

'Exactly, "uh-huh", that's about the level of your contribution to our relationship, Johnny. Do you know anything about our bills, our out-goings?' As per usual, I decided on silence as a response. 'Yes' was incorrect. 'No' was suicide. Silence was a fair stake.

'Do you know anything about the wedding, Johnny? Do you?'

'Well . . . yes.' I felt this was an accurate reply. I did, at the very least, know the date, and I could name a few of the guests.

'Where's the bloody electronic organizer I bought you?'

'Er.' *Lost*.

'Lost?'

'No.'

'Which of these tasks are you responsible for, Johnny?' She pointed at the long list on the chalk-board, and I squinted.

'Er . . . cars . . . ushers, photographer,' I read, rather than remembered.

'And what do they have in common?' BTB interrupted before I could finish the list.

'Er . . .' I racked my brain. Surely she couldn't mean that they were all tasks that Uncle Alfie could do? Photos, sure, DJing, maybe, but cars? His car was OK, but I didn't think BTB would want to arrive at the church in a tan Sierra.

'What does this symbol mean?' She pointed at a tick. The tick was next to all the tasks on the board that weren't mine.

'Oh,' I said.

' "Oh"! Is that it?'

'Make sure you have Balls for breakfast.'

'Right, listeners, you're back with Chris Balls on Fun FM, and do we have a treat for you. Polly, put your beaver away. It's a real beaver, listeners. Billy the Fun FM beaver. Don't want you thinking we're cheapening the show. Right, we're here with a new feature, and it's day one of Desperados. Play the jingle, Polly.'

The theme tune to *A Fistful of Dollars* whistled out of the radio. BTB and me had stopped, mid-row, to listen.

'Colin, are you there?'

'Yeah . . . yes, Chris . . . er . . . I'm here.'

221

'OK, we're going to see if we can persuade the lovely Trish to come on the show and set you a luuurve challenge tomorrow, for you to prove just how desperate you are, OK?'

'Er . . . yes, Chris, that's right.'

'OK, so today we've had to come up with a Herculean task ourselves, and I understand you reckon it would be romantic to sing her favourite love song with no accompaniment, live on air, to two million listeners?'

'That's right, Chris.'

I put my head in my hands in embarrassment.

'Do you hear that, listeners? Colin has no shame. Right, what's the song?'

'Er . . . the song is her favourite song, which we played as our first dance for our wedding in nineteen ninety—'

'Just name the song, Colin,' Chris Balls butted in.

' "My Heart Will Go On".'

'By?' Balls prompted.

'By . . . er . . . Celine Dion.'

'OK, you ready?'

'Yeah.'

'Listeners, this is Colin Carter's rendition of Celine Dion's "My Heart Will Go On", which goes out to Trish, his wife, as a message of love from a desperate and undignified man.'

Colin was more tuneless than it was possible to imagine. Chris, Polly and Billy the Beaver left their mike on maliciously, so the listeners could hear their laughter and disbelief. Halfway through the song, Chris Balls cut in.

'Enough, enough. Trish, please, for the sake of the show and the listeners, take this man back. If that's what he does on day one, what will he be doing by Friday? See you tomorrow, Colin. OK, that was the first in a new feature. Now, if you're a true desperado, if you would do literally anything to win your loved one back, give us a call on . . .'

'I can't believe he did that,' I muttered, head in hands.

BTB turned from the window to face me.

'Like I said, Johnny, at least he's trying.' I glanced at BTB to make sure she was being serious.

'Is that what you want me to do? Sing friggin' shite songs on the radio like a wazzock?'

'No, Johnny, you are completely missing the point. God, why do I bother?' BTB walked past me, aiming for the kitchen door.

'What? What am I supposed to do?' It was too dangerous to allow her to walk away. She was way too stubborn. If she left, that was it, she would keep on walking. Past experience proved she could go the distance. 'What can I do? Come on, don't do this to me,' I pleaded. She turned around in the doorway, thank God.

'Work it out, Johnny. Grow up, pay bills, be responsible, finish something you've started. You never finish anything, you're pathetic. At least Colin's doing something. You and Merl and the rest of them, you just dither your way through life. You're like a gang of bloody ostriches, running around in circles, sticking your heads in the ground when anything complicated comes along.'

'I do . . . I will . . . I . . .'

'What did you ever do about that film contact, Norbert wotsit?'

'Well I . . .'

'You did nothing, did you? You tell me scriptwriting is the only thing that drives you. You run away and hide in your room when we're supposed to be sorting bills or fixing the wedding, to scribble your scrawl in those bloody notebooks. Along comes the only chance you'll probably ever get, and what do you do?'

'I . . .'

'Fuck all,' she answered for me.

'Let's talk tonight. I'll buy you dinner.' Yet another transparent tactic.

'We're skint, Johnny.' She waved the bills and pointed at the board.

'I'll cook us dinner.' *We have a cooker and some pans, I can't fail.*

'I'm out with Ruth tonight, she's buying me dinner, so sort yourself and your mutt out.'

As BTB walked away, my bowels triple-jumped. This would be the first time she'd seen Ruth since Ruth had seen . . . well, whatever the hell she thought she'd seen. After BTB had left for work in angry anti-Tigger mood, I tried to work things out. After a shower, I sat on the edge of the bed, dripping in a grey bath towel, with Muttley at my feet.

'So do I tell her, Muttley? Do I get in there with reality before Ruth hands her a grenade?' Muttley yawned, obviously unaware of the seriousness of the situation. Unaware that Ruth could be about to wreak havoc on BTB and me.

'I mean, what would I say? "Listen love, I've secretly been visiting Maddy for private lessons"? Bollocks, I'm dead. I can't win, can I?' Muttley looked up at me, broke wind and fell asleep.

Dung Beetle's Virtual 360

'What the fuck's going on on this planet?' Johnny sat in front of Colin's portfolio, flicking through the plastic sheathed pages.

Colin paced around his living room, phone clamped between ear and shoulder. 'Yeah, sure, I'll do *The Big Breakfast* ... Yeah, that's fine, no probs ... OK ... Car picks me up at six a.m., no worries.'

'Merlin, how did this happen?' Johnny turned to the tartan boxer-shorted mess draped over the sofa, immersed irretrievably in VR Rally. Merlin shrugged, uninterested. It was Saturday afternoon and Merlin had just forced himself out of bed, tempted by the armful of pizza boxes and crate of beer that Johnny had arrived with, fighting his way through the press.

'Fuck off, piss off, get out of here!' Johnny rose to harangue another journalist flashing cameras at any available window space. He pulled ill-fitting red curtains across the bay windows to stop them peering in.

Colin had always been the dominant design force in the house he shared with Trish. She had moved in with him after they'd married, and hadn't yet managed to eradicate Colin's style-blind taste. Colin had spent a decade nurturing his video library, crafting his entertainment unit and feeding the babe-of-the-month altar in the downstairs loo with new cuttings and clips.

Number 77 Elbourne Grove was a physical representation of Colin Carter. For this reason, visiting him was a trip back in time, to sock-smelling lockers at school and stale student bedsits. The naff, the impractical and the unhealthy all vied for supremacy.

The house itself wasn't hard for the journos to find. Squatting in a side road to the north of the Common, it was an unobtrusive Victorian red-brick semi, lost in a grid of similar streets. First-time-buyer land for young professionals, awash, commuter-time, with pinstripe and black shiny leather. At weekends, the same herd shed suits for jogging pants and fleeces, baseball caps and deck shoes.

Trish hadn't dented Colin's thickly glossed lad haven in their eight months of marriage. Maybe this added to the pile of reasons to leave him. Unfamiliarity makes leaving easy. How simple it feels to walk on through some unknown train station, how hard to part with a place of significance – a home, a hideaway, a cherished happen-site.

Since Trish had gone, just before Christmas, the Colinness of Elbourne Road had overflowed and spilt across the house, like ivy. Videos and CDs, cable and satellite-TV guides, crosswords and jigsaw puzzles represented the floating trash of Colin's haphazard mind.

Penthouse and a Scrabble dictionary battled for sunlight on the coffee table along with take-away detritus and beer cans. Dirty socks and crusty cooked pants clung to different parts of the radiator.

Yet here was the proclaimed hero of our times. Colin Carter, Mr Lover-Lover.

Merlin started lodging informally in early January, when Ruth kicked him out, rapidly doubling the demolished state of the house. He had overlain his own brand of mess as a complement to Colin's chaos.

The fake-leather cover of Colin's A3 portfolio had his

favourite headline pasted on the front: THE LOVE MACHINE, the *Sun* called him.

'Merlin, don't you feel we've entered a funny parallel universe sometimes?' Johnny frowned from the depths of the once-beige sofa.

'Hmm?' Merlin managed somehow to manhandle the PlayStation controls, while balancing a cigarette on his bottom lip.

'Some sick invention of Colin's mind, in which the world has mistaken him for the most romantic man alive? And we are the keepers of the dark secret – that he is, in fact, as romantic as a dung beetle?'

'Fuuuckk!' Merlin hurtled out of control, flipping his car into a 360 on a hairpin. He threw the controls down in disgust. 'Want another beer?' Merlin trotted off to the kitchen, clearing a path through strewn clothes, empty crisp packets and cans.

'Yeah, but I'm gonna make a pot of tea in just a second,' Johnny replied.

'Dung beetles could be romantic, for all you know.' Colin put the phone down and it rang immediately. 'Yeah . . . Speaking . . . *Loaded*? Yeah, no problem.' Colin had become matter-of-fact about the media.

'Dung beetles live in shit, too.' Johnny warmed to his allusion, looking around the living room.

The latest *Mail on Sunday* sat atop a pile of papers on a shelf below the coffee table. Johnny had stopped bothering to check on the exploits of his doppelgänger in 'The Life of Riley' column. Picking it up, he reluctantly chuckled as he read that the bride-to-be had called it all off because his namesake had accidentally hoovered up her niece's guinea pig. 'Where does he get this stuff from?' Johnny shook his head as Merlin wandered back in with a four-pack of Bud. 'What, the hoover thing?' Merlin asked cagily. 'Well, I did that to Ruthie's niece, Cassandra. Poor little fella had a heart attack.'

'Jesus! He's like a friggin' magpie, picking up everybody's bits and pieces, and yet here he is, being lauded as some sort of icon.' He threw the paper on the floor.

'Thing is, see, Johnny,' Merlin cracked a can, sipped it, slumped back into the armchair and pressed reset on the PlayStation in one single, worryingly slick movement, 'that society needs its ordinary heroes, right.' He lit another cigarette while the game went through its warm-up sequence.

'Here we go, Professor Merlin, bloody amateur sociologist.' Johnny opened his beer and put his feet up on the coffee table, sliding the cheap portfolio on to the sofa next to him.

'It's true, look at him.' Johnny and Merlin looked at Colin, standing in the bay windows in tattered jeans and his 'Colin & Trish 4 Ever' campaign T-shirt. He was peering out at the band of journalists, thinning in the failing light and falling temperature. 'He is the common man, see,' Merlin continued.

'Can't argue with that, mate.' Johnny nodded.

'And the common man needs icons, but if all their icons are rich and famous and beautiful, well, there's nothing to relate to, like.' Merlin had been developing his theory gradually, since it all kicked off on the Chris Balls breakfast show two weeks ago. 'They want to know that the underdog can win in the end, that normal people can change their circumstances and end up on top. Not win money, or long-term fame, you understand, just win wives and lives back, a return ticket to normality.'

'But there's millions of people in the same boat as Colin, Merl.' Johnny carried on flicking through the plastic-coated news clippings.

'Yeah, but he went public, didn't he? He wore his heart on his sleeve in front of millions of listeners and, the next thing you know, he's a fuckin' national hero. The fact that he writes about a fictional bemused groom on a wedding countdown just adds to the romantic myth. They don't care if Colin's overweight, thick-skinned and balding. In fact, that makes them love him even more. That makes him more accessible, more representative. He could be a part-time pornographer who's into bestiality and no-one would care.' Merlin started the game, instantly freezing his brain cells.

Johnny glanced at *Penthouse* and considered the camel-coat incident. 'I reckon I could make a pretty strong case for both. Hmph, put that in your bloody papers,' he swore at the portfolio, as though the clips embodied the whole mixed-up media world.

The *Evening Standard* picked up Colin's cause on day two of the Chris Balls show. Trish, staying at her mum's house in Croydon, rang the show right after Colin came off air. She had missed him, and was willing to see where Fun FM would lead her. Anyone who knew the couple could tell it was staged and scripted, but to everyone else they sounded real enough. Two real people, living out their life, their separation, for the nation. It was addictive for a nation bred on fly-on-the-wall soaps and docu-dramas. Chris Balls spoke to Trish before giving Colin his challenges. Usually, Colin had to do something embarrassing live on air and something ludicrous over the course of the day, which Chris Balls would encourage the press and TV stations to pick up on. It was a mutually beneficial PR frenzy. Balls created his own romantic hero for the nation, and the media fuelled the fire with yet more publicity, followed everywhere by Billy the Beaver in Fun FM furry suit. More listeners, more readers, more money. Colin's journalistic career had always veered towards the tacky, culminating in the column, and he knew how to play the crowd like an old hand. He knew what the papers and their readers wanted. He ought to, he'd written it often enough.

An ode to Trish was read out by Colin, live, on Wednesday morning. Johnny read from the version printed in the *Evening Standard* that day.

I love you Trish, please take me back,
I really miss you in the sack.
Around the house and down the pub,
At Tesco's and the snooker club
'Where's Trish?' they ask. 'She's gone,' I say.
They shake their heads as if to say
Shouldn't have let her get away . . .
You spanner.

Over the week, Colin swallow-dived off London Bridge, broke the world record for sitting in a bath of custard – twenty-four hours and a nasty rash ever since – did a *Full Monty* strip at the Limelight with Peter Stringfellow, got his left nipple pierced, sat atop Canary Wharf and joined the Foreign Legion. All challenges laid by Trish – planted by Chris Balls and his PR team – as proof of his undying love. His image was littered through the media as if he were the Second Coming. The *Sun* gave out plastic Union Jack bowler hats saying, 'Colin 4 Trish'. Colin's website had more than a million hits in a week. He was booked on *The Big Breakfast* and *The Richard and Judy Show* in the run up to Valentine's Day. The theme was the same throughout the media; like some great Colingate conspiracy, everyone asked the same question: 'Will Trish take Colin back by Valentine's Day?'

'I just can't bloody believe this, Merlin.' Johnny couldn't understand how it had happened. How his sad friend, who was the butt of most of the jokes at the Blue Boy, had been elevated to national hero in a matter of days, while in the same time frame, his own relationship seemed to be collapsing around him.

'Mmm,' Merlin grunted at the TV. 'Fuuuckk!' he shouted, totalling his car into a tree and turning to Johnny.

'Yeah, it's mad, isn't it. But, you know, fifteen minutes of fame and all that,' he muttered.

'So it's all just a cynical media thing?' Johnny had a hint of bitterness in his voice.

'Listen, Johnny lad, whatever this is about now, whoever's hijacked and manipulated it all, it started for the purest of reasons.' Merlin seemed to have developed a level of wisdom and freedom of expression since his separation from Ruth. 'Colin just wanted Trish back. That's all. No harm in that now, is there?' Merlin's tone seemed to quietly chastise Johnny for his bitterness.

'So, d'you think it'll work? Think he'll get her back?' Johnny tried to shake away the envy.

'Oh aye. He loves her. She knows it. And the world knows it now. He'll get her back.'

'What about you?'

'What? Me and Ruth?' Johnny expected Merl to nervously toy with his white streak, but he didn't.

'Yeah. I mean, no offence, Merl mate, but you're just sitting here, playing computer games, eating pizza, drinking beer and' – Johnny picked up January's already well-leafed *Penthouse* – 'bashing the bishop.'

'Uh-huh,' Merlin confirmed, almost smiling.

'Well, that's not going to get Ruth back is it?'

'You're presuming I want her back, Johnny lad.' Merlin crumpled his empty can and tossed it over his head. Johnny let this sink in for a second, nodding his head gently, realizing that his friend seemed more complete, more confident and calm than he had seen him in years. Merlin looked a state, unshaven, scruffy, short of clothes. He ate shit, drank reservoirs of beer and was fixated on computer games and junk videos. But all of the garbage seemed part of the cure. Colin reckoned this was Merlin's way of detoxing, Merl's version of a seaweed wrap. But underneath it all, the clarity and focus of Merl's eyes were a polished pair of zoom lenses.

'So what about Ruth?' Johnny asked tentatively.

Merlin shrugged. 'Don't know, boyo. Don't even know if

she's at the house. Maybe she's doing what I'm doing. Staying with a friend, staying with her folks. I hope she's happy, like. I'm sure she's happy. Maybe she's already left the country, I don't know. I guess I should find out, pluck up the courage, like, an' go home.'

'Colin says you haven't been to work, either.'

'Yeah, you know, can't be bothered, mate. Told them the dog died.'

'You haven't got a dog.'

'No.' Merlin nodded.

'So you're not even going to try . . . with Ruth, I mean.'

'It was just us, Johnny, together. You know we clashed. It all started so madly. We just fucked each other senseless and exploded like chemicals mixing, totally un-fuckin'-stable, we were. Never even stopped to think about what we would do when we got bored of fuckin', an' had to talk, like, an' had to live together an' all that. London was about saving up the cash to travel round the world. For Ruth, too, but I wasn't sure she really wanted to, you know. I sort of thought she'd just latched onto what I wanted to do, copied my dream, like some software. But I'm sure she's fine. I'm sure she feels like I feel – like we just stepped out of a sauna, where we thought the heat and pain and sweating was normal life. But out here it's fine; it's not painful. It's all OK.' Merlin picked up a fresh beer, and looked hard at it before opening it. 'Am I making sense, Johnny?'

'No, you're talking total bollocks, mate.' Johnny smiled, dissolving the tension. Colin continued to chatter in the background incessantly.

'An' what about the great Johnson Riley. How's that old tosser doin'?' Merlin was playing tit for tat. He'd spilt his emotional guts to Johnny and was offering a free return to sender.

'What?' Any question put Johnny on edge.

'If I was to say I've seen happier death-rowers, would you

be surprised?' Merlin dug, disregarding Johnny's reticence.

'Nothing's wrong.'

'Wedding all going to plan and everything?' Merlin hit the target with ease.

'You're the best man, you tell me.' Johnny rubbed his thighs in nervous frustration as he spoke.

'Ouch.'

'Apparently I'm not pulling my weight.' Johnny drained his beer.

'For the wedding?' Merlin turned in his chair to give Johnny his full attention.

'For the wedding . . . and life in general. Half of me thinks she might even call it all off, just like doppelgänger Riley.'

'Really?'

'We're pretty distant, Merl, mate. Not really on talking terms. Apparently I'm a loser, a child, a no-hoper, who finds it nigh on impossible to finish making a cup of friggin' tea.'

'Now where is that cup of tea you were making?'

'Bastard!' He threw the empty beer can at Merlin, who ducked as it bounced off the back of the armchair.

'She's got a point, mate.'

'I do not need mates taking her side, for fuck's sake, and I think your bloody Ruth chucked a bomb in for good measure.'

'What d'ya mean?' Merlin frowned.

'She saw me and Maddy, and I think she read a lot more into it than there was.'

'What, you an' Maddy? No way, mate.' Merlin sounded surprised but calm. 'You're not marrying an idiot . . . not you and Maddy, mate. No way.' Johnny looked puzzled by Merlin's certainty.

'Anyway, it's all piling up – the Maddy thing, the organizing, the eternally unfinished *Mr Saturday Night* – I'm just your basic dunderhead in her eyes.' Johnny stood and tried to look purposeful.

'You're seeing that film geezer soon, aren't you?' Merlin dragged the memory from some hazy, pubbed-up conversation.

'Exacta-bloody-mundo. I mean, how many people can say they've got an appointment with Lord Norbert Camberly, eh? Mr Hollywood, meeting me. Geordie boy made good. Read my script, wants to talk to me. So how about that for bloody finishing. And while I'm at it, who wants tea?'

'Yeah, go on, mate.' Merlin messed with the controls again, muttering, 'Right, you bastard, I'm gonna have you,' to the console.

Colin finally hung up and immediately said, 'Did I hear you say you're seeing Norbert Camberly?' Johnny had left the room as Colin shouted after him, 'Well, do us a favour, would you, mate.'

'What's that?' Johnny shouted back from the kitchen.

'See if he fancies doing this as a film.' Johnny re-entered the room, poking his head around the door.

'Doing what, Colin?' Johnny looked confused.

'Doing this . . . you know, Mr Lover-Lover.' He pointed at his portfolio. Johnny laughed dismissively.

'You're a fucking one and only, Carter.'

'Guaranteed audience, Johnny. Just think about it, mate.'

Disengaged

It was one of the weirdest days of my life. Round about mid-day in late February, standing in the rain outside the shoddy offices of EF&Co on Hanway Street, just off Tottenham Court Road. I clutched my mobile, wearing my best black suit and least-offensive Christmas-gift tie, the latest script draft tucked under my arm in a brown envelope.

I suppose it was inevitably huge, but I was still shocked by the size of Mr Big's limousine. You know the opening scene in *Star Wars*, when the space cruiser cuts in from top right, quickly fills the screen and goes on and on for ever. It was like that. The metallic blue, US-style limo took one look at the side street where EF&Co were based and decided against try-ing to turn into it, parking instead on the main road, gradually grinding to a halt, like some sort of supertanker.

I stood stock-still and witless. I hadn't really expected him to turn up, even after his PA had confirmed by phone.

'Yes, Lord Norbert has a slot between noon and one; he'll pick you up outside your offices and leave you at Gatwick.'

'But I don't need to go to Gatwick,' I said, like a fool.

'I know, sir, but Lord Norbert does.'

Eventually, in the distance, one of the windows in the rear hemisphere of the car opened, and a vast, familiar hand, like a boxing glove, beckoned me over. I realized I was standing still, in shock. Childishly, I responded by breaking into a run, as though the car might change its mind and drive away unless I hurried along.

I'd wondered, in the months that had passed since I'd last seen him, whether I had an exaggerated memory of Mr Big. Whether the enormous blustering nutter was as much a product of my own alcohol consumption as his.

'Getinthefuckincarlike, yer daft twat.' I wasn't disappointed. Mr Big occupied the latter half of the limo. This was his haven, his made-to-measure nirvana. Everything fitted around him like a pilot in a cockpit. His phone was a minuscule headset and microphone. Several screens floated in front of him, and a keyboard-cum-remote-control was strapped ergonomically around his waist. A drink – a gin and tonic I think – rested on a tray, where his hand naturally lay, and he sipped from time to time.

I have since discovered how the interior of the limo was created. Mr Big sat in a great big vat of plaster. A delightful brilliant-white mould was made of him, and reproduced in foam, like some sort of joke iceberg. The limo company, in co-operation with Lord Norbert's personal designers, created the perfect mobile office for their paymaster, based around the presumption that all movement was nasty.

In the beginning, he said nothing. Outside, London choked on grey rain. Crowds rippled past the window and the hum of traffic was ever present.

'Fuck off! Not now,' he shouted suddenly. I jumped, wondering if our meeting was terminated, or worse. He pointed at his headset by way of explanation. 'No more calls,' he barked. I think I preferred the sensitive Mr Big who was scared of flying.

Mr Big was holding a crumpled piece of paper between his thumb and forefinger. I recognized it as the letter I had penned in angry response to BTB's insults about me being an ostrich. It was a normal-sized letter, on EF&Co headed A4, but in his paw it looked like a postage stamp. Mr Big was rereading the letter, refreshing his memory and sipping his gin and tonic.

I tried to remember what I'd written. The letter had gone off with a copy of *Mr Saturday Night* the day after BTB's barracking about my finishing skills; the day after Chris Balls launched Colin on Fun FM. So it was written prior to the Valentine's night massacre, when me and BTB were still a living, unbludgeoned thing. I touched the painful, bruised bridge of my nose at the memory.

Strange, I thought, how coincidences conspire to cause such opposite outcomes. Colin's and my own relationships, and the dynamics that affected them, both went critical on the same day. Satellites glancing asteroids on interplanetary orbits. Yet Colin's glance had sent him off on a glory-bound trajectory, through new vistas of galaxies, while mine had sent me crumbling apart, like chalk in the vacuum of space.

Mr Big dabbed his mouth, using my letter as a napkin, before crumpling it softly, unconsciously. I looked around for signs of my script, wondering if he wanted the copy I had brought.

'You helped me, Riley,' he said. 'First flight for a long time, and you helped me through it. I never forget help. On a plane again today, you know.'

'Really?' I said, nervously banal.

'Yes, fuckin' really, think I'd joke about it? Fuckin' planes. I hate the bastards. Jesus! What're you doing today?'

'Er . . .'

'Wanna come to Rio?' Mr Big's moon of a face lit up at the spontaneous thought.

'Well . . . I, er, sort of have things planned. I haven't got a passport, anyway.'

'Course not. Not lost your firefly, anyway, so why the hell would you want to chase mine round bloody Brazil for me?'

'Well, it's not that, I just—'

'Not what? Got married, didn't you, Riley?'

'Er . . . no . . . Well, we were going to . . . I mean, I asked, but she left . . . last week, so it's all off.'

237

'WHAT! What did I tell you on the plane, you twat?'

'Um . . . not to miss my chances, Lord Norbert, sir,' I stammered nervously.

'Damn fuckin' right, and call me Norb, not Lord fuckin' anything.'

'Well, that's why I'm here, that's why I sent the script.' I held up the envelope, shakily.

'What script?' His pasty face crinkled with confusion.

'Um . . . with the letter. *Mr Saturday Night*. I've got a spare one here, if you want it.' A big mitt swiped the envelope from my hands, ripped off the brown paper and glanced at the cover before flicking through the pages.

'Oh . . . this . . .' He seemed to recognize the words.

'Yeah, you know, I didn't want to miss the opportunity for you to see it.'

'Daft fucker. I'm not your opportunity, I'm not the chance you don't want to miss. Stupid southern pillock, more stupid than bloody monkey hangers or the bloody aristotwats in the House of Lords.'

'You're not my chance?' I repeated, trying not to excite the unstable Mr Big.

'This is a shit script.' He opened the window and threw the clump of pages out.

'Oi, what the hell?' I could see my pages scattering in the wind and rain across Shaftesbury Avenue.

'I've read better wank mags.'

'But I . . . you . . .' Mr Big must have seen the bemused fear and confusion written across my face. And maybe, just maybe he could see a bit more besides. Maybe he could see the sadness below. He cocked his head to one side and raised his hands in a calming gesture. I wasn't sure if he was calming himself, or me. He leant towards me. 'You've got talent, lad, sure, but that pretentious bollocks isn't worthy of my sphincter.' He said this gently, as if it was well-earned praise. He shifted back in his chair and folded his arms. I sat, awkwardly, not sure what to say or where to look. After a while I made eye contact. Mr Big's curious button eyes were framed by inquisitively raised eyebrows, waiting for something. After a while, I realized they were waiting for me. Awaiting my explanation.

'What? You want me to tell you what happened?' I was unsure, feeling my way through.

'Johnny, this film stuff is as significant as a fart' – he farted loudly – 'compared to the big things in life. Tell me what happened. Tell me what happened to *her*.' As he said the word 'her', he cupped his big hand gently, as though holding something fragile, small and breakable.

So I told him. He drank more gin, never offering me one, and I told him what had happened on Valentine's Day. He wanted the full works, even, seeing as we were near by, a trip to Agent Provocateur in Soho. It was embarrassing enough the first time round, without a return visit accompanied by Norb.

I know I shouldn't have listened to Maddy, but I did. It was Friday the thirteenth, predictably, and I was already late for a night out at the dogs with Ratty and Stef. I blustered into the trendy lingerie shop, just off Berwick Street, red-faced and out of breath, determined to buy the best present I could for BTB. Sexy underwear said all the right things; it said, 'I still fancy the pants off you after all these years.' It said, 'We might be about to become husband and wife, but we can still shag like rabbits and laugh and love and lust and enjoy.' BTB had gone to St Helens in a rage, and would be back on Valentine's Day, for what, I decided, would be the dog's bollocks of a romantic night.

'Can I help you?' The assistant looked like she'd stepped out of the imagination of a schoolboy. I felt as though I'd been caught with my hand on the top shelf at the newsagent's, standing on tiptoes. My cheeks burned and tingled, my eyes flitted from item to item, trying to avoid alighting on anything and revealing an unhealthy interest in waspies, PVC, or the assistant's cleavage.

'Would it be a Valentine's present, sir?' How astute, I thought, but, looking around the small shop at the handful of blushing men being assisted, I realized it was an easy guess.

'Um . . . I, er . . .' I stammered, wondering what the form was. The shop's policy was to assist lone men and leave other shoppers to sort themselves out. A couple browsed together, tittering, experimenting, pushing back boundaries. A stylish, understated woman in her forties was left to shop undisturbed, and had already gathered an armful of silk.

I quickly realized why this was the policy. Without assistance, I would have cut my losses and done a runner. Maybe because of the beguiling array of sizes, combinations, styles and patterns, or just the sheer embarrassment. I'm pretty sure me, and most of the men in the shop, would suddenly have thought, *Hmm, come to think of it, chocolates are a damn fine idea.* But now I was captured, cuffed to the bedpost.

'Girlfriend? Wife?' The tall assistant had hair like Cleopatra, cut in stark lines and angles. Her pale face was lost to violently scarlet liquid lips, which looked so full they might explode at any second, without warning.

'Fiancée,' I said, bizarrely. It was a word I'd never used, but somehow it arrived on my tongue like unwanted spittle. 'Tying the knot . . . in, er . . . in May,' I elaborated, and realized I was trying to remove all threat from my situation. I was saying, We may be in an underwear shop, you are indeed a very attractive lady, my, that is a short skirt you are wearing, but I am not, I repeat not, weird, nor am I up for it.

'Good for you,' she said indifferently. 'Now, does she like crotchless, or G-string?' I gulped. Somehow, over the next ten minutes, we managed to select a bra and knickers. I steered a course, with stoic determination, towards the discreet and away, as far as possible, from the gauche.

'No, no, she's just not the pink leopard-skin type. Yes, I know it looks good when you drape it over you like that, but . . .' It all got fairly difficult when it came to sizes.

'So those are the small panties? With the crotch?'

I nodded firmly.

'And her bra size?'

I swallowed and panicked. How could I not have thought to check this out? How could I have left the house without quickly peeking in a drawer?

'My sort of size?' The assistant, thoroughly enjoying my awkwardness, cupped her own breasts proudly.

'Um, yes,' I said, not knowing what else to say.

Mr Big rubbed the steamed-up car window pane, peering at the shop front of Agent Provocateur. The rain blurred the view. Eventually, he pushed a button and the window slid down. By now I was used to the constant rubbernecking caused by Norb's blue whale of a car. He squinted at the window display, which centred around a giant, fluffy strapped stiletto and a diamanté whip. Estimating that the doorway was a little too small for Norb, we decided to remain limo'd, saving me a repeat red-faced performance. I thought I could just make out the assistant who had belittled me, peeking out of the doorway and pointing at me and Mr Big. Stuff that up your crotchless knickers, flubber lips, I thought, trying to look as though I was sitting in my everyday car.

We headed south, towards Gatwick, veering west to Clapham Common on another diversion, so that Mr Big could soak up the atmosphere as I told him about Colin's triumph.

'And he's your friend?' Mr Big bounced excitedly in the back, testing the car's suspension.

'Yes . . . Yes, he is.'

'Now there's a man committed to his cause.' It didn't take much explaining. Norbert, like me and BTB and everyone else in the world, had seen it all unfold on TV.

With relative secrecy, Interflora had sponsored Colin's attempt to create a world-record-winning bouquet of flowers on Clapham Common, appropriately, on Valentine's Day. Trish was kept occupied by her mother all day, before Fun

FM's eye-in-the-sky helicopter arrived in Croydon at around about teatime. Trish's reaction to the 200-yard-square bouquet was caught live on camera and beamed out to millions of homes on the early-evening news. 'Colin & Trish, 4 ever' was picked out in white among the field of roses, tulips and carnations. Colin, meanwhile, wearing an Interflora T-shirt, *Sun* hat and Fun FM stickers, was being interviewed on the ground as Trish descended. 'Any last words before you see Trish, Colin?'

'I love her, and, you know . . . that's all that matters. I just hope she'll have me back.' Colin turned to speak directly to camera, tears welling up in his eyes. 'This is it, Trish. Have me back. I'm sorry I was a plonker, just take me back on Valentine's Day.'

With the world's media tuned in, the chopper landed, Trish and Colin rushed towards each other and she leapt into his arms, twirling around and around. It was perfect television. Colin was a natural. All of his junking out on crap TV and B-movies, his tabloid training and his addiction to American daytime talk shows paid off in that moment. Colin had an absolute understanding of what the mass psyche wanted to see.

Lord Norbert wept, openly, as I recounted the story to him once more. I remembered how BTB had also sobbed helplessly through the Valentine's Day news. 'It's lovely,' she repeated, over and over.

'But it's all staged, set up, faked,' I protested.

She sobbed more, muttering things like, 'That just sums you up, Johnny Riley. How could you think that? Look how much he loves her.'

'And he's your friend?' repeated Lord Norbert, using my letter to blow his nose.

'He's an usher . . . Sorry, he was going to be an usher at my wedding,' I corrected myself, bringing yet more sobs from Norbert.

'One day, perhaps I could meet him; he seems to me a very special individual.' I realized, in his words, that reality is irrelevant. Colin had become Mr Lover-Lover. He was now the most romantic man in Britain, if not the world. My view, the real view of Colin Carter, was inconsequential. The media and the public, Mr Big and even BTB, didn't want to know about the real Colin, they wanted the hype and invention. That's what they wanted and that's what they got. You had to give it to him, Colin might have sacrificed his dignity and transformed himself into a national hero of Eddie the Eagle ilk, but he had achieved his goal. He had, for the time being, at least, won back Trish's heart and salvaged his marriage. There can be few worthier causes.

Now, I guess I can't blame Colin for my result, but science does reason that, for every action in the universe, there is an equal and opposite reaction.

I had good motives, too. All I was trying to do was breathe a little oxygen on the fast-fading flames of me and BTB. I'd planned a Valentine's night that would snuff out all doubt from BTB's mind. It would be a celebration designed to leave her with unwavering certainty about me, about us and our togetherness. At once an apology and an announcement of the arrival of the new Johnson Riley. Johnson the husband, Johnson the hunter, the provider, the anti-arse.

Between Clapham and Gatwick I explained about the Valentine's night massacre to Mr Big. Outside, through the rain, the low-level south-west terraces thinned out, replaced by bands of council blocks. Later, on the M25's graceless boundaries, the scenery became large mock-Tudor semis and big detached houses with misplaced delusions of the country estate. The traffic was always slow, the driving unrushed and comfortable. The gentle rock, the scent of leather, the engrossed captive audience, created the perfect environment to tell my story. I found it a release, cathartic, but I suppose that was how he wanted me to feel. Maybe

Lord Norbert felt some debt to me after the Barcelona flight? Maybe he really was a wandering saint of missed opportunity. A man possessed by his own loss and obsessed with averting the suffering of others.

BTB had escaped to the comforts of her family at the tail-end of the week. I did nothing but frustrate her, so she had to leave. Our relationship was left hanging by the tiniest of threads. After visiting her mum and dad on Thursday and Friday, BTB arrived back with me as irritated and angry as a rash, after the long drive. She'd been listening to the Colin and Trish story unravelling during the day on the car radio. On her return, she was interested in nothing but watching TV and trying to get through to Trish on the phone. BTB wandered around the house saying, 'They're so lucky,' shaking her head and sobbing, 'I'm so happy for them.' Then she'd look at me, or shove Muttley out of her way with her shin, tutting and cursing.

Her mood could not have been clearer, or more ominous, if she'd worn a sandwich board painted with the words 'I'm pissed off' on the front and 'I hate Johnny' on the back. But, somehow, yet again, I had the incompetence to ignore all the warning signs. I didn't mean to, I wasn't being a knob, I just didn't want to inflame anything. Not blind, but with my eyes tight closed. I know this is always a dangerous game to play, but I'll choose the safety of silence above the hazard of direct action any time. Muttley knew the score, and sensibly went into hiding.

While BTB had fumed and stormed and battered around the house, before finally buggering off to her parents, I'd realized something. I may have been silent, I may have avoided confrontation like a coward, but I had been through an awakening. I had watched BTB. Watched her green eyes smoulder and spark, watched her pale fists clench and flail, watched her lips drain of blood as they pressed tense to keep a coiled and sprung tongue. The colour, speed and dizzy effort of observing made me think of a dragonfly trapped in a glass house.

What I'd realized was simple. It was that I wanted to keep her. I wanted her to be mine. And every angry movement, every thump of dragonfly on glass, made me more aware of my certainty. Do you remember the genie in the cartoon, *The Arabian Knights*? He would clap his hands and say 'size of an elephant' and 'speed of a cheetah' in a deep voice, and then morph into that creature? Well, you might think I had met this genie years ago and he'd said 'speed of a snail' or 'mental agility of a sprout', and I was still waiting for the effects to wear off. I confess, I have not been quick off the mark. It's been a meandering realization of the preciousness of BTB. A dithering, dawdling, reluctant proposal; a feeble crawl across the line to finally understand how much I wanted to catch and keep my angry dragonfly, and yet, for me, it was an epic awakening, an evolutionary leap of the scale of sight, or flight, or consciousness.

But what could I to do? To catch her in my hands was to be stung. To leave her alone was to allow her to batter herself to death on the glass. And to open a window was to lose her for ever.

I should have tackled BTB on Thursday, when she abruptly informed me she was off to see the Mersey Mafia – probably to get a contract put out on my head. She didn't invite me and I didn't argue. Thinking back, watching her on the white tiles of the kitchen as she said, 'I'm off to Mum and Dad's for a couple of days,' she was probably angling for a fight. I should have clocked the tight tendons in her neck, should have realized she wanted passion and disapproval. She probably wanted to hear, 'What the hell do you mean? What about me? Aren't I bloody invited?' Or 'But it's Valentine's Day on Saturday. When will you be back?' Something, anything but, 'Oh . . . that means I can go to the dogs with Ratty and Stef Friday night,' which is what she got.

I should have tackled her at any of a thousand obvious moments over the previous week, during which BTB had spoken to me in little more than monosyllabic grunts. I now know she was trying to produce a response, trying desperately to cattle prod my cow's hide of a skull into action. But I chose to say nothing, do nothing. Well done, Johnny, that's got to rank up there with, 'Nah, can't be an iceberg,' in the league of things you shouldn't ignore.

The trouble was, I knew I'd done something wrong, and I reckoned if you put all of the hundreds of errors, mistakes and misjudgements into a big boiling pot of fuck-up stew, you could reduce the bubbling mess down to the two real problems driving BTB's anger.

Either Ruth had told her about Maddy and she was about to confront me, or this was more aggro about my wedding failure. Either way, I had a single, fail-safe plan, which was to blow her away with Valentine's night and tackle the issues later.

A poor response to both problems, I agree. I should've known better. I honestly thought that, if I created the right environment, I'd have a better chance of explaining myself. I would take the blank canvas of our pine-floored, open-plan living room, and convert it into something magical. I thought that if I could cloak her in candlelight, prime her with soothing music, subtle wine and pleas for forgiveness from the moment she sat down, then I might avoid disaster. I just might side-step the sting in her tail by telling the truth about me and Maddy.

I didn't know she was about to go nuclear, did I? I didn't know she was at boiling point.

She ignored my little Saturday night insect trap, pretending not to even notice me laying the table and decorating the room with an army of candles, as she finally made contact with Trish.

'. . . It's wonderful, darling . . . Yes, isn't he a superstar . . .

You're so lucky having him.' She glanced at me for the first time that day, with an acid look that caused me to flinch. She carried on talking: 'Oh, I'm OK . . . No, he hasn't . . . No . . . No, I'm not surprised . . . I think I'll have to, as usual.' She walked the phone upstairs to the bedroom, shutting the door behind her. I heard Muttley squeal, discovered in his hiding place, and pad downstairs glumly, pausing to give me a dour this-is-your-fault-Johnny look, before flopping into his basket gloomily.

Later, once she was all gabbled out with Trish, BTB returned, another layer of hardened anger set over her face like fired clay. She ignored the clanging and clattering noise I made in the kitchen, banging pots and pans around in a desperate look-at-me-I'm-doing-something-nice effort.

She sat down at the table reluctantly, pushing my gift-wrapped present to one side. She shovelled the smoked salmon around her plate and downed her champagne in one. I raised my glass too late.

'Happy Valentine's, sweetheart.' That was it. The detonator. That sentimental soundbite was like dropping a bomb into a fault line, or sticking your thumb up the arse of a bull. BTB went off on one.

'Johnny, open your eyes, you stupid little boy. We've had it.' BTB pushed her food away.

'Well, that's what I . . .' I tried to find rehearsed lines.

'We don't speak. When we do, we row. The wedding's a complete farce. You spend your time either trying to get away from me, or hiding behind *Mr Saturday Night*, or just not being here, Johnny.' The accusations were racking up too quickly and I couldn't keep pace.

'Hang on, slow down . . . I . . . It's not that bad.' This was not how I'd planned things.

'Johnny . . . I don't want to marry you. I don't know you any more, and I'm not sure I even love you. ' It was a soul-destroying trio of statements and it stopped me in my tracks.

247

My rehearsals, my thought-through lines and apologies, were blown away like dust from a gravestone. 'J. Riley, born 1969', it said below, as the wind whistled.

'But I . . .' I looked around, trying to find perspective, trying to find something to cling to, to stop me spiralling downward. 'But I bought you a present.' I pointed at the gaudily wrapped box on the table.

Even as she opened it, I began to realize the inappropriateness of the present. The terrible timing and the triviality of the contents.

'And what's in a present, Johnny? Some material crap? Isn't our problem a little deeper than . . . Oh, Agent Provocateur.' She recognized the pink box and seemed to twitch suddenly. 'Maddy's favourite shop. What a co-fucking-incidence Johnny.' I juddered nervously, as though a whole congregation had walked over my grave. I swallowed, thinking of the implications, trying to find an escape, an answer. BTB was ripping the box open and tearing at the black crêpe paper violently.

'Well, Johnny, what better when our relationship is on the rocks than some cheap, whory . . . red bra and knickers.' BTB's serene pale face was gone, lost, unrecognizable behind the contorted, violent replacement. She stood, holding the bra and panties against her body. 'Is this what you want, Johnny? Is this what they wear in your nasty pornographic magazines? Is that how you want me to look for you? Shove my bum in the air and stick my tits in your face? Is that it, Johnny? My, how fucking deep.'

I was silent, watching the red silk blur into BTB's face, veins pulsing, eyes burning, voice shaky and breaking. Again, maybe intervention was what she wanted. Maybe for me to stand and try to hold her, control her, interrupt and explain myself was what she wanted. But, to me, that looked as safe as stroking an injured tiger. So I stayed, pathetically rooted, potato-like.

'Eight years down the pan and your answer is that I dress up like . . . like fucking Maddy.' The word carried a sharp spiny emphasis, as BTB's lips spat it like venom and I cowed. 'Your solution is a quick shag, is it, Johnny?' She looked at me, pausing for a response for the first time.

'I . . .' It was a chance, an opportunity to try to put things right. But I was too slow, missing it like the hairline slash of a shooting star that someone else wishes upon.

'Shall I put them on now, Johnny? Maybe a good fuck right here on the table will sort us out?'

'No . . .' I was about to launch into my series of apologies and explanations, but the pause was too brief for my strangled mind. Last chance lost to BTB's anger-powered, chainsaw mind.

'No . . . no, you don't want to have sex? Why? Because we never have sex any more, do we, Johnny?'

I managed to shake my head, hoping it was the right thing to do.

'But then, that must be because I don't look like a whore. Is that it, Johnny?'

'No . . . I . . .'

'Mind you, why should you care? You probably wank away happily to yourself with Colin's porn, isn't that right, Johnny?'

'No . . .' I tried to keep up with the non-stop barrage of questions, exploding like flak clouds all around me.

'No? You don't wank?' She was on an unstoppable melt-down, a one-woman cavalry charge. 'Don't wank? Don't have sex with me? My, what do you do with all that testosterone, Johnny?' She paused for impact. For a second, we were inside the eye of the hurricane. The silence settled, feathers after a pillow fight. My snail brain caught up with what she was going to say.

'Oh, let me guess, you're fucking Maddy, aren't you? And I bet she loves this cheap shit, loves playing the whore. Does she wear this for you, Johnny?' She waved the red silk. 'Does she wear this while you take her from behind? Does she tie you up and sit on your face?' It was like watching a demonic possession as she spat and swore.

'No . . . there's nothing—'

'Don't deny it, Johnny, what do you take me for? I know it's true, you bastard. Ruth told me all about you and Maddy. Why don't you give this to her? She loves it. In fact . . .' For the first time, BTB looked at the underwear closely, scrutinizing the label on the bra; her reaction was like a damn bursting. 'In fact . . .' Hot, prickly tears streamed down her distorted face, as if it was final confirmation of the truth, the last damning piece of evidence. Finally, all of BTB's doubt and anger welled up inside her like lava, overflowing the brim and releasing itself in a huge melancholy back-draught. Between deep, lurching sobs, she managed to say weakly, 'It's her size anyway, Johnny.' With the same will-lost resignation, she threw the underwear at me. 'It's her size, Johnny. Did you get our presents mixed up?' She sniffed. 'Or is this an outfit she's already got?' BTB had backed against the wall, leant and raised her arms to cover her face. She looked like a lost little girl. I decided to make my move, my gesture.

Standing and moving towards her, I said, 'It's not like that. There's nothing between me and Maddy.' I reached out to try to hold her shoulders, shaking in time to her sobs. 'You should know that. For God's sake, she's your friend. I mean, just ring Maddy. Ask her.'

'Don't you dare touch me, Johnny.' BTB's tiny fist rose like a startled bird and jabbed the bridge of my nose, sending a sudden rush of pain through my head. Raising my hand to my nose, the blood filled my palm. 'Now get out. Get the fuck out of my life, Johnny Riley,' she said coldly. I stood, stunned and motionless. 'Johnny, I'm leaving you. Now get out,' she repeated.

*

Looking outside, the rain had stopped. Everything was the colour of lead. Inside, Mr Big's cheeks were wet and his button eyes were red-rimmed, like wounds. The car stopped outside the entrance to the Gatwick Express. A plane flew low overhead and Mr Big looked nauseous. I wondered who would help the now-drunk bulk through his troubled journey. The door unlocked automatically. 'I'll be back. And if you have not recaptured her, then I will take your silly little neck in my hands and throttle you as though you were a sparrow. Do you hear?' I nodded, confused by the sudden change of tone from Norbert. I got out hurriedly.

'What about the script? Shall I rewrite it? Do a new one?' I remembered the reason, or at least my reason, for our meeting.

'Fuck the script, lad, it was bollocks.' A vast hand grabbed me by the collar of my crumpled grey suit, hooking a finger into a buttonhole, and holding me there in a vice. 'Firefly. Catch it, Riley. She sounds too precious, too fleeting. Get her back . . . OR I'LL RIP OUT YOUR TONGUE WITH MY PINKIE!'

He let go and pulled the door shut. I stood, shocked, on the pavement. This was not a peaceful saint. This was an axe-wielding crusader. The car began to pull away, then stopped and reversed back towards me. I considered running. The window opened once again, and Mr Big peered out, proffering another of his rare business cards. 'And perhaps you would give this to your friend, Colin. I think there may be a film in him.' The window shut and the car pulled away. I watched it roll around a long, slow corner in the distance.

I stood on the pavement in the cold, and the mobile I'd clutched all afternoon in the same hand rang. I recognized the number on the display. 'Hello, Mum, you're not going to believe what's just happened to me.'

Mum sounded weary, and fixed on forcing out her words rather than listening to mine. 'Granny Victor's died, Johnny.

I'm sorry, love. She passed away just a few hours ago, this morning, at the hospital. Her heart finally gave in. Dad was with me.'

I stood in the rain, looking for somewhere to shelter, somewhere to sit, listening to Mum. 'We were there together, your father and I. He was lovely, Johnny, your father. I was proud of Henry. He just held her hand and mine, and encouraged me to tell Mum stories of how happy I'd been as a child. And he told us both how hard he'd tried to win her over when he was courting me, and how he knew she'd disapproved. But that he was glad he'd never let me go. She smiled when he told her he'd always look after me, and that she should forget about our arguments, as we would always be together. And she asked after you, Johnny. Said we should all look after each other, and that you were a good lad, even though you reminded her of Dad and Jonah. And that you mustn't let that young lady of yours get away; she said she was far too special.'

I don't know how long I stayed on the pavement, in the cold, listening to Mum. I don't know when I started, or stopped, crying. Nor when I finally said goodbye, and that I'd be there as soon as possible, sounding brave for Mum.

I could think of only one place of safety. I knew the landscape, the geography, of BTB's body as if I had created it myself. But there was one special place, the place at the base of her throat, that delicate hollow between her collarbones. And I knew, I knew after eight years, that I could rest the base of my own chin in that hollow, and slot my crown beneath her chin, and there feel an all-encompassing comfort that must be equivalent to the completely protective surroundings of an unborn child. BTB would blow on my cheeks and stroke my eyelashes with her fingertips, and there, nothing could harm me. I stood on the pavement and wept for my hollow, my place of safety.

Departed

I'd never been a pall-bearer before. Never carried the delicate, morbid calling card in the top pocket of my best suit jacket before. A black-crossed reminder of the position you should take when the time comes and the priest calls your number.

The responsibility of the role weighed heavily, distracting me from my grief, from the cold facts of the situation, smooth pebbles in my pockets. The setting, too, defied expectations. The Cornwall cemetery crowned a small hill, a good hundred yards from the church and its original crowded ground, on the edge of the town. An overflow, built to accommodate the war dead, the stone dyke-walled grave-yard already jostled with headstones.

Beforehand, I'd imagined it all as dramatic, funereally majestic. Imagined rain and greyness, imagined tolls and tears and slow movements. But our small gathering of family and friends was bathed in spring sunshine like a bank holiday break. Buds clumped and edged nervously at the walls and beds, the fresh smell of the wind carrying the taste of the sea, the ever-present gulping of gulls. It was light and bright, with a pale-blue sky and a white, uncertain sun which lit the sea with silver.

It was the first time I'd seen BTB since I'd found out about Granny Victor. I'd seen her arrive, graceful and pale in a formal black suit, flanked by her father and two tougher brothers, Jack and Paddy. Leaving them at the back of the church, she slipped like a whisper into the pew next to me, gently pushing a gloved little finger into my clutched angry hands.

Through the bellyful of emotional sickness, through the memories of Granny Victor, I realized I owed her something additional in death. Only a happening this severe could have impacted upon my floundering relationship. We weren't speaking. I had moved out. BTB was on the verge of dismantling everything, unpicking the threads of our togetherness.

We had spoken, of course. Eventually, the day after I'd found out about Granny Victor, BTB had called me on the mobile, when I was already rattling on a train to Cornwall. Sat at Gatwick, in the rain, the night before, I had tried her everywhere – at home, at Ruth's, at Trish's, at her parents' – without success. Devoid of my hollow, I had packed and left for Cornwall, in autocoma-shock.

'Johnny, I'm so sorry.' Strangely, in the rock of the carriage across the Bristol plains, her voice brought no comfort, purely because it was so distant.

'Where the fuck were you?' A shocked old lady opposite shuffled as I swore.

'Johnny, I'm sorry I wasn't in. I'm sorry I wasn't there, but . . .'

'Where were you?'

'Johnny, I'm sorry, I'll be with you as soon as I can.'

She refused to answer, and I still didn't know where she'd gone that evening. Where to and why my guardian, my safety net, had suddenly disappeared. I still didn't know, but suspicion clouded my mind, like a shadow on an X-ray. I spoke to her over the days leading up to the funeral and she continued to sidestep my question and, as a result, to spite her, I put her off coming to Cornwall.

'Don't bother, I don't need you there,' I'd said, stubbornly, the reverse in my mind. In the event, she'd ignored me and spoken to Mum, who had insisted she come down, and knew that I'd need her.

BTB threaded her arm through mine and walked with me behind the hearse, from the church to the grave. 'I'm glad you're here,' I said. Ahead of us, Mum and Dad braced each other.

'I couldn't not be, Johnny. She was an extraordinary woman.' She reached up, stroking the haphazard fringe from my eyes.

'What about us?' I asked. 'Are we OK? You know.' I tripped on my words, but she knew what I was asking. She knew, in my wordless way, I was asking if we were together, if we were getting hitched or not. She smiled gently and turned her head into my shoulder, tightening her hold on my arm.

'Let's talk about it later, Johnny.' I determined not to waste precious moments with BTB being vague. This could be a final chance to straighten things out, to be direct and ask those ugly questions lurking in the back of my mind before it was too late. Today, BTB would hear only the essentials, only the black stuff left behind when all the water was boiled away.

Like the beach, like the fields and cliffs and crannies around Cawsand, the cemetery was yet another place of mis-spent youth. An escape place from adult eyes, to indulge in things adult. We used to call it Boot Hill, but I don't think I ever realized where I'd stood. Alone, or with friends or girl-friend, trysts and truants, we had looked hard, looked so hard it hurt, but never at the ground beneath our feet. Always elsewhere: deep into the eyes of the latest love, words poetic, mind on the brassiere catch. Surreally, into puff-smoke clouds, making shapes from nothing, no sense of the preciousness of time. Longingly, at the crack of sea/sun horizon in the distance, aiming for beyond, bored of the here

255

and now. Profoundly, at the speckled vast everness of stars, a hunger for the unanswerable. Pupil-stretched, at whisky and cider and cigarettes and solvents, at grass and resin, at porn and football cards. But never to the soil, never considering the significance of the place. Back then, it was simply shelter, a wall, a seat, a haven from the wind whipping off the sea.

Now it would always be the place where the memory of Granny Victor lay. Now the clutter of granite and marble clamoured for attention, stating names and lives in chiselled summary, distilled to simplicity.

In loving memory of Victoria Elizabeth Stephenson, born 1902, died 1999, wife of Jonah James Stephenson, born 1892, died 1968, leaving a daughter, Janet.

In twenty-three words the unimaginably huge catalogue of a life. But what really was the sum total of Granny Victor? Granny Victor, who'd latterly lost her marbles and sworn at me comically, who'd scolded and spanked the living daylights out of me as a six-year-old, left a dying blue bony cat called Wedgwood behind, like a ghost. Despised the liberated thoughts of the generations below her own. Taught me the ivory secrets of mah-jong with a tender patience. Nursed me tirelessly through a fever when I was ten. Married a man ten years her senior, who'd swept her off her feet and drank himself to death. Seen a world without cars, danced with King Edward, journeyed on the *QE2* and refused, with her husband, to accept that men had ever landed on the moon or evolved from apes.

Sentences from a single perspective on a life; like one tiny surface among the millions on a random hunk of quartz.

The reality, the heaviness of coffin, the body, as you lower, cord through hand after hand, is the exhalation of finality. If, against the odds, you haven't considered what is happening, it is then that it brutally registers. You know that you are lowering the totality of a previous existence into the cold earth. The strain on your palm, which runs through your arms and into your shoulders, is caused by nothing but body and bone and casket. Nothing but Granny Victor.

That was the point at which I lost it, stepping back into the space beside BTB, my chin quivering, shoulders shuddering, the brevity of life, the importance of living, being, doing, loving, spinning around my head.

BTB placed me in her hollow and the tears flowed. My thoughts and emotions converged on the concern that the life cycle of a dragonfly is unimaginably fractional.

'It's not right. We're not right apart,' I mumbled.

'No . . . no, Johnny, I can't stand it, either.' I was sure I could see hope and relief in her eyes, too. Sure I could sense that she, like me, wanted, needed repair.

'Are you staying?' I whispered hopefully, through the embrace.

'For the wake? Or do you mean after, Johnny?' she answered.

'Both,' I said.

'I'm going home with Dad and the boys tonight, but I'll stay a while, Johnny. I guess we need to talk. Are you all right?' She held me back, her hands on my shoulders, looking me up and down to see if I passed the test.

'Yeah. Yeah, I think so.' I rocked back, legs rubbery, body dislocated.

Around me, the dark suits and powdered faces dispersed softly. Dad, formal and stiff, was thanking the priest and shaking hands with a few mourners. Mum stood near by, looking other-worldly.

'I'm just going to see Janet, Johnny. You sure you're OK?' Standing in the bright light, I watched BTB touch my mother lightly on the shoulder, watched Mum smile suddenly, revived, and overheard their conversation from a distance.

'I am glad you're back together. So pleased. Mother was so happy you were to be married.' Mum glanced at me as she spoke. BTB's words, out of earshot and lost in the wind, escaped me. For once I was pleased to have Mum's direct approach, the same approach that had embarrassed me so often as a child: *'My Johnny seems quite taken with your daughter, Mrs Giblets.'* Secret love instantly shattered.

I watched BTB comfort Mum, and then Dad, who joined them and let BTB hug him, possibly pulling an unseen tear, glimmering in the sunshine. I noticed Clark, the orange neighbour, looking edgy and well pressed in his best suit. He hovered uncertainly on the boundaries of the family, before reconsidering and fading back into the crowd, leaving my family to our grief for the time being.

Standing in the graveyard, having laid a batty, magnificent woman to rest, I knew now, more than ever, my needs. All these stones covered lives, the brutal basics. A headstone bearing nothing more than twenty words or so: born, died, wife, children. That's all. Not born, died, wife, children, four girlfriends at school, two at college, EF&Co and a couple of mediocre film scripts. And why not? Why no elaboration? Because life is the simple things. Life is births, marriages and deaths. And that can be beautiful or tragic, absurd or mundane.

And there, standing on the wet trampled grass ahead of me, was my life. The three adults chatting and consoling, the sea glittery in the distance – that was my headstone, my simple summary.

About to walk over to join them, I became aware of a presence at either shoulder. Two too-close overcoats.

'Jack, Paddy. How are you?'

BTB's brothers nodded, muttering politely. 'Sorry about your grandmother.' We stood in a row, silently, hands held respectfully to our front, heads bowed. Jack stepped aside and I felt a powerful lean hand grip my right shoulder, vice-like. I didn't need to turn to know who it was. Gerry Donnelly leant in close and whispered, 'At times like these family becomes important, eh, lad?' The whiff of whisky and the deep rattle in his throat were familiar.

'Mmm,' I said solemnly.

'You join our family and we'll always be there for you, lad, you know that?' he continued.

'Thank you,' I said weakly.

'Nothing to do with you, son, but that's my daughter over there. She's upset, I'm upset. She's happy, I'm happy. Understand?' His hand gripped more tightly.

'Yes . . . yeah, I understand,' I said, shoulder buckling slightly. I tried not to grimace as BTB, Mum and Dad waved at us from the far side of the grave. Mr Donnelly waved with his free hand.

'Wave, lads.' The two brothers and myself waved awkwardly.

'Be right over,' he shouted, before finishing, whispering throatily in my ear. 'Now, I don't know what you've done to my daughter, but I do know that if it's something you can't fix, you'll need fixing yerself soon enough. But like I say, if marrying you makes her happy, and you join our family, all you've got to do is keep her that way and we'll look out for you, son. You understand?' He released his grip and patted me on the shoulder.

'I . . . yes I do,' I stuttered.

'Right, I'll pay my respects to your parents, lad.' He turned to face me, his eyes wild through deep fissures, straightening his tie and reaching out to shake my hand. 'Only met your grandmother the once, lad, but I'll never forget her. If I get past ninety with a pinch of her passion, I'll be happy, son.' Temporarily blocking the sun, the three men walked slowly away.

I paused before following, trying to unravel my thoughts on family, on mortality and on the Donnellys. Had I just been embraced, welcomed into a family? Was this the Donnelly way of showing me respect? Or was it a straightforward threat? Hurt my daughter and we'll hurt you. And while I was shaken, was that so wrong? Or just natural, just flesh and blood? As they walked into the frame of my headstone summary and mixed with my own family, I saw the strength, the loyalty, the permanence of the Donnelly way.

Wedgwood sat sullenly on the mantel, brittle and stubborn, dying. Waiting for Granny Victor to return, the cat sneered at the sherry-sipping, snack-munching crowd, gradually gaining the confidence to talk loudly and tell stories about Granny Victor.

With BTB on my arm, we toured the room like honorary guests at a function. Adopting learnt stances, repeating practised niceties, we smiled and shook hands, accepted consoling pats on the shoulder and hearty handshake congratulations in advance of the wedding. BTB disappeared now and then to help refill plates of sausage rolls and vol-au-vents, while I refilled glasses with sherry and whisky.

Smoke, from cigars and pipes and the crackling fire in the grate, rose and clouded the room. Muttley snuffled and snuck between legs, finding treasured scraps of food or plates and drinks, unguarded on the floor, to steal.

Grief came like tiredness, in sudden sickening waves, wearing me down and blackening my eyes. I was conscious of BTB watching me closely, concerned.

Midway through a wave, caught rubbing my eyes into their sockets, trying to massage them back to life, I felt her catch my arm; 'You need some fresh air. Come on, love.'

'He's happy.' BTB laughed at Muttley's capers. We sat, entwined in the cooling light, together on an old favourite flat rock, an overgrown, pitted lump of shortbread, sheltered at the back of the beach. Muttley ran in circles, stopping and starting suddenly, leaping and diving, chasing his shadow and splashing in pools. Every once in a while he would return to us, challenging us to play, head on paws, nose in the sand, a manic look on his face, seemingly uncontrollable snorts bursting out of him. Our breath billowed in the cold as the little warmth the spring sun had mustered lost its heat in the late afternoon.

'Hasn't seen us together in weeks, has he? That's what he's dancing about,' I mused, BTB's head resting on my shoulder as we watched Muttley gallivanting. 'I'd be doing the same if I thought we were permanent,' I continued, conscious of the need to know, to clarify. 'Where were you the other night?' I clenched my jaw and looked hard into eyes that matched the sea.

'When? When Granny Victor died?' The question had hung over us all day, as if we both knew something we wished we didn't. As if we knew a murder had been committed, or a wrong-doing done that we couldn't discuss.

'Yes.' I had a clarity of thought and action that had no need of elaboration and waffle, rambling and disorientation. BTB was visibly thrown by my attitude and tone, by my focus.

'With Stef,' she said, simply.

'What?' I wasn't shocked. It had to be something sinister, something out of the ordinary, for her not to have told me instantly. For BTB to have waited until we were face to face and certain of one another's emotional state.

'Out with Stef, for a meal. A meal with Stef.' She held my eye contact, knowing it was how I would measure her truthfulness.

'What for?' I was determined not to show panic or anger or jealousy. Determined, with my new-found certainty, to approach this problem with appropriate discipline. I had to give BTB the chance to defend herself that she had denied me in the emotional furnace of Valentine's Day.

'We've been out for meals before, Johnny. He's my friend, too, you know.'

This was absolutely true. As was the fact that Stef had never made it a secret that he fancied BTB. At times, when it suited him or her, and in a mainly light-hearted and non-threatening way, these sentiments were played out in public as a joke. You know, the if-you-get-bored-of-Johnny-you-know-who-to-call crack.

'What happened?' I held my calm, looking across the waves as the sun courted the sea, toying and tempting.

'What do you mean, What happened? Nothing happened. We ate pizzas at Pizza Express is what happened.' BTB was firm, answering questions, holding my gaze, offering transparency.

I sat for a long time, considering this. Out with Stef. Why should I be even slightly bothered by this? She and Stef had been out together a hundred times, so why should it bother me now? It shouldn't, but something nagged, like an itch, under a wound's new skin, something felt wrong. Maybe it was circumstance. BTB had never been out with Stef when she was single, when she had thrown out her fiancé, whom she'd accused of sleeping with her best friend, when she was vulnerable. This state of mind was an unknown, for me and for her, and importantly, particularly importantly, for Stef. I would have felt safe if she was with Colin or Merl, just not with Stef. It was an instinct, a character judgement. 'Look, I need to know. I need to know that nothing happened, that it was all platonic stuff,' I pressed.

'Johnny, it was . . . it was in my mind anyway.' It was a waver, a wobble, a lapse in concentration which I pounced on.

'What the hell does that mean? "In my mind." What did he . . . ?'

'Look, forget it, Johnny. Nothing happened; just leave it.' She realized her mistake and worked hard to regain control, closing the shutters quickly. 'Nothing, Johnny, just forget it. Nothing happened, OK.' Palms held to my face, instructing me to drop it, to trust her. I had to. Think about my situation here. Imagine a diplomatic incident between countries. I simply couldn't continue my current line of questioning indefinitely without wrecking the relationship permanently *'So you're sure you're not supplying arms to the horrible dictatorship? You're certain? Sure? Absolutely sure? Cross your heart and hope to die? Stick a needle...'* At some point you have to let go. I had to avoid condemning BTB in the way she'd condemned me. I had to hold the moral high ground, for there was precious little else I owned. BTB was surprised by my directness, but the day had dragged me that way.

'OK, I'll leave it. I trust you. I'm not sure about him, but I trust you, and, likewise, you should trust me. Do you?' I returned to my original plan of action.

'What, you mean you and Maddy? . . . She came over yesterday.'

'So you know there's nothing,' I confirmed.

'I guess.' BTB squirmed, reluctantly.

'Come on.' I forced the issue.

'OK, I believe you, Johnny. I still don't know what on earth you do over there but—'

'Look, I'll tell you if you want. It'll ruin the—'

'The surprise. Yeah, I know, that's what she said, and forget it, if it's a surprise for me, fine, I trust you . . . I think.' She smiled mischievously.

'So, where does that leave us?' A bored, wet, shivering Muttley returned, pushing himself between our legs, expecting attention.

'Where do you want it to leave us, Johnny?'

'Am I moving back in? Are we getting married? Is everything OK again?' I looked at BTB calmly, certain of my aims and intentions. Clear on what I wanted and needed. BTB looked confused, and I realized I'd been speaking with a different tone and had said the 'M' word without even thinking.

'Er . . . well, I, suppose . . . I . . . I'm not sure, Johnny.'

'Listen, nothing happened between me and Maddy, there's nothing going on with me and anyone. Just you. That's it, understand?' I held a hand to her cheek, feeling the burn of blood vessels below the surface.

'Johnny . . . I . . .'

'No, listen, you ran the show last time, you threw me out without letting me get my words out, and I'm not having it this time. Life's too short, I know that now . . . after today. Life's way too short to let your . . . to let things go . . . so . . . so I know buying underwear was bollocks but . . .'

'It's not that.' BTB shook her head, a vague smile playing on her lips.

'Yeah, hang on, let me finish. And I know I'm useless with the wedding and the bills, and telling you what I think, and being a grown-up and . . . and everything . . . but I'll try to be better; I'll try to grow up a bit.'

Muttley barked loudly in support.

'You will?' BTB laughed, surprised by my show.

'But I'll always be Johnny Riley. You know that, don't you?' She cocked her head and frowned a little, reminding me of Muttley.

'I'll always be me. I'll buy you the wrong-sized bra, insult your parents, forget our anniversary, I'll . . . I'll try, but I'll always be me.' She looked away, watching the sunset fizzle and creak in amber and gold.

'I don't know, Johnny . . . I don't know.' She stood to walk away.

'No.' I caught her cuff and pulled her back on to the rock, and was met with yet another look of surprise.

'Not this time. No walking away, no having the last word, no uncertainties. We're on, or we're not. I've lost you, or I've got you for ever. Nothing in between.' BTB's eyes softened in a way I'd never seen before, watery in the half-light. It was the first time I remembered being so determined, so resolute. She melted into my arms on the rock.

'Will you marry me?' No stuttering, no Spanish, no joke.

'Yes. Yes, Johnny.'

Depraved

The men stood in a huddle, joking, shuffling, knocking back the standard Oranjeboom served in the Dutch pub. The sun was weak and grey, and the air carried the sickly whiff of monosodium glutamate, rising from the drains, bins and basements of the rows of Chinese restaurants on Gerard Street.

I had to admit they'd done a fine job, Merlin and Maddy. The hen and stag were both in Soho, kicking off on Saturday lunchtime the week before D-Day, both separate yet interwoven, tacky, hip, sordid and sophisticated. A couple of nasty lurid cocktails: a Strawberry Daiquiri for her and a Long Island Iced Tea for me.

Thinking about it, it was well engineered, well planned. Maddy and Merlin must have stolen a fair amount of time together sorting it all out. I only kind of know what happened to the girls, but as I discovered, updates were an all-too-vivid twist to the day. I remembered how it started – harmless and normal, like any Saturday afternoon with the lads.

Mixed in with the smell of rotting noodles and special fried rice was the scent of expectancy. Like soldiers lying in the peaceful dawn mist of jungle grass, the certainty of battle ahead; like cowboys draining treacle coffee from tin cups, a cattle drive and a horizonful of rolling plains before them.

That was me and the boys outside De Hemms in China Town. Me, Merlin, Ratty, Colin and Stef, all soldiers or cowboys . . . or maybe just a bunch of rough-looking lads with a day of drunken debauchery ahead?

The men had followed their instructions, turning out in shirts, trousers and shoes; smart enough to get into sad establishments, trendy enough to get into cooler venues. It was a hard call, which Merlin really had to push, especially with Colin, who ended up being dragged out for a forced threads-sorting afternoon. The result was that everyone looked slightly too spangly. Slightly too well pressed and off the shelf.

'You know, I still can't believe you won't move the bloody wedding so we can watch the match.' Inevitably, Stef's lament returned.

'Act of God, Stef. Can't blame Johnny it was put back. Anyway, saves you the trouble of deciding who to support for another week.' Merlin patiently batted the whinges away.

'Gotta be the Eyeties, surely, Ronaldo. I'm supportin' 'em anyways, and the only Italian in me is a touch of herpes I caught in Tenerife.' Ratty happily catalogued his remarkably long list of STDs given any opportunity.

'That's not Italy, Ratty, mate.' Colin stated the obvious.

'No, the bird was though . . . an Eyetie, like,' he explained.

'Ratty, you'd support anyone over England. I heard you make up some bullshit Dutch ancestry when they were pasting us in that friendly last September.' Colin pointed the top of his green bottle accusingly at Ratty.

'Even the friggin' Krauts. Anyone above England,' Stefano agreed.

Ratty shrugged. 'Och I canna help it, it's in ma blood. I hope youse get panned next week.'

I was already bored with the ear-battering pretty much all the men invited to the wedding had given me in the last week or so. 'Look, it was an earthquake warning, right. Blame the friggin' Italian government, not me.' Mind you, it was more than a minor glitch. The stag was supposed to overlap gloriously with the match, providing a focal point, a theme. Now it clashed cruelly with the wedding and just caused trouble.

'Come on, Johnny. For your country, man, just bung Father Derek a few quid and we'll pop up a big screen in the church and start the wedding an hour and a half later, job done.' Stef was the chief whinger.

'Johnny's tried, honest. Look, we'll keep track of the score live, and have beers and a replay round at mine on Sunday. Deal?' Merl loyally defended me as the lads shrugged and muttered.

Merlin's mobile rang, 'Yup, hello love . . .' Merlin strolled off and sat on the dull, burnished metal barrier below the red mini dragon gate that cordoned off China Town. Colin whispered to me, 'Thought Ruth and him was all off.'

'Yeah it is, she's in the US. Going coast to coast in a Cadillac with two other hairdressers.' I kept my voice low.

'Fuck! Two hairdressers in a Caddy – sounds like a film. And Merl's back in the house. Is he OK?'

'Yeah, he seems happy as Larry. I mean, it could do with a good clean out, and I think most of the bills are glowing on the doormat, but I can't remember him being this happy.' It was true, Merlin was a testimony to matrimonial failure.

'So who's this? A new woman?' Colin asked, and I shrugged, ducking the response, but with a fairly good idea who it might be. What was interesting was Merlin's body language and behaviour. He was buzzing, like he'd just worked out or won a football match or something. Merlin put his phone away as he returned to the group.

'Right, lads, here's where the fun starts. That was Maddy, she knows where we are, and the girls are gonna send something over, then later on we'll repay the compliment.'

'Send what over?' Stef asked.

'I don't know, that's up to them. A message, gift, who knows. The girls get to decide, same as we will when we send one back.'

'What? What's this all about?' I was more confused than anyone and, on top of that, severely worried that, seeing as it was my stag, I'd be the butt of any scams on the go. I did not want to go home with a shaved head, or naked, or dipped in paint or . . .

'Don't worry, Johnny boy, it'll all become clear. By the way, your other half's having loadsa fun with some male strippers round the corner. Who's got the kitty?' Merlin spoke matter-of-factly while an image formed.

'Off, off, off, off!' BTB and the girls clapped and jeered as strippers dressed as firemen (London's Yearning) waved yellow helmets around.

Halfway through the second round of Oranjebooms, a disturbingly large, square-jawed, shiny man appeared in a cream mac. Looking slightly uncomfortable, he seemed to be wearing no more than a pair of trainers, a rash of lipstick marks on either cheek and bugger all else below his beige gabardine.

Keeping his distance, wary, shy or unsociable, he called over, 'Johnny Riley?' I was shoved to the front of the group as the culprit.

'Thanks, guys.' Nervously, I wondered what might be expected of me and considered the consequences of a mad dash up Shaftesbury Avenue. 'Just keep your mac on, big guy,' I called, walking slowly towards the shiny man.

'I've been asked to give you this.' The stripper stayed rooted to the spot, with no intention of taking what he must have considered a risky step towards a group of half-cut lads drinking heavily in the afternoon. He spoke plummily, and I

wondered if this was the barrel bottom in the career of a
RADA-trained actor. He handed over a flimsy white envelope
with 'The Boys' smeared in lipstick across the front. Opening
the envelope, I began to stroll back to the group, relaxing
slightly.

'One other thing,' he said. I turned, and the shiny man
furtively whipped his mac wide open, revealing a muscle-
bound, suspiciously hairless body.

'Steady, lad!' shouted Merlin, laughing.

'We don't know this man. We didn't ask him to do this,'
Colin cried out at the passers-by, tourists and shopkeepers,
who had began to pause and look on, intrigued.

'Think you huv tae work out for a physique like 'at?' Ratty
pondered, possibly to himself.

With relief, we realized it could be worse: tight rubbery
cycling shorts attempted to cover the shiny guy's crotch.
Across his stomach was a big bold cerise lipstick message.
Merlin read aloud, 'Girls just have more fu . . .' the remainder of the message was below the shorts line, and
no-one was going to ask him to reveal any more of himself.

'Reckon 'at says fun or fucks.' Ratty was always a sordid
step ahead.

'Or furniture?' Colin said thoughtfully.

Satisfied we'd had enough time to read the message, the
stripper bolted in the same direction I'd been considering
seconds before. Opening the envelope, I pulled out a fresh
Polaroid, showing BTB draped across the oiled biceps of the
five-strong London's Yearning crew. I was slack-jawed,
already feeling out-stagged by my fiancée.

'Right, lads,' Merlin rallied. 'That's it. The gauntlet has
been thrown.'

It took a good ten minutes to hatch a plan. Around the
corner, in the Trocadero, Merlin struck a deal with an instant
digital T-shirt maker. We grouped in close behind. 'Go on,

mate, we'll pay double.' Merlin and the shifty ginger shop-keeper haggled.

Happy with the price, Merlin turned back to the lads. 'See, we use these digital cameras at work, right, for brochures, like. You can take a snap and load the shot straight onto a PC, and then do whatever you want with it. And he's got one.' Merlin pointed at the shifty T-shirt man. 'Normally he uses it to superimpose, say, Johnny's face over the face of Clint Eastwood, and then prints it off as a poster or a T-shirt.'

'So we're gonna take a daft shot of Johnny, are we? And print it on a T-shirt?' Colin enthused.

'Well, we could, but basically, we can do whatever the hell we want, boys.' Merlin grinned wickedly, a plan already in mind.

After much amusement while taking the photo, and an argument about who would wield the big blue marker pen essential to the shot, the T-shirt was eventually printed. Like Maddy with her Polaroid, Merl had given plenty of advance thought to the game, with ideas for a message and means of delivery. 'Right, how about a stunning lap-dancer to deliver it?'

Two phone calls later, Merlin was speaking to a Kiwi called Tina – admin girl in Merl's company by day, moon-lighting lap-dancer by night.

The lads looked on, open-mouthed, as a svelte blonde woman wearing faded skin-tight denims strolled through the arcade, spotted Merlin and pecked him on the cheek.

''Atta boy, Merl,' Ratty muttered.

'Let's send Merl off with the T-shirt and keep Tina for our-selves,' Stef drooled.

'So I just have to wander up to these women and ask them directions?' Tina clarified.

'Yeah, yeah, that's all. Oh, but you have to wear this.'

Tina held up the T-shirt. 'B–L–U . . . hey, is this written on your . . . Awesome.' The lads looked on proudly as Tina worked out that the message, in bold blue marker-penned letters, was spelled across an ugly line-up of arses, cheek by cheek. BLUEBOYSFC glared out from the mooning butt-cheeks, printed in vivid technicolour on the photo T-shirt. Ratty held up the blue pen proudly, like a trophy, and winked at Tina. Tina examined the picture. 'Mmm, I like the end arse with FC on it, but BO in the middle's a bit spotty, and I think UE is showing a little turkey.' Colin blushed. 'Easiest fifty quid I've ever earned.' She pulled the T-shirt over her head, and blew a goodbye kiss to Merl.

'And they're in Café Boheme right now?' she checked.

'That's it, Tina. Off you go, girl.' Merlin, the stagmeister general, saluted.

Half an hour later, in the middle of a mass Formula 1 race in Segaworld, a call came through from Maddy. We swore and gesticulated from our row of black bucket seats facing flashing console screens. Merlin, losing anyway, used the distraction as an excuse to try to call the race off.

'That's it, red flag. False start. Hello?' He fumbled with the phone while Ratty and Colin, also too far off the pace to have a hope of winning, joined in with the protests for a replay.

'Bollocks!' I shouted. 'I'm winning and there's a ton riding on this.' We'd all chucked twenty quid into a sweep.

'No surrender, I'm with Johnny, keep racing.' Stef was right behind me, nudging my wheels on chicanes and trying to edge past on the straights. I veered left and right, shimmying the car on-screen to try to block Stef from overtaking.

'You bastard, Stef, that's illegal.' Stef, desperate and failing with speed or manoeuvring, piled his nose cone into my rear wheel on a corner and flipped me into a crowd of cheering pixels, which exploded dramatically. 'All's fair in love and war, eh, Johnny?' Stef accelerated away, taking the chequered flag and laughing manically.

'Bastard. Shame the race was called off,' I stirred. Nothing had been said about him and BTB, but there was an edge between us that could slice a friendship in half.

'Uh, uh.' He shook his head. 'I won, who's got the sweep?'

'Your fiancée wants a word, Johnny.' Merlin handed me the mobile, avoiding any argument between me and Stef.

'It's all off.' BTB was laughing down the phone.

'What, the wedding?' A month ago, trust fractured, love questioned, I'd have believed her.

'Yup,' she confirmed.

'Good. Why?' I chuckled.

'We've studied your T-shirt and decided that none of you has a bum as firm or as good-looking as Gary's or, in fact, any of London's Yearning.'

'That's not what Tina said when she was writing on them,' I lied.

'Oh really; that'll be Tina who's joined us for a drink. I'll just ask her, shall I?'

'Er . . . no.'

'Oh, apparently, Tina says some short Scottish bloke seemed to quite enjoy wielding the pen! You'll be hearing from us.' She alluded to our next delivery and hung up. I handed the phone back to Merlin, realizing the row about the race remained unresolved.

'Rerun,' I shouted, trying to distract my mind from the anxiety caused by the knowledge that BTB was now drinking with a lap-dancer and a herd of naked firemen.

'Really. Yeah, course I'll teach you how to lap-dance. We need some more girls down at the Windmill. OK, first you need a theme, what d'you reckon, boys?' Tina encouraged BTB.

'I think she'd make a smashing dominatrix, don't you, Brad?' Sebastian held his jaw in his hand as he spoke.

'Nope, schoolgirl – natural freckles, blond pigtails – it's you, it's perfect.'

'So where exactly d'ya buy flock wallpaper, like?' The booze was taking effect now, and Merlin was happily rambling about the first thing that came into his head. Tandoori Dreams was decorated highly originally in dark burgundy, fake brass and lit sympathetically for the assorted curry, vomit and cigarette-smoke stains.

'Come on, Johnny, just admit it, yer no' really gonna shag the same woman yer whole life, are ye?'

'Yes, Ratty.'

'Come on, I mean, I'm no' even sure the entire female gender can satisfy me.' I frowned at Ratty, presuming he was considering bestiality. 'Look, just imagine I'm yer psychologist, what are you gonna say now?'

'The same.'

'Shite. It's just no' possible.' Ratty spat tikka masala at me, refusing to accept my answer.

'Ratty, the lad's getting married in' – Stef thought for a second – 'less than a week, he has to say that.'

'Whoa, hang on, this is not "have to". I believe in this.' I was riled by Stef's dismissive tone.

'Yeah, right.' Stef raised his eyebrows and gestured a wrist-flick of disbelief. I was beginning to struggle to contain my anger.

'Listen, lads,' I held my ground, 'you are in charge, know what I mean? You fucking decide what you do or don't do, nobody else. It's all too easy to reckon your cock's some malign mind-control organ that runs the rest of your body.'

'Uh-huh.' Stef and Ratty nodded blankly.

'OK, OK, so I'm the fucking lunatic, but I'm gonna give this a go. I can't get married presuming it won't work out. What's the friggin' point!'

'Kids.' Colin had overheard our conversation, and collided head on.

'Eh?' I asked, the beer settling and setting now, jelly injected into our skulls like a mould.

'Kids,' he repeated. 'Listen, listen, before I get too comatose.' Colin staggered to his feet, Kingfisher in hand, 'I have an announcement.' Colin was swaying badly. 'As you know, Trish and me have had our ups and downs.' Colin spoke formally, double chin lodged in his chest to stem a belch.

'Aye, she gets down trying to get you up,' Ratty heckled.

'And we're back together now.' Colin waded on through the jeers.

'Thank you, Billy the Fun FM beaver,' I joined in.

'But . . . well . . . I'm going to be . . . a dad.' The word didn't really fit into the curried surroundings.

'Jesus!' I swore through sag aloo.

'Oh fuck! Cloughy's kids, that sounds like a dangerous gene-pool problem.' Stef blithely took the piss and made me want to punch him.

'Excellent . . . that's just . . . wow!' Merlin incoherently summed up my thoughts. None of us had a benchmark here. We didn't really have any experience of this event as a group. Colin was the first father-to-be, and it was a strange moment. A life-changer with no instructions.

'So . . . so here's to life, love and happiness. Here's to Johnny next weekend. May your rod be long, firm and well staffed.'

Colin's smile and sense of humour were well worn these days. His brief flame of fame as the nation's Mr Lover-Lover had already faded from the public's fickle attention span. What was left behind was a confident, sorted Colin. As thick-skinned and emotionally myopic as ever, but happy, positive, accepted.

We raised glasses and bottles. I stood, automatically, to

give some sort of ad-libbed return toast. 'To Colin, Trish and the best news I could imagine for the pair, soon to be three, in fact, of them . . .' I faltered. 'Congratulations, Colin, mate.' Another chink-clink of glasses, lager slopping over bhajees and naan bread.

The table quickly disintegrated into muttering. 'Think I'll get me tubes tied 'fore that.' Ratty winced.

I leant back, removing myself from the mêlée, and looked across at Colin. He stared into the middle-distance, a Cheshire Cat's grin spreadeagled across his face. His eyes, his bearing, his manner, all those of a convert, someone who has worked out all the answers, or perhaps the right questions. Someone who knows the measure of the world that surrounds him, and is happy with its dimensions.

'You are the luckiest man alive, Johnson Riley.' Tina slumped on to my lap, still svelte, but now sweetly trolleyed after an afternoon with the hen party.

'Wey-hey, Tina's back. Do us a lap-dance then, love.' Stef leered, beerful and lairy.

'Piss off, you dirty sod, I'm off-duty.' Tina subtly stuck two fingers up at Stef, before adding, 'Alternatively, come and see me later at the Windmill,' as if remembering her business conscience. 'But no lap-dancing for you, Mr Riley.' Tina playfully tweaked my cheek. 'Oh no, your wife-to-be's all too lovely for that.'

'Great, just great. Merl, my wife-to-be's the lap-dancer's best mate. I don't think this was s'posed to happen, was it?'

'This is for you.' She handed over another expected envelope, addressed plainly, with the word 'Johnny' in signature cerise lipstick.

'So they liked the T-shirt?' I asked Tina, opening the envelope.

'Oh yeah, but I think London's Yearning preferred it. She gave it to one of them; Sebastian I think his name is. He's wearing it tonight. Asked if you could get some more copies;

reckons it could become quite culty down at Club Slippy,' Tina babbled.

'What?' Stef made an offended grunt. 'Hang on, you're saying our arses are now on the chest of a gay bloke who's clubbing tonight?' Stef really wasn't happy with this prospect.

'Yes, at Club Slippy. My, you're a fiery one. What's your name?' Tina winked at Stef.

'Clubbing? In Soho?' Stef was incredulous.

'He's Stef, by the way,' Ratty answered for him.

'Yes, Stef, Sebastian has your pert little butt plastered against his nipples and six-pack, and is probably already sweating it see-through to some hard-core dance.' Tina took great delight in the detail as Stef moaned and buried his bald head in his hands.

'So . . . er . . . we'll be sort o' famous, like? In this . . . er . . . this gay place?' Ratty addressed Tina intently. 'And . . . er . . . where is this Slippy place exactly?'

'Jesus! What's she done? Bloody hell!' I stared in shock at the two photos in my hand.

'Ha ha,' Tina laughed. 'She said you'd lose it.'

'Oh my God. What's her mum gonna say? Jesus!' The first photo was BTB outside a tattoo parlour on Berwick Street. The second quite clearly showed BTB's shoulder adorned with a bright-red love heart and the word 'Johnny' in black Gothic script scrolled diagonally across it, as BTB smiled with pride, like some biker's babe.

'Look. Fuck!' I passed the photos around.

'Foxy,' said Merl drunkenly.

Colin was more conservative. 'She can't do that,' he said.

'Too late, boy, she's gone and done it.' Tina giggled.

'Fuck! What about her dress? You know, she must have a dress that covers her shoulders next week, otherwise it'll be on show, and I'm not sure they're not still scabby after a week, and . . .' I wittered, bewildered.

'Dress?' Ratty was as confused by my concerns as any non-groom would be. Blissfully unaware that, to the bride, the dress takes on an importance that would overshadow an alien invasion. 'Yeah, you know she keeps it locked away in the spare room. The room I can't enter, so I've no bloody idea what it looks like, but—'

'Mr bloody boring. Tattoos are great.' Tina strutted. 'I've got one.'

'Yeah, I thought you liked tattoos, Johnny?' Ratty was right, I did. I'd always thought they were sexy, and had spent hours trying to persuade BTB to have one at Eddie the Rainbow's parlour. In fact, an early dream wedding for me was a tacky Vegas Elvis-impersonating priest and a tattoo-swapping ceremony. I don't think I ever managed to get the bottle together to suggest this before everything went all white and sepia and trad.

'Let's see your tattoo then, Tina?' Stef slavered pathetically.

Tina bounced off Stef's lap and began to unbutton her jeans, stuck her backside in Stef's direction, to his obvious pleasure, and hooked her thumbs into the belt loops. She looked back at Stef with a cruel smile and said, 'It's in a very special place, Stef.' Tina dummied pulling the jeans down before jumping back up, turning around and saying, 'Whoops, I'm off duty. Like I said, see you at the Windmill.' She kissed her fingers and planted her hand on Stef's cheek, who was left looking boyishly frustrated. Buttoning herself up, she turned to me. 'You behave, Johnny Riley, you're a lucky man.' Tina kissed me on the cheek as she sauntered out of the flock and burgundy cave.

After two pints, to wash down the curry, in the spit and saw-dust of the Glassblower, Stef became uncontrollable. 'Come on, we might be missing Tina's set. Let's go, let's go.' Staggering through the alleyways, neon noise and flickering puddles of Soho, I found myself walking next to Stef, as

Colin, Merl and Ratty straggled behind, or stopped to look and laugh through tasselled doorways and seedy club entrances.

'Stef.' Stef strode like a man on a mission. 'You know you went out that night when we'd split up, me and the . . .'

' "Wife". Ha, you nearly said "wife", me and "the wife". Jesus, Johnny, this is seminal stuff. Fuck! Me and the wife.' He laughed, shaking his head. My anger continued to well, silently.

'Well, I . . . You've always fancied her, haven't you?' Stef looked at me sideways, searching for anger. He shrugged. I kept my emotions and expressions in check, sealed tightly in a cellophane wrap.

'I guess, Johnny. She's got something about her, y'know . . . but nothin' happened, Johnny. I'd never do that. We're mates, all of us, mates.' Stef swept his arm in the vague direction of the lads dallying behind. 'Never diss your mates, you know that, Johnny.' I nodded, clenching my teeth, swallowing the wrap. 'You know, mates are a for ever thing. Never fall out over women, Johnny.' Stef put his arm around my shoulder and hugged me hard. We paused briefly, looking up at the huge neon Windmill.

'I guess we're here,' I said. We waited for the lads to catch up.

'Heads up, lads. Look sober and sophisticated, we are about to enter the sweetie shop.' Stef brushed himself down as two hefty bouncers in black bomber jackets clocked us.

'Hope it's no' too tame,' Ratty muttered as we filed through the club doorway and were checked to ensure we were properly attired and not too improperly pissed.

Inside, it felt like a Hollywood gangster flick, moody lights, pulsating music, a long sweeping mirror-and-chrome bar, surrounded by table after tableful of men, mainly focused on a large pole-impaled stage, or distracted by their own show as a girl gyrated privately for their table.

The light veiled the tawdry surroundings supremely. The men, when you looked hard, were not gangsters, but Japanese tourists, pasty-faced brokers on stag dos and birthdays, and dodgy-looking bulldogs. These guys, the middle-aged men in immaculate suits, heavyweight, pockmarked, with shaven heads, looked like regulars. They also looked in need of a lot more than topless dancing before they'd get their fix and head back to dreary London suburbs, wives and children.

Likewise, from a few feet, aided by the light, spatula-applied make-up and drink-broken focus of the men's eyes, the women were goddesses. Peroxide wigs, sequinned boob tubes, impossibly tight short skirts, long leather boots and stilettos, all squeezing and prodding, jutting and cutting into bodies.

'Nirvana,' Stef muttered, now pretty much arseholed.

'The best table, please, madam.' Merlin thrust a twenty into the palm of the hostess, who guided us, sliding on rollers, to a vacant round table in the middle of the club.

From the depths of the circle of sunken red-leather seats, Merl attempted to police the rapidly deviating men. 'Look, guys, you're on your own now. The kitty's bought the entrance fee and the first round, but that's a hundred and fifty gone already. So whatever else you want, you'll have to pay for yourself. Then there's beer back at Johnny's later, OK?'

'Where's all the friggin' women, like?' Ratty was right to point out that, for a lap-dancing club, the essential ingredient seemed to be a bit thin on the ground. A few minutes later our question was answered as a sort of show kicked off. It involved all the dancing girls coming on stage *en masse* as spotlights swung across them, followed by freestyle dancing as the music blared out. It was like watching a single-sex fantasy disco from the naff heights of the Eighties. Lots of women dancing in far less than they would normally wear and no daft-looking blokes getting in the way, dancing like pillocks or trying to cop off with the women.

As the spotlight ranged across the waving girls, wearing false smiles, glazed eyes and battered dignities like costumes, you could see that they had themes and styles which maybe they'd invented, or maybe were one of the club's stockpile of standard sexy outfits. Hand-me-down costumes, from girls gone upward and onward to Paul Raymond's revue bar, with dreams of the West End, or downward, shunted off the ladder by a younger body.

Stef's blurry eyes somehow managed to spot Tina, buried at the back, swaying a little too much after a day's drinking, dressed as a cowgirl, dancing badly and hanging onto one of the metal poles.

'Right, I'm saving her till last,' Stef planned, and I was reminded of childhood paper bags of penny sweets, eaten in worst to best, painstakingly thought through and ordered. Cola cubes last and powdery-pink candy shellfish first.

Stef and Ratty quickly found out just how profitable the place was. It was like turning a tap on in your bank account and watching the money pour out. After two tame table dances, they realized, fifty quid too late, that the dancers' tops stayed on, and discovered that, for double the money, all their kit came off in a room at the back. From that point on, the two would shuffle off through a sequin-covered curtain every half-hour, looking more jaded and jagged every time.

'So how do you feel, mate?' I was fascinated by Colin's changed circumstances.

'I don't know, just feels weird.' He carried a wistful look.

'Weird, but good sort of weird, like, mate?' Merlin lit another cigarette.

'Everything's different, you know.' He pushed his drink aside, so that he could use his hands to gesture. 'Everything changes. All this, like,' he pointed at us, the bar and the velvet and leather surround, 'just doesn't matter.' I tried to break through Colin's opaque words.

'Like what changes? How does it change?' I probed.

'I don't want to do this. No offence. I mean, I'm having fun and all that, Johnny, but I want to be looking after Trish. I want her to be OK, kept safe and sorted.' We nodded, trying to understand.

'And also, I feel all wary . . . worried, you know. Worried about me being healthy and being able to look after the kid. I don't want to not be there, not just because I want to provide, to support, you know, but also I want to see it all. I don't want to miss anything.' We continued to nod. I remember feeling the passion in his words but, at the same time, feeling disconnected from what was happening inside his head. It wasn't something I could empathize with or fully grasp.

'It's hard to explain, maybe you'll understand if it happens to you. I don't know.' Colin sighed and grinned.

'Hello, boys.' Another jumble of flesh, sequin and lipstick jiggled at the table's edge. We'd become used to the constant offers of table dances from girls trained to make you feel special.

'And did you plan it, Col, mate?' Merlin asked, ignoring the girl.

'Plan? Well . . . well, I didn't plan it. Trish maybe did, you know. We've been chancing our arm for a while now anyway with this Persona stuff. I mean, I don't really follow it, like, but I know if I had to pee on something every morning to be sure I wasn't fertile, I'd be as reliable as Merl is in goal. No offence, mate.' He apologized to Merl.

'Oh, none taken, lad.' Merlin wasn't precious about his goalkeeping skills.

'I said, hello, boys.' The girl had raised her voice now and Merl, who was the closest to her, turned.

'Sorry darlin', but we're smack in the middle of something

here.' He turned back to the conversation.

'So when's she due?' I asked, trying to remember the right list of questions to ask.

'She's due November the twenty-first.'

'So when does that mean you actually . . . you know . . .' Suddenly sex took on a whole different meaning.

'Valentine's Day.'

'What a surprise. Bloody hell, if the papers get onto that, it'll be round two of Mr Lover-Lover,' I said.

'No more media bollocks. I've had enough, back to journalism. Been offered a regular features slot on *Esquire*, so I'm gonna take that,' Colin explained calmly. 'As for the "Life of Riley" stuff . . . well, just the stag and the big day – all a bit predictable really – then it's run its course. Someone even approached me about publishing the lot as a book.'

'Excuse me!' the girl shouted. She was petite, with cropped black hair and a pale face, wearing a disco-diva pink crop-top and hot pants. We all turned to face her, startled.

'Why are you here? This is a strip club. I am a stripper.' She had a pained twang in her voice.

'Sorry, love,' Merlin spoke gently, 'it's just that our friend here has just told us he's going to be a dad, and was telling us about it.'

Her face lit up. 'A baby! Wow, your wife's having a baby?'

'Yes,' Colin smiled broadly, proud and dad-like.

'My sister's just had one. When's she due?' The girl slotted herself in next to Colin, and the two started nattering about parenthood and children. I was struck by how incongruous a conversation about conception, pregnancy and parenthood felt in a strip club.

'It's my first day. My name's Maggie,' the teenager said. 'I don't think I'll last, I'd rather have a chat than jiggle my tits about. I'm training to be a manicurist. Let me see your nails.' We handed her our cracked cuticles for inspection. 'Anyway, the only people spending real money are a table of apes that look like retired hit men and two sad fuckers in the backroom.'

'Who?' I questioned Maggie, worry burrowing through the beer.

'Some dodgy bald bloke pretending to be an Italian footballer, who gropes anything that comes within two feet of him. If he doesn't keep his hands to himself the bouncers'll be on to him,' she explained.

'And . . . ?' I asked.

'And they'll kick his head in.' I tried to prevent myself from thinking, *Good*.

'No, I meant and who else? You said two lads.' As if we needed confirmation.

'Oh, and this nasty little Scottish geezer who just keeps saying really disgusting things, asking us to say stuff and do things, and calling us sluts and whores 'cos it's not doing anything for him.'

'You mean those two sorry fucks.' Colin nodded at the curtain as Stef fell through and Ratty angrily pushed him aside.

'Shit, you know them. I didn't mean . . .' Maggie stuttered.

'Don't worry, love, we should be apologizing, dopey bastards.' Merlin shook his head. Maggie smiled briefly and dived away before Ratty and Stef staggered over to the table.

'Youse borin' buggers finally havin' a go?' Ratty peered into the gloom after the shrinking shape of Maggie. 'I dinnae think I've tried her. Looks a bit tomboyish. Am I right? Fuck, I'm skint, an' I've no' even got a proper stiffy yet.' Ratty was swaying and slurring. 'Someone lend us a hundred. Actually, forget it, I'm wastin' me money.'

'I've gotnuffforTina and thassit.' Stef's eyes were rolling.

I caught Ratty edgily twiddling his thumbs and staring at the table-top, his leg tapping up and down like a piston.

'You need to take a break, mate?' I said.

'I need somethin', 'ats fer fuckin' sure.'

'Ratty, calm down. What's your problem?'

Ratty turned to face me. Red-faced and sweaty, he whispered, 'It's no' fuckin' workin' fer me any more. I've got tae do something, Johnny. Where's that Slippy Club, d'ya ken?'

'What?' I thought I'd misheard him.

'You know, that place where London's Yearning are wearing our arses on their chests, like?'

'Ratty, what the fuck are you on?'

'Johnny, I cannae get it fuckin' up. I have tae try summit, an' if a wee bit o' AC/DC's fit the doctor ordered, then there you go.'

'But . . .' I realized Ratty hadn't really noticed who or what he'd shagged for years, and that the attraction wasn't men, but promiscuity and the hope of a new high.

'Dinnae say anythin', like, eh, Johnny?' It was inevitable really. Ratty had objectified sex to such a degree that he'd entered a downward spiral of sordid excess. 'Right, see you, lads. Good luck, Johnny. Look after him, Merl.'

'Wherethefuckreyougoin'?' Stef mumbled, slumped on the seat. Ratty paused, looking at me, presumably to check whether I'd play along or not. He nodded a silent thank-you.

'Skint, pissed and knackered. Off to get some kip. See youse, like.' He waved and left, a noticeable urgency in his walk.

'Well I'll be buggered,' said Merl. 'Never thought Ratty'd be first out.'

'You know, yeraluckybastard, Johnny.' Stef was totally gone now, slurring and rolling dangerously.

'I know, I know I'm lucky.' I was pissed, but nowhere near as far gone as Stef.

'Teen . . . Tina . . .' he shouted indiscriminately at some poor girl passing.

'No, but I'm sure you'd never know the difference. Want to go out back?' Stef looked like easy money.

'Oh fuckit, whynot.' Maggie passed by, saw what was

285

happening and whispered in the girl's ear. She sneered at Stef. 'On second thoughts, fuck you, ya bastard.' Stef shrugged in slo-mo.

'Fuckin' sluts.' He slumped on the table.

Maggie leant over, talking to the rest of us. 'Your friend here grabbed a girl so hard she's in tears. I'd get him the fuck out of here if I was you.' Two bouncers loomed into view like bombers, sights on Stef.

'Teen . . . Tina . . .' Stef called out to any woman passing. 'You know, Johnny, I reckon Tina has an arse just like your wife-to-be.'

I cut the bouncers off before they reached the table. 'Look, we'll sort it out. He's our problem.'

Back at the table, I pulled Stef to his feet. 'Shorry, Johnny. Never meant it, you know, about her arsh.' I tried to control my clenched fists.

'We should get him out of here, Johnny.' Merl was pissed, but clung to a reminder of sobriety.

'I'm gonna throw . . . goin' to the loo.' Colin helped Stef to the gents.

'Look, we'll meet you outside, Col, OK. We'll get a cab back to Johnny's.' Merl stuck doggedly to his job as stag-controller. We sat together outside on the kerb, waiting for Colin and Stef to arrive, chain-smoking battered Silk Cuts.

'I'm gonna take a walk, Merl. There's somethin' I need to do,' I said.

'I'll stay with you, man. Can't go home alone, mate.' Merl tried to look after me. Three people stumbled into us, two of them laughing, drunk and loud.

'I 'ave us a privatedancer,' Stef slurred. Somehow, Stef had found Tina, and the pair of them were irretrievably blitzed.

'Fuckinfuckorrrf,' Tina swore back and swayed in time with Stef.

'Someone's got to look after this lot, Merl. Take 'em back to mine. I'll see you in an hour or so.'

'No. Come on, Johnny, the taxi's got room. I'll stay with you, Johnny.'

'No, honest, there's something I've gotta do, mate,' I shouted.

'Johnny!' Merlin called as I darted into the crowded Soho night, which closed around me.

On the way to Berwick Street, I thought I saw the silhouette of a long limousine patrolling the streets like a great shark in deep waters, leaving me yet more certain of my design.

An hour later, shuddering through the rainy night in a black cab, I clutched my shoulder and felt suddenly sober.

Unlocking the door back in Clapham, I half expected total chaos, but instead was met by MTV blaring out Trevor Nelson's late-nighter, and Stef and Tina slumped on the sofa, half asleep. Muttley was lapping at a puddle of beer on the floor next to an upturned can. The room was cold, and through the hall and beyond the kitchen I could see the French windows flapping in the wind.

'Johnny, ya fuckwit, we've been waiting fer you, ain't wee, Teeeen?' Stef roused himself. 'I bet Teeen's got better tits 'an your bird.' Tina woke and whacked Stef with a cushion. I wished it was a breeze-block.

'Fuckooorffff, ya sod.' Tina and Stef were both as pissed as when I'd left them.

'C'mon, luv, get yer kit off,' Stef pleaded, necking more beer, red eyes all lit up.

'Jesus!' I shook my head.

'C'mon, Teen,' Stef whined.

'Whaasit worth, you sad bastard.' Tina wasn't too drunk to do business. I left in search of Merl and Colin as Stef fumbled for his wallet.

'Where's Col, mate?'

Merlin was sat on the step, staring at the stars, tugging happily on a joint. 'Family man these days, Johnny. You know how Col throws himself at stuff.' Merlin spoke in a slow, stoned drawl. 'Where you been?' He asked after a long pause.

'Nowhere,' I said. 'Just something I wanted to do, like I said.'

'You OK, Johnny boy?' Merlin was ever-wary, even when stoned.

'Yeah. You?' We were beginning to conquer our trapped-in-amber thoughts.

'I was wrong about something, Johnny. It's a good thing, a good thing for you two, marriage.'

'I know,' I replied. And I did know. We watched the stars for a while longer. I pulled on the joint and watched them fur.

'So I s'pose she's staying at Maddy's tonight, is she?' BTB's image filled my thoughts, smoke like speech bubbles.

'No, back here, mate. Didn't think you'd mind, like.'

'You what?' I laughed nervously. Merlin simultaneously realized his mistake. I stood, suddenly feeling unanchored and flimsy.

'It's Stef's problem, mate. Er . . . I thought they'd just end up in the spare room, the two of them, like.'

'That's where she keeps her fuckin' dress!' I staggered back through the French windows, but sort of knew fate was about to fuck me over. Walking into the lounge, through the kitchen, I could hear several things simultaneously: Muttley barking excitedly, Stef singing the stripping song, badly – 'Na na na . . . na na na' – the door unlocking and women's voices.

The picture that greeted me will haunt me for ever. My eyes locked with BTB's across the room, her face agog. In between us, Stef clapped drunkenly on the sofa. Muttley, similarly, sat captivated, a blue garter clutched in his innocent teeth. He and Stef stared up at Tina, hips swaying, tits jiggling, wearing nothing but a white veil.

Blind-sided. Just when you think everything's OK, something you didn't expect comes at you. There was a second of

deathly quiet. Tina stopped stripping, Merlin looked hor-
rified, Muttley wagged his tail and BTB left. I thought I heard
'It's off.' Maddy ran after her, spitting at Stef, 'I'd expect
nothing less from you, but Jesus, Johnny, what have you
done?' She slammed the door behind her.

'Oh my God!' Tina, as drunk as she was, realized the
magnitude of what had just happened.

'You said she wasn't coming home, you bastard.' Tina
walked towards Stef, who automatically reached for her
breasts.

'You see,' he said, grabbing, 'Tina's tits are unbeatable.
Ooophhhh!' Tina landed a shin in his groin, picked up her
clothes and aimed for the door, dressing hurriedly in the
corridor while Stef squirmed on the floor.

'Just go, Stef.' I sighed. Eventually, he stood. Merlin was
behind me, watching. 'Just leave, you don't know what
you're doing.'

'She might be marrying you, ya fucker, but if she'd thought
she could have had me for more than a shag, she wouldn't be
walking up the aisle with—'

The swing came from deep inside my mind, like a thought
or emotion, entirely uncontrollable. I caught Stef directly on
the belt buckle, but followed through the hard metal into his
stomach, ignoring the pain in my hand. Stef bowled forward
on to his face, thudding heavily on to the floor.

I went outside to smoke, while Merlin picked up the pieces.

I sweated through the week. While BTB refused to engage me
in conversation, my only feedback was 'You'll be lucky,' from
Maddy. But whenever I said, 'So is it off?' I was told, 'That's
not your decision, Johnny.'

I lobbied Maddy, I pleaded with BTB's mother, I even fed
her dad a line about a minor error of judgement on the stag,
but I was still left in the dark. They all knew the truth about
that night, and that it wasn't what it looked like, that it was

entirely out of my hands. Behind the scenes a UN-style peace negotiation was taking place. From Merlin to Maddy to BTB and back again.

Maddy finally rang on Thursday. 'She says she doesn't want you there on Friday night, Johnny.' A family get-together had been planned in Soho Soho the night before the wedding.

'Oh, but the wedding's on, though?'

'Well . . .'

'What do you mean, Well? She can't happily have a meal with my parents, her parents, Merl and you the night before no bloody wedding, can she? Anyway, won't it look weird if I'm not with the family on Friday?'

'She's going to tell them she's superstitious.'

'Maddy, she's not gonna do it, is she?'

'I don't know, Johnny, she keeps laughing and saying, "I'll leave him at the altar," and I can't bloody tell if she's having me on or not.'

'Oh fuck.' I sighed.

'Johnny, listen, just do what I tell you, OK.' I listened carefully to my instructions.

After a trouble-free family do, Maddy managed to persuade BTB to go for a final drink with her and Merl at a club where she often sang. Maddy was at home in the oak-panelled walls of Soho House, where shady people looked famous, lurking in shadows and speaking in hushed voices.

Maddy had hired a small private room – the study – on the top floor of the club. It was a split-level room, overlooking Dean Street, with a few armchairs and a sofa littered casually and, on the raised half of the room, a piano squatting impatiently, sleek and black.

I was drinking large whiskies a little too quickly in the bar downstairs. Maddy found me sitting, depressed, on a stool. 'So this is it, Johnny.'

'Let's forget it, Mads. She hates me.'

'No way, Johnny, she loves you. She knows it was Stef's fault; me, Merl and Col, we explained it all. You are doing this, Johnny.'

'No . . . I just can't . . . Thanks and everything, but I'll do it another time, you know, when we're on our own. Some other time . . . I just can't . . .'

'Johnny, shh.' Maddy held a finger to my lips and put her hand to my jaw. 'Johnny, you're good at this. I never told you before, but you're really good at this . . . and I think it might be your only hope.' Maddy guided me up the stairs, the tower talking a pilot down in a storm.

Looking like some high-society hostess, BTB lounged in an armchair, legs crossed, champagne dangling from her limp wrist. She looked made for the club, wearing a stylish black shift dress, and with a tiny grey cashmere cardigan draped across her shoulders, covering her enigmatically, with a hint of the tattoo padding hidden below.

'Oh, Johnny, what a nice surprise,' she said flatly, as though I were a war criminal. At first, BTB refused to make eye contact with me. I walked towards her and kissed her on the cheek. She was still wearing her poker face; no hugs and reconciliation, but no scenes or shouting, either.

'It's off,' she whispered, but deep down, inside her eyes, a smile twinkled and gave me hope.

'I should be going,' BTB said to Maddy.

'Hang on, just a sec,' Maddy cut in, 'there's something we wanted to do before.'

'Of course,' BTB said, 'you've gone to all the trouble of arranging a piano so a song—'

'Well,' Maddy looked nervously at me, 'I know you think I'd deliberately plan the night before your wedding around me singing, but that's not the real reason the piano's here. Johnny?'

I stood, silently, and walked towards the piano.

'What are you doing, Johnny?' BTB snorted. 'Johnny only knows how to play chopsticks.' BTB laughed.

'Badly,' Merlin added.

Maddy and me had worked towards this for months, but in the space of a week, since the lap-dancing débâcle, its importance had suddenly grown. It had become a last-hope rescue plan, when previously it was, literally, the icing on the cake.

I took a deep breath and tried to remember words I'd previously thought appropriate for this moment. *Bollocks. Bollocks, bollocks, bollocks. Get up, give up, go home, you fool.*

Maddy dimmed the lights, leaving me conspicuous in a soft pool of white. I'd like to think I looked Dean Martin or Sinatra-like, to say I was hip and cool and calm, but I've no idea, no real image of myself, it all just rolled.

'Listen, I can't remember what I was going to say, I hope I remember how to play it, but . . . well, I learnt this for you.' BTB looked unimpressed. 'I learnt it because you love it, because it says what I wish I could say, but most of all because it's the last thing you'd expect me to do.'

The drink must have helped. My nerves were replaced by the notes, which came unconsciously. The same understated tinkling introduction, leading unavoidably to the words, which can't be spoken, let alone sung without emotion.

'The very thought of you makes my heart sing,
Like an April breeze,
On the wings of spring,
And you appear in all your splendour,
My one and only love . . .'

I hope she liked it. It's impossible to explain the feeling of spending so much time doing something you're not naturally gifted at in an effort to surprise, to express feelings which would fail to carry the weight of the sentiment by using any other means. They clapped, but then friends do. Maddy whistled, shouting, ''Atta boy, Johnny,' and Merlin shouted, 'More,' annoyingly failing to realize that this one song, BTB's favourite song, was the limit of my repertoire. But BTB's damp cheeks were the only reward I wanted, the only response that mattered. Beyond that, who could tell?

D-Dayed

So that's it. That's the story so far. Here I am, sitting on a pew at the front of St Luke's, in Clapham, sweating. Gothic arches straddle the plain wooden seats and simple white flower arrangements are spread throughout. A stiff collar silently scythes into my neck, while hard, shiny black shoes strait-jacket my feet. I'm not at all convinced that Merlin has attached my buttonhole correctly, nor, more importantly, that BTB will turn up.

I'm trussed up like a penguin – not an emperor or a king penguin, or the grand aloof penguins that stand tall like the aristocrats of the bird kingdom, more of a rock hopper penguin. Have you seen them? They look sort of scatty, a bit like joke penguins, with odd yellow tufty bits on top and colourful markings on their beaks. Penguins wearing Groucho masks, the clowns of the bird kingdom.

I hope my flies are up. I hope I don't barf, or faint or fart. I hope I don't look too much of a wazzock in this garb. But most of all I just hope she bloody well arrives. Come on . . .

Come on, Merl, give me the signal. Give me the thumbs-up that means the car's here, and then get your Welsh arse down the aisle, pronto. This is like . . . being an astronaut after the bloody T-minus has finished, still sat on my backside in the rocket, wondering what the hell's going on. She's half an hour late and I'm losing it, logic going AWOL.

I mean, I know I shouldn't worry. She'll come. At least I think she'll come. Will she come? I was worried back in March. Granny Victor's funeral was a watershed that coloured our minds in different ways. We both arrived at the simple fact that life's too short, but seemed to latch on to opposite conclusions about what to do next. I realized how important it was to spend a life doing the things that matter with the people you love. While BTB's version went, 'Ever and ever, Amen, is a long, long time, and is Johnson Riley (the boy-child) the right guy?'

And then there was the Italian incident. For a long time I wondered if it was fair to entirely blame Stefano. I mean, BTB had flirted with him; she hadn't exactly discouraged all the innuendo over the years, the 'Ditch Johnny, love, and come and see what you're missing' lines that I'd learnt to laugh off. But I don't really reckon anyone else but me was behind her doubt.

And then there was Tina's dance. I'll never forget the image of Muttley, jaw clamped on garter, swinging his head, a nodding dog, moving in time to a sordid strip show.

Come on. Jesus, hurry up. Trying to hold a cool, assured expression with the congregation watching my every move was getting harder by the second.

With the May sunshine streaming through the stained-glass windows, the familiar faces look almost luminous at the thought of a wedding. Broad smiles, nods and winks cascade down on me like confetti, and I try to respond individually, helping me to relax and forget BTB's increasing lateness.

I guess the people you would expect to be here are here. At least, I think they are. Merlin, Colin and Ratty are lingering at the back, watching their watches, looking official and formal, and huddling around the earpieces of Colin's personal stereo. I glance at my bruised knuckles and wince at the tenderness which reminds me of Stef's absence. I don't regret what I did on the stag last week – I'd do the same again – but it still feels weird. In my mind's eye, he was always going to be here, one of the morning-suited ushers. Now he is a place name scrubbed off a map, not just today, but maybe permanently. I mean, I can't exactly see myself popping down the Blue Boy for a pint with him, but who knows, time might soften me, like old leather in the rain.

At the back of the church, Mr Big bobs like an iceberg, sitting alone in his pew, everyone else unaware of how much he's contributed, unseen. In front of Norbert, we step through rows of Blue Boy football lads, wives and girlfriends, Frankie the landlord and Jean, colleagues and friends, and Uncle Alfie, camcorder at the ready.

Crowding me at the front, my parents are looking on proudly. Mum with a gentle smile, whispering, 'Don't worry, Johnny, brides are always late.'

Earlier, Dad had patted me on the shoulder and leant close. 'Your gran, and dear old Dad, too, they'd have all been proud of you, son.'

I don't think they knew just how much Granny Victor had done, and I hoped her ghost was smiling and swearing somewhere, *'Well done, Johnny-bloody-bladder-pants! No dawdling, oveny-bun time for tea.'*

On the bride's side, Mary Donnelly looked fragile, with Paddy and Jack on one side and Seamus on the other, next to Trish, tissues at the ready. They, too, had all smiled and shaken my hand when they arrived. I'd got a warm, welcoming hug and a kiss on the cheek from Mary, unaccompanied by the *Jaws* theme.

Behind me, the round, jolly Father Derek fusses behind the altar, popping over sporadically and whispering, 'Don't worry, Johnny, plenty of time. Don't have to be at another wedding until four.'

I gulp and look at my watch. Twenty to three, forty minutes late, with the seconds ticking away loudly in my mind like a platform clock. It was the first sign of weakness in a previously confident groom. Eyes front, a wave of watch-checking spreads through the pews as I check mine.

'Yeeeesssss!' Ratty leaps about at the back as Merlin tries to calm him, forcing his hand over his mouth while smiling pleasantly at the people who turn round, women tutting, men holding back the urge to ask the score. Great, my wife-to-be isn't here and Italy are in the lead. Great, we're off to Italy tonight, the fans will all be leaving and the Italians will have bloody won. Two weeks of piss-taking Italians, or am I being paranoid? Bloody great.

Come on, where are you?

Maybe I scared her off last night with my singing. Maybe London's Yearning offered her broader horizons than I could. Maybe she's done a Ruth on me and buggered off abroad.

In fact, she could have gone already. The tickets, the packed bags, the car, the currency are all with BTB at our house. Maybe she's gone to Italy without me . . . and with . . .

'We are the self-preservation society
We are the self-preservation society.'

Stef drives the red-and-white Mini Cooper through the back alleys of Turin, while BTB navigates, twisting and skidding past coachloads of England fans and horn-blowing Italians stuck in the city's gridlocked streets, chased by tinny-looking Fiat Poliza cars and macho motorcyclists.

'Left. Left, Stef. Right . . . up the ramp.' The Mini sweeps over a ramp, revving wildly, and jumps between buildings, cars and bikes crashing and colliding in their wake.

'We did it, Stef. We fooled him, we pulled it off . . .' The Mini drives across a weir, before joining empty roads leading to the Alps, leading to escape and Michael Caine on a cliff-teetering coach saying, 'Hang on a minute, lads . . . I've got a great idea . . .'

*

'She's here.' I hadn't even noticed Merlin walk briskly down the aisle to join me.

'You what?' I jump, shaking away paranoid dreams.

'You know, wife, wedding. Hello, Johnny?'

The organ music takes a while to crank up, and I can't resist turning to watch her enter the church. No way are this rabble seeing her before me.

I gasp. I think everyone did, but I couldn't see anyone else, or hear anyone else, or think anything else. The image will stay with me for ever, but I don't think I could ever recreate it in the mind of someone who hadn't seen it through *my* eyes. She shone, shone with her eyes and her smile and her skin. Shimmering, silvers and greys and white, marble shot with quartz.

The details take a while to break through, but eventually they begin to register. Gerry Donnelly is proud, like a lion on her arm, his own arm through hers, delicate and pale in the low-cut dress. Maddy, subtle and demure some distance behind, noticeably holding all of Merlin's attention.

Rewind . . . low-cut dress? Tattoo! Scab, mess, blood, bruising. Believe me, I know, thanks to Eddie the Rainbow, they might look great after a month, but only a week after the needle, it is not a pretty sight.

But I can't see it, I can't see it anywhere. It must be plaster-covered on her left side, hidden by her father, or some decorative armlet or bangle, or silk tie, or something. Something must be hiding it. Please, Jesus. Her mum'll keel over on the spot.

As she arrives at the altar, unable to help myself, I crane my neck trying to look at her left shoulder. Nothing. Make-up can't be that good. As the congregation bustle behind I whisper in her ear, 'You look staggering. Where's the tattoo, though?'

She smiles and winks. 'Didn't fall for a bit of body paint, did you, darling?'

'Please be seated.' Father Derek begins the service.

A second of silence.

'Yeeeessss.' Colin leaps out of his pew at the back. 'Sorry . . . sorry.' *One all.*

I smile to myself. I wouldn't have it any other way. It's all perfect, in a flawed, clobbered type of way. The image of my tattoo, permanent, for ever there, hidden beneath the white cotton and gauze padding on my shoulder, forms in my mind.

Caitlin

In Your Dreams

CHARLIE ROSS

BANTAM PRESS

LONDON • NEW YORK • TORONTO • SYDNEY • AUCKLAND

TRANSWORLD PUBLISHERS
61–63 Uxbridge Road, London W5 5SA
a division of The Random House Group Ltd

RANDOM HOUSE AUSTRALIA PTY LTD
20 Alfred Street, Milsons Point, Sydney
New South Wales 2061, Australia

RANDOM HOUSE NEW ZEALAND
18 Poland Road, Glenfield, Auckland 10, New Zealand

RANDOM HOUSE SOUTH AFRICA (PTY) LTD
Endulini, 5a Jubilee Road, Parktown 2193, South Africa

Published 2000 by Bantam Press
a division of Transworld Publishers

A catalogue record for this book is available
from the British Library.

ISBN 0593 045432

Typeset in 10½/13½pt Sabon by Falcon Oast Graphic Art

Printed and bound in Great Britain by
Mackays of Chatham plc, Chatham, Kent.

1 3 5 7 9 10 8 6 4 2